Wide Awake

"[T]he pacing is brisk and the bloodshed cinematic enough that a first-timer can wolf down this entry without having knowledge of the first two. This sends the series out with a bang."

—*Publishers Weekly*

Coming Dawn

"A deft cat-and-mouse novel that keeps the action moving and the reader guessing."

—*Kirkus Reviews*

Deep Sleep

"Techno-thriller fans will delight in military vet Konkoly's obvious expertise when it comes to the authenticity and intensity of the numerous action sequences."

—*Publishers Weekly*

"A lively, roller-coaster thriller that moves like lightning."

—*Kirkus Reviews*

"Nobody's better at spy craft, action, and intrigue than Steven Konkoly. Thrilling entertainment from the first to the last written word."
—Robert Dugoni, *New York Times* and #1 Amazon bestselling author
of *The Eighth Sister*

"Steven Konkoly has blown my mind! *Deep Sleep* is an intelligent, intense, and completely unpredictable high-concept spy thriller. I'm hooked!"

—T.R. Ragan, *New York Times* bestselling author of *Her Last Day*

"Fast paced, suspenseful, and wildly creative. A modern-day masterpiece of spy fiction."

—Andrew Watts, *USA Today* bestselling author of the Firewall Spies series

"A pulse-pounding conspiracy tale in the finest traditions of Vince Flynn and Nelson DeMille . . . *Deep Sleep* is a must-read roller coaster of a thriller."

—Jason Kasper, *USA Today* bestselling author of the Shadow Strike series

"Devin Gray is the hero we need in our corner. Relentless in pursuit of truth, vindication, and saving his homeland, he is the perfect protagonist for Konkoly's newest dive into the techno-thriller world. Again Konkoly proves his mastery of the genre, drawing from real-rowed events to create a plausible and frightening glimpse into what's happening underneath our feet and behind the walls of power."

—Tom Abrahams, Emmy Award–winning journalist and author of *Sedition*

"Steven Konkoly delivers a conspiracy thriller unlike any other and proves he's at the top of his game. With a deft hand and an eye for plot intricacies, Konkoly will take you into a web of deceit that will shake you to your core and keep you turning until the very last page. The Lost Directorate has set a new bar in the world of thrillers, and Konkoly has taken his seat at the head of the table."

—Brian Shea, *Wall Street Journal* bestselling author of the Boston Crime series and coauthor of the Rachel Hatch series

"Steven Konkoly's new Ryan Decker series is a triumph—an action-thriller master class in spy craft, tension, and suspense. An absolute must-read for fans of Tom Clancy, Vince Flynn, and Brad Thor."

—Blake Crouch, *New York Times* bestselling author

A CLEAN
KILL

OTHER TITLES BY STEVEN KONKOLY

DEVIN GRAY SERIES

Deep Sleep

Coming Dawn

Wide Awake

RYAN DECKER SERIES

The Rescue

The Raid

The Mountain

Skystorm

THE FRACTURED STATE SERIES

Fractured State

Rogue State

THE PERSEID COLLAPSE SERIES

The Jakarta Pandemic

A CLEAN
KILL

STEVEN KONKOLY

THOMAS & MERCER

Published by Thomas & Mercer, Seattle

www.apub.com

Amazon, the Amazon logo, and Thomas & Mercer are trademarks of Amazon.com, Inc., or its affiliates.

ISBN-13: 9781662509247 (paperback)
ISBN-13: 9781662509254 (digital)

Cover design by Faceout Studio, Elisha Zepeda
Cover images: © Pawel Radomski / Shutterstock; © Shelley Richmond / Arcangel; © Roy Bishop / Arcangel

Printed in the United States of America

To Kosia, Matthew, and Sophia—
the heart and soul of my writing

PART I

CHAPTER 1

Alejandro released his tight grip on the overstuffed contractor bag and crossed himself. He'd long ago rejected the church, but the sacred gesture, drilled into him as a child, involuntarily surfaced on rare occasions like these. When remarkably fortuitous circumstances conspired to protect him. To keep his life's unfinished journey intact—and the *tríada* legacy alive. He shook his head at the irony of the moment, his hand mechanically finishing the sign of the cross. Just a few minutes ago he had enthusiastically cursed the same spirit's name.

A sizable tear in one of the contractor bags had forced him to return to the Suburban to retrieve another. A cracked tibia or ulna— whatever—had stabbed through the thick material while he dragged it through the grass. The small hole had snagged an immovable root or rock and ripped a gash in the plastic. Sizable enough to empty some of the bag's contents along his route. The time he'd spent correcting the situation had delayed his labors long enough to alert him to an unforeseen danger—a set of oncoming headlights—during his last trip across this waterlogged field.

A few more seconds and he would have dropped into the shallow ravine that ran roughly parallel to the road, oblivious to the potential threat to his less-than-holy calling. A possible endgame scenario if things went substantially wrong. Alejandro ignored the headlights for now and concentrated on the task at hand. Lugging the last of the bulging contractor bags over the edge of the rift and out of sight. He didn't bother to arrange the bag next to the others. He had more pressing business to attend to.

A vehicle traveling this isolated stretch of road at one thirty in the morning—during a vicious rainstorm—suggested a potential complication. The kind of complication that probably wore a uniform, wielded a gun, and carried a radio. The radio being Alejandro's biggest concern. The uniform meant little to him. The gun even less. Like in his own country more than a thousand miles to the south, most police officers here spent a day or two on the gun range every year. Hardly enough to give him even the remotest concern.

Alejandro put in several hours of firearms training a week on his private range. Rifles. Pistols. Submachine guns. Shotguns. A gun engagement was the least of his worries. But a police radio represented a different threat altogether. Even out here, in the middle of nowhere—during a torrential rainstorm—a call for backup would complicate matters.

If the approaching headlights turned out to be a state or local police cruiser, things could go in one of several directions. Few of them good. Alejandro wiped the thick sheen of rainwater off his face and studied the dark shape behind the headlights. An SUV, if he had to guess.

As the vehicle closed the distance to his Suburban, which he'd parked facing north, it slowed for several seconds—a powerful light suddenly lashing out to probe the Suburban's windows. Definitely a police vehicle. He instinctively tucked the bottom of the waterproof rain shell tight into his waistband behind the concealed holster on his right hip, where it wouldn't interfere with a quick draw, if that ultimately became necessary.

The police SUV passed the Suburban and stopped, the spotlight now sweeping across the grassy, waterlogged field he had just traversed for the fifth time. The trail left by the heavily burdened contractor bags had worn an obvious path through the low grass. Obvious to Alejandro, but hopefully not so easily observable by the officer scanning a rainswept scene through water-speckled windows.

He made a quick mental calculation just in case. Roughly thirty yards lay between Alejandro and the police vehicle. Easy shooting distance, even in the rain. If the officer got out of the SUV and started to look around, he'd be forced to act. Forced to add another body to the scene. Only time would tell.

CHAPTER 2

Deputy Keller scanned the area beyond the Suburban with the spot-light. Nothing noteworthy. The heavy downpour concealed most of the landscape, but he knew it all too well after patrolling these roads for a few years. The low grass would connect to an endless field of soybean plants. Same on both sides of the road. Same throughout the entire county. Soybeans as far as the eye could see—the occasional, distant farmhouse breaking up the horizon like an oil rig on the ocean.

He directed the light back toward the black Suburban. Not that he could see much through two sets of rain-blurred windows from this distance. Or any distance for that matter. He had to admit—it was an odd vehicle to find abandoned out here. No doubt about that. But the strangeness of the situation ended there. Keller hadn't observed any exterior damage to the vehicle. The tires and windows were intact. No tools next to the vehicle. No handwritten SOS sign affixed to one of the windows or lying on the dashboard. Just an empty SUV with Minnesota plates, in the middle of nowhere Minnesota. Not exactly a big deal—especially when he was on his way home at one thirty in the morning after a double shift.

He extinguished the spotlight and considered his options. First and foremost—all he wanted to do right now was drive another ten minutes to his house in Ellendale, take a quick shower, and crawl in bed with his wife. This was his second double shift in a week. Back-to-back shifts to be precise. The Steele County Sheriff's Office had been hit with a flu bug, which someone had likely passed along during Chief Deputy Hanson's retirement party last week.

To say that Keller felt exhausted would be a grave understatement. Borderline mission-incapable might be a better description. If he called this in, he'd be stuck out here for hours. And the last thing he needed right now was to give up some desperately needed sleep to babysit a rich asshole's abandoned SUV—which was how it would play out. Walker, the duty sergeant, would drive down from the station in Owatonna with a few other lookie-loos to assess the situation, dragging him out into the rain to search the soybean fields. Hours would pass before a tow truck arrived. The sergeant might even ask him to drive back up to the station to file paperwork. He could kiss most of his sleep goodbye.

Or. He could head back to this spot early tomorrow afternoon, on his way north to Owatonna. Before reporting for his next shift— which was another double. If the Suburban was still here, he'd call it in. It really wasn't much of a decision. Sleep trumped babysitting an eighty-thousand-dollar SUV. Keller took his foot off the brake and pulled away from the scene. A few hundred yards down the road, he started to have second thoughts.

But how would he explain why he'd diverted from Interstate 35 to a side road if the SUV hadn't moved by the time he headed back to the station? County Road 3 ran roughly parallel to the interstate, but it was located east of the interstate. He lived in Ellendale, to the west. Then again, he was unlikely to be questioned about his choice of route— unless something funky turned up in the vicinity of the Suburban. And if that happened, GPS tracking data would reveal that his patrol vehicle had stopped near the Suburban tonight and moved along. He started to slow down.

Did he miss anything obvious? It was hard enough to see in the darkness, even with the spotlight. The rain made it nearly impossible. Maybe he should have gotten out of his Interceptor and taken a quick check around the abandoned SUV or taken a better look inside the vehicle. Keller pounded the steering wheel and cursed. He was about to lose precious sleep because some jackass probably ran out of gas several hours ago, called a friend to pick them up, and neglected to leave a courtesy note on the dashboard saying they'd be back tomorrow.

"Son of a mother," he mumbled, before stopping his vehicle.

Keller executed a three-point turn on the two-lane road and sped north toward the Suburban. He'd do a quick search of the vehicle and the area surrounding it. If the search turned up nothing suspicious, he'd head home without calling it in. And he'd take Interstate 35 to the station tomorrow, forgetting about the Suburban altogether—with nobody the wiser. Out of sight. Out of mind.

A hundred yards or so away from the abandoned vehicle, his headlights caught something in the grass next to the Suburban. Something moving fast. Someone running.

"No shit," he grumbled, before turning on his police strobes.

A hooded figure crossed in front of the Suburban, momentarily vanishing before reappearing to open the driver's-side door. *Definitely up to no good!* Keller hit the siren, hoping to freeze the person in place. Nope. They shut the door—the taillights glowing red a moment later.

Keller slowed the Interceptor, not wanting to get too close, too soon. This could be anything. From a guy taking a piss on the side of the road to a prearranged drug drop. Better safe than sorry. When the Suburban took off, its taillights vanishing into the darkness, he hit the accelerator and grabbed his vehicle radio transmitter.

"Dispatch. This is Keller. I'm about two miles south of Oak Knoll Campground on County Road 3, heading north in pursuit of a black Suburban. Minnesota license plate. Didn't catch the full number. Started with *XR*. Black Suburban had been parked on the shoulder of the road, facing north. When I approached from the south, a single subject appeared in the field next to the vehicle and proceeded to take off in the Suburban. Request backup."

He left out the part about having previously approached it from the north and passing it.

"This is dispatch. Copy your last. Sending Duncan and Shuman your way. They'll be heading down from Owatonna. I'll coordinate an intercept based on your updates. Be careful, Rich. A fancy truck like that parked out in the middle of nowhere on a night like this sounds fishy."

He recognized the voice as Sheryl Eggers, who must have just taken over dispatch for the night. Karen Shay had been the one to send him all over the county prior to this call.

"Copy that, Sheryl," said Keller. "I plan on maintaining my—"

His Interceptor rumbled violently, then slowed to a crawl. He gunned the accelerator, pitching the vehicle forward—without gaining any significant momentum. The Interceptor crawled along the slick road, a high-pitched squealing sound filling the cabin. Keller took his foot off the pedal, letting the Interceptor grind to a halt, presumably on its rims. The Suburban's taillights disappeared in the storm.

"Keller. You still there?" said Sheryl.

"Yeah. I'm still here," he said. "But something's wrong with my vehicle. Hold on a second."

Keller put the Interceptor into park and hopped out, the heavy rain instantly flattening his hair and getting into his eyes. He reached back inside the cabin and retrieved his ball cap, pulling it tight over his head. Raindrops pattered against the hat's bill and his rain jacket as he examined the driver's-side tires with his flashlight. Not only flat but shredded. Just as Keller had suspected. He walked around the front of his vehicle and confirmed the same situation on the passenger side. Had to be a spike strip. There was no other explanation.

A short jog down the road validated his theory. An expandable, accordion-like spike strip spanned the two-lane road, originating from a luggage-size container on the eastern shoulder. A remotely activated system, like the one their department had purchased a few years ago. He grabbed his shoulder-mounted radio microphone.

"Sheryl. My vehicle has been disabled by a remotely triggered spike strip. All four tires are gone. I'm headed back to where the Suburban was parked to see if I can figure out what this yahoo was doing out here in the middle of the night."

"Stand by."

Stand by for what? He started walking south on the road. His radio crackled a few seconds later.

"Deputy Keller. This is Sergeant Walker. Stay with your vehicle until we can get some backup out there. The spike strip thing is highly unusual. Same with the high-end Suburban. Nothing run-of-the-mill about this."

"Understood, Sergeant," said Keller, relieved not to be traipsing around in the rain and slogging through the muddy fields. "I'll wait for backup."

"Better safe than sorry," said Walker. "I'm scrambling some auxiliary patrol deputies from nearby towns. They should be there within ten minutes. The rest of us will be headed south from Owatonna, looking for the Suburban."

"Sounds good," said Keller.

"I'm not gonna sugarcoat this. You're in for a long night, Rich," said Walker. "I'll find someone to cover your shift tomorrow."

"Thank you. Either way, I'm good, Sergeant. Seriously. I know the roster is low right now," said Keller. "Maybe one of the auxiliaries could fill a thermos with coffee?"

"I'll make sure some hot joe arrives on the scene," said Walker.

"Much appreciated, Sarge."

"Hey, Rich. Did you notice anything peculiar about that Suburban? Other than it being parked where it shouldn't be?"

"No," said Keller. "Full disclosure—I passed it coming down from my last call at the Oak Knoll Campground. The rain kicked in a few minutes before I got to the campground and pretty much extinguished the drunken commotion I'd been called to break up. I stuck around Oak Knoll for about thirty minutes, to make sure everyone was tucked in for the night, before heading home down County Road 3. I took a long look at the Suburban on my first pass. Nothing out of place except for the Suburban being there—like you said. I drove about a quarter mile past before turning back around. Didn't feel right to not give it a second look. The driver must have been hiding in the soybean fields."

"Fair enough," said Walker. "You may not have noticed in your previous travels, but there's a sizable ditch running along the west side of that road. My guess is he—or she—was up to something in that ditch. It's at least fifteen feet deep. Irrigation or something. Probably flooded with this rain."

"Good to know. I'll take a look when the auxiliaries arrive," said Keller.

"Might be a better idea to hold off," said Walker. "Rain is supposed to ease up in a few hours. Gone by sunrise. Why don't you seal off the scene for now and wait until the weather clears up—so you can see what you're walking into. I don't like the whole spike strip thing. Might be something worse waiting for you down in that ditch."

"I was thinking the same thing," said Keller, before turning toward his Interceptor.

CHAPTER 3

Alejandro killed the headlights and slowed the Suburban to a crawl, scanning both sides of the dark, rain-swept street for the right opportunity. He needed a reliable replacement vehicle and somewhere to hide the Suburban where it wouldn't be spotted until the sun came up. By then, he should be tucked away in his safe house west of Minneapolis, the stolen vehicle parked inside the safe house's garage, where it would never be seen again.

What a night. He knew his lucky streak would run out eventually. He just hadn't expected it to happen at one thirty in the morning, during a torrential rainstorm, on one of the most isolated stretches of rural road imaginable. He'd driven similar roads in southern Minnesota and other states hundreds of times and had never seen a police vehicle. Barely any other vehicles, either. Why a local cop would be out in a rainstorm, in the middle of nowhere, so late at night would likely remain a complete mystery to Alejandro. A random coincidence.

He found what he needed a few houses down the street. A lone pickup truck parked in the grass next to a double-wide trailer. No lights on inside or outside the home. The dark shapes of several trees rose above the trailer, indicating a reasonably private backyard. Perfect for his needs—assuming the owner wasn't a shoot-first, ask-questions-later type. In his experience, few were, even when faced with overwhelming, clearly presented evidence that they were in grave danger.

Alejandro eased the Suburban off the street and onto the grass in front of the truck, then carefully maneuvered it between the home and vehicle. Once past the house, he turned the oversize SUV into the near-pitch-black backyard and momentarily activated the fog lights. A dark form beyond the hood transformed into a picnic table covered with beer bottles; the patchy grass under it was littered with cigarette butts. With any luck, the trailer's occupant or occupants were passed out drunk.

He steered clear of the table and turned off the lights, parking the Suburban directly behind the trailer, where it wouldn't be visible from the street. Alejandro removed a flashlight-equipped, suppressed pistol from the glove compartment and got out of the vehicle. The moment his feet hit the squishy ground, a light illuminated the trailer window just above the hood of the Suburban. He shut the door and aimed at the window.

When the dark shape of a head appeared directly behind the thin, translucent curtain, Alejandro didn't hesitate. He pressed the trigger twice, the double snap of his pistol barely louder than the crack of the two bullets punching through the glass—and the occupant's forehead. In this storm, the sound was presumably inaudible to even the most alert neighbors.

He waited a few moments for any immediate sounds that might suggest the house posed more trouble than the car swap was worth. Screaming? A slammed door? More lights? No problem. A shotgun racking? A panicked voice yelling at a 911 operator? *No bueno.* He could find another vehicle in any of the hundreds of sleepy, one-stoplight towns dotting the vast farmlands of southern Minnesota.

When nothing of concern materialized, he opened the rear driver's-side door and took a compact crowbar out of the footwell before making his way to the trailer's back steps—several cinder blocks stacked below a sliding glass door. He triggered the pistol's flashlight and examined the sliding door's interior.

Fortunately, the owner hadn't installed a security bar, or even jammed a simple piece of wood along the inside track, to prevent the door from opening. He set his pistol down on the makeshift stairs and pried the slider open, its lock mechanism breaking with surprisingly little effort. A heavy odor of stale cigarettes poured through the opening, competing with the musty stench of a neglected, filthy home.

Once inside, he swiped the pickup's keys from the kitchen table before conducting a quick search of the structure, which confirmed that the man he'd shot through the window was the trailer's sole current occupant. A second bedroom with a bunk bed set and dresser suggested the man was divorced and shared custody of two children, who weren't present today. Lucky for the kids. Alejandro allowed nothing to get in the way of his work—and his work was nowhere near finished.

CHAPTER 4

Special Agent Garrett Mann slowed the Lincoln Navigator and lowered the tinted window as they approached the police roadblock—two Ford Interceptors parked in a V blocking the two-lane road. A good sign in the grand scheme of things. The Steele County Sheriff's Office wasn't screwing around with security surrounding the crime scene.

A far cry from what he'd seen in other counties, where hastily arrayed orange safety cones often sufficed as the only barrier until you nearly ran over the bodies. In his experience, small details like that made a big difference. He expected the same attention to detail and professional handling across the entire crime scene. Mann didn't want to get his hopes up, but this looked promising.

He pulled the SUV up to a weather-worn, crusty-looking deputy wearing a light-tan cowboy hat, who had lazily ventured forward from his perch on the hood of one of the vehicles blocking the road.

"Afternoon, Deputy," said Mann, extending his FBI badge through the open window. "Sheriff Young is expecting us."

The deputy barely examined his badge, or the woman in the passenger seat, before turning his attention to the rest of the convoy.

The vehicle behind Mann's was a Ford Expedition, featuring the largest Yakima roof box available on the market. Twenty-one cubic feet of extra space dedicated to their deployable surveillance gear.

A four-door, soft-top Jeep Wrangler came next—to get the team into hard-to-reach places. Since most of the bodies hadn't been located too far from the road, they primarily used the Wrangler for distant, armed overwatch of the crime scenes. You could never be too careful in this business, especially when you were closing in on a serial killer.

Technically last, but certainly not least, a medium-size recreational vehicle brought up the rear of the convoy. The modified "camper" served two purposes. Its first, and most important, role was to house Dr. Jimmy Trejo, the team's resident forensic pathologist, and his workshop, which occupied close to two-thirds of the vehicle's rear cabin space. The RV retained the kitchen, a small foldaway table, and a bathroom, all of which provided a welcome luxury when they were stuck in the middle of nowhere—like today. It also served as a basecamp whenever they needed to stay overnight at a crime scene. They'd unwind the side awning and roll out their sleeping bags.

"Looks like you brought the whole circus with you," said the deputy.

Mann stifled a laugh and smiled. "All three rings."

The barest of grins crossed the deputy's face. "Don't blame you, I guess," he said. "This one's shaping up to be a class-A shit show."

"What's your read on the situation?" said Mann.

He liked to solicit the rank and file's opinion when practical. The most valuable information or context often came from the dispassionate observations of a veteran or the raw, unfiltered opinions of a rookie.

"My read is that you got a nasty situation on your hands," said the deputy. "I've been on the job for twenty-eight years, and I've only thrown up twice. First time was a farmer's suicide just a few miles west of here. Twelve-gauge, double-barreled shotgun under the chin. They gave this one-month rookie two plastic buckets and sent me into the hayloft above the body. One bucket for the bits of skull and brain. The other to catch my lunch—and breakfast. Needless to say, I filled one much quicker than the other. You can guess which one."

"And the second time was this morning?" said Mann.

"Oh. No. Second time was when Jerry Miller ran over one of his kids with a combine about eighteen years ago, before they started requiring them to be built with all kinds of cameras and safety features. Damn thing spit his head into the grain bin. I most definitely wasn't ready to see that," said the deputy, his gaze shifting back toward the crime scene down the road.

"And you think this is worse?" said Mann.

"Let's put it this way. After watching Sheriff Young and Deputy Keller empty their stomachs earlier this morning, I ain't in any kind of hurry to examine the contents," said the deputy.

"I wish I could say the same," said Mann. "Did they open all the bags?"

Young had mentioned five contractor bags. Two more than were discovered at the killer's previous dump site. The Piano Man had been busier than usual on this trip. This sick fuck had started out with one kill on each trip, then quickly progressed to two. Then three. Then four. Mann's team had found that dump site outside Santa Fe, the victims taken from cities and towns along the killer's southbound route. He always dumped his entire trip's haul in one place.

They'd traced the Piano Man's general travel routes—north and south—but with thousands of miles of isolated, rural roads adjacent to the killer's path, the best they could do was put the word out to all the county sheriff's departments and local police departments along the way. Which was how they'd found the previous dump sites.

Today's discovery had gone down the same way, with one major difference. Instead of somebody eventually stumbling on festering bags of human remains, sometimes weeks after they'd been dumped, the killer had messed up. Or his luck had simply run out. Sometimes the line between the two was too hazy to tell the difference.

Either way, dragging five heavy bags, instead of three or even four, to the ditch along County Road 3 had undoubtedly put him in contact with one of Steele County's deputies, who had the presence of mind to give the killer's Suburban a second look. Mann's team stood a solid chance of recovering more evidence from this crime scene than the others. The bodies wouldn't be fresh. Not by any stretch of the imagination. But they'd be weeks newer than all their previous finds.

"No. Sheriff Young only sliced open one of the bags, just to confirm what he already suspected," said the deputy. "The puking started right after they took a look."

"I bet it did," said Mann.

"Well. Don't let me get in the way of all the fun," said the deputy, before speaking briefly into his shoulder-mounted radio transmitter. "Head on up. Sheriff Young is waiting. Deputy Keller, too."

"Keller found the bags, right?" said Mann.

"Yep. Around two in the morning."

"I think Keller got lucky last night," said Mann.

"Lucky to stumble on this mess?" said the deputy, glancing back toward the dozen or so vehicles parked a few hundred yards down the road.

Mann shook his head. "No. Lucky that he didn't linger too long on that first pass."

"Yeah. That's what I was thinking. The spike strip trick is a new one," said the deputy. "Never seen one deployed against a police vehicle."

"Whoever's been dumping these bodies isn't messing around. They'll rock and roll at the drop of a hat," said Mann.

"Sounds like he did get lucky," said the deputy.

One of the police Interceptors blocking the road backed up, giving Mann's convoy enough room to continue toward the crime scene.

"That's promising," said Catalina "Cata" Serrano from the front passenger seat.

She clutched a pack of cigarettes in one hand, stopping herself just short of crushing them—door handle in the other hand. Her body coiled up to spring out of the vehicle the moment they reached their destination. She'd gone five hours since her last smoke, the team driving nonstop from Kansas City after receiving the call from Sheriff Young.

Mann could have offered her a nicotine break at some point, but the team was in a hurry—and the five-minute stop would have brought the stench of tobacco back into the vehicle. Her breath, long after her last cigarette. Her clothes. Selfish of him, but he couldn't stand the smell of it. And she always had the option of riding in the smoker-friendly vehicle with Turner and Mayer.

But not really. She needed to stick as close to Mann as possible. Her presence on the ARTEMIS Task Force was far from official. More like completely illegal. Sanctioned by Mann. Begrudgingly accepted by the rest of the team at his insistence, which meant she probably didn't expect anyone but Mann to stick his neck out for her. And Mann didn't expect it from anyone on the team, either. He'd made it perfectly clear that he'd accept all responsibility for her presence, if the Bureau somehow discovered he'd integrated her into the team.

The problem wasn't her capabilities as an investigator. Not by a long shot. Nobody questioned her skills and determination. The problem was even more basic—without a remedy. Serrano wasn't an FBI agent. In fact, she didn't serve in any capacity as a law enforcement officer. Not anymore. And back when she'd been on the job a few years ago, she had worked as a cop outside the US. Serrano had been a Mexican state police officer.

"You want to walk the rest of the way?" said Mann, nodding at the pack of cigarettes in her hand.

Serrano rolled her eyes. "I think I'll survive a few more minutes."

"What if the sheriff banned smoking at the crime scene?" he said, mostly in jest.

"Then you'll just have to overrule him," she said—without the slightest hint that she might be joking.

CHAPTER 5

Mann maneuvered the Navigator through a gauntlet of sheriff's department vehicles, taking directions from a deputy who had broken away from the gaggle of law enforcement officers standing on the road. Behind them, a line of yellow crime scene tape staked to the ground extended from the soybean field to the east, across the road to the west shoulder. A second line of tape fluttered in the breeze roughly fifty yards down the road, enclosing the primary crime scene.

The spike strip site was a few hundred yards north of here, which was why his team had approached from the south, even though it cost them some time. The sheriff had left everything in place for Mann's people to examine.

"Not bad," said Serrano.

"Yeah. The sheriff gets it," said Mann, easing the Navigator directly behind an oversize, black rectangular van labeled STEELE COUNTY FORENSICS UNIT.

The rest of his team's vehicles parked in a single-file line behind him, on the east side of the road. The moment the convoy came to a stop, the group of deputies by the tape started to make their way over to the Navigator.

"Remember," said Mann. "Be nice. Diplomacy is the key to success with our local friends."

Serrano already had her door open, cigarette in mouth and lighter in hand. "I'll join everyone in a minute. Don't want to get off on the wrong foot," she said, lighting the cigarette before shutting the door.

"Funny," mumbled Mann, dropping down onto the dirt shoulder.

The first thing he noticed was the heat radiating from the road. And the humidity—still steamy from the previous night's rain. Behind him, car doors slammed shut as the rest of his team started to assemble. He walked around the front of the Navigator and waved at Steele County's finest, who approached at a rapid pace. The two groups met next to the forensics van, Serrano furiously fixing her nicotine situation on the opposite shoulder of the road, downwind from the get-together. Mann extended a hand to the man he'd identified as Sheriff Lonny Young from the county's website.

"Sheriff Young. Special Agent Garrett Mann," he said. "I'd introduce everyone on my team, but nobody will remember anyone's names anyway."

Young shook his hand and chuckled. "I'm with you on that. I'll forget the first two names by the time we're on the fourth. The rest go just as quickly. No reason to burn any daylight on that. *Deputy* or *sheriff* works just fine for us."

"Huh. I suppose *special agent* or just *agent* sounds a little odd. A tap on the shoulder or a *hey* should suffice. This is a very informal crew," said Mann. "As you may have guessed from the lack of suits and ties."

"I never judge a book by its cover," said Young. "Task Force ARTEMIS? Doesn't sound informal. What is ARTEMIS?"

"Greek goddess of the hunt. And trust me. We're more of a rogues' gallery than you might think," said Mann, glancing over his shoulder to examine his team for any signs of unfriendliness.

Not everyone on the team had Serrano's charming personality. And the wrong look at the wrong time could spark a turf war—the absolute worst possible scenario for their investigation. The last thing he wanted to do was pull rank and take control of the entire crime scene with a phone call to DC. Word traveled fast in these rural counties.

They could find themselves transporting five bags full of body parts to the FBI field office in Minneapolis, where the special agent in charge would have to burn a big favor to get them into one of the local medical examiners' offices. He'd much prefer they did the preliminary work in Owatonna, at the Steele County medical examiner's facility.

"So. How do you want to do this? The only people who have been inside the yellow tape are me, our county medical examiner, and Deputy Keller. Keller and I walked the scene last night. We waited until the rain stopped around eight this morning to bring Dr. Rostov down to take a look. That's when we opened one of the bags. Just to be sure of what we were dealing with. I mean . . . I think we all knew, but—"

"There's absolutely no need to apologize, Sheriff Young. This situation is so far outside the realm of normal, there's no standard operating procedure. You did good sealing off the scene like this. I can't thank you enough for that," said Mann. "Why don't we start by introducing Dr. Rostov and Dr. Trejo—"

"No relation to the movie star," said Dr. Trejo, getting a laugh out of a few of Young's deputies.

"Never gets old," said Mann, before continuing. "We'll let them take a look at the scene first. Dr. Trejo is an FBI forensic pathologist. We also have Special Agent Mills, who's a criminal investigator with extensive forensic experience. They walk all our scenes before I do. I worked transnational crime most of my career. Big-picture cartel stuff."

"Dr. Rostov is the county's medical examiner and forensics lead. Jack-of-all-trades type. I also have my two investigators," Young said, nodding over his shoulder at the two men in country-casual attire, well-worn work boots and badges on their belts. "If it's all right, I'd like to send them out on that first look. We haven't had a murder in as long as I can remember."

"And no multiple-body dumps?" said Mann, grinning.

"None of those, either," said Young. "Maybe they'll learn something."

"Hopefully something they'll never have to use," said Mann. "Dr. Trejo? You good with a few more sets of footprints out there?"

"I'm fine with—"

The door to the forensics van flew open to reveal a short, aged man with gray hair—wearing rubber, thigh-high waders and tan overalls.

"I don't need those two bumblers tripping over themselves out there," he said in a thick Russian accent. "It's bad enough that Keller almost stepped on a hand, in broad daylight—before nearly going ass over teakettle into the ditch!"

"Did I mention he's also a jack-of-all . . . asses?" said the sheriff. "And an eavesdropper?"

"Don't you mean *Russian spy*?" said Rostov, stepping down from the van.

"Oh yeah. Lots to spy on in Steele County," said Young, before nodding at Mann. "I probably should have warned you about Dr. Cold War. You might have saved yourself the trouble and taken over jurisdiction from the get-go."

"Ha! And take over moving the bodies to god knows where?" said Rostov. "He's not stupid, Sheriff. He needs us. He needs our—correction—*my* facility. Remember: I don't work for you. I work for the county's board of commissioners."

"Hard to forget with you reminding me every ten seconds," said Young.

Mann tried hard not to laugh but couldn't help himself. Neither could pretty much everyone standing on the road next to the forensics van.

"Laugh all you want. Fortunately for you, the board is a bunch of self-serving, incompetent idiots, so I do as I please. Which is why I'm

21

willing to . . . how shall we say it, play along? Those two can come, if they help move the bags into my van. Assuming our FBI friends don't want the bags for themselves."

"Holy shit . . . this guy is something else," said someone behind Mann.

He intervened before less complimentary comments aired and spoiled the moment.

"Dr. Rostov. We'd appreciate your help transporting the bags to *your* facility, where we'll examine the bodies together," said Mann. "And yes. We do need your help. Given what we've previously encountered, we're not looking at five distinct bodies. More like a jigsaw puzzle that's going to take some time and intestinal fortitude to solve."

"Well spoken, FBI guy!" said Rostov, before turning his attention to Young's two criminal investigators. "And no fading out on me when it comes time to get dirty! The G-man is right. This is going to be a real mess."

One of the investigators chimed in. "We'll be fine."

"Yeah. We'll see," he said, before turning his attention back to Mann. "Where is this Dr. Trejo?"

Trejo stepped forward. "Right here. I should probably fill you in on a few things before we proceed."

"I've already figured it out," said Rostov.

"Oh boy," said Young. "Here we go."

"I scour the forensics bulletins across the Great Plains all the way down to the border. Talk with dozens of contacts everywhere. My wife left me several years ago. I have way too much time on my hands," said Rostov.

"It's been painful for us, too," said Sheriff Young dryly, cutting him off.

"The sympathy is overflowing as always," said Rostov. "Anyway. Your killer collected these bodies on a south-to-north route and dumped them here. Not the first time this has happened."

Mann glanced at Trejo, raising an eyebrow. "I think the two of you will get along just fine."

"We'll see," said Trejo.

"And we'll see about you sinking three feet into the mushy ground in your fancy shoes. The irrigation ditch is like quicksand," said Rostov. "I have a spare set of waders in the van if you'd like to borrow them."

"I would. Thank you," said Dr. Trejo, before making his way to the van.

"Looks like they're getting along," said Young. "Which is all that really matters at this point, I guess. The rest of us are basically scarecrows."

"Yes. Just stand where you are, and today's outcome will be the same," said Rostov, glancing toward the sun. "Let's get moving. Unless someone wants to drive back to Owatonna and drag the lights out."

"One quick question before we get to work," said Mann.

"Make it a good one," said Rostov.

"Whose idea was all of this? Taping off the entire area? Waiting for us to arrive before really going to town on the crime scene?"

"Sheriff Young's," said Rostov. "I would have done the same thing, but he was very insistent last night that we preserve the scene, as best as possible, for your team."

"Well. I want to thank both you and the sheriff for taking my bulletin seriously," said Mann. "We may be looking at a big break here. This is the freshest scene we've come across to date."

The bulletin was the formal request Mann repeatedly sent to every county sheriff and police department from the Mississippi River to the Sierra Nevada Mountains, Canada to Mexico, requesting that his team be immediately notified of body dumps that fit a certain profile. Multiple bodies at one site, especially if stuffed in contractor bags, being the number one criterion.

"*Fresh* isn't a word I'd use. Not after opening one of the bags," said Young. "The bodies are pretty ripe."

"One of them is bound to be fresher than anything we've come across before. Depending on how long he took to make his northbound journey, of course. But regardless of their state of decay, we've been able to ID close to seventy percent of the bodies. Enough to establish the pattern Dr. Rostov just verbalized."

"We're burning daylight," said Rostov, before nodding at Dr. Trejo. "Let's get you geared up."

Trejo made his way over to the van and disappeared inside.

"I hope we see him again," said Young, before winking at Mann.

"I heard that!" yelled Rostov.

"I'll get a drone up to scan the area," said Callie Jackson, the team's primary surveillance operative.

"I'll help Jax with the drone," said Jessica Mayer, an FBI Special Surveillance Group castaway.

"Drones?" said Young, nodding his approval. "Nice. I wish we had the budget to train a drone team. We don't have a ton of use for aerial surveillance, but it sure would come in handy when chasing folks through these endless fields."

"Any of your deputies play video games?" said Jackson. "*Call of Duty. Battlefield.* Anything like that?"

The youngest of the deputies raised his hand. He looked like he might be twenty-one.

"If the sheriff doesn't mind, we can show your deputy the ropes," said Jackson. "Unless he absolutely sucks at flying, all you'd have to do is fork out between five hundred and a thousand for a quadcopter. Then another fifteen hundred bucks for a good IR camera. There won't be a place in the county for the bad guys to hide from you."

"Go for it, Crawford," said Young, nodding at the deputy.

"The rest of us will hang back and wait for the medical examiners to do their initial work," said Mann. "We brought some coffee from

Kansas City. Dunkin'. Box O' Joe. Probably cold by now, but we can heat up individual cups in the RV's microwave."

"Caffeinated?" said Young.

"Is there any other kind?" said Mann.

"No. And there's no need to heat it up," said Young. "Cold coffee is better than no coffee."

Mann chuckled. "Truer words have never been spoken."

CHAPTER 6

Catalina Serrano finished her third cigarette and snuffed it out on the road, then tucked the butt into a small Ziploc bag she kept in her pocket for this very purpose. She never littered. Ever. Few things ranked higher on her list of personality defects than littering.

She rejoined the group just as the investigation team departed to walk the crime scene. If anyone took issue with or noted her absence during the meet and greet, they didn't show it. Serrano typically made herself as invisible and silent as possible—for a good reason—during protracted interactions with local US law enforcement.

Serrano spoke fluent English, having studied the language with a passion for the past decade and a half, suspecting that her future lay north of the border at some point. But her Mexican accent was still thick. As in "let me see your ID" thick, depending on who pulled her over in the US—and where.

"Sorry about that," she said. "Five hours without a smoke nearly killed me."

Sheriff Young chuckled, a knowing smile crossing his face. "I quit three years ago. Lifelong smoker."

"I haven't really tried to quit yet. Not with this job," she said, settling in next to Mann.

"Oh. I don't blame you," said Young. "Took me a half dozen or so serious bouts of bronchitis before I finally decided to give them up. Let me rephrase that: until my wife made me give them up. Wasn't easy."

"Yeah. I know they're no good for me," she said, her hand playing with the pack in her jeans pocket. "Just waiting for the right time. Which seems to be never."

"What's your poison?" said Young.

Interesting question from a former smoker. Did he smell the difference? Mann gave her a quick glance, like he was reading her mind. She generally didn't care what she smoked, but in all the excitement this morning, Serrano had forgotten to run into the gas station before the convoy left Kansas City. She'd had to break into the slightly stale emergency stash she kept in the glove box. It was always the small details like these that got you busted. Fortunately, she'd long ago prepared a story.

"My father used to smoke unfiltered Delicados. From Mexico," she said. "The guy came over to the States when he was twenty, worked his ass off to become a citizen—and sent money back to Mexico for cigarettes. I keep a pack around to remind me of him."

"He's gone?"

"No. I'm just so busy with this assignment that I rarely get to see him anymore," said Serrano.

"We knew each other from the Southwest US Joint FBI-DEA Task Force," said Mann. "I finally convinced her to give up the good life in LA and live out of motels for a few years with this team. We also spend a lot of time by the border, so—"

"My accent and fluent Spanish come in handy quite often. All the time. You see—nobody else on the team can *habla español* beyond a high school level," she said. "You'd think it would be a requirement for a team operating on or near the border as often as it does."

"A small oversight," said Mann. "Which I corrected."

"*Overcorrected* might be a better way to put it," said Serrano.

Sheriff Young's cell phone chimed, mercifully putting an end to the scripted conversation Mann and Serrano had mastered over the past year. Young answered the call, his eyes opening wide several moments into the exchange. He glanced up at Mann and Serrano.

Steven Konkoly

"The Suburban turned up about thirty miles west of here in a small town called Waldorf," said Young. "Waseca County sheriff's deputies found it parked in a backyard. The property owner was shot dead. Two bullets to the face—and his pickup truck is missing."

"Probably won't be his last vehicle swap," said Mann. "Plates?"

"Plates were stripped. VIN scraped. No identifying information found in the vehicle," said Young.

"Shit. And Keller's dashcam? Any luck clearing up the plate image?" said Mann.

This was the first time that Serrano had heard of any dashcam footage. She shot Mann a look, which he noticed but ignored. Mann played his cards a little too close to the vest sometimes. Sharing information was one of the few weaknesses she'd identified since she'd first met him. Other than the booze. He certainly didn't mind having a drink or several under the right circumstances. Or the wrong circumstances, depending on how you looked at it.

Same for her, though the two of them never had more than a beer or two at dinner with the rest of the team. Mann had been careful about that. And not just with her. At least half of the team also hit the bottle pretty hard. Serrano knew the signs. She lived them. The booze never got in the way of work. She was careful about that. Enough of her days stretched far longer than necessary because of the bottle. Enough to give her pause. An occasional pause.

"Negative," said Young. "The plate must have been coated with some kind of video-spoofing film layer. The light from Keller's vehicle instantly blurred the plate."

"And Keller can't remember more than *XR*?" said Mann.

"Not yet. He pulled a double prior to last night's encounter. I sent him home to get some rest, hoping it might jog his memory," said Young. "Minnesota plate and *XR* is all he reported last night, and all he could remember this morning. Nothing in the state system matches. Not even a custom plate."

"*XR*? Sounds like a diplomatic plate prefix. The State Department assigns two-letter country codes to the plates they issue diplomats. Nobody messed with those vehicles, even if they just ran over a gaggle of preschoolers in a crosswalk," said Mayer. "I remember that *XF* represented Turkey, but *XR* doesn't ring a bell."

"Maybe he didn't get it right," said Young. "It was raining sideways, and he'd just come off a double shift."

"But he's sure it was a Minnesota plate?" said Mayer.

Young nodded. "I'm confident he got that part right. He's been chasing down Minnesota plates for the better part of a decade. Why?"

Mayer shrugged. "Diplomatic plates are exclusively issued by the State Department. They haven't been issued by individual states for over thirty years. And they're very recognizable. They either have DIPLOMAT or CONSUL in prominently featured bold letters. And either a *D* or *C* before the country code. Diplomatic staff feature an *S*."

"Maybe you should call O'Reilly," said Serrano. "She might be able to shed some light on the *XR* thing."

"Yeah. I'll give her a call," said Mann. "Sheriff Young. Can you ask the Waseca County sheriff to tow the Suburban to Dr. Rostov's office? We'll scour it for fingerprints. Anything useful. I'm not hopeful. Our perp has been very careful over the years."

"Been going on for that long?" said Young.

"Sorry to drop the curtain on this conversation, but many aspects of our case are considered classified—for various reasons beyond my control," said Mann. "That said—yes."

"Yes, what?" said Young.

"This has been going on for a while. Progressing from one dismembered body to who knows how many have been stuffed in the bags out there," said Mann. "This might be our big break. Or another dead end. I'm hoping for the former. We've been at this for a year and a half."

"Jesus," said Young, shaking his head. "I'll get on the horn with Sheriff Kadence. Explain the situation. We'll get the Suburban towed over to Dr. Rostov's office. And just so we're clear here, Dr. Rostov gets to play with the bodies, but we—I mean you—own all the evidence. So don't let him fuck with you about any of this. He's a good medical examiner. But he can be a pain in the ass."

Serrano laughed. "In my experience, personalities like Dr. Rostov's yield the best results. They're not beholden to anyone or anything—except their own demons."

"And I have zero interest in meeting Rostov's demons," said Young. "I can't even imagine."

"Same," said Mann, before pulling out his phone. "Gonna call O'Reilly—and kick the hornet's nest."

"If we're looking at a 'can't touch this' diplomatic plate—in Minnesota," said Mayer, "this might get really interesting. Really fast. Could be someone in witness protection."

"That would be a nightmare," said Mann.

Serrano removed the pack of cigarettes from her pocket. Screw it. This was too much. They were closer to the killer than ever before.

"Hope you don't mind," she said. "I'll stand downwind."

Young laughed. "Doesn't bother me. I'm done with those."

"Downwind would be nice," said Mann, giving her cigarette pack the stink-eye.

"Sure thing, boss," said Serrano.

Mann turned to Young. "When you get a chance, can you circle back around with Keller? See if he remembers anything else about the plate. And if you don't mind, give the Waseca sheriff a call and let him know I'd like to send a two-person team over to take a quick look at the crime scene in Waldorf."

"No worries. I'll let the sheriff know she can expect your people," said Young. "Then I'll give Keller a ring. Do you want me to bring him in so you can talk with him in person, as a witness?"

"How much sleep is he working with?" said Mann.

"A few hours," said Young.

"Is he scheduled for a shift anytime soon?" said Mann.

"He was originally scheduled to be back at the station in a few hours, but I swapped him out. He's not on until tomorrow morning," said Young.

"If he doesn't mind swinging by your station or the medical examiner's office tonight, I'd love to talk with him sooner than later," said Mann. "We'll be providing dinner for the department tonight. Pizzas. Or whatever is good up in Owatonna. It's been a long day, and for some of you . . . it's gonna be an even longer night. I don't take your time for granted. And I promise we won't take up much of Keller's time. Does he have family?"

"Wife. No kids yet."

"I'll order him a pizza to bring home," said Mann.

Mann and his coffee-pizza one-two punch. The amount of goodwill he'd generated over the past year feeding cops coffee and pizza across a dozen states could power a small city.

"That's mighty kind of you. I know the deputies will appreciate it. Probably draw more of a crowd than you want," said Young, laughing.

Serrano took a long drag, inhaling—and savoring—what she knew to be a toxic combination of a thousand different chemicals. A fact Mann made sure to point out whenever he could.

"You should send most of the pizzas to the station," said Serrano. "Nobody wants to eat pizza while assembling a human jigsaw puzzle."

Young grimaced in agreement.

"Good point. I've very sadly gotten used to it," said Mann, before turning to Young. "We'll figure something out and get everyone fed."

"Sounds good. I'll make those calls now," said Young.

Mann made his way over to Serrano, while the sheriff scrolled through the contact list on his phone.

"You want me to put this out?" she said, holding up her cigarette.

"Nope," he said, shaking his head. "And sorry for pushing us all the way through without a break. I should have been a little more flexible."

"I can manage," she said. "It sucks. But that's my problem."

"Still," said Mann, leaving it there. "So. What do you think?"

"I think this might be the break we've been looking for," she said.

"The body dump?" said Mann.

"No. The bodies won't tell us anything we don't already know about the killer or his methods," said Serrano. "The license plate might be the key to busting this wide open."

"Or shutting it down," said Mann. "If that's some kind of diplomatic, get-out-of-jail-free license number—we're kind of screwed."

"Fuck that," said Serrano.

"There is no 'fuck that' in the FBI, Cata," said Mann. "Not exactly."

"So, you'll just ignore the plate—if it comes back untouchable?" she said.

Mann shook his head. "No. But we'll have to take a far less direct approach."

"What if they just shut us down?" said Serrano. "What if our killer is important to them?"

"To them?"

"To whoever. You know how it works," she said. "Why would our killer be driving around with diplomatic or protected plates?"

"We don't know it's a special plate," said Mann. "Could be a total fake."

"True," said Serrano. "But you don't believe that. Do you?"

"No," said Mann.

Let the games begin.

CHAPTER 7

Gerald McCall, AXIOM's director of special activities, ended the call with Alejandro and rubbed his temples. They had a potential nightmare on their hands. Could be nothing. Could be the end of it all. And from what he could tell, there was zero daylight between the two on this one. The real kicker was that they had no way of knowing which scenario they were looking at. For now.

"Fuck," he muttered, pounding the desk. "What the hell was he thinking?"

He started laughing a moment later. Laughing at his own dumb question. *What the fuck was Alejandro thinking? Ha! The guy is a damn serial killer—who works for AXIOM at the LABYRINTH. What the hell did they expect?* They knew the guy hadn't stopped killing, and he had no reason to stop. He lived a gilded life inside the US. Immune from our laws—mostly—and overindulged. Of course he wouldn't stop! That much they accepted. But six victims in one trip!

"Over the top," he mumbled.

They'd inherited Alejandro from SINKHOLE. The CIA had rendered him out of Mexico in 2015, after determining that he was likely responsible for most of the killings and body dumps in Ciudad Juárez from the early nineties onward. Two decades of brutal murders that made the international news at one point, spawning several widely distributed documentaries that drew some seriously bad press to Ciudad

Juárez and the cartel that controlled the border area south of western Texas.

The CIA saw a unique opportunity in Alejandro. He wasn't just a random serial killer. The man had served as a notoriously brutal and effective enforcer for the Juárez Cartel for close to ten years. His reputation didn't just precede him. It cleared a path in front of him. Everybody in Ciudad Juárez knew Alejandro. And everybody feared him. Which was why his addition to the CIA's SINKHOLE operation had made so much sense. Turning one of Mexico's most dreaded cartel enforcers against his home cartel was a serious win for the CIA—until it wasn't.

Actually, SINKHOLE's failure was far more complicated than that. It was a fiasco in the making from the get-go. The CIA just couldn't see it. Using a well-known cartel enforcer to turn low-level cartel members into moles to work against the Juárez Cartel sounded like a feasible idea at the time. And it worked for a year or so, until the entire program unexpectedly unraveled. Almost overnight. With AXIOM's help—of course—at McCall's direction.

Langley had outsourced most of the security and maintenance work at the SINKHOLE site to AXIOM. As an upstart in the military-security contracting world back then, McCall approached all potential government contracts by engaging in labor-intensive "due diligence." Most of that diligence revolved around one key tenet: don't do anything that will sink the company.

The initial risk assessment of SINKHOLE held water, but several leaks sprang up during the first year of the contract. Most of them being leaks to the Juárez Cartel. Low-level shit at first. Testing the waters. Then full-out treachery. Few of SINKHOLE's "graduates" wanted to commit to double-crossing their former employer, regardless of the promised rewards and protection. And who could blame them? Betraying any cartel was a veritable death sentence.

The original SINKHOLE idea had been sound enough. On paper. Grab lower-level cartel members, hold them in a simulated cartel tunnel complex environment, and convince them that they were still working for their own cartel, as an internal investigator reporting on the activities of their own local network.

Ambitious, "loyal" moles who thought they were sniffing out and snitching on thieves and traitors were actually providing cartel operations intelligence to the CIA. A solid agency effort to undermine the cartels' operations, without putting too many US government boots on the ground in Mexico. But it was doomed from the start, and nobody seemed to understand why—until it was too late.

The cartels' single-mindedly brutal stranglehold on all its "employees," past and present, almost immediately triggered counterbetrayals. SINKHOLE "graduates" began to talk, voluntarily and involuntarily. Mostly involuntarily. Combine loose lips with the cartels' unlimited budgets to employ sophisticated counterespionage methods to root out traitors, and you had a sinking ship.

Once the CIA program started unraveling with the glaringly suspicious murders of several SINKHOLE "graduates," McCall caught his first glimpse of AXIOM's future, which he immediately helped to usher in. A future where AXIOM took over the SINKHOLE complex in New Mexico—and turned the entire operation's focus north of the US-Mexico border. Fertile ground for AXIOM's slowly growing clientele of ultrapatriotic politicians, business leaders, and political thought leaders. True Americans willing to do whatever it took to save the United States and set the country on a new course toward greatness.

McCall pulled out his smartphone and scrolled through his contacts list for Mr. Clean. He dialed the number on the secure phone in his private SCIF (Sensitive Compartmented Information Facility), a surveillance-proof space the size of a walk-in closet that was attached to his sprawling seventh-story corner office in Foggy Bottom.

"Powell here," said the voice that answered.

They'd lured Jeremy Powell away from the CIA right around the time AXIOM acquired SINKHOLE. Powell had run the CIA's infamous "black site" program for close to a decade at that point, establishing illegal prisons around the world to hold and interrogate terrorists deemed to be critical threats to the US and its allies, without observing any of the pesky "rights" afforded to prisoners of war, or prisoners in general, by US and international law. A perfect fit to oversee LABYRINTH, the ultimate black site facility, and to coordinate DOMINION, a plan designed to permanently change the American political landscape—for the good of the people. And AXIOM's bottom line.

Powell had earned the nickname Mr. Clean because of his razor-shaved bald head—and the fact that he never left a mess behind when given a task. Another reason why he was a perfect fit for the job. McCall's plans for AXIOM left almost zero margin for error, and Alejandro's mistake last night would require one hell of a cleanup.

"Jeremy. Call me back from a secure location," said McCall.

"Right away."

CHAPTER 8

Jeremy Powell ended the call, before swiftly making his way to the SCIF at the end of the hallway. A small inconvenience in the grand scheme of things, but enough to annoy him, given his job. The construction of a broom closet–size SCIF inside his office was scheduled to begin in a few weeks. Within a month, he'd have immediate, unfettered access to the kind of secure communications required to execute his duties as DOMINION's nationwide coordinator. Until then, he had to share the SCIF with everyone else on the floor, who mistakenly thought they were important.

He shut the reinforced soundproof door behind him, which activated additional lighting in the room and triggered the door's serious lock-and-seal mechanism. The door could be opened only from the inside at this point unless an executive at Gerald McCall's level initiated an override with a unique key card. AXIOM took their information more seriously than the CIA did theirs.

Powell sat down behind the small, square table in the middle of the compact room and contemplated the secure phone attached to the table. He picked up the receiver and dialed a number he'd committed to memory.

A series of clicks and beeps followed, filler while the room's IR and facial recognition sensors confirmed what the call's recipient, Gerald McCall, had requested. Powell's sole presence. Several seconds later, the call was connected.

"Confirmation code," said McCall.

"Seriously?"

"The code, please."

"Cubs win. Cubs win. Eight to seven. Tenth inning."

McCall was a die-hard Chicagoan, but not the White Sox kind.

"Jeremy. Alejandro has been a bad boy," said McCall.

Powell considered a smart-ass response but decided against it. He detected fear and doubt in his boss's voice. Unusual for McCall, who had the world at his fingertips and could pretty much make anything happen—anywhere. He'd tread lightly for now.

"How bad?"

"He took six on his most recent travels," said McCall. "And botched the dump—less than an hour from his home."

Jesus. Powell thought he had an understanding with Alejandro. The former Juárez Cartel enforcer had been a very prolific serial killer back in the day. Made the news at one point, shortly before the CIA grabbed him and put him to work converting Juárez Cartel members into intelligence sources.

When AXIOM "inherited" Alejandro after taking over SINKHOLE, they honored the CIA's agreement to let him continue to indulge his twisted needs—but with the same limits. Six to ten kills per year outside the LABYRINTH compound, spaced out between trips back and forth from his cushy lair outside Minneapolis, which translated to one to two per trip back and forth. Nothing that would attract too much attention, or any attention at all if he played it smart.

On top of that, he had access to a nearly unlimited supply of victims at the LABYRINTH compound. A third of the candidates brought to the compound eventually turned out to be unsuitable for DOMINION, AXIOM's stateside program. Liabilities that could not be returned to Mexico or their actual cartel duties in the southwest United States. Playthings for Alejandro's kind. But apparently not enough to satisfy his bloodlust.

Like most predators, he preferred to hunt wild game. So, his trips back and forth from Minneapolis quickly became a problem, attracting the wrong kind of attention. Specifically, ARTEMIS. A shadowy FBI task force focused on serial killers. AXIOM knew next to nothing about ARTEMIS, which was led by Garrett Mann, who had no previous experience pursuing serial killers.

That said, Mann did have a rather long and notorious history of pushing the wrong buttons at the Southwest US FBI-DEA Task Force, where he rather consistently and stubbornly pushed programs and operations targeting the Juárez Cartel. AXIOM's personal profile workup on Mann suggested that his obsession with the Juárez Cartel, and Mexican cartels in general, was spawned by a college spring break incident in Cancún fifteen years ago, in which his fiancée-to-be disappeared under extremely unusual circumstances—unquestionably related to the cartels.

Given his stubbornly passionate stance toward the cartels, specifically the Juárez Cartel, AXIOM successfully lobbied FBI leadership to have him removed from the task force. What they hadn't counted on was the connection Mann had somehow formed with Dana O'Reilly, the head of the FBI's Critical Incident Response Group. Within days of his ousting from the Southwest US FBI-DEA Task Force, he had been given carte blanche to form a small task force to investigate serial killers along the US-Mexico border.

For a year or so, Mann's task force posed no threat to LABYRINTH or DOMINION, his attention and success on the Gagliani case keeping his focus away from the border—until it wasn't. Which was why they had been watching him as closely as possible for the past year and a half. Confident that he had little chance of connecting any of the dots and catching Alejandro. All that had changed overnight.

"His latest antics could very well bite us in the ass," said McCall.

"What's our current level of exposure?" said Powell.

"For starters, Mann has Alejandro's Suburban. A local sheriff's deputy passed the SUV while he was dropping the last of five bags filled with body parts. He managed to get back into the SUV and elude the deputy, using a remote-activated spike strip," said McCall. "After ditching the Suburban a few towns over, he removed the license plate and cleaned out any identifying paperwork, like the registration. All VIN tags had been removed prior to providing him with the vehicle. They might pull some fingerprints, but those will come back unidentified."

"Did the deputy get the SUV's tag number?" said Powell.

"The tag number hasn't been queried in Minnesota's license plate database."

"Mann isn't stupid," said Powell. "He'd pursue the tag number more discreetly given the circumstances."

"True. But the Steele County Sheriff's Office would have run the tag if the deputy had caught it. Nearly twelve hours elapsed between the late-night encounter and Mann's team arriving at the scene."

"Should we terminate Alejandro?" said Powell. "Remove any possible link to DOMINION and LABYRINTH?"

"No. DOMINION isn't fully staffed," said McCall. "We're close, but we still need him to work on several more batches of candidates—to fill the entire nationwide roster. Alejandro is not going to like this, but he's grounded until further notice."

"Like a teenager," said Powell dryly.

"Exactly. Transport him to LABYRINTH immediately. He can fulfill the rest of his contract in the comfort of his underground accommodations. A small price to pay given his transgressions," said McCall.

"And . . . what about Mann's team?" said Powell, hoping for some kind of execution edict he could implement.

"Leave them alone—for now," said McCall. "We can vanish Alejandro without any repercussions. We can't wipe out a team of ten FBI agents without attracting serious attention."

"We probably could. If we blame it on the cartels," said Powell. "Which is an entirely reasonable course of action given Mann's history of pressing for stronger action against them."

"It'll still draw too much attention," said McCall. "Which we don't need on any level. Mann reports directly to Dana O'Reilly, who heads the FBI's Critical Incident Response Group. Her history is very checkered."

"As in?"

"As in—she's an enigma," said McCall. "I get the impression from various contacts in the FBI and DOJ that she doesn't give a shit about her career and hasn't ever given a shit about it. She was a favorite of Ryan Sharpe's, the former director of the FBI, which is probably why she's sitting in one of the more coveted positions within the Bureau."

"I'd never heard of her until Mann got involved," said Powell. "Now she's suddenly somebody?"

"That's the thing," said McCall. "She was literally a nobody—until she wasn't. Bottom line? We don't mess with Garrett Mann unless he proves to be a clear and present threat to our bigger operation."

"But we keep a close eye on him," said Powell.

"I'll take care of that," said McCall. "Your job right now is to bring Alejandro to LABYRINTH. Come hell or high water."

"And if Mann tries to intervene?"

"I don't see how he would—but we can't have any violence if Mann somehow shows up. You have all the authentic enough–looking credentials necessary to take Alejandro into custody—right in front of the FBI if it comes to that. Threaten violence if you must, under your perceived authority, but do not engage," said McCall. "They'll back off long enough for you to get Alejandro out of there and vanish."

"Easier said than done with FBI guns pointed in your face."

"Well. That's why I pay you an exorbitant amount of money," said McCall, pausing for a moment before continuing. "Are we good? Are your orders clear enough?"

"We're good. And your orders are crystal clear," said Powell.

Why rock the boat? What he wanted to say was that it wouldn't be their credentials that defused any potential law enforcement situation or interference. The immediate threat of overwhelming firepower by his team would buy them the time they needed to move Alejandro to the private jet that would fly him south.

"Good. Get your people out there immediately. Secure Alejandro's property and move him to LABYRINTH, where he will be required to stay for now. And please search the property for any trophies that sick fucker may have kept over the past few years. The last thing we need is for Mann's team to be able to connect any more dots. Not that he's connected any so far."

"I'll put Zaleski on the job."

"Uh. No. Absolutely not," said McCall. "Tara is a bona fide psychopath. She's not the right person. Especially if Mann's team somehow shows up. Do it yourself or send Gary."

"Litman might not have what it takes to handle this situation if it goes sideways," said Powell.

"Then fire him."

"He's not that bad," said Powell. "Just not—"

"Fucking crazy? I know. I hired him. Send Litman to Minneapolis. He'll do fine. He's resourceful," said McCall. "Send Tara to Owatonna to take possession of Alejandro's Suburban. Should be an easy job. It's a rural county police station. Not Fort Knox. I want that vehicle back in our possession sooner than later. The less evidence Mann's team has to work with, the better."

"What are her rules of engagement?" said Powell.

"Well. I'd prefer if she didn't lay waste to the entire sheriff's department," said McCall.

"Obviously," said Powell.

"But if she has to crack a few local skulls in the process, that's fine. But no FBI skulls. Clear? We don't need that kind of heat. Not now. Not ever."

"Clear."

"I'm holding you up," said McCall. "Flight time to Minneapolis is a little over two hours."

"I'll get Litman and a SAG team airborne within the hour," said Powell. "Same with Zaleski."

"Sounds like a plan. Keep me in the loop, especially if things look like they might go sideways," said McCall, ending the call.

"Fucker," muttered Powell, after confirming that the call had indeed ended.

He hated being micromanaged like this, but he understood why, particularly given the unusually risky circumstances they faced. Tara was the best operative for the Minneapolis job, as far as he was concerned, but McCall wasn't wrong about her. She could be unpredictable and impulsive given the wrong set of external stimuli. Guns pointed at her face being the worst-case scenario imaginable.

Litman, on the other hand, was entirely levelheaded. Often too even-keeled for Powell's liking—but he could be trusted to keep the peace under stress. Which was what the situation demanded. And McCall required. And whatever McCall wanted, Powell strived to deliver. He wasn't in any position to do otherwise. Not yet.

CHAPTER 9

FBI Assistant Director Dana O'Reilly excused herself from the department head meeting to take Garrett Mann's call. He'd been at the latest Piano Man crime scene for a few hours now. Normally, she wouldn't interrupt a meeting to take a seemingly routine field call, but last night's discovery had been unique. For the first time in the year-and-a-half-long investigation into this killer, Mann had a fresh drop site on his hands. And the possibility, however remote, that the Piano Man might have left usable evidence behind during his hasty, forced departure. She answered the call as soon as the door closed behind her.

"Got anything?" said O'Reilly.

"Yes and no," said Mann. "The scene looks pretty much the same as the others, except for the spike strip. We might be able to trace that. It's not something readily available to civilians."

"They're not available to civilians at all," said O'Reilly. "Let me know if you need any help with that. Not many distributors out there for remote-activated spike strips, and none of them want to piss off the FBI."

"That's what I figured. We should be able to identify the company that made it," said Mann. "Other than that, I have five bags stuffed with body parts—and a partial license plate number."

"First things first. Five bags?" said O'Reilly.

"Yeah. More than usual," said Mann. "I don't expect to find anything new or helpful in the bags—other than at least two more bodies than before."

"Six victims?" said O'Reilly.

"Definitely more than four. Probably why the dump site is farther north than before. He got greedy and extended his killing spree," said Mann. "One of the bags broke open at some point. The sheriff's department found a hand in the grass between the irrigation ditch used for the dump and the road. My guess is that the killer would have been gone by the time the deputy passed by if the bag hadn't busted apart."

"So. More of the same?" said O'Reilly.

She didn't mean to come off as gruff or abrupt, but she wasn't hearing anything new. Nothing in the bags would prove useful. The killer had never left Mann's team anything to work with, other than DNA evidence, which Mann had used to identify most of the victims—and establish a travel pattern. A repetitive pattern that the team used to position themselves along the killer's most likely path and get to the site as quickly as possible.

"Basically," said Mann. "Except the killer abandoned his Suburban in a neighboring county, after killing a local. He stole that victim's pickup truck and disappeared. We've always known that the killer wasn't a run-of-the-mill murderer, but the scene over in Waseca County suggests the level of sophistication of an assassin. The victim was shot twice in the head with a pistol, through a window—from the backyard."

"Any evidence left behind in the Suburban?"

"We're having it towed to the medical examiner's office in Owatonna for a thorough sweep," said Mann. "Plates, VIN, and paperwork are gone. But we have a partial plate number from Deputy Keller. Hoping to get more from him later. He was coming off a double shift last night when he ran into our killer, so the sheriff sent him home to get some sleep."

"Are you going to keep me in suspense about the plate?" said O'Reilly.

"I thought you'd never ask," said Mann. "All Keller could recall so far is *XR*. Minnesota plate. Young ran *XR* through the state system and came up with nothing. Special Agent Mayer said the two-letter combo resembled a country code used for diplomatic plates but wasn't familiar with *XR*."

"States don't issue diplomatic plates," said O'Reilly.

"I know," said Mann. "But since *XR* didn't show up in the state database, I was hoping you might be able to dig into the federal database."

"You mean the State Department's database?" said O'Reilly.

"I know you can access the system," said Mann. "If you want to."

"That's the million-dollar question," said O'Reilly. "Do I really want to piss off the State Department for a Minnesota state plate featuring two letters? It's not like letters are unusual on license plates—and I don't see how State could possibly be involved."

"I'm not saying they are," said Mann. "But the fact that there's not a single license plate combination in the Minnesota State system using *XR*, I thought it might be worth asking around. We cracked the Gagliani killings by identifying a WITSEC-issued plate—with your help."

The Gagliani case put ARTEMIS on the map. They'd gotten lucky with a gas station security camera hit that identified the killer's license plate, but that's how these investigations tended to go. The smallest details cracked open the biggest cases, and sheer persistence by investigators kept those details under constant scrutiny, until they revealed their secrets.

To say that Mann had been persistent would be an understatement. His team meticulously scoured camera footage taken at parking lots and gas stations from Santa Fe to Las Cruces. Roughly a 280-mile-long, thirty-mile-wide corridor running north–south along Interstate 25. Hundreds of cameras. Thousands of hours. A chore most investigators would have pared down to major travel hubs and called it good. But not Mann. His team spent months traveling the region, reviewing all the footage they could get their hands on and recording license plate numbers—looking for a pattern. And it paid off brilliantly.

Tommy "The Slicer" Gagliani, a mob enforcer turned federal witness, had been relocated to Albuquerque, New Mexico, through the United States Federal Witness Protection Program (WITSEC)—where he immediately went back to work killing prostitutes and escorts, female and male, that he solicited online. When Mann matched the killings' bizarre MO to a string of unsolved murders throughout eastern Connecticut and Providence, Rhode Island—strangulation followed by necrophilia—he dug deeper into the New England killing spree.

Mann discovered that the murders out east had stopped cold, right around the time the FBI had arrested a dozen or so big players in the Patriarca crime family. The Mafia family that had controlled most organized crime from Boston to Hartford for over a hundred years. He floated a theory that sounded as far-fetched as anything O'Reilly had heard before—and she'd seen some improbable shit in her career.

Mann simply didn't accept that the Providence serial killer randomly moved to Albuquerque. He suspected that the killer had turned federal witness, in the wake of the Patriarca family arrests, and had been relocated by the US Department of Justice through the Witness Protection Program. A long shot by any stretch of the imagination, but one that made sense on a number of levels. Enough sense for O'Reilly to put her reputation, whatever it was still worth, on the line to make some inquiries.

Several bruised egos later, mixed with a few career-threatening phone calls, she had a license plate number for Barry A. Jones—previously known as Tommy Gagliani. An unmarried Albuquerque resident with no previously known history of residency, work, or family in the state prior to 2017. Mann's team began surveillance on "Mr. Jones," coming up with nothing. The guy appeared to keep to himself, living frugally off a modest WITSEC stipend. But Mann wasn't convinced, which led him to focus on the security footage they had collected.

Eventually, he identified Gagliani's license plate at a Sonic Drive-In restaurant in Socorro, New Mexico, about an hour south of Albuquerque. A few miles from the home of a recently declared "missing person." A woman with profiles on several escort sites catering to clients along the Santa Fe to Las Cruces corridor.

The Department of Justice took over from there, the investigation and all criminal proceedings buried under WITSEC rules and regulations. Gagliani went to jail for life, and ARTEMIS went from O'Reilly's "pet project" to "legendary" status with the bang of a gavel—along with a significant increase to the ARTEMIS budget. Another gamble that paid off. The story of her career.

She'd been doubtful of Mann's initial proposal. A task force dedicated to hunting down serial killers in the Southwest? Sounded like a career killer for Mann and anyone involved, including herself, but O'Reilly was a veteran of career-killing moves, so she dug a little further. The results gave her pause at first.

Mia Alvarez, his fiancée-to-be and fellow student at the University of Texas at Austin, had disappeared in Cancún during their senior-year spring break—about fifteen years ago. She'd vanished during an early-morning beach run. Mann had tried to file a missing person report with the Quintana Roo State Police Department, but something had gone wrong.

The police had held him overnight and put him on the first flight out of Cancún the next morning—along with the rest of his friends from UT Austin—after falsely accusing him of being involved in her disappearance. Mia's body was never recovered, something Mann obviously hadn't let go. All the better. *Never letting go* tended to get results. Something she could attest to as the only reason she sat in one of the most coveted positions in the FBI.

"Okay. I'll put some feelers out," she said. "Does feel a little odd. Suburban in the middle of nowhere. Spike strip. Sophisticated vehicle dump. It doesn't add up."

"It doesn't," said Mann. "Which is why I'm worried."

"Worried about what?" said O'Reilly.

"Worried that we may be looking at another cover-up of some kind," said Mann. "Which is why I'm asking you to dive deep into the license plate thing. Could be nothing."

"Could be everything," said O'Reilly.

"Exactly."

"All right. Just keep all this shit to yourself," said O'Reilly. "Understood? Do not, under any circumstances, expand upon your theories with the Steele County Sheriff's Office. Or any other department."

"They've heard our general speculation," said Mann. "Sheriff Young ran the letters through the system."

"Yes. And that's where it ends," said O'Reilly. "You don't say another word about the license plate. You don't hazard guesses in front of anyone outside of your team. And they don't say shit, either. I'm not kidding around. If your instincts are even remotely on target, we're looking at something way bigger, and far more dangerous, than the Gagliani case. Are we clear?"

"Crystal," said Mann.

"Good," said O'Reilly. "I'll get back to you as soon as I have anything."

"Same here," said Mann. "I feel like we're getting closer. And I strongly suspect that the Piano Man lives somewhere in the Minneapolis area. This is the farthest north we've ever found a dump site, and the general south-to-north trend points to Minneapolis."

"Keep doing the grunt work. Forensics, for what it's worth. Victim IDs. All of it," said O'Reilly. "If the latest batch points farther north than before, we have something more to go on."

"Agreed," said Mann. "And thank you."

"For what?" said O'Reilly.

"For continuing to support the team," said Mann. "I know ARTEMIS has been a bit of a stretch for you."

"Just slightly," said O'Reilly.

Actually—way more than slightly. When Mann first approached her with the idea, she liked the concept, but had no idea how she'd justify attaching a highly unorthodox serial-killer investigative team to the Critical Incident Response Group's already robust and successful Violent Criminal Apprehension Program (ViCAP). Fortunately for Mann, the powers that be in the FBI wanted him sidelined, and they were more than willing to grant him an assignment out of the regular chain of command. Somewhere to effectively hide him. And there was no better place to bury a wayward soul than CIRG.

O'Reilly knew this better than anyone. Her FBI career had been unorthodox to say the least. Much of her work was classified at the highest level thanks to a bizarre series of domestic conspiracies that the US government would prefer to forget. Her unexpected appointment to head of the FBI's Critical Incident Response Group had as much to do with her previous experience handling uniquely high-stress cases as her boss's insistence that she be given the job—FBI directors past and present tended to have some sway regarding personnel assignments.

That and the FBI's overall desire to keep her in check. O'Reilly wasn't delusional or self-flattering. She was good at what she did, but her past—and by default the FBI's past—was a closet filled with skeletons that the government would prefer to keep out of public view. CIRG fulfilled an important role within the Department of Justice, but most of their work took place in the shadows. Exactly where they wanted her. CIRG was the FBI's "break glass in case of emergency" department.

Hostage rescue. Hostage negotiation. Special intelligence gathering. Serial killer investigations. Not your garden variety stuff by any stretch of the imagination. ARTEMIS fit the CIRG bill perfectly in so many ways. A rogues' gallery of FBI agents. Misfits and management challenges cast away by their superiors—and immediately swooped up by Garrett Mann. She had to give him credit. He picked the right people, from the wrong pool of candidates, ultimately assembling a surprisingly effective team. And O'Reilly knew a thing or two about unorthodox teams. To say the least.

"I'll keep you posted," said Mann.

"Same here," said O'Reilly, before ending the call.

She stood in the empty hallway outside the conference room for a few moments, contemplating her next move. A call to her contacts in the Special Surveillance Group? They should be able to shed the most light on the diplomatic license plate theory, since they spent much of their time following diplomats. A call to the State Department? She'd need a precall from her former boss to grease those skids. Her WITSEC contacts? She'd burned those with the Gagliani bust.

Or someone outside the government? Someone who followed people in the DC area for a living—outside the FBI's purview. Yep. She knew exactly who to call. O'Reilly scrolled through her list of contacts for a few moments, before dialing a number she hadn't used in years.

"Assistant Director Dana O'Reilly," said her contact. "To what do I owe the pleasure of this call?"

"How familiar are you with diplomatic license plates?"

"Thank you for asking, Dana. Marnie and I are doing well. And you?" he said.

"Not now, Devin," she said. "Diplomatic plates?"

"I just happen to be staring at one right now," he said. "What do you want to know?"

"Ever hear of a state issuing a diplomatic or protected license plate?" said O'Reilly.

"Never a diplomatic plate. But some kind of protected plate? Yes. But it's rare. At least from what I've seen," he said. "What's this about?"

"We had a bit of a break last night in one of our cases," said O'Reilly. "Along with a possible partial license plate. A deputy saw the letters *XR*, which sounds like a diplomatic country code, but he swears it was a Minnesota plate. The state vehicle registration database doesn't have a single plate with *XR*."

"Do you have any more of the plate number?"

"No. We're talking with the deputy that reported the SUV in a few hours," said O'Reilly. "Hopefully he'll remember more."

"Sounds like the plate is either fake or it's a one-of-a-kind, specialty tag number—issued by the state," he said.

"You've seen one-of-a-kind plates like this before, Devin?" said O'Reilly.

"We've come across them a few times in the past," he said. "Unless you have the entire plate number, nothing comes up in the state system."

"Who arranges these? The feds?" said O'Reilly.

"We don't know. We had zero luck piercing that veil," said Devin. "I could see the feds arranging these plates for VIPs or high-value witnesses? At the same time, a state could issue a plate like that for its own purposes."

"And what did you do when you came across these plates?"

"What do you mean?"

"I mean, how did you proceed?" said O'Reilly.

"We didn't. Officially," said Devin. "You don't mess with those plates. At all."

"Uh-huh," said O'Reilly, smiling to herself. "But unofficially, what did you do?"

"Unofficially—we only pressed the issue through proper channels once. A Delaware plate that spent a little too much time near some folks we were investigating," he said. "Got our surveillance shut down quickly."

"Wait. It got you shut down?"

"Yes," he said. "A small swarm of DOJ lawyers hit the home office within an hour of our calling in the plate."

"WITSEC?" she said.

"That's what we thought at first, but no," he said. "Something different."

"How different?" said O'Reilly. "What am I dealing with here?"

"I sincerely have no idea," he said. "We never found out what was going on with the plate we followed. Complete DOJ blackout. But we did eventually identify the woman driving the SUV. A dual US and Lithuanian citizen with an apartment in Silver Spring and a condo in Rehoboth Beach. Traveled back and forth from Lithuania at least a dozen times a year. Her parents are retired Lithuanian diplomats."

"A spy?" said O'Reilly.

"We were thinking a possible honeypot operation, given the nature of the countersurveillance mission we were running at the time," said Devin. "She most likely started following our client around with the intention of compromising and ensnaring him. Or she could have been hired to kill him. We'll never know. She disappeared faster than the lawyers appeared. She was definitely up to no good—driving around with near impunity thanks to someone, somewhere with enough pull in Delaware to get her behind the wheel of a shielded vehicle. What brand of criminal are you dealing with?"

"Serial killer."

"Shit."

"Exactly," said O'Reilly.

"Need any help?"

"No," she said. "Not yet. Hopefully never."

"We're always here if you need us."

"I appreciate it," said O'Reilly. "But I think my crew has it locked down."

"Famous last words," he said. "Nothing is ever fully locked down."

"I know," said O'Reilly. "Anything else you can share about these mystery license plates?"

"Yeah," he said. "Watch your back."

"I figured that much," said O'Reilly.

"Then you're already way ahead of the curve, Assistant Director."

"Funny."

"Not really. Tread cautiously on this one, Dana," he said. "I guarantee the connection to that plate, if it indeed turns out to be one of these one-of-a-kind tags, will not be a savory one. Not if the plate is protecting a serial killer."

"I will," she said.

"Call if you need help."

"I have a task force that can get the job done," she said. "I just need to figure out what the job is."

"Stubborn."

"Don't you have something better to do right now other than shit on me?" said O'Reilly.

"You called me. Remember?"

"Fair enough," she said. "So. What would you do in my situation?"

"You have to press the plate issue," he said. "I assume the killer is still active?"

"Very active," she said.

"Then turn on the lights and watch the roaches scatter. See where they run," he said. "Let *them* shut *you* down first. Then go after *them*. If you can identify *them*."

"This is going to be painful," said O'Reilly.

"Finding a serial killer who is potentially hiding behind some kind of special Minnesota license plate?" he said. "If you're lucky, they'll just shut you down. Easy peasy. If not? I'd say you're in for quite a ride."

"Wonderful. So. After getting burned following the *proper* channels, I assume you found a work-around?" said O'Reilly. "I could poke around like you did the first time—and piss a lot of people off—but I'd rather do this a little more discreetly. At least for now."

"Always better to minimize the number of people you've pissed off," he said. "Are you looking to remain entirely within the realm of—you know—what's legal?"

She remained quiet for a few seconds, hoping he got the hint. She couldn't possibly answer that question inside FBI headquarters, on an FBI-issued phone.

"Okay. Texting you the number right now. Wait until I give you the go-ahead to call him," said Devin. "He owes me a few favors, but I'll need to remind him first. He tends to selectively remember what he owes."

"Thank you. I appreciate the help with this. Hopefully, I'll have more of the plate number later," said O'Reilly. "So. How is everything going on your end? Marnie is good?"

"All good. Thank you for asking," he said.

"Any kids on the way?" she said.

"Not that we know of," he said. "Why? You looking to become a godparent?"

"I don't even have a pet," she said. "I'm probably not the best candidate."

"We have a new sailboat if you're interested. Less of a commitment," he said. "Sunset drinks on the bay?"

"Very interested, actually," said O'Reilly. "Once I've cleared this very unorthodox investigation. I remember what happened the last time you took friends out on the bay with some things pending."

"Fair point," he said. "Well. You're always welcome out on the water with us. I know Marnie would love it."

"She's the best," said O'Reilly.

"Agreed."

"Anything else you can think of that might help me with this license plate?" said O'Reilly.

"No. Other than—be very careful. Seriously."

"I will. We will. Thank you again, Devin," she said, before disconnecting the call.

Fuck. We have a problem on our hands if the license number turns out to be a protected plate. A nightmare, possibly. A serial killer protected by the government? Why? And how the hell will we proceed?

CHAPTER 10

Mann dispatched Jessica Mayer and Tony Baker to examine the crime scene in Waseca County and collect basic evidence before the sheriff's department towed the Suburban to Owatonna. Neither one of them possessed formal crime scene investigation training, but that wasn't why he sent them. He had picked them over any of their more seasoned investigators for a few reasons. The most important being that he needed both of his forensic experts focused on the roadside scene.

Their killer had been meticulous in the past, leaving no useful evidence for his team to process—but he'd been caught off guard out here last night. That much was certain, and Mann couldn't afford to blow what might be their first and last opportunity to move the case forward. Trejo and Mills had scoured the Piano Man's previously discovered dump sites together. Ten in total—yielding twenty-seven victims. He doubted they would find anything, even considering the killer's hasty departure. But if anything was off, they'd know it. And the devil was always in the details. Even the smallest screwup on the killer's part could break the case.

The second reason was even more of a long shot. Mayer was a surveillance expert who'd spent close to two decades tracking and trailing suspected spies in the US. On the extreme off chance that the killer circled back to glean information into the investigation, she'd be the most likely member of the team to detect his presence.

He'd sent Baker to watch over Mayer, not that she needed protecting. Far from it—but the team couldn't afford to become complacent on any level. Not when they still didn't know what they were up against. All they knew for certain was that the killer was a brutal and exceedingly meticulous murderer. And who the hell knew if they were looking at one murderer. Two murderers. Or three? Could be an entire syndicate for all they knew.

And after last night, nothing could be taken for granted. The spike strip represented a "next level" boost to their killer's repertoire. A newly exposed skill. A high level of planning and preparation Mann hadn't expected. So, having a former member of the FBI's elite Hostage Rescue Team like Baker on hand wasn't overkill. Quite the contrary. Mayer would detect the threat . . . and Baker would eliminate it. That was the plan, anyway. He couldn't imagine any scenario in which the killer got by their combined defenses.

The two had taken the Wrangler and been gone for a good hour and a half, with nothing unusual to report about the Waseca County crime scene. Gone long enough for the medical examiners and investigators here to do their work and return to the road to debrief the rest of the team. Rostov's new minions had already retrieved a collapsible litter to start transporting the contractor bags to the forensics truck—the work to be overseen by Ray Mills.

Everyone gathered next to the Steele County "crime scene" van for the initial medical examiner debrief.

"Same as before?" said Mann, nodding at Dr. Trejo. "Jax's drone surveillance didn't show anything unusual out in the fields behind the ditch."

"I'm not surprised. The scene itself looked the same as the others," said Trejo, before glancing back toward the irrigation ditch. "But I think our guy is getting greedy and impatient. We may be looking at six victims here. And not all of them have been handled the same as before. We identified some very raw, brutal detachments. Machete or hatchet work."

"Interesting," said Mann. "Maybe he bit off more than he could chew toward the end of his trip?"

They still hadn't figured out how the killer pulled off the time-consuming torture and dismemberment of his victims while on the road. Where did he take his victims once he grabbed them? How did he conceal moving live and dead bodies back and forth to his vehicle? Did he pick his victims from specific cities or towns based on known access to isolated locations for his gruesome work? These being just a handful of the hundreds of questions that had gone unanswered.

"Well. Six victims would be an escalation, if that's what we determine after emptying the bags?" said Trejo. "The most we've previously seen is four."

"But how else do you cut off a major limb," said Young, "without using a sharp-as-hell weapon?"

Rostov jumped at the opportunity to school the sheriff. He hobbled over to join the group—his limp a recent development.

"If you'd been paying any attention to the bulletins—" he started.

"Oh, for shit's sake," mumbled the sheriff.

"Hey. Don't shoot the messenger. Or don't hate the player, hate the game. Whatever the saying is," said Rostov.

"It's neither," said Young. "But don't let that get in your way."

"I won't," said Rostov.

"So. What are we looking at in your opinion?" said Mann, interested to hear Rostov's take, since he seemed knowledgeable enough about the murders.

"The usual MO on maybe three or four of the victims. Garotte or piano wire slicing to the bone around the major joints, followed by sawing to disconnect," said Rostov. "The rest were hacked down to size, so to speak."

Dr. Trejo nodded in agreement. "The good doctor knows his stuff."

"And here's where I can shed some new light on the subject. The method is consistent with a brutally slow form of torture—perfected in the USSR," said Rostov.

"The killer isn't Russian," said Serrano.

"Really? I've heard of this method being used by the KGB. Agonizingly painful as you can imagine. Used for the highest-level interrogations. The kind where you don't want the victim to leave out any details," said Rostov. "To be quite honest, I never expected to see it in the real world. It was the stuff of nightmares back in Russia. All rumors of course, but one of a hundred reasons that I left as soon as the wall came down."

"This isn't the Russians. Maybe inspired by the Russians somehow, but not a Russian job," said Serrano.

"How can you be so sure?" said Young. "Maybe this is some Russian bigwig that the FBI granted immunity to. Diplomatic plates and all. It kind of makes sense."

Mann looked at Serrano for a moment, signaling that she needed to be careful with this question.

"On the surface, without the context we bring to the investigation, you're one hundred percent right," said Serrano. "But this same method of torture and murder has been used for the past two decades in Ciudad Juárez. Are you familiar with those murders?"

"Actually. Yes. They called it a femicide. Hundreds of unsolved murders. Mostly women. Mutilations. Never caught the killer or killers," said Young.

"I'm impressed," said Rostov. "Which doesn't happen very often around here."

Young rolled his eyes.

"Me too," said Serrano. "Not much reason to know or care about what happens down in Ciudad Juárez when you're running a department in Minnesota."

"Contrary to the good doctor's predisposed beliefs, I do read many of the same bulletins he does. I just don't go jabber jawing about it day and night," said Young. "So, this is all somehow related to what happened in Ciudad Juárez?"

"Yes and no. We don't think the killings are a direct extension of what's *still* happening south of the border," she said. "But the methods of dismemberment and mutilation are too similar to be a coincidence."

"All the women were killed the same way?" said Young.

"He didn't read the bulletins that closely," mumbled Rostov.

Serrano glanced at Mann, a question of *who should continue?* in her eyes. He nodded that he would take over.

"Not all of them," said Mann. "But a lot of them. Especially during the decade-and-a-half stretch from 2000 to 2015. One MO in particular."

"The piano wire," said Rostov.

"How have you kept all of this quiet for so long?" said Sheriff Young. "The connection between the body dumps is plain to see."

"Bribes. Pizza and coffee," said Serrano, getting a laugh from everyone.

"Effective enough, I suppose," said Young.

"That and we don't advertise the connection. We silo the information and only dole out what's needed for departments like yours to do their job. It's plain to see, but easy to miss if you're not looking for it," said Mann.

"I suppose you're right," said Young.

"And we stress the importance of keeping a lid on certain information. The last thing we want to do is spook the killer, because he won't stop. He may go dormant for a little while, but he'll never quit," said Mann. "The killer has claimed twenty-seven victims, that we know of—not including those lying at the bottom of that ditch. Or his victims in Mexico. Our mission is to put a permanent end to these murders."

"Well," said Young. "You can count on my department's discretion."

"And mine, obviously," said Rostov.

"We sincerely appreciate it," said Serrano.

"Speaking of keeping a lid on things, the sooner we wrap this up and get the bodies out of sight, the better," said Mann.

"Looks like Tweedledee and Tweedledum are already working on that as we speak," said Rostov, nodding toward the crime scene.

The two Steele County Sheriff's Office investigators struggled to keep the stretcher level with the ground as they worked their way out of the irrigation ditch with the first of five bulging contractor bags. Mills directed them around the path the killer had left in the low grass between the ditch and the road, to preserve that part of the crime scene for closer examination once the bodies had been moved.

They reached the shoulder of the road, where the lead carrier stumbled on the edge of the asphalt, his knees buckling to the road before he dropped his end of the stretcher. The black bag hit the road hard and disgorged its contents. Six bloodied heads rolled in different directions across the sizzling pavement, the investigator scrambling out of their way like they might explode the moment they stopped moving. The other deputy dropped his end of the litter, before turning and vomiting into the grass. Serrano looked away and crossed herself. Mann took note of her sudden, seemingly involuntary turn to God and filed it away for later.

"That's a first," said Dr. Trejo.

One of the heads rolled to a stop in the middle of the road, just several feet away. Young and the deputies gathered next to the van backed slowly away from it as if it were radioactive.

"Definitely a first," said Mann. "I really hope nobody saw that. Jax?"

"We're still alone out here," said Callie Jackson, suddenly appearing next to him with the drone controller in her hand. "Nobody for miles according to the last drone sweep a few minutes ago. Did that really just happen?"

"Yep," said Mann.

Rostov put his hands on his hips and made a proclamation to nobody in particular—but everyone.

"My guess is six bodies," said Rostov matter-of-factly.

Mann stifled a laugh, despite his best effort not to react to Rostov's gallows humor.

"Good guess, Dr. Rostov. Good guess," said Mann.

CHAPTER 11

Catalina Serrano took one step into the sweltering garage and turned right around, retreating to the air-conditioned hallway inside the medical examiner's building. The heat hadn't driven her back. She grew up without air-conditioning, and the crappy window unit in her tiny apartment back in Ciudad Juárez struggled to keep the temperatures tolerable for most of the year. The stench of six decomposing bodies stuffed in a confined space, all in varying states of decay, had driven her back.

A first for her. She was no stranger to death and decay. Serrano had seen more than her share of mass graves and body-part piles over the past decade. Back in Mexico, all the mass graves they dug up, or contractor bags they cut open, contained bodies that had been rotting for weeks. Some longer. But all that had been outside. Here in Dr. Rostov's ninety-plus-degree garage, she'd finally met her match. That and the buzzing of flies. The flies always found a way in, or they were already growing as larvae inside the bags.

A cigarette would take the edge off the sickly smell—and her nerves—but that wasn't an option here. Instead, she removed a small plastic container of Vicks VapoRub from the back pocket of her jeans and applied a dab under her nose. An old but effective trick. The strong menthol scent competed with the odor of rotting flesh and organs just enough to get her by. She took a few deep breaths to fill her nasal passages before reentering the garage, which had been temporarily converted into a cadaver reassembly area.

Serrano approached Mann, who stood in front of the closed garage bay doors, silently observing the gruesome undertaking. Mann didn't look well, even with a thick, shiny streak of Vicks visible under his nose. A quick glance at the work in progress on the garage floor explained why.

Twelve tarps lay in two rows of six across the three-bay garage, the contents of the contractor bags already separated by body part on the top row. Heads. Arm pieces. Leg pieces. Hands. Feet. Miscellaneous or unidentifiable chunks. Six piles of carnage to be eventually matched with one of the torsos placed on the bottom row of tarps. In the end, they'd be lucky to reunite half of the parts with one of the torsos. But that was usually all it took to identify most of them.

Dr. Rostov, Dr. Trejo, Ray Mills, and one of Rostov's assistants, dressed in loose-fitting white hazmat jumpsuits, moved between the tarps trying to match the body parts. Trejo and Mills had played this puzzle game several times before, always more than eager to co-opt and train the medical examiner unlucky enough to have bodies dumped in their city or county. Though in this case, it looked like Rostov was thoroughly enjoying the grisly task.

The work looked crude—grab a body part and see if it matched any of the torsos—but there was a scientific method to it. The two roughly hacked-up bodies, a new MO for the Piano Man, should be the easiest to piece together. More or less. At the very least they could immediately narrow down the body parts that would match one or two of the torsos. The rest would be complicated.

They started with hair color—always trying to match a head to a body—which was a tricky business when dealing with American women and all their hair dyes. At first glance, scalp hair rarely matched pubic hair these days, but a close examination of scalp roots typically gave away the game. Almost nobody dyed their pubic area to match their head. Almost. They'd seen a case of pink hair up top and down below before.

Tattoos were next. If a torso featured tattoos, they could reasonably assume, based on their previous work, that similarly themed tattoos would be found on the limbs. Or just any tattoo. People tended to be tattoo people or not. Most of the time, there was no rhyme or reason to the pattern of tattoos. The casually tattooed got one here and there over time. The more serious inkers told a story on their body. They'd come across a few of those. The easiest to identify in the long run. The easiest to put together on the tarps. And the easiest to pinpoint along the killer's route. Full tattoo sleeves or serious body ink drew attention. Even the smallest tattoos were known to someone—and their team almost always found that someone.

Serrano had no tattoos. She could never afford a good one. Her only options back in Mexico were back-alley scumbags with sketchy needle guns that nearly guaranteed skin infections or fuzzy tattoo images. Plus, she'd been told from day one at the police academy not to get a tattoo, or at the very least, a tattoo that would suggest she was a cop—in case she was randomly snatched off the street and "interrogated."

Smart advice overall. Not that her job as a cop was a big secret. She wore a uniform and stood on one of the busiest intersections in the city for most of the day. But you never knew what might happen on the streets of Ciudad Juárez after-hours. After-hours was when the barely enforced laws of Mexico disappeared, not to be seen again until midmorning.

Then came the rest. The small details. Nail polish bringing two hands, and maybe two feet, together. Piercing holes. Not the actual jewelry; the killer always tore that out and presumably buried it where it would never be found. In a few cases, they'd managed to match ear piercings to breasts to belly buttons—and beyond. Same as the tattooed.

Of course, they always worked with the obvious. A fingerprint here and there sealed the deal, but that was a rare occasion. The killer always dipped the victims' hands in acid, effectively erasing any fingerprints, and he meticulously scrubbed their personal belongings—but occasionally he botched the job, and the team would eventually find a fingerprint that identified the victim.

Same with facial features. The Piano Man routinely poured acid over his victims' faces, rendering identification very difficult. But the kind of modern facial recognition and reconstruction software available to Mann's team rendered the killer's efforts somewhat useless. They had close to a fifty-percent identification rate based on facial pattern recognition alone. The teeth were a different story altogether.

"Need a refresh?" she said, presenting Mann with an open Vicks container.

"Yes. Please," said Mann. "Do you have a Q-tip?"

"For what?"

"For the Vicks?" he said, nodding at the container. "I didn't want to assume I—"

"Jesus. Just use your finger," said Serrano. "It's a petroleum jelly. Not a bowl of queso."

"Just being polite," said Mann, smearing a healthy glob of Vicks under his nose.

"Anyone else need a hit?" she said.

"I'll take one," said Mills.

"Same," said Trejo. "This batch is particularly ripe. Rostov?"

"You're kidding, right?" said Rostov, holding one of the heads in his gloved hands like it was a soccer ball. "I thought you people did this for a living."

Serrano rolled her eyes. Nobody sane got used to this kind of charnel house display.

"Did he remove all the teeth?" she said while Trejo reapplied his Vicks.

Previously, their killer had been meticulous about yanking out the teeth, but he'd also taken his sweet time with the victims in the past. The rough machete or axe cuts on two of the bodies gave her hope that he may have been in too much of a rush to patiently pull between twenty-eight and thirty-two teeth—the average number found in most adult jaws.

"The usual brute force extraction job on four of the victims," said Trejo. "He poured acid into the mouths of the two freshest corpses. Must have been in a hurry. Burned the gums and loosened the teeth, but didn't damage them enough to prevent dental ID."

"Teeth are the most durable parts of the human body," said Rostov. "A tooth would need to be submerged in acid for at least an hour to change its morphology enough to prevent forensic identification. Assuming the use of hydrochloric acid or nitric acid. Sulfuric acid could take half a day or longer."

"We lucked out and got Mr. Wizard," said Ray Mills, smearing more Vicks under his nose.

"I assume that's some kind of pejorative, inside joke?" said Rostov.

"Pejorative? No. Inside joke? Not really," said Mann. "*Mr. Wizard* was an old TV show that showcased scientific exploration—for kids. Very informative."

"So. You're the kids that I'm informing?" said Rostov.

"Something like that," said Mills, rolling his eyes.

"Any prints?" said Serrano.

"Dusted everything," said Trejo. "Rocha is uploading all the prints we pulled to IAFIS."

Kim Rocha was the team's computer forensics specialist. Although she specialized in pulling evidence from computers, Mann had put her in charge of all things digital, which included uploading fingerprints into the FBI's Integrated Automated Fingerprint Identification System. Mexico implemented a national digital ID system a few years ago, the government aggressively registering its citizens across all states. Cédula

Única de Identidad Digital now served as the official domestic ID for all Mexicans, containing names, surnames, date of birth, place of birth, nationality, and—most importantly—biometric data.

"Can she help me upload prints to the new Mexican database?" said Serrano.

"Do you have access to the database?" said Mann.

She shook her head. "Of course not. But I heard that Rocha could make it happen."

Mann seemingly ignored her.

"She can. Can't she?" insisted Serrano.

"It's okay. I won't say a word," said Rostov. "And neither will my assistant, who I can fire at a whim and send back to his family's failing soybean farm."

His assistant, a tall, thin, ghostly pale young man in his midtwenties raised both hands—showing them his palms.

"I didn't hear a thing," he said.

"Smart kid," said Rostov.

"Smart indeed," said Mann, before nodding at her. "We'll see what Rocha can do. Though I highly doubt our killer is in the system. He's smarter than that."

"I agree, but you never know," she said. *"Gracias."*

"De nada," said Mann.

"What else?" she said.

"Nothing for now. Blood has been drawn from each torso and all parts for eventual DNA matching. Pictures have been taken. Prints processed. Requests for all missing persons reports, from here to the border, have been filed," said Mann. "We're in our usual holding pattern, but with a little more to go on than usual."

"A lot more," said Trejo.

"True. Relative to what we've had to work with in the past," said Mann. "But we're still looking at a scant amount of evidence in the grand scheme of things."

"But we're in Minnesota for the first time—a few hundred miles north of the last dump site," said Serrano. "Which suggests that our killer lives farther north than we initially suspected. His previous dump sites had never gone north of Des Moines. Any word on the license plate prefix?"

"Not yet," said Mann, stealing a glance at her while subtly shaking his head.

Message received—don't push the topic. Interesting. Mann had something going on behind the scenes. Hopefully something entirely illegal, because that was the only way she saw them breaking this case open. A complete bypass of the system. But she didn't think Mann was up for it. Maybe he was, but nothing she'd seen so far gave her that kind of hope. He was too by the book for this kind of work, from what she had seen over the past year. But Serrano had also heard rumors. The kind that had drawn her north of the border to join his team.

From what she understood, Mann had previously diverted enough of his time to looking into *certain aspects* of the Mexican cartels to get sidelined on the Southwest US Joint FBI-DEA Task Force. Benched. Not banished. Which was why he bypassed the FBI chain of command and took the ARTEMIS concept directly to Assistant Director Dana O'Reilly—who signed off on the concept immediately. Serrano had no idea how Mann managed to pull that off, but he must have had someone's ear. Someone important.

She had first met Mann in 2019, when she was still a Mexican state police officer for the State of Chihuahua. She'd approached him "off the books" at his hotel lobby bar while he was in Mexico City attending a capabilities and cooperation summit between US and Mexican law enforcement agencies. Mexico had recently combined all federal agencies into Guardia Nacional, a single entity, and wanted to assure US officials that they meant business on the border.

Her pitch hadn't been as compelling as she'd hoped. He'd nodded and listened, but ultimately wouldn't commit to anything other than handing her his business card and telling her to "stay in touch." A disappointing result given that she'd spent most of her paycheck on the trip. But not unexpected. At least it shouldn't have been. She'd approached a senior FBI agent with a proposition he couldn't possibly have made happen at that point. Hope and naivety had gotten the best of her.

Serrano had learned about his task force from a law enforcement contact in the El Paso Police Department, and bluntly asked him if he might be able to convince his federal Mexican counterparts to persuade state officials to start a more focused task force to investigate the ongoing femicide epidemic in Chihuahua.

Thousands of women had vanished or been murdered in the past three decades, with no serious leads or convictions. Her mother was one of them. A single mother and worker at a nearby electronics factory who never made it home from a late shift one night in 2008. Her dismembered body stuffed in a contractor bag and dumped a few miles down the road from the factory when Cata was seventeen.

Four years later, after finishing her university degree a year early, she joined the Chihuahua State Police force, quickly wrangling her way onto the understaffed team of reluctant detectives working the murders. They were more than happy to have the help, until she started making dangerous waves. Everyone on the force knew the Juárez Cartel had some kind of connection to the murders. Nothing went down in the cartel's territory without their knowledge. And apparently, nothing got investigated too closely without their permission.

Her repeated attempts to convince state and federal police to do more than assign a few reluctant detectives to the murders never gained any traction, and she was moved to traffic control in downtown Ciudad Juárez, where they probably hoped she'd choke on enough car exhaust to give up and quit the force. But she hadn't. Serrano and a handful of incorruptible police officers, who had lost loved ones to the killers, quietly worked the murders during their off-duty time until all of them were either fired or "killed in the line of duty."

When she reached out to Mann for the second time in 2023, she had something concrete to offer him. After having been reassigned to traffic patrol, and eventually fired from the police force, she'd spent several months investigating and hunting down a Juárez Cartel *sicario* she believed to be responsible for the serial killings, finally catching him in the act. Literally.

She'd posed as a local factory worker, like her mother, stranded outside the factory after missing the last bus back to town. The killer approached her with the offer of a drive home, which she pretended to reluctantly accept.

Two days later, she'd extracted a confession and discovered that he hadn't been working alone, which hadn't come as a surprise. The scale of the murders was entirely too massive to be the work of one killer. She quickly hit a wall trying to find his accomplices. The killings stopped after she burned his body, but he hadn't been the only killer. She had a confession and some evidence that strongly suggested otherwise—which was why she reached out to Mann again.

Mann hired her on the spot when she reached out to him with news of her most recent "off the books" activity. His task force had recently come across a string of murders north of the border that bore a chilling resemblance to the serial killings in Ciudad Juárez. All he could promise her was an unofficial role on his task force. A role he believed might eventually bring her some closure. The same thing he had so desperately sought for close to fifteen years. She wasn't the only person on the team to have lost someone dear to them in Mexico—at the hands of the cartels.

Mann had used his highly sought-after position on the Southwest US Joint FBI-DEA Task Force based out of Los Angeles to do his own digging into his girlfriend's disappearance in Mexico. And the same thing happened north of the border when you pushed a little too hard against the system. Except he wasn't fired or murdered.

Mann's ARTEMIS task force was hardly different from Cata's fume-dizzying traffic circle, where they sent the unruly and disobedient to keep them from digging in the wrong places. The sole difference being that the FBI had unknowingly put him right where he wanted to be, opening the door for Serrano to continue her mission to avenge her mother and the hundreds of women put under the blade by a depraved team of serial killers.

CHAPTER 12

Mann's phone buzzed a few minutes into their gruesome puzzle-solving fun.

He checked the number, then made eye contact with her. "We need to take this."

"We?" said Serrano.

"You can stay here and reassemble bodies instead," said Mann.

"No gracias," said Serrano, following him.

Mann took the call and immediately headed for the door leading back into the medical examiner's office.

"Hold on," said Mann, ushering her out of the garage.

When the door slammed shut behind them, Mann put the call on speakerphone. "Okay. We're clear. You're on speakerphone with me and Catalina Serrano."

"Hey, Cata. How are you?" said Dana O'Reilly.

"Dealing with this asshole," she said.

O'Reilly laughed. "Ha! Exactly what I was thinking."

"Thanks," said Mann.

"Don't cry, Garrett," said O'Reilly. "I still like you enough to stick my neck out on your behalf. In fact, right now, my neck is in a guillotine waiting for the blade to drop. Because what I dug up regarding the license plate is . . . sensitive, to say the least. Not sure either of you want to fuck with it, to be honest."

"How sensitive?" said Mann.

"The license designation *XR* in Minnesota corresponded with a high-level, federal government request. My contact thinks it's CIA, based on his experience," said O'Reilly. "But it could be something else entirely. Either way, we're looking at something the government would probably like to bury. Immediately. Along with you and your team—I suspect."

"They wouldn't dare," said Mann. "Whoever *they* might be."

"Garrett?" said O'Reilly.

"Yes?" said Mann.

"I've seen things over the years that would directly challenge your assertion that 'they wouldn't dare.' Seriously. If the CIA is somehow involved—as my contact suspects—this could get really messy, really fast."

"The CIA isn't sponsoring serial killers in the United States," said Mann. "This is something else."

"Maybe," said O'Reilly, pausing for a few moments. "Hopefully. But we can't discount the possibility. I have an address in Minneapolis. Do you want it? Could be total bullshit. A complete misdirect. My contact couldn't say."

"Couldn't or wouldn't?" said Mann.

"I didn't press the issue," said O'Reilly. "This was a deep favor. As in we're all likely to be in deep shit when this is over."

"Should we wait until I get a chance to talk with Deputy Keller?" said Mann. "He might remember more of the numbers or letters on the plate. Help narrow things down a little, so we don't raid some bigwig's house."

"My contact found only one protected plate with *XR* in Minnesota," said O'Reilly. "Federal sign-off. No trail. But definitely not WITSEC."

"Any chance we could get a warrant?" said Mann, already knowing the answer.

No judge would sign off on this, for at least a half dozen obvious Fourth Amendment reasons that didn't require a law degree to understand.

"I can always try," said O'Reilly. "But without probable cause, evidence, and all of those things . . ."

"Never mind," said Mann. "We're good."

"Ready to copy the address?" said O'Reilly.

"Go for it," said Mann, pulling a small notepad with attached pen out of his pants pocket.

"Cata. You didn't hear any of this," said O'Reilly.

"Hear what?" said Serrano.

"Exactly," said O'Reilly, before giving them the address.

Serrano inputted the address into her phone.

"One hour north," she said. "On a lake. Looks nice."

"What do you need from me, Dana?" said Mann.

"Plausible deniability," said O'Reilly. "Restraint. If possible. Mostly, I want this asshole taken out of circulation. I can deal with the fallout if the takedown is . . . one-sided."

"One-sided?" said Mann.

"One-sided. As in only one side lives to tell the tale," whispered Serrano.

"Oh," said Mann.

Damn. Maybe all the stories he'd heard about O'Reilly were true.

"Let me know what happens," said O'Reilly. "I'll run all the interference I can, once the deed is done."

"See you on the other side," said Mann. "Thank you."

"My pleasure," said O'Reilly, before ending the call.

Serrano raised an eyebrow. "So?"

"We hit the address after doing a thorough recon. Later today, if the mission looks safe enough," said Mann. "Leave Trejo and Mills here to keep working on the bodies."

"If our killer is there, the capture should be easy enough. Unless he has some kind of security team," said Serrano. "The hardest part will be figuring out what to do after we capture him. If we bring him in, he'll be back on the street in a day or two. Gone forever shortly after that."

"We're not bringing him in," mumbled Mann, while texting Jax.

"I was hoping you'd say that."

Callie Jackson joined them a few moments later.

"Nice. I thought you might be at the station already," said Mann.

"I was about to head over with Rocha to take a closer look at the Suburban and the spike strip," said Jax. "Do a sweep for trackers. Check out the vehicle's onboard computers for navigation data. Basically, one big digital sweep, and some more fingerprinting."

"Let's step outside," said Mann.

He led them back through the hallway and outside the medical examiner's office, where the sun and oppressive humidity blasted their faces.

"Brutal," said Serrano.

"Not the soothing dry heat you get down in Ciudad Juárez?" said Jax, winking.

"Oh yeah. It's very good for you. Like a dry sauna," said Serrano. "Except there's no getting out of the sauna—for like eight months."

While Mann and Jax laughed, she produced a cigarette and moved downwind of them before lighting it.

"So. Why the secrecy?" said Jax. "Don't tell me Dr. T and Ray are out of the loop."

"No. Not at all," said Mann, looking pained by her question. "I'm just thinking a little further out than usual, given the potential complications we face. I just received some interesting information from a deep source."

"How interesting?" said Jax.

"Interesting enough that we need to start covering our tracks and watching our backs," said Mann. "We have the killer's address."

"Possible address," said Serrano.

"Right," said Mann.

"That's great news?" said Jax, raising an eyebrow. "Right?"

"If it's real," said Serrano.

"Exactly," said Mann. "I'm skeptical, but it came from a source I trust."

76

"Okay? So, I assume we're going to hit the address?" said Jax.

"Yes. But before we go anywhere, I need you to turn the killer's Suburban into one giant GPS transmitter," said Mann.

Jax cocked her head for a moment. "You think they—whoever they might be—will grab the Suburban?"

Mann shrugged. "No idea. But the plate designation suggests that somebody, very well placed somewhere, will not want us tearing that vehicle to pieces to gather evidence."

"Gotcha. I'll give it special treatment. An obvious transmitter or two. A few well hidden, but findable by anyone competent. One nearly impossible to find. Boost their confidence. And one that nobody will find unless they tear the vehicle into one-inch pieces. That one will daisy-chain to other electronic devices once it's cut off from a GPS signal."

"What does that mean?" said Serrano. "Sorry. I'm just a traffic cop from Mexico."

"Nice try. You're more than a traffic cop, and everyone here knows it," said Jax. "So. What we're looking at is cutting-edge industrial espionage technology. Once the device loses GPS signal connectivity, it gets creative. First thing it does is wirelessly transmits a virus to any Bluetooth- or Wi-Fi–enabled device within a certain range. This is a low-power transmitter, to avoid obvious detection. Limited range—but once the virus infects one device, it'll daisy-chain across other devices it encounters. Phones. Tablets. Computers. The goal is to infect one or more systems with external access, to report the location. If any of the individually infected devices, like a phone or tablet, sees the wide-open sky, the virus will do what it can to triangulate the location via cell towers."

"What happens if they're underground or in a remote location with no cell coverage?" said Serrano.

"It's a very sophisticated virus," said Jax. "Kind of like *The Little Engine That Could*. If there's a way—it'll find the way."

"I always liked that story," said Serrano. "My mother used to read it to me when I was a child."

"How long do you need?" said Mann.

"An hour or two. To do it right," said Jax. "To make sure they don't find the final bug."

"Two hours max," said Mann. "The target address is an hour's drive away. I'd like to get there before rush hour. Definitely before sundown. Give us some time to surveil the land and water approaches to the property without night vision. I assume the property is expansive?"

"Good guess," said Serrano, studying the satellite image on her phone. "A decent amount of waterfront. Pier. Boathouse. Landside is mostly obscured by trees on Google Maps. I see a common road winding through the houses, but I can't tell if it's a gated community."

"That's important," said Mann.

"We can put a drone up and map out both approaches," said Jax.

"Not if you're still here, planting bugs," said Mann, tapping his watch. "Ticktock."

"Jackass," said Jax, flipping him the middle finger. "I'll keep you apprised of my progress. Two hours should do it. Just to be sure."

"Don't rush. Seriously. Even if we manage to grab our killer, I'd like to know who's behind all of this. Who's bankrolling and supporting him," said Mann. "My guess is they'll do whatever they can to get the Suburban back. Maybe it'll tie up one of our many loose ends."

"If you really think someone might come to reclaim the Suburban, we should make sure that the Steele County Sheriff's Office knows to back off on security. Just leave the SUV alone. Same with Mills and Dr. T if they stay behind," said Serrano.

"Very good point," said Mann. "I have no idea if anyone will try to forcibly take the Suburban from police custody, but it's a possibility given the circumstances."

"I'll rig some hard-to-find motion detectors in the sheriff's department garage," said Jax. "We'll know if the Suburban goes missing."

"Why are you still here?" said Mann.

"I'm not," said Jax, mock saluting Mann before heading out.

Serrano laughed, apparently inhaling too much smoke from her cigarette. A coughing fit was the result.

"Told you those things were bad for you," said Mann.

"Funny," she said, kneeling to snuff out the cigarette on the pavement in front of her. "Back to one of my earlier questions?"

"Depends on the question," said Mann.

"No warrant. Only an address provided by who the fuck knows who," said Serrano. "How does this go down? If we find our killer—"

"I know. I hear you," said Mann. "I'm still trying to figure it out."

"What does your gut say?" said Serrano.

"My gut?" said Mann. "My gut says this guy doesn't go free. Doesn't get a lawyer. Doesn't get due process. Doesn't get anything more than a few hollow-point bullets to the head or a well-placed knife jab to the upper neck. But we have to tread cautiously if we go down that path. Whoever we ultimately find at that address may have nothing to do with any of this. That's a distinct possibility we'll have to consider. As much as I want to put an end to our killer's reign of terror, we must be one hundred percent sure that we have the right person."

"But how will we know?" said Serrano. "Seriously. How will we know—one hundred percent?"

"At least one of us will have to sell our souls," said Mann. "And do the unthinkable—to make him talk."

"How much can you get for a soul?" said Serrano.

Mann laughed and shook his head. "Not enough."

CHAPTER 13

Garrett Mann had never felt more unsure about himself in his life. Standing in front of the team he'd spent over two years assembling, he suddenly felt like an impostor. More like a saboteur. A killer of careers. He'd skirted the rules and slid along the boundaries throughout his entire FBI career, but this was decidedly different. He was about to ask everyone to throw away what little might be left of their careers. Their only consolation being that they wouldn't be alone. Mann would be right there with them, taking a very hard nosedive into the ground.

What he was about to propose had little legal basis. Actually, one could successfully argue that it had zero legal basis. It was a massive stretch on every imaginable legal and rational level. But the payoff could be epic. If they somehow managed to find the owner of the Suburban abandoned in southern Minnesota, they could stop the killings. Within the law or outside the law.

He didn't care how it went down in the end, as long as their efforts at least stopped the triannual cycle of murders that their killer had firmly established over the past few years. That much he was committed to. Hopefully, his team felt the same way. Though Mann wouldn't begrudge anyone who demanded a cleaner, more legal approach to what he was about to propose—or anyone who wanted to walk away after his proposal. He'd give them the opportunity to move on, guilt free. It was only fair. Not everyone carried his burden.

Mann scanned the crew gathered in the room. The only person missing was Jax, who was busy rigging the Suburban with tracking devices.

"Jess. Will you please shut the door?" he said.

Jessica Mayer, a former Special Surveillance Group investigator, reached over and pulled the door shut.

"So. Here's the deal, in case you haven't heard," said Mann. "A source of mine took the partial license plate provided by Deputy Keller and came up with an address in Minneapolis. Don't ask how."

"How?" said Mayer.

"Seriously?" said Mann.

"Seriously. How?" said Mayer.

"By somehow hacking some kind of classified network—somewhere," said Mann.

"That's not exactly definitive," said Luke Turner.

"The address is definitely linked to the plate," said Mann.

Mayer shrugged. "But the link between the two could have been purposefully created to send us on a wild-goose chase."

"It's entirely possible, which is why we have to tread cautiously," said Mann. "But this is our first, no-shit direct lead since we started—and it sounds solid to me. Our data source and the intermediary who authorized the deep data-dive both feel the same way. We have to pursue this."

"How can we possibly do any of this without a warrant?" said Tony Baker.

"Sometimes doing the right thing doesn't mean doing what's perfectly legal," said Serrano.

"Raiding someone's house without a warrant is pretty far from legal," said Baker. "Even in Mexico."

"Nice," said Serrano.

"Hey. We're on the same team here," said Mann.

"Sorry, Cata. I didn't mean to make that personal," said Baker. "But we're talking about a serious trampling of rights here, which may not be your forte—given your background."

"No offense taken, Tony. I understand," said Serrano. "Due process in Mexico can be extremely screwed up at times—if not all the time. But I think the situation here is nuanced enough in our favor."

"I don't know about that," said Jennifer MacLeod.

MacLeod was one of the team's two SWAT-trained field agents, Turner being the other. The two of them combined gave ARTEMIS the punch they needed in high-risk situations—like today's.

"Without a warrant we're operating without authority. And without authority, we're nothing in the eyes of the court, which is all that matters in the end. Don't get me wrong. I want to nail our killer to the wall like everyone else, but if we do this the wrong way—the killer goes free."

Mann took a deep breath and exhaled. He'd always known this day might come. MacLeod was right, but that wasn't how he planned to proceed. It was time to lay it all on the line.

"We're going to immediately match the fingerprints lifted from the Suburban to whoever we find at the target address," said Mann. "We'll use our digital kit."

"Okay," said Baker. "And then what? We're still talking inadmissible evidence."

"If we match the prints," said Mann, "I'll take care of the rest."

"What does that mean, exactly?" said Luke Turner.

Mann glanced at Serrano, who subtly nodded her approval. She knew exactly what he intended to do if the prints matched, and their perp fit the profile. They'd talked about this moment dozens of times in the past, their discussions spanning multiple scenarios. If they had a blatantly open-and-shut evidentiary case, they'd go the traditional arrest route. Seek a warrant. Serve the warrant properly. Dot their i's and cross their t's. Place their faith in the system. Let the justice system do its work.

Unfortunately, they weren't looking at an evidentiary slam dunk. Far from it. The situation they faced right now fell into the haziest of areas, which would require them to take one of two approaches—with no middle ground.

The first approach involved placing a lot of trust in the system. Possibly too much. His team would basically break the law to grab the killer—but hopefully provide enough evidence to the courts to keep their killer incarcerated. They'd face a serious uphill legal battle later. A crazy fight to keep the killer off the streets, the team's "less than legitimate" actions scrutinized and analyzed on every level. The outcome in question.

Or Mann's team could take matters into their own hands, if the SUV fingerprints matched whoever they grabbed at the house. A bullet to the perp's head, and then they'd move on. Nobody the wiser. Nobody seriously questioning what happened to a seemingly random guy living in an exclusive lake community. The easier and cleaner option in Mann's opinion, but ultimately not his choice. He couldn't put his teammates in that kind of legal and career jeopardy without their consent.

"What it means is that I have no intention of letting our target just slip away on technicalities," said Mann.

Dr. Trejo stood up and pushed his way through to the front of the packed conference room. "What exactly are you saying here, Garrett?"

"You know what I'm saying, Jim," said Mann.

Trejo shook his head.

"I'm not on board with an execution. Sorry."

"Same," said Mayer. "No fucking way."

Tony Baker put both of his hands up. "Count me out."

Jennifer MacLeod stood up and turned for the door. "Nope. I'd rather flip burgers."

He glanced at Serrano, who maintained her usual poker face. Mann already knew where she stood on the issue. She'd cut the killer's throat right in front of the task force if given the opportunity.

"Hold on. Hold on. Just let me explain," said Garrett, stopping MacLeod's exodus. "I completely understand your sentiment—and that's not exactly what I'm implying."

"Not exactly?" said Kim Rocha, getting up from her chair.

"Please. Let me explain," said Mann.

"This better be good," said Rocha.

"Really good," added Ray Mills.

Luke Turner was the only member of the team Mann couldn't read right now. He remained just as quiet and detached as Serrano, despite the fact that he was typically anything but stoic or restrained.

"Here's what I'm proposing. If—and only if—we're certain we have the right person, then I say we deliver him to the Juárez Cartel. I have the feeling they'd like to have a few words with him," said Mann. "I need to know where everyone stands on this idea before we hit the address. Because to be completely honest with all of you, I don't see any reason to pursue the license plate lead unless we intend to take this guy out of circulation. I understand this still isn't a clean option, but I don't see any other way."

"I'm fine with it," said Serrano, a little too quickly, though he appreciated the support.

"Of course you are," said Luke Turner.

"What does that mean?" said Serrano.

"You have nothing to lose," said Turner.

"How do I have nothing to lose?" said Serrano, standing up.

"You can slip away from all of this and disappear at any time," said Turner.

"Really?" said Serrano, taking a few steps toward Turner. "So. I should just head back to Ciudad Juárez—with no job and a price on my head—and just live happily ever after?"

"No. That's not what I meant. I think. I guess. I don't fucking know," said Turner. "But the rest of us need to be careful. Some of us have careers to think about."

Mayer broke out laughing. "Nobody here has a serious career in the FBI or the government ahead of them. That's why we're basically on a dead-end team. No offense, Garrett."

"None taken. And you're not at all wrong," said Mann. "It's not like any of us are going anywhere fast in the Bureau. Hey. At least we're not chained to desks deep inside obscure field offices—with bureaucrats counting our keystrokes."

"Quite the inspirational statement coming from our leader," said Turner.

"The truth stings," said Mayer. "But it still doesn't make us judge, jury, and executioner."

"Exactly," said MacLeod, who had returned to her seat. "If we turn the killer over to the cartel that he betrayed, we're pretty much signing his death warrant."

"He's tortured and murdered several hundred women over the years. There's no way he's just going to stop on his own after a little scare," said Serrano. "He's somehow found a home here in your country, where he's apparently free to kill dozens of women a year without any consequences. The questions we should be looking into are why and who's behind it."

"We'll never get to the bottom of that," said Mann. "Not if his guardian angel is as well placed and connected as I suspect. There's apparently nothing even remotely normal about his license plate or the fact that he's living *la vida loca* in a mansion in an exclusive lake community just outside Minneapolis."

"He's right," said Baker. "I feel like our hands are tied here."

"Then screw it," said Serrano. "If we all believe this guy is untouchable, then it's time to either shut down ARTEMIS or turn the task force's attention to some low-hanging fruit—so you can all get your careers back on track. I mean if that's what's truly important to everyone."

Harsh words. He expected some immediate backlash, but instead—the room went dead silent, everyone hopefully absorbing the truth bomb Serrano had just dropped on their heads. Maybe it was time to let

Cata take the stage. She not only had their attention, but he suspected she had their sympathy. Her story was far more compelling than his.

Losing a fiancée-to-be on spring break in Cancún to low-level, local cartel thugs was one thing. Losing the mother who had raised you alone for over a decade to a cartel-sanctioned serial killer was another thing altogether. Mann's career choices, from joining the FBI to lobbying for this task force, were all driven on some level by the loss of Mia in Cancún, but Serrano's entire life's focus was on avenging her mother's murder. He gave Cata a subtle nod, yielding the rest of the conversation to her.

CHAPTER 14

Serrano acknowledged his gesture with a simple wink. The shift in the room had been palpable. Not hostile by any stretch, because she'd spoken the truth. Skeptical perhaps. But definitely the start of a difficult conversation for a group of law enforcement agents who had slightly—if not entirely—bent the rules they had sworn to uphold. The perfect transition for Serrano.

MacLeod spoke up first. Not surprising given the fact that she hadn't been *banished* to ARTEMIS like most of the team. She'd volunteered after learning about Mann's intentions for the group. MacLeod's Cornell University roommate had vanished while attending a Phish concert in Watkins Glen, New York, in the summer of 2011. Her body was never found.

"I don't know. I mean—we obviously can't just kill this guy. Right?" said MacLeod.

"Uh. Correct," said Ray Mills; a few others immediately reinforced his sentiment.

"Or just line him up in front of a cartel firing squad," said Rocha.

"Or that," said Mills.

"Not to mention the fact that we're considering a completely illegal arrest, which could very well be interpreted as a kidnapping," said Baker.

Serrano stood up and faced the team. Time for a reality check.

Steven Konkoly

"And we can't just let this fucker go free, which is exactly what will happen if we hand him over to your Department of Justice," said Serrano. "Someone very well placed in your federal government set him up with the equivalent of an untouchable diplomatic license plate. We can't lose sight of that. They had a vested interest in protecting him at one point—and maybe still do—for whatever reason."

"Hey. Maybe they'll just get rid of him," said Mills. "Save us the trouble. He's one hell of a liability."

"No. I don't think so," said Mann. "They would have disposed of him already if he served no further purpose."

"Maybe he has some kind of leverage that makes him untouchable," said Mayer.

"It's entirely possible, but I think there's more to it," said Mann. "The guy has traveled back and forth from Minneapolis to New Mexico—or somewhere near the US-Mexico border—three to four times a year, leaving a trail of dead bodies in his path. It's a brazen pattern, to be honest. He could travel in any direction to claim his victims, but he always takes pretty much the same route back and forth. The killer feels secure for some reason. I think the reason has everything to do with the legal or political clout hiding behind his magic license plate."

Now we're getting somewhere, thought Serrano, though she didn't dare reveal why she believed this to be true. She tempered her response.

"This is bigger than just a single killer," said Serrano, muddling the truth.

"Serial killers are creatures of habit," said Dr. Trejo.

"True," said Mann. "But in this case, I agree with Cata's assessment."

"Shocker," said Turner.

"Whatever," said Mann. "The bottom line is—if we hand him over to the DOJ, we'll see more body dumps in the news within a year. Maybe sooner."

"And we'll process the crime scenes, like we always have," said MacLeod. "And we'll keep doing that until we can nail this guy with unimpeachable evidence—which we don't have right now. That's the process."

Mann shook his head. "If we turn him over to the DOJ, after an unlawful arrest based on unverifiable information, we'll all be flipping those burgers you mentioned earlier."

"Or directing traffic," said Serrano, catching Mann's eye.

Only Mann knew her full backstory. Turner and MacLeod both started to say something, but Dr. Trejo cut them off—forcefully. And surprisingly.

"Everyone shut up! No more *what-ifs*, *maybes*, and *I don't knows*. Bottom line is we have to do something to take this scumbag out of circulation," he said. "I don't like it any more than any of you do, but handing him over to the DOJ isn't an option. Not unless everyone wants to go home right now and forget the whole thing—like Cata said. Save our hides. Turn our attention to another killer. Hunt down some guy who's killed a few hookers in Omaha—not that those victims aren't equally worthy of our attention. They are. But we have a chance to stop guaranteed future massacres here. We have to do something."

Once again, complete silence in the room. Followed by another shocker. Turner changing his tune. *The team is beginning to see the light!*

"Okay. Yeah," said Luke Turner. "So, who's going to liaison with the cartel? Not that I'm entirely in favor of that scenario."

"I have contacts that should be able to help," said Serrano.

"Of course you do," said Turner.

Serrano shook her head, muttering a few choice Latino curses under her breath.

"That could get you killed," said Mann.

"I don't really care—if it stops this killer," said Serrano.

"Are we really doing this?" said MacLeod.

Time for the moment of truth.

"I can't speak for the rest of you, but I'm hitting that address. By myself—if that's what it ultimately comes down to," said Mann. "Maybe it turns out to be nothing. Maybe nobody's home. Maybe our killer has already evacuated, or never returned after almost getting busted last night. Maybe he's sitting in the house surrounded by twenty Black Ops fuckers from the NSA—and I get smoked a few feet onto the property. I have no idea. But what I do know is that I won't be able to live with myself if I don't try to take this guy out."

"I'll be right next to you," said Serrano.

"That's just plain stupid. Tactically," said Turner. "A few well-aimed rifle bursts or a competently placed antipersonnel device could take both of you out simultaneously. Rookie move. Game over."

"Do you have a better plan?" said Mann, clearly baiting him.

"Obviously," said Turner.

"Care to share it with the rest of us?" said Serrano.

"Only if you ask nicely," said Turner, smirking.

"Por favor?" said Serrano.

"And please?" added Mann. "Is that good enough?"

"If you had to ask, probably not. But I suppose it'll do," said Turner, before standing to address the rest of the team. "So. For planning purposes, who else do I have to work with?"

MacLeod raised her hand. "You'll get everyone killed if you plan this by yourself. Count me in. Tony?"

"Could be a hostage rescue situation involved, right?" said Tony Baker.

"Very possible," said MacLeod.

"Then you're gonna need someone with hostage rescue experience," said Baker. "I'm in."

Mayer muttered a few obscenities under her breath, before speaking up. "This whole thing doesn't get off the ground without proper aerial surveillance. Not to mention police and target scanner monitoring."

"Anyone can fly a drone," said Turner. "Or tune in to a radio frequency."

"Ay mi madre," mumbled Serrano.

"Really? You're going there?" said Mayer. "You ever stealthily operate a low-to-medium altitude, fixed-wing drone over a target during broad daylight?"

"Not my job," said Turner.

"Uh-huh," said Mayer. "Can you even name the type of drone we use?"

"Fixed-wing or quadcopter?" said Turner.

"Either. But let's go with fixed-wing, unless you think flying a buzz saw over the target property is stealthy."

"The Pelican," said Turner. "The one we have in the top carrier?"

Mayer chuckled. "The Albatross."

"Exactly. Some form of seabird," he said.

"Yeah. I think the team is gonna need Jax's help on this one," said Mayer. "Speaking of Jax. Shouldn't she be in on this conversation? Given that we're debating the merits of committing extrajudicial murder."

"She wouldn't be on the property," said Mann. "Plausible deniability."

"True. We'd just be completely shattering her trust in the team by not telling her she's technically an accessory to murder," said Mayer.

"Fair enough. I'll give her the straight-up when she gets back. What about the rest of you?" said Mann, glancing back and forth between Mills, Rocha, and Trejo.

"Since everyone else seems to be fine with just shredding the Fourth Amendment in its entirety, I may as well put the icing on this illegal cake, and forensically examine our alleged killer's digital footprint," said Kim Rocha. "Take a deep dive into all of his electronics."

"Now we're talking," said Mann.

Gracias a Dios. Serrano took a deep breath and exhaled. Incredible. *They're all on board!*

"Shit. Digital is only half the picture. Probably need someone to work the physical forensics side of things. Prints. Fibers. DNA. Never know what I might turn up," said Ray Mills. "Count me in."

"Son of a mother . . . ," said Trejo, the obscenity trailing away while he shook his head. "I suppose we might run into a dead body or two on the property. Body parts in a freezer. Taxidermy. Who knows. These killers tend to take trophies. Having a medical examiner on hand might be useful."

"Then we're all in agreement? Tentatively?" said Mann. "To head up to Minneapolis and check this place out? With specific parameters in place?"

Everyone nodded and mumbled their agreement, the enthusiasm level low. A three or four on a ten-point scale in her estimation. But far better than she'd anticipated.

"Look. I appreciate everyone's support on this," said Mann. "I know that most of you regard your assignment to ARTEMIS as a punishment. A purgatory of sorts. Or maybe a permanent hell—until you retire."

"Retirement is a long way off for most of us," said Turner. "Not sure any of us will make it that far given the current circumstances. Dr. T might have a chance, given his age."

"Laugh all you want. I'm already eligible for retirement," said Trejo. "I'm doing this because I believe in the work."

Serrano nodded at Trejo. A tacit thank-you. The two of them had spoken extensively before. Trejo's daughter had been abducted from the Mall of America in Minneapolis over twenty years ago, presumably trafficked—then murdered. His wife left him less than a year later. Not an uncommon result in these cases. Mann reached out to him the moment ARTEMIS was activated, insisting that a forensic pathologist was critical to the team's success. He couldn't have been more right.

"You didn't sound very convinced about that a little earlier," said Turner.

"There's a big difference between believing in the greater good of the work and expressing reservations about a single plan in the grand scheme of that greater good," said Trejo. "I still believe we're doing the right thing overall. I'm just not entirely happy with the path we're taking to get there."

"And I don't disagree with you on that last point," said Mann. "Without a doubt, this case has been a shit show from the very start. I think we can all agree on that. But don't forget how jacked-up the Gagliani case seemed at first. Nobody thought we had that right. But we did."

Mann was right. Too many aspects of the case didn't add up. The special license plate. The regular travel back and forth between New Mexico—or possibly western Texas—and a mansion in one of Minneapolis's most exclusive lakeside communities. The killer's methods of torture and murder precisely matching those that took place for more than a decade in Ciudad Juárez. The most bizarre circumstances and coincidences on seemingly every level. If she had to guess, she'd say that the CIA was somehow involved. All the more reason to be careful.

"But we never had to break the law to nail Gagliani," said Trejo. "That's where I'm hung up here. I want this guy off the street. I just wish there was a cleaner way to pull it off."

"Maybe there is. Let's break for thirty minutes and pack up for the trip north. I have an idea I need to put a little more thought into. It might just solve our legal dilemma," said Mann. "Serrano. Dr. Trejo. Hang back for a minute?"

After the room cleared, Mann shut the door. *Shit show* was an understatement. She had no idea how they might pull this off without breaking the law, running afoul of whichever powerful government or private entity was working against them behind the scenes, and basically handing the killer a get-out-of-jail-free card.

"What's up?" said Trejo.

"First. Thank you for your support. The team respects your opinion," said Mann. "Probably more than mine."

"Believe me when I say that they trust you implicitly," said Trejo. "This is just our first foray into a serious gray area."

"Still. Thank you," said Mann, a pained expression on his face.

Trejo shrugged and raised an eyebrow. "But?"

Mann chuckled. "Nothing gets by you. Does it?"

"You're not that hard to read," said Trejo.

"I want you to stay behind and continue working with Dr. Rostov," said Mann. "We still have to identify the victims, gather evidence—the works. It's crucial to our overall case."

"Even if you entirely torpedo the case with your little stunt in Minneapolis?"

"Especially if I screw things up in Minneapolis," said Mann. "If our raid goes sideways from a legal standpoint—"

"It will go sideways on some level," said Trejo. "Guaranteed."

"Yeah. Well. Then the six victims in Rostov's garage and the killer's SUV at the sheriff's office represent the last untainted evidence we've collected. I really need you to shepherd that process," said Mann. "Regardless of whatever happens up north, I want whatever happens down here to be by the book. And you're the right person for the job."

"Everyone looks up to you," said Serrano. "As the outsider, I really see it."

"I don't know about all of that, but I'm thankful to be here. Beats working out of a field office, that's for sure," said Trejo.

"You mean just sitting in front of a computer and shuffling digital files around all day?" said Mann.

"Or working a traffic circle?" said Serrano.

"Precisely. On both counts," said Trejo. "So. What's your idea for a cleaner way to pull this off? Or was that just theater?"

"I was really hoping you'd forgotten about that," said Mann.

"Nope," said Trejo.

Mann rubbed his temples for a few moments before responding. Even Serrano had no idea where he might be going with this, and she didn't care, as long as they headed north to take a shot at their killer.

"If we can confirm that our suspect is present—with high confidence—I want to draw him off the property somehow. Maybe we fake a lakeside raid and get him to flee out of the front gate of his property. Or vice versa. The bottom line? If we apprehend him on public property, that changes things from a legal standpoint. I can think of a dozen scenarios that I could use away from his property gates to justify an arrest. At least we won't be starting off in a legal quagmire."

"This guy isn't going to give you what you want," said Trejo. "Neither are the people using him."

"Yeah. We'll see," said Mann. "So—what about Mills? Do you need him here or can I use him up north?"

Trejo stifled a laugh. "What are you really asking?"

Serrano cut him off, hoping to wrap this little discussion up sooner than later so she could take a smoke break.

"Will he be a liability up there?" said Serrano.

"Will you?" said Trejo, hitting back harder than expected.

"Fuck off," said Serrano.

"Sorry. Cheap shot. But I can't be the only one thinking that your presence might complicate things when or if this case comes to a head. You're an ex-Mexican cop with a sizable price on her head. A rogue, illegal asset, basically. I think," said Trejo. "I don't actually know what your status is here in the US—and I don't care. You're solid. You do good work. But Garrett hasn't exactly been honest with any of the locals we've dealt with over the past year and a half about your standing. And that could come back to bite us in the ass if we're not careful."

Mann glanced at Serrano. "He's not wrong."

"I'm not hanging back for this one," she said. "And you know why."

Whoever they found at that address could be the man who killed her mother.

"I do," said Mann.

"Regarding Mills," said Trejo, bypassing any further discussion of Serrano. "He'll be fine. He's efficient. If you're short on time up there, which I assume will be the case, Mills works extremely well under pressure. You'll get whatever there is to be gotten, forensically, with him on the job."

"Sold. Mills comes with us," said Mann. "You'll run the forensics show down here, with Dr. Rostov. Everything by the book. Leave no stones unturned. If I mess things up in Minneapolis, your work here will be essential to the continuity of our case."

"That's how I roll," said Trejo.

"I know," said Mann. "Go give Mills the good news. Or bad news, however he interprets it."

"I think he'll view it as good news," said Trejo. "He's a far better forensic investigator than door kicker, but everyone likes to bust a door down from time to time. Right?"

"See you in thirty minutes," said Mann. "And Jim?"

"Yeah?"

"I need you to do me a favor, without asking any questions," said Mann.

"Name it," said Trejo.

"Leave the Suburban alone until further notice. Don't go anywhere near it. Just let it sit in the Steele County Sheriff's Office vehicle lot," said Mann. "I'm going to pass the same message along to Sheriff Young, but I need you to make sure none of his deputies take it upon themselves to guard or watch the vehicle lot."

"Bait?" said Trejo. "Is that what Jax has been working on?"

Mann shrugged. "The less you know—the better. Just stay away from it for now."

"I hear nothing. See nothing. Know nothing," said Trejo as he headed to the door.

"Thank you, Sergeant Schultz."

"You're velcome," said Trejo in a terrible German accent.

When the door shut, Mann took a seat, burying his head in his hands. "I hate leading everyone on like this. I'm worried we're going to get some of them killed."

Serrano sat next to him and took his hand. "Yeah. But *it* . . . must be done. If the opportunity presents itself."

It being an execution. Their killer didn't get to navigate the legal system. Whether they had to hunt him down on his exclusive Cedar Lake property, or stop him in public, inside or outside his gated community,

Serrano would kill him. That much she'd already decided. How they got there was the big question. A lot could go wrong from now until then.

"*It* will be done," said Mann. "You have my word on that. We just need to figure out the best way to pull it off, without screwing the team over. I owe them that much."

Cata briefly squeezed his hand, letting go just as quickly.

PART II

CHAPTER 15

Gary Litman scuttled down the Gulfstream 600's staircase, followed closely by the AXIOM Special Activities Group team he'd assembled less than an hour after Jeremy Powell had tasked him to fly to Minneapolis in person. Thirteen of AXIOM's top-tier operators, including himself, carried oversize duffel bags through a light rain across the tarmac to the hangar where they'd gear up for the recovery mission.

Frank O'Brien, head of AXIOM field operations for the upper Midwest, met them just inside the open bay door. Based out of Chicago, he'd arrived on very short notice with a small contingent to arrange the hangar and local transportation needs for Litman's operation: three full-size SUVs for the trip to and from the target address, plus an emergency extraction option. Litman shook O'Brien's hand before scanning the double hangar. The three SUVs sat in the adjacent hangar bay, arranged side by side facing the closed door.

"Are they bringing the jet inside?" said Litman.

"Negative," said O'Brien. "The plan is to keep the jet spooled up and ready to whisk you out of here the moment you return."

Litman nodded his approval. "Then let's close this bay door for now so nobody gets a peek inside while we're getting ready."

"Yeah. Looks like you're rolling heavy for the Minneapolis suburbs," said O'Brien, glancing at the no-nonsense team assembled in front of him.

"Surprisingly heavy," said Litman. "The absolute last thing we need is a nosy private pilot or airport maintenance worker sniffing around. I imagine we've already attracted some attention."

"Without a doubt," said O'Brien, before signaling for one of his people to shut the hangar bay door.

"How many did you bring with you from Chicago?" said Litman.

"Six. Including myself," said O'Brien. "I would have brought more, but this is all I could muster, given the short notice—and the clearance level required."

"That should be more than enough to handle any issues that might arise here. Hopefully, we'll be back in the air within the next ninety minutes. The target address is about a half hour away with traffic," said Litman. "Just keep them on their toes. Headquarters doesn't make us jump through hoops like this unless there's a problem."

"Will do," said O'Brien.

"And Frank?"

"Yeah?" said O'Brien.

"How does the emergency extraction plan look?" said Litman.

O'Brien checked his watch.

"Cutting it a little close, but that option will be in place if you need it," said O'Brien. "The plane is no more than ten minutes out. Pilot said he'll need to refuel, because he flew straight here after dropping off a fishing group on one of the lakes up north. We were lucky to find a pilot on short notice, even with the amount of money I was offering."

"What does he know?" said Litman.

"I told him I was a local businessman, looking to take a last-minute trip north to the lakes around Brainerd to join a few friends," said O'Brien.

"How long will it take him to refuel?" said Litman.

"He said it's usually about a twenty-to-thirty-minute turnaround, depending on how busy they were," said O'Brien. "He already made arrangements with the airport—and it doesn't look very busy out there."

Litman did the math. Should be plenty of time to refuel and taxi over to the hangar. If anything, O'Brien might have to stall the guy for a little while. The problem would be the takeoff. The airport might not be busy, but if things went sideways at the target, the success or failure of the mission could be measured in seconds. The trip from the airport to Cedar Lake was short. A few minutes at most. But that would be a long few minutes for the ground team if the property were to turn into a shooting gallery.

"Frank?"

"Yeah?" said O'Brien.

"I'm going to need you on your A game when it comes to that pilot," said Litman. "If things go south at the house, I need you in the air immediately."

"I understand," said O'Brien. "My plan is to board the plane but hold him up at the last moment with a fake call. Tell him that I might have to cancel the trip. Just waiting on word from a business partner. A possible complication."

"Make sure he knows he's still getting paid," said Litman. "So he doesn't try to bail on you."

"The trip is already paid for, plus a generous kicker for the last-minute notice and possible overnight in Brainerd. His wife took the payment over the phone. I'll tell him he can keep the full payment, regardless of whether I fly north."

"And if I need the plane for an emergency extraction?" said Litman. "What's your plan to get him in the air and willing to make a highly illegal landing?"

"Easy enough," said O'Brien. "I have my contingency cash bundle stuffed in a backpack that I'll bring onto the plane with me. I'll open the backpack and quickly explain what I need him to do. If he balks, I'll put a gun to his head and tell him he can fly home to his family with fifty thousand tax-free dollars or be shipped home in a body bag—and buried next to his wife and children, who we'll be paying a visit to if he doesn't cooperate."

Litman nodded his approval. There wasn't much else O'Brien could do to coerce the pilot.

"What if he calls your bluff?"

"Then the pilot gets a bullet to the head and today will be my first water landing," said O'Brien. "They say it's easier than a hard runway— once you get used to it. I'd rather not take on that steep of a learning curve under the circumstances."

"You can fly a plane?" said Litman.

"I've been flying for years. A couple times a month on weekends," said O'Brien. "Single- and twin-propeller. Mostly single. But never a seaplane—or I'd just drag him into the hangar after he taxis over and fly the mission myself."

"Do you think you can land his plane on the water?"

"No idea," said O'Brien. "But I'll give it a try if it's the only option to get a plane to you."

"Let's hope it doesn't come to that," said Litman.

"I plan on convincing him to do the job," said O'Brien, taking a satellite phone out of one of his cargo pockets. "Speaking of the pilot. He should be landing shortly. Said he'd give me a call when he's on the ground. I'm gonna step outside so I don't miss it."

"We'll be out of here in fifteen minutes. Make sure he doesn't decide to swing by before refueling," Litman said, before turning his attention to his team.

Litman quickly rehashed the plan he'd created with the team leaders on the flight over. He'd separated the twelve-person SAG unit assigned to him into two groups. ALPHA team consisted of four operators, whose sole focus would be to retrieve and escort their VIP back to the SUVs or to the emergency option if it came down to that.

He reinforced the fact that they would be on the tightest of timelines at the property and couldn't afford to spend any time negotiating or arguing with their target. Voluntarily or involuntarily, they had to move him out immediately. He'd been assured by his boss, Jeremy Powell, that their VIP would be contacted shortly before their arrival by his handler—and should come along willingly. But just in case, each member of ALPHA carried restraints, a blackout hood, variable voltage ZAP Sticks to literally prod him along, and if all else failed, ketamine autoinjectors. They'd drug him and carry him out.

BRAVO team, made up of eight operators, would provide site security and keep the SUVs ready to roll the moment ALPHA stuffed their VIP inside one of the vehicles. If forced to use the contingency plan to extract their target, BRAVO team would remain behind to buy ALPHA enough time to get their man out of there.

He still had zero idea who they'd been sent to grab. The target's I&I (Identification and Intelligence) package had contained little more than an address, several high-resolution photographs, and three simple code-word exchanges that would authenticate the extraction. One for initial contact at one of the community's two exterior gates to get the team inside the neighborhood. The second for contact at the property gate. And the third for the team's face-to-face with the VIP. If their target refused to grant them access at any point in the process, BRAVO had all the gear necessary to breach any kind of gate or barrier.

AXIOM clearly didn't want this guy falling into the wrong hands, whoever he might be. Powell had made it crystal clear that he was never to leave the VIP's side, and that if the mission somehow went sideways before they got him airborne on the Gulfstream, or if they were forced to land by law enforcement, Litman was to "neutralize the asset."

"All right. We roll in fifteen minutes," said Litman. "ALPHA goes with a light armor kit for mobility. Helmets, basic plate carrier rigs with a few spare magazines, prisoner handling equipment, and self-inflatable life vests, in the unlikely event we're forced to go for a swim. I want the inflatable vests worn *over* your gear. BRAVO goes in heavy."

"Any changes to the ROE?" said Osbourne.

A seemingly innocuous, off-the-cuff question, but critical in the grand scheme of their mission. If things spun out of control on the property, she would be the first to feel the weight of the world on her shoulders. Establishing solid boundaries for her team's rules of engagement wasn't a bad idea. He'd be in constant contact with her throughout the operation, but if a hostile threat suddenly materialized, she could be faced with an immediate, mission-critical decision whether to engage or hold fire.

He'd asked Powell about what they could expect in terms of threats, and all he got was "the feds." Followed by, "which doesn't change any-thing. You get our VIP out of there, no matter what it takes or costs." In other words, if the FBI showed up at their target's gate, the likelihood of a shoot-out was high. He left that part out of previous mission briefings. BRAVO team understood the risk of being left behind to fend for them-selves against federal and local law enforcement, but the fewer times he reminded Osbourne and her team of that harsh reality, the better.

"Negative. Stay in contact. Keep me apprised of the situation," said Litman. "But you do what you have to do to keep any threats away from our VIP. No restrictions on force escalation."

Osbourne shrugged. "Easy enough."

"Really?" said Litman.

"Not really. But orders are orders," said Osbourne, turning to both of the teams. "And AXIOM stands behind their people. Even under the shittiest of circumstances. We do our jobs so AXIOM can do theirs."

Nicely done. Ms. Osbourne would go places in the company. If the FBI or some quasi-federal military agency didn't show up to spoil the afternoon. The other tidbit shared by Powell, which Litman had strategically withheld from the team? AXIOM would disavow anyone captured by law enforcement. He studied Osbourne for a few moments, looking for any sign that she didn't believe what she'd just said. Poker face. Very good. Definitely a bright future in the company—assuming things didn't go to shit today.

O'Brien burst into the hangar through the access door. "The plane just landed. It's headed for the fuel depot."

"We roll in ten," said Litman.

CHAPTER 16

Garrett Mann called Jax on his satellite phone. She'd parked the team's RV as far out of sight as possible at the Cedar Lake Point Beach parking lot, on the opposite side of Cedar Lake from the target house, twenty minutes ago—and launched the Albatross drone from the longest packed-dirt road at the park.

The launch itself had attracted the attention of pretty much every early-evening beachgoer at the park, though the crowd that had witnessed the sudden takeoff hadn't yet zeroed in on the RV. She'd been careful enough to discreetly start the drone's journey in a separate parking lot, then taxi it onto the road before takeoff. For now, a few dozen people stood in the sand at the waterline, trying to spot the drone overhead.

Not ideal, but not a disaster. Even if someone called the police for whatever reason, Jax and Crawford, the young Steele County sheriff's deputy who had shown an incredible aptitude for drone operations and begged to come along, would likely remain undiscovered. Worst-case scenario: they might have to ditch the drone in a nearby lake, a costly line item to report to O'Reilly, but better than trying to recover the drone on a nearby road or parking lot—and getting nabbed by local cops.

The FBI badge held some sway, but not enough to brush off FAA regulations, local drone ordinances, and federal surveillance laws—all of which applied to their drone flight. Not to mention the warrantless search raid he was about to execute in one of the area's most prestigious gated communities. Yeah. Local law enforcement wouldn't be happy on any level. And Mann would be forced to hang Jax and the deputy out to dry. He couldn't risk tanking ARTEMIS.

"How are we looking?" said Mann.

"Good," said Jax. "Busy time on the lake. Lots of kayakers, canoers, and a few small motorboats. MacLeod and Mills will fit right in."

"Are they in the water?" said Mann.

"They launched the skiff a few minutes ago," said Jax. "Turner is parking the SUV and trailer."

"And our target?"

"Daytime thermal imaging has confirmed one person on the property, inside the house," said Jax. "That one person strayed close enough to the floor-to-ceiling windows adjacent to the deck for about ten seconds, then disappeared. I'm not seeing anyone else on the property, or anything I consider suspicious. I think you're clear to move on the target."

"Copy," said Mann. "Position the drone to watch the overall neighborhood, while keeping some situational awareness of the property. I know that sounds easier said than done."

"No problem. I'll put our drone in a long racetrack pattern a few thousand feet above the eastern shoreline. That'll give me a full view of the community and most of the target. My only blind spot will be the west side of the house, and I won't be able to see into the house. My angle will be too high."

"That's fine. Whatever's in the house is our responsibility to handle," said Mann. "I just don't want any surprises coming from outside the house."

"That's why I'm here."

"How's Deputy Crawford doing?" said Mann.

"He's actually flying the drone. Been flying it all along," said Jax. "Well. The drone is in a fixed flight pattern right now, but he's been on the stick the entire time. And now he's about to learn how to send new flight orders to the Albatross. Steele County might lose one of their deputies to the feds. This kid is good."

"Is he listening?"

"Yes, sir," said a male voice over the net.

"Deputy Crawford, I promised Sheriff Young that I wouldn't get you in trouble," said Mann. "That was a condition I agreed to. Understood?"

"I don't mind a little heat," said Crawford.

"Uh-huh," said Mann. "Just making sure you understand that we're not exactly operating on the most legal grounds here."

"I'm good with that," said Crawford.

"Jax?"

"He's dressed in civilian clothes. If things go really sour, he walks out of here without anyone the wiser."

"Deputy?"

"Sir?"

"You heard what she said, right?" said Mann.

"Yes. I did."

"No bullshit," said Mann. "You walk away if this goes to shit."

"Understood, sir," said Crawford. "This is purely a skills-building opportunity. So maybe, I don't have to spend the rest of my life in bum-fuck southern Minnesota."

"Fair enough," said Mann. "Welcome to the team."

"Meaning?" said Crawford.

"Meaning that if Jax vouches for you," said Mann, "I may offer you a job. Jax could use the help, unless she disagrees."

"I don't," said Jax.

"Great. Thirty minutes until we hit the house," said Mann. "Watch all approaches. Land and water."

"We're on it," said Jax, ending the call.

He turned to Serrano, who took the longest drag on a cigarette Mann had ever witnessed.

"I feel good about this," she said.

"Are you sure? That was quite a hit," said Mann.

"Making up for lost nicotine," she said.

"Big-time," said Mann, before turning to his assault team. "Ready? Anything we're forgetting?"

Tony Baker shook his head. "We're lean but mean. Ready to roll."

Lean was right. Just the six of them. But they were *mean*, too. And that counted for a lot under the circumstances.

Tony Baker—former FBI Hostage Rescue Team leader—was pretty much the most efficient close quarters battle operator he'd ever met. He "may or may not" have summarily executed a serial kidnapper on what turned out to be his final rescue operation within HRT.

Luke Turner—SWAT trained, with a complicated career history that made the rest of them look like new hires at the FBI. Started his career in Los Angeles. Got engaged to an aspiring model who got caught up with some unsavory types and landed in the soft-porn industry. Abused his authority and ceaselessly hassled her Van Nuys–based "employers," until she vanished without a trace. Transferred to the Salt Lake City office with the thought that he was a "vice avenger," where he was eventually booted for "drinking-related field aggression." A no-no in the heart of Mormon-land. The Bureau transferred him back to Los Angeles, where he was assigned a shit job at the Southwest US Joint FBI-DEA Task Force, under Mann.

Jessica Mayer—not a door kicker by trade, but she'd trained extensively with Baker and Turner over the past year and could hold her own. A Special Surveillance Group castaway, after outing a Turkish diplomat she identified as a possible DC-area serial killer, which turned out to be true. O'Reilly scooped her out of the federal netherworld and sent her to ARTEMIS. A match made in heaven, which Mann readily accepted.

Kim Rocha—not a shooter or a door kicker. Zero aptitude for either. Strictly a digital forensics expert. She'd join Mills inside the house for a quick evidence sweep. Kim's skills had the potential to be the most useful once they retrieved their target's electronic devices. She'd performed more than a few digital miracles for the team in the past. They'd keep her in the background until the site was secure.

That left Mann and Serrano—two scarred souls with serious, judgment-impairing grudges that they both fought to keep under control. Extensively cross-trained by Turner, Baker, and MacLeod, the team's special operators. Avengers in their own minds, but neither of them proven in battle.

The six of them would secure whoever they found at the address, while Mills and MacLeod disabled the pontoon boat at the target house's dock to prevent an easy water escape. If their target somehow made his way to the dock or the waterfront, they'd apprehend him. The bottom line? A mixed bag of agents spread about as thinly as possible. It wouldn't take much to upset this applecart.

"We'll head out in five minutes," said Mann. "Give Jax a little more time to fully scan the neighborhood, lake, and surrounding areas."

Serrano lit another cigarette and took a seat on one of the concrete parking lot bumpers across from their two SUVs. A compact M4 rifle lay across her thighs. Turner sat next to her, bumming a cigarette. He'd never seen Turner smoke before. Nerves? The curtains in one of the windows above them swept to the side, an ancient face staring down at them. Mann pointed to the chest-wide, rectangular patch at the top of his tactical vest that spelled *FBI*. The man—or woman, he couldn't tell—gave him a thumbs-up and shut the curtain.

He'd chosen the back parking lot of a nearby nursing home for their staging area. Less than a mile from the target address and surrounded by trees. Their only exposure appeared to be the residents. They'd had more than one lookie-loo since the entire team arrived about a half hour ago, but no problems so far. Mann had gone inside the senior living center's lobby when they first pulled in to let the front desk staff know that they just needed a secluded spot to prepare for a local arrest, and that if any of the residents called down to complain or express concerns about their presence, they had nothing to worry about.

He'd also given the front desk staff his cell phone number and asked them to let him know if any of the residents called down and suggested contacting the local police. He told them that their investigation involved a high-level Mexican drug trafficker living on the lake, and that one or more of the local police officers might be "in cahoots" with the drug dealer. "Better to shield everyone here from any possible retribution," he told them. "Beg them not to get involved. It'll all be over in less than an hour." As far as he could tell, the ploy had worked. Local police units hadn't screeched into the parking lot—yet.

His sat phone rang. Jax again.

"Miss me already?" said Mann.

"Funny," said Jax. "No. I have three SUVs approaching the north gate, in way too tight a formation to be a group of neighborhood soccer moms bringing their kids home from practice."

"Fuck. Here we go," said Mann. "Switch over to push-to-talk comms. Let MacLeod and Mills know to switch over. We're heading out."

"Copy that. Switching over now," said Jax, ending the call.

Serrano and Turner were already up, their cigarettes extinguished underfoot. The rest of the team had mobilized just as quickly. Everyone was primed, reading each other's body language—or more likely just eavesdropping on his call.

"Someone may have beat us to the punch, or our target travels with a serious security entourage," said Mann. "We have a tight, three-SUV convoy pulling up to the north gate. Switch to push-to-talk and earpieces. We roll now."

As everyone scattered for their vehicles, he thought of something.

"Hold up for a second!" said Mann, stopping the team in their tracks. "We'll use the south gate and take a right instead of a left at the split just inside. That'll put the passenger sides to the target's gate when we pull up. If you're not the driver, you're in the second row—and you exit on the driver's side. I want everyone to have cover the moment we arrive."

"What's our ROE again?" said Turner.

"No different than any other day as an FBI agent," said Mann. "Deadly force is only authorized to prevent death or grievous bodily harm to yourself or others. Verbal warnings will be issued if practical, prior to the use of deadly force."

"Yeah. We'll see," said Turner.

CHAPTER 17

Gary Litman stepped down from the SUV and studied the lakeside mansion's front entrance. Double doors with no windows anywhere—on the doors or around them. A dome camera sat in the middle of the wide porch roof, directly in front of the entrance, but set back from the doors by at least ten feet. Smart. The camera could be used to identify anyone who approached the door, before they stepped onto the porch, and it could be used to see what they might be holding behind their backs. And there was no way to block its field of vision without making it extremely obvious.

He nodded at the camera before ordering ALPHA team to disembark and join him on the porch. Weapons shifted to positions along their sides or backs. They gathered around him at the door, where he pressed the doorbell.

"Can I help you?" said a voice through the speaker on the doorbell panel.

"Alejandro? Jabba the Hutt sends his regards," said Litman, reciting the final code-word sequence.

"Jabba no badda," said the voice.

"De wanna wanga," said Litman, having no idea what that meant.

Some kind of *Star Wars* bullshit. That was all he knew. The other code words had been sci-fi movie exchanges from what he could tell.

"How much time do we have?" said the voice.

"My orders are to get you out of here immediately," said Litman.

"I'll be out in five minutes. I need to pack a few more things. Your boss didn't give me much of a heads-up."

"I don't want to sound rude, but I have orders to keep you in sight at all times," said Litman.

The door opened to reveal a thin Latino man of average height with thick, jet-black hair. Too black to be real—especially when contrasted against his deeply tanned, weathered face. The man had to be in his late fifties or early sixties.

"Alejandro," he said, offering his hand to Litman. "I have several suitcases. I hope that's all right."

Litman reluctantly accepted his firm handshake. "As long as we're on the road in under five minutes."

Alejandro pulled him inside the house with an unexpected strength, putting him in what felt like an inescapable bear hug.

"Very trusting," said Alejandro, before releasing him. "Did they tell you anything about me?"

"No," said Litman, after taking several steps back.

Alejandro nodded. "Just following orders?"

"Something like that," said Litman, resisting the impulse to shift his rifle into a more ready position.

"Well. Let's get this show on the road then," said Alejandro, motioning for them to enter the front door. "Don't worry. I don't bite. I do much worse—but mostly to other people. Why are you wearing life jackets?"

"Just in case," said Litman. "How can we help?"

"Suitcases are in the master bedroom," said Alejandro. "Follow me."

Litman's earpiece crackled.

"ALPHA-1. This is BRAVO-1," said Maeve Osbourne over the radio net. "I just got a call from the south gate. FBI inbound. Two SUVs. Three, possibly four, agents per vehicle."

"FBI? Are you sure?" said Litman, grabbing Alejandro's arm to keep him from heading any farther into the house.

Alejandro shot him a murderous look but didn't try to shake his grip.

"The driver of the first vehicle identified himself as an FBI agent. Badge and all," said Osbourne. "That's all the gate attendant told me. They'll be here in half a minute. I have one vehicle at the gate with four of our people."

"Head to the front gate with one additional BRAVO team member," said Litman. "Send two to the dock to secure the boat."

"Copy. Repositioning team," said Osbourne. "Same ROE?"

"ROE remains the same," said Litman. "And to be clear, if they try to breach the gate, you're authorized to use whatever force is necessary to repel them until the VIP is clear. I'll send the boat back for you. Motor directly across the lake or north along the east side of the lake to one of the public beaches and steal some vehicles. Make your way back to the airport—if you're absolutely sure that nobody is following you."

"And if someone's following me?" said Osbourne.

"You're on your own until you either lose or neutralize them," said Litman. "Give me a call when you're free and clear of any surveillance. I'll arrange a way to get you out of the area."

"Understood," said Osbourne. "Heading down to the gate."

He turned to Alejandro. "Sorry. Change of plans. No luggage. We're heading straight to your dock. Where are the boat keys?"

"I have a set here in the house and one in a key-coded lockbox on the dock," said Alejandro.

"Code?"

"1993."

"Like the year?"

Alejandro nodded. Litman triggered his radio.

"BRAVO-1. We're heading to the dock. There's a lockbox on the pier with the boat keys. Code is 1-9-9-3," he said. "I want that boat running by the time we get there."

"Copy," said Osbourne. "BRAVO-4 acknowledge."

"This is BRAVO-4. We're on our way," said one of the operators headed to the dock. "Code 1-9-9-3."

Litman turned to ALPHA-2, the team's actual leader. "Start moving him to the dock. I want a lifejacket on him before he reaches the water." Litman let go of Alejandro. "I'll be right behind you."

"Moving out," said the team leader, before pointing at Alejandro. "We good?"

"We're good," said their VIP. "Get me the hell out of here."

Litman followed ALPHA team through the house, while dialing O'Brien, who answered a few moments after he pressed "Send" on the call.

"So. Am I going on vacation or putting out your fires?" said O'Brien, pretending to be talking to a business partner.

"Both. Get your ass over here ASAP. Look for the red smoke," said Litman.

"Yep. Oscar Mike," said O'Brien. "ETA three to five minutes. Assuming everything goes right here."

"Make it go right," said Litman. "It looks like ARTEMIS had some help finding our VIP."

CHAPTER 18

Garrett Mann pulled the Lincoln Navigator parallel to the target address, continuing slowly forward until both the Navigator and the Expedition behind him had equal real estate on the street directly in front of the black sliding gate that barred entrance into the estate. A black Suburban sat in the driveway about ten feet back from the gate, three heavily armed, body armor–clad figures standing at the ready halfway in front of the SUV. One of them held up what looked like a badge.

"Dismount," said Mann, while opening his door. "Stay behind cover until we get a feel for what's going on here. Weapons down for now."

His team quickly hit the street and took positions behind the vehicles. Turner and Serrano followed him to the back of the Navigator, where they knelt in a tight stack, rifles ready. Baker and Mayer took positions behind the Expedition's hood a few feet away; Rocha headed to the back of their SUV to cover their blind side.

"Homeland Security!" yelled the man holding up the badge. "Identify yourselves!"

"Turner. What's your read?" said Mann.

"Homeland my ass," said Turner. "I say we smoke these fuckers and breach the gate. No way they're real."

"Baker?" said Mann.

"I don't know," said Baker. "If they're Homeland agents, we'll be in a world of shit if we provoke an engagement. We need to verify."

"How?" said Serrano.

"I'll call the badge in," said Mann.

"How you gonna get a close look at the badge without turning yourself into bullet bait?" said Turner.

"Like this," said Mann, stepping in between the two vehicles holding his own badge high. "FBI! Stand down! We're on the same team."

"Original," said Turner, getting a sharp elbow in the back from Serrano.

"Do you have a warrant?" said the man holding the badge.

"Do you?" said Mann.

"I'm going to reach into my right cargo pocket to produce the warrant," said the man. "Is that okay?"

Mann nodded, and the guy dug a thick, neatly folded packet of papers from one of his pockets.

"It's a complicated one," said the man, offering it to him. "Might take some time to read."

"Who are you here for?" said Mann.

The man waved the warrant paperwork in front of him. "I can't say without checking your badge. Probably should call it in."

Mann's earpiece came to life. "Garrett. This is Jax. You have three hostiles crouched behind the SUV at the gate. They just came into view between the trees. Sorry for the late notice."

"Better late than never. Thank you," said Mann. "Did everyone copy that?"

As soon as everyone at the front gate acknowledged Mann's question, he made a quick change to their tactical stance.

"Serrano. Switch positions with Mayer," said Mann.

Serrano and Mayer dashed between the vehicles, taking opposite positions. Now he had three serious shooters with a clear line of sight to the SUV inside the gate. He directed Mayer to watch the southern approach, from a position at the hood of the Navigator.

"Turner. Baker. Serrano. If anyone we can see right now raises a weapon, or if any of the three hidden behind that SUV step into the open with a weapon raised, we take this whole checkpoint down. No need to respond. Just get ready."

"Hell yeah," said Turner, inching toward the back of the Navigator.

"Are we doing this?" said the man holding the supposed warrant.

"Yes!" said Mann, slowly walking forward with his badge held high. "Homeland, huh?"

"Homeland Security. Special Activities Division," said the man, not making any move toward the fence.

"Based out of where?"

"Based out of camp—go fuck yourself," said the man, dropping the papers and reaching for the pistol nestled into his thigh holster.

The man's head snapped back before his hand touched the pistol, a bright-red spray covering the hood and windshield behind him. Mann dropped to the pavement and brought his rifle to bear on the scene in front of him—amid a maelstrom of suppressed gunfire. Bullets snapped overhead and clanged off the gate, some audibly thumping into the vehicles behind him.

By the time he flipped his rifle's selector switch off SAFE and searched for a target, the deed was done. Six bodies lay prostrate, in various twisted poses, on the ground around the Suburban. He glanced back at the three agents who had been covering him, their rifles smoking from the intense volley of gunfire. The Navigator's rear compartment side window now an opaque, milky bluish white. Two bullet holes were evident in the middle of the glass. Turner was already on the move, sliding between the two vehicles.

"Breach?" said Turner, stopping next to Mann.

"Yeah," said Mann. "Is everyone all right?"

"Yep. We got the drop on them." Turner removed a cigarette pack–size plastic explosives charge from a pouch on his vest.

"Baker and Serrano, cover the gate approach. Rocha and Mayer, watch our flanks," said Mann, hopping to his feet. "We're blowing the gate."

Turner burst forward and attached the small explosive charge to the mechanism box on the brick post that kept the gate locked in place. A few seconds later, Turner sprinted back, and the two of them took cover behind the vehicles.

"Fire in the hole!" he said, crouching next to Mann before detonating the charge.

The SUV shook violently, the sound of shattering glass the only thing he could hear over the explosion.

"Shit. Sorry?" said Turner. "Might have been overkill."

"Let's hope you didn't warp the gate, or we'll never get in," said Mann.

The two of them returned to the gate, which showed surprisingly little damage from the explosion. Turner knew what he was doing. They gave it a tug, but the massive steel frame barely budged along its track.

"Team effort here!" said Turner.

A few moments later, with everyone pulling, they had opened the gate far enough to slip through individually. Mann pocketed the warrant and badge without examining them. Even if they were somehow real, the agents or operatives at the Suburban had tried to kill them without provocation. He passed down the driver's side of the vehicle, taking note of the precision shooting. No holes in the windshield or hood—just foreheads or faces.

"Talk to me, Jax," said Mann over the radio. "We're heading up the driveway."

"I have two hostiles futzing around with what looks to be a lockbox attached to the shack at the foot of the dock," said Jax. "Five more moving toward the dock. Four of them armed and wearing body armor. The fifth dressed in regular clothes."

"That's probably our target," said Mann.

"I have a sixth armed hostile trailing them by about fifty feet," said Jax. "He's talking on a satellite phone. The weird thing is that they're all wearing life vests."

"They're planning on taking the boat," said Mann. "MacLeod? You hearing this?"

MacLeod's last report had put them alongside the target's pontoon boat—presumably undetected.

"Yeah. I copy," said MacLeod. "You want me to scuttle the boat? We've already attached a charge to the engine."

"Affirmative. Disable the boat and get the hell out of sight," said Mann. "You're super exposed in that skiff, and these people aren't messing around. We beat them to the punch at the gate, but I get the feeling that was a one-time deal."

"We're out of here. We'll detonate the moment we're clear," said MacLeod.

"Perfect," said Mann. "Let me know when it's done."

"You'll know," said MacLeod.

Automatic gunfire erupted in the distance as they approached the top of the driveway. The gunfire seemed to go back and forth for several seconds, before tapering off to nothing. A sharp crunch followed the brief silence, shaking the birds out of the trees above them.

"MacLeod? Mills. You guys good?" said Mann.

No response. He repeated his call. Still nothing.

"Jax? What are you seeing?" said Mann.

"Hard to tell what happened with all the smoke," said Jax. "Wait. I have one shooter down at the end of the dock. Definitely KIA. The pontoon boat is sinking. And . . . uh . . . shit, the skiff is motoring in a circle. I don't see anyone moving on board."

"What?" said Mann.

Serrano glanced over her shoulder; a look of pain spread across her face. Turner kept pressing forward, side by side with Baker. Turner was the wild card here. MacLeod and Turner had been tight. Diametrically opposed, personality-wise, but locked at the hip when it came to tactical operations. An unbreakable bond of respect, forged by their mutual SWAT training and experience but hardened by the shared trauma of the backgrounds that brought them to the team. They'd both lost loved ones to unsolved disappearances.

"Hold on. Looks like the skiff is straightening out. Headed north," said Jax.

"MacLeod. Mills. Report your status," said Mann.

"This is Mills. Jennie's gone. The team on the dock spotted us speeding away and opened fire. I thought we were good, but a bullet punched right through the side of the skiff and hit her in the head. I'm headed back to the launch site."

"Are you okay?" said Mann.

"I'm fine. I think. I haven't checked. I mean . . . this isn't my thing. But I don't . . . yeah . . . I think I'm good?" said Mills. "The pontoon boat is gone, by the way."

"Yeah. Nice job on that," said Mann, his voice trailing off for a moment. "Leave the skiff on the beach and get out of there. We'll coordinate a rendezvous. Given the explosion and gunfire, I don't think we're going to have time to search the target's house and do any forensics work."

"Okay," said Mills, pausing for a few seconds. "I think I'll make my way over to Jax's position. Provide backup."

"Do you want to bring Jennie to a local hospital?" said Mann. "I mean—is that even realistic?"

"No. She's gone. No question about it," said Mills. "I'm headed to Jax."

"Understood," said Mann, not sure what else to say to him right now. "Jax. Did you copy that?"

"Uh-huh," she said absently. "Two hostiles are headed in your direction."

"What about our presumed target and his entourage?" said Mann.

"They just reached the dock," said Jax. "One broke off to join the hostile headed your way."

"Can you route us to flank the inbound threat?"

"Yeah. The trees are thick along the top of the driveway and north side of the property," said Jax. "Once they reach those trees, I won't be able to see them. I can't see you right now. What's your location?"

"We're already at the top of the driveway," said Mann.

"Perfect. Keep moving forward to the edge of the tree line," said Jax. "They'll never know what hit them."

"Copy. I'm leaving four at the top of the driveway for the ambush," said Mann. "Serrano and I will access the house and engage the group on the dock from the deck. Pass all information regarding the inbound threat to Baker. Keep me apprised if anything changes on the dock. I need to know if any boats approach to pick them up. Anything that looks like a potential escape for our target."

"Got it," said Jax.

Mann tugged Serrano in the direction of the open front door, while pointing at Baker.

"Neutralize the two inbounds, then take covered positions along the tree line, facing the dock," said Mann. "Let me know when you're in position."

"ROE?" said Turner.

"Weapons free," said Mann, which meant they could freely fire on any target not identified as friendly. "Except for our target. I want to take him alive if possible."

Baker gave him a thumbs-up. But more importantly, Turner nodded his agreement. He needed Turner's buy-in more than anyone's at this point to keep the target alive. Mann acknowledged Turner's unspoken acceptance of the terms he'd just laid out by silently mouthing *thank you*. He hoped that would be enough to keep Turner from going on a shooting rampage that killed their target.

CHAPTER 19

Gary Litman took one look at the burning pontoon boat and muttered a curse. He had no idea how things had come to this, and he didn't care. His only concerns at this point were surviving the next few minutes and accomplishing his mission. The two concerns being mutually dependent. Gunfire erupted nearby. Just a few bursts. Probably the guy they sent up to the house.

"BRAVO-7, come in," said Litman.

Nothing. Fuck.

"ALPHA-3, come in."

Several seconds passed. No response. ALPHA team leader shook his head in resignation. *Fuck! Who the hell had shown up at the gate?* This didn't feel like an FBI team. Garrett Mann's infamous ARTEMIS team should have been bogged down for hours by Osbourne's bullshit, if not longer—even if they had a warrant! But Osbourne's last transmission hadn't mentioned an FBI warrant, and everything had gone sideways within a half minute of the SUVs arriving at the gate.

A few seconds of gunfire, followed by an explosion—that was all he had to go on at this point. Too damn fast. Something was more than just off. Had Mann gone rogue? How did he even find this place? Or had DOMINION been betrayed? None of that mattered right now. He needed to focus on getting the VIP and himself out of there.

First things first. He needed to establish some kind of defensible position until the plane arrived. After a few seconds of analyzing the situation, he determined that the dock's boat shack provided the best cover they could hope for right now—with a bit of a twist. Litman grabbed Bob Shaw, ALPHA team leader, by the shoulder.

"Here's the deal," said Litman. "Position one shooter behind the boat shack to cover the house and one in the water at the foot of the dock to cover the tree line due west of us."

"Which side?"

"Doesn't matter, as long as they can cover the trees directly west of us," said Litman.

"Copy that," said Shaw, before issuing orders over the radio to the last remaining AXIOM operators. "I can move back and forth behind the boat shack to support both of them."

"Negative. You're coming with me," said Litman. "We're going for a swim, and I'm going to need your help."

"Understood," said Shaw.

"I can't swim," said Alejandro.

"That's why you're wearing a life vest," said Litman.

"Ah. Very reassuring, given the current circumstances," said Alejandro.

"This isn't exactly what I had in mind, either," said Litman. "But despite appearances, we have everything under—"

Shaw stumbled backward and toppled over the side of the deck, blood spraying from his neck. Litman grabbed Alejandro and pulled him behind the boat shack, a torrent of bullets snapping through the space they'd occupied just moments ago.

"Under control?" said Alejandro.

"Who the hell are you, exactly?" said Litman.

"You have no idea."

"Obviously," said Litman, taking the satellite phone out of his vest and dialing O'Brien.

"We're less than a minute out!" said O'Brien. "What's your status?"

"My status?" said Litman. "It's pretty much fucked."

"I'm sorry. I didn't catch that," said O'Brien over some serious propeller noise. "Something about fucked? What's happening down there?"

"The situation is fucked!" said Litman. "Did you copy that?"

"Affirmative!" said O'Brien. "How bad?"

"BRAVO team is gone!" said Litman. "We're down to three, plus the VIP."

"Okay. I didn't catch that!" said O'Brien. "But I can see the lake! Pop the red smoke! I'm coming in fast. Might not get another chance."

"O'Brien?" he said. "Are you flying the plane?"

"Uh. Yes. The pilot refuses to land on the lake," replied O'Brien. "Said he'll lose his license."

"Did you make it clear that he'd lose his life if he didn't land on the lake?"

"I did!" said O'Brien. "But he wasn't budging—and you needed the plane immediately, so I relieved him of his duties."

"Can you pull this off?" said Litman. "You didn't sound very confident about a water landing."

Fuck. He glanced at Alejandro, who didn't seem to give two living shits about the lopsided situation they faced at the moment. Litman resigned himself to having to put a bullet through the guy's head, before trying to swim to freedom. What a mess.

"It's all good!" said O'Brien. "The pilot is talking me through it. He said that if I was at the controls, he wouldn't lose his license."

"Wait. What?" said Litman. "The pilot's with you?"

"Damn right!" said O'Brien. "I'm flying from the copilot seat."

Jesus. This might actually work.

"Where are you?" said Litman. "I don't hear the plane. Shouldn't I hear the plane?"

"I'm about thirty seconds out," said O'Brien. "Coming in low, but I can see the lake. You should hear and see me in a few."

He shook his head. Was this whole thing some kind of test? A very realistic, utterly convincing operational exercise? What else could explain this level of fuckery? He glanced at the dock, just beyond the boat shack, examining the blood sprayed out of Shaw's neck. Looked pretty real. *This can't be a test. Right? Why would AXIOM do that?* He noticed a sizable drop of blood on the barrel of his rifle—and decided to taste it. Nope. Coppery. Real blood.

He turned to ALPHA-4, crouched behind the opposite corner of the boat shack.

"Is this real? Nobody's messing with me?"

The operator gave him a worried look. "What are you talking about?"

Litman's head jerked sideways, followed by a sharp crack. He backed up a few feet and took a knee; bullets smacked into his corner of the shack, splintering and punching through the wood. His hands instinctively went to his helmet to check for damage.

"Is that real enough for you?" said the operator.

"Where's it coming from?" said Litman.

"Has to be the house," said ALPHA-4. "I can't see the tree line from here."

Shit. They'd infiltrated the entire property.

"Copy that. Load up one of your drums!" said Litman. "Time to lay down some serious suppressing fire!"

ALPHA-4 gave him a thumbs-up, then retrieved a drum magazine from the pouch hanging from his tactical vest. Seventy-five rounds of 5.56mm ammunition. Hopefully enough to keep the FBI guns off the inbound aircraft.

"ALPHA-6. Load up a drum magazine and start working the tree line. Burn through all your ammo. We're going to need the cover."

"I'm way ahead of you," said the operative in the water at the foot of the dock. Automatic gunfire broke loose from both ALPHA team members.

Litman removed the smoke grenade attached to his vest and pulled the pin, waiting until he finally heard the buzz of an approaching plane to release the safety lever. Instead of trying to roll or throw the grenade down the dock, he set it down next to the corner of the boat shack and backed up a few feet. Once the red smoke started billowing from the grenade, he called O'Brien.

"I popped the red smoke. Do you see it?"

"Got it!" said O'Brien.

"The smoke is on the dock. Bring the plane as close as you can," said Litman. "We'll be in the water, waiting. This will be a hot extraction. Copy?"

"Copy! Hot extraction!" said O'Brien. "You should be able to see us now. We're over the southern edge of the lake."

Litman glanced over his shoulder, spotting the plane—coming in low. He grabbed Alejandro's life vest.

"This is it. No screwing around. If you don't get on that plane, you answer to the FBI," said Litman.

Alejandro nodded. "I can doggy paddle and frog kick."

"Good," said Litman. "Because I'm not a very strong swimmer. Grab the back of my vest when we're in the water and kick your heart out. ALPHA team—throw your smoke grenades as far onto the property as possible. We're going to need every bit of help we can get."

CHAPTER 20

Serrano sighted in on the corner of the boat shack, waiting for her target to reappear—or for someone to take their place. She'd undoubtedly hit whoever had poked their head out, but the outcome was far from conclusive. The target wore a ballistic helmet, and she couldn't say whether her shot had hit the helmet or his face. She'd taken a helmet shot before—and it rang her bell like nothing before. A tenth-of-an-ounce projectile traveling at 3,200 feet per second felt like a jackhammer blow, no matter where it hit you.

Several seconds passed. Nothing. Then an arm, tossing something onto the grassy slope leading down to the waterline south of the dock. She snapped off a few shots, knowing they'd probably gone to waste.

"Do you hear that?" said Mann, crouched nearby. "Propeller plane. Really close."

"Probably just—"

The hard-plastic composite railing post in front of her suddenly splintered, a dozen loud cracks snapping past her—until she was punched backward a moment later. Serrano hit the deck flat on her back, unable to take a breath or make a sound. Mann was over her before she could form a coherent thought, dragging her back into the house. Glass shattered around and over them as he pulled her through the open deck slider, until they were deep enough into the house to avoid direct gunfire.

Mann didn't ask her any questions. He immediately went to work checking for bullet wounds, stopping several seconds later.

"You're good! Vest stopped the bullet!" he said, tapping the armor plate inserted in her vest. "Stay here and stay down!"

Mann took off for the deck before she could respond or even bring herself to move. *He'll get himself killed.* A sustained hail of bullets drove Mann back into the house, none of them hitting him somehow. He crouched behind the wall next to the slider and signaled for her to stay down. *Yeah. Hope you take your own advice.*

The deep buzz of a propeller plane filled the room.

"They're taking him out by seaplane!" she croaked, still struggling to breathe from the bullet-hit to the chest plate.

Mann risked a glance outside, before he was driven back by gunfire. She struggled to get up, finally making it to her knees.

"Stay down!" he said, before getting on the radio. "Jax. Do you see an aircraft flying low over the lake?"

"Hold on. Panning my view around," she said. "Shit. Affirmative. Seaplane coming in from the south. Low over the treetops."

No way Serrano was going to let their killer get away. She pushed herself to her feet and lurched toward the deck, still unsteady. Mann pulled her down and out of the way as another sustained burst of gunfire hit the house. Someone down there had undoubtedly identified them as a serious threat to the extraction. She tried to break free, but Mann held her in place.

"Turner and Baker will take care of the shooters!" he said over the snapping bullets. "Then we'll all take care of the plane."

The automatic gunfire didn't let up; two guns from what she could tell by the staccato timing of bursts.

"Doesn't sound like they're any better off than we are!" said Serrano.

Mann triggered his radio. "Baker. We're pinned down inside the house. Heavy automatic fire. What's your status?"

"Same situation!" Baker replied. "Automatic gunfire from the dock. It's keeping our heads down. I'm going to flank north a little bit while the shooter is busy. Take him down once I'm in position."

"I don't think we have time for that," said Mann. "There's a plane inbound."

Serrano took advantage of the distraction and broke free of Mann's grip.

"Hold on!" said Mann. "I'm trying to coordinate an attack."

"They're going to fly him out of here right now!" said Serrano, changing rifle magazines. "That'll be the end of this. *Adios, muchacho!*"

"Then we better make this count," said Mann, before transmitting over the net. "On the count of three. Everyone opens up on the dock. Half a magazine. Serrano and Baker are the designated sharpshooters. Three."

He helped Serrano up and led her back toward the deck.

"Two."

A mix of red and gray smoke obscured the dock and boat shack, the chemical cloud drifting south—just as a seaplane burst into view over the southern edge of the lake. The plane hit hard at first and bounced, but quickly leveled off and skimmed the surface—before firmly planting its pontoons in the water. It was only a matter of time before the cloud of smoke blocked the plane.

"Garrett. The seaplane!"

"One," said Mann.

Serrano pushed him away and rushed to the edge of the deck, where she rested her rifle's handguard on the top of the railing and started pouring long bursts of gunfire into the corner of the shack, forcing the shooter to take cover.

"Open fire! Open fire!" said Mann, joining her a moment later.

In her peripheral vision, the reed- and cattail-infested water at the foot of the dock erupted in dozens of small geysers as Baker's team attempted to neutralize their shooter. Serrano kept her attention focused on the boat shack. The smoke had almost completely obscured it, but she wasn't convinced that the automatic gunfire threat had been extinguished. Their adversaries seemed hell-bent on protecting whoever lived at this house.

The shooter reappeared at the corner, aiming a rifle at the house. She pressed her trigger once, the holographic reticle firmly centered on the target's face this time. The shooter dropped to the dock instantly, then tumbled into the water.

"The shooter behind the shack is down," said Mann.

Automatic gunfire continued to explode from a concealed position at the foot of the dock, Baker's team still taking a beating.

"Still working on the other guy," said Baker. "He's dug in good. But not for long. I got his number."

She reloaded and shifted her aim to the foot of the dock. The sooner they silenced the automatic fire, the quicker they could focus on the seaplane. She was about to start firing, when the rifles in the tree line went quiet for several seconds. What the hell happened to Baker's team? Three evenly spaced gunshots rang out from the forest—and all the gunfire ended.

"Second shooter is neutralized," said Baker.

"Reload and concentrate all gunfire on the seaplane," said Mann, over the radio net. "That's their only way out of here."

"Copy that," said someone. Sounded like Turner.

Serrano sighted in on the seaplane, which was barely visible beyond the wall of smoke, and started rapidly pressing her rifle's trigger. If they took out the plane, their killer had nowhere to go—other than try to swim across the lake—where they'd pluck him from the water when he finally reached the shore. The volume of rifle fire increased almost instantly, the water around the seaplane kicking up from bullet strikes as it approached the dock.

"Want us to make a move on the dock? I think our target is hiding behind the boat shack," said Baker. "I can't see shit with all the smoke."

"Negative. Too risky," said Mann over the radio. "Hit the plane. They're stuck here without that plane."

Serrano wondered if Baker had the right idea. She was basically firing at a barely visible silhouette through the smoke at this point. She'd watched a few more sail over the shack and land in the grass along the shoreline. Someone knew what they were doing.

"Maybe we need to get down there!" said Serrano.

"They could have the dock rigged with a Claymore. Explosives. Or another shooter waiting to go full auto," said Mann. "We stop the plane and take our time with whoever's left down there."

"You better be right about this," said Serrano, reloading her rifle.

She was down to two magazines. They'd gone with light loadouts, none of them guessing that a small army would arrive at the property just ahead of them.

CHAPTER 21

Litman tossed his last smoke grenade a few feet down the dock and waited for the thick red smoke to blossom. From what he could tell, it was just the two of them now. His guns had gone silent, the last of ALPHA team floating face down in the water. It was now or never.

"O'Brien. How are we looking?" said Litman, his eyes stinging from the caustic smoke. "I'm about to make a run for it. It's imperative that you pull up as close as possible."

"Almost there," said O'Brien. "This needs to be a quick pickup. They're turning the plane into swiss cheese."

"We're moving out," said Litman. "But we're going to need help getting into the plane if you want this to go quickly."

"The pilot doesn't want to—"

"To what? Get involved? He's already fucking involved!" said Litman. "Tell him he has two choices. He can take the controls while you help us get on board or he can be the one to help us on board. If he's unwilling to do either, he's dead weight. Shoot him and push him out the door. I'm not fucking around here. We're on the move!"

He turned to Alejandro, who didn't look worried. *Who the hell is this guy?*

"Ready?" said Litman.

Alejandro shrugged indifferently.

"I need you to listen closely. We're going to sprint to the end of the dock and jump into the water behind the pontoon boat," said Litman.

"We'll have full cover from all this shit once we hit the water. Your life vest will automatically activate. Start doggy paddling toward the plane right away. Someone will help us on board. Don't mess with them."

Alejandro rolled his eyes, before nodding in agreement. Damn. This was like dealing with a teenager. Litman had already "been there, done that." Well, his ex-wife had done most of that work, which was why they weren't together anymore. But he'd seen enough of it to know the behavior. Something was off with this guy. As in, seriously screwed. And if Litman's career wasn't on the line right now, he'd put a bullet through this guy's face and make up a story along the lines of "shit happens."

But that wasn't an option based on his conversation with Jeremy Powell. Not unless Litman was fine with being captured or killed by the FBI. He'd been given permission to kill the VIP, but only as a last resort to prevent his capture. The VIP's capture. If Litman returned without Alejandro, there would be questions. And most likely a bullet—at the end of a long torture session. No. The two of them were joined at the hip.

"Let's go," said Litman. "I'll follow right behind you."

The two of them took off, Alejandro moving surprisingly fast. Too fast. Unencumbered with body armor, ammunition, and a rifle—he was pulling ahead.

"Slow the hell—"

A torrent of bullets snapped all around Litman, one catching him in the meaty part of his left shoulder. Another hit him in the back, smacking into the metal plate inserted into his vest and propelling him forward. He kept his balance and miraculously closed the distance to Alejandro. The gunfire intensified the closer they got to the end of the dock, the bullets zipping inches away—all around them.

Litman didn't skip a beat. He ducked a little and hit Alejandro in the lower back, lifting him over his right shoulder before careening left and launching them both off the dock into the water. His thirty-plus pounds of gear sent him straight toward the bottom of the lake for a few seconds, before his vest automatically activated and yanked him to the surface. He bobbed up and down a few times before steadying himself. Alejandro had already started swimming for the seaplane, which sat about thirty feet away—idling like an angry table saw.

The pilot stood on the float skid, beckoning them toward the plane, while bullets smacked into the aircraft's aluminum frame. Windows shattered. Holes riddled the fuselage and tail. Litman didn't see how the damn thing could possibly take off by the time they got everyone on board, but they had to try. The pilot pulled Alejandro onto the skid and pushed him through the open door into the rear passenger compartment, before turning his attention to Litman, who grasped the edge of the pontoon with his right hand. His entire left arm had been disabled by the bullet that passed through his shoulder.

After a short struggle, Litman stood on the pontoon, bullets cracking and snapping all around him—but none striking home. The pilot shoved him inside the plane and shut the door, banging on the copilot window before performing a near perfect dive off the pontoon into the lake. Good for him. The plane pitched forward, picking up speed, as bullets punched through the thin fuselage. All the windows, except for the forward windshields, were long gone.

Litman made his way to the cockpit, to find O'Brien bleeding from a deep gash along his right forearm.

"You good?" said Litman.

"Somehow I'm still alive," he said. "You?"

"Same here!" said Litman.

The gunfire died off as they raced across the lake, scattering kayaks and canoes on what looked like a terminal approach to the wall of trees on the northern shore of the lake.

"Do we need to turn around?" said Litman.

"Just need a little more room to build up speed," said O'Brien.

"It doesn't look like we have any more room," said Litman.

"Trust me," said O'Brien, edging the throttle forward.

"I think you're going to need more than that!" said Litman.

"I'm channeling Zeke right now."

"Who the hell is Zeke?" said Litman.

"The pilot," said O'Brien. "Hang on! He told me this wasn't a good idea, but it was the only way off the lake."

"What?"

Litman jumped into the pilot seat a moment before the plane rocketed skyward. There was nothing subtle about the takeoff. They were skimming the lake at highway speed one moment—clawing through the air at what felt like a completely unsafe angle the next. The aircraft pitched up and down a few times, the view through the windshield switching from bluish-cloudy skies to green trees—until everything leveled off.

"How far to the airport?" said Litman.

"Three minutes," said O'Brien.

"I want the jet ready to go now," said Litman. "As in taxied onto the runway and ready to take off. We'll land on the same runway and ditch this plane close to the jet."

O'Brien handed him a satellite phone. "Do you mind calling Franklin for me? He's running the show back at the airport. I think I need to focus my attention on flying the plane. It's feeling significantly different than the ride over."

"Probably has something to do with all the bullet holes," said Alejandro.

"Exactly," said O'Brien.

CHAPTER 22

Garrett Mann watched the plane take off, wanting to scream at the top of his lungs. It just didn't seem possible. They'd fired hundreds of rounds at the aircraft, yet somehow they couldn't stop it. He knew why. Mechanically, the plane wasn't very complicated. A system of chains, cables, and pulleys connected the basic cockpit controls to the flight surfaces—the elevator, rudder, and ailerons.

A bullet would have to sever one of the cables running through the plane or damage a junction box to impact the aircraft's flight, each quarter-inch bullet slicing through the fuselage, wings, and tail with barely a hope of hitting one of those critical components. The engine, located in front of the cockpit, was the other point of weakness. A much bigger target—and highly susceptible to damage. His mistake for not suggesting that they concentrate their gunfire on the front of the aircraft.

Like the rest of his team, Mann suspected that they'd all been drawn to the human targets climbing onto the skids. The smoke severely limited their visibility, but everyone saw the two targets sprinting up the dock. And that had become their focus. Mann's especially. He fired nearly every shot at them. On the dock and in the water.

"Shit!" he said, slamming the butt of his rifle on the top of the deck railing.

"Do you see that?" said Serrano, following the plane with her rifle. "See what?"

"Jax's drone is following the plane," said Serrano. "Wait. It's like almost on top of the plane now."

"Jax. This is Mann," he said over the radio. "Do not crash the drone into the aircraft. You're over a populated area."

"That's not what I'm doing," said Jax. "The drone is equipped with the same virus transmitter we planted on the SUV. The difference being that I can activate the transmitter remotely. I'm trying to keep it close enough to pass along the virus to any devices on the plane. Ah, shit . . . they just leveled out and picked up speed. I can't keep up."

"Will it work?" said Mann.

"Depends on how close and how long she kept the drone next to the plane," said Mayer, over the radio. "It's not exactly a powerful transmitter."

"Why didn't anyone tell me about this?" said Mann.

"Because it's a total jerry-rigged operation," said Mayer. "I have no idea if it'll work. We'll see."

"Fair enough. Let's keep our fingers crossed," said Mann.

Serrano turned to him. "Fuck all this technological bullshit. What's the nearest airport?"

"I don't—hold on," he said, pulling his cell phone from his back pocket.

"We need to have local authorities swarm that plane when it lands," she said.

Serrano was right. They had the juice to make that happen, even if they'd spend the next three years in court trying to explain exactly what they had been up to today. Things like raiding a house without a warrant and getting into a gunbattle that resulted in a dozen or more deaths. Not to mention the hundreds of bullets they'd basically fired into and across a public lake. Kind of a prosecutorial slam dunk, really. They'd be lucky if they didn't spend the next decade or two in federal prison.

"Yep. I'm on it," said Mann, searching Google for the nearest airports.

Minneapolis–St. Paul International Airport came up first, but he highly doubted that they had used such a visible airport. Especially since they utilized a seaplane for the extraction. Had to be something smaller.

Serrano jumped on the radio net. "Jax. Were you able to track the plane at all? See where it was headed?"

"Due north. I just lost sight of it," said Jax.

"Here. Crystal Airport. About eight miles north," said Mann. "It's a regional airport capable of handling smaller jets."

"Shit. They'll be gone before we finish explaining the situation to the local police," said Serrano.

"I'll call the airport directly and tell them to shut down all traffic," said Mann.

"Over the phone?" said Serrano. "On whose authority? How will they verify your identity?"

"I'll call O'Reilly," he said, bringing her number up on the phone.

"You sure you want to loop her in on this?"

"Do we have a choice?" said Mann.

His radio earpiece came to life. "Garrett. This is Turner. Looks like we have someone in the water, swimming to shore. North side of the dock. We have him sighted in. He stops swimming every few seconds and waves both hands toward the shore. I don't think he was part of the team sent to pick up the target."

"Copy," said Mann. "Send two down to grab him when he reaches the shore, but keep him covered the entire time until he's secured."

"I'll head down," said Turner. "Baker will provide overwatch."

"Sounds like a plan," said Mann. "I'm working the airport angle. They got here too quickly. They can't be going far."

"Yeah. I don't know if you could see it from your angle, but the plane left a trail of smoke behind it. They're definitely not going far."

"I couldn't tell through all the smoke along the waterfront," said Mann.

"This is Jax. I can confirm that the plane sustained damage to its engine. Light smoke. Still flying pretty steady before I lost it."

141

"Jax. Time for you to pack up and get out of there," said Mann. "Can you land the drone at the beach parking lot?"

"Negative. Too many people running around," said Jax. "I'm sending the drone to a soccer field about a mile south of here. It can land itself. We'll pick it up and meet you wherever."

Police sirens drifted over the lake.

"Jax? How long until police units arrive at our doorstep?" said Mann.

"Two minutes?" she said. "Maybe sooner."

Damn. He really wanted to spend some time sifting through the target's house, but the last thing he needed was to get entangled with local law enforcement. His FBI badge would only hold so much sway in the face of a shitstorm of this magnitude.

"Forget the guy in the water. Everyone back to the vehicles. I want to be out of the neighborhood in under a minute," said Mann. "Mills. What's your status?"

"Loading MacLeod into the back of the SUV," said Mills, his voice shaky.

"Copy. Head south back to Owatonna. We'll bring MacLeod to the Steele County Medical Examiner's office. Keep all of this among people we can trust."

Mills barely responded. "Okay. Yeah. Owatonna."

"Jax. Same for you. Head back to Owatonna after you retrieve the drone," said Mann. "How's Deputy Crawford handling all of this?"

"Surprisingly well. I gotta get out of here before the police seal off the beach exits," she said. "There's talk on the radio about cordoning off all the roads around the lake."

"All right. Get moving. Everyone gets moving," said Mann, before nodding at Serrano. "Let's go."

Mann's cell phone buzzed. Sheriff Young. Shit. News traveled fast. Sounded like young Deputy Crawford had found time to make a call. He answered the phone without slowing down. Judging by the police sirens, they'd be lucky to get to one of the neighborhood gates before half of the police department arrived.

"Sheriff. I'm a little busy right now," said Mann. "Can I call you back in a few minutes?"

"No. I need your full attention right now," said Sheriff Young.

"Sorry about the skiff," said Mann. "We'll get you a new one, even if I have to pay for it myself. And your deputy is safe. He was never in the line of fire."

"What are you talking about?" said Young.

"Wait. Why did you call?" said Mann.

"You need to pull your people in tight up there," said Young. "You might be in some serious danger."

He could have used that warning about ten minutes ago. But what could Young possibly know to prompt this untimely warning? Something was way off.

"What do you mean?" said Mann.

"Well. I don't know how to say this exactly, so I'm just gonna say it," said Young. "The medical examiner's garage is on fire, and the Suburban that was towed back from the body dump site has been stolen. One of my deputies and an Owatonna police officer are dead, killed right in the police department parking lot during the SUV heist. And Rostov and Trejo are missing. They're the only people that didn't muster outside the medical examiner's building. I hate to speculate, but my guess is they're dead. Burning inside the building with the rest of the evidence."

A clean sweep. What the hell have we stumbled on here? None of this is even remotely normal. He kept jogging, even though he had fallen behind the rest of the group trying to evacuate the property before the police arrived. That's what it had come down to here. The FBI running from the police—and something sinister. Bigger than anything they imagined. Something they'd somehow prodded hard enough to retaliate.

"Things went very badly here, too," said Mann. "I have one KIA and a public shit show on my hands. It's bad enough that I don't think my badge is going to satisfy things here, if you know what I mean. I need to focus on getting my people out of here. I'm very sorry about your deputy and the local police officer. I don't know why any of this happened, but I can promise you one thing. We'll get to the bottom of this—and make whoever is responsible pay dearly."

"I appreciate hearing that," said Young. "And your team can consider Steele County a safe haven. You have my word on that."

"Thank you, Sheriff," said Mann. "I have a feeling we're going to need it. One last question."

"Go for it," said Young.

"We're bringing back our KIA. Jennifer MacLeod. I was hoping to store her in the medical officer's morgue. Will that be an option?"

"The fire shouldn't threaten that part of the facility," said Young. "We'll take care of her body."

"Thank you, Sheriff. That means a lot to us," said Mann.

"It's the least I can do," said Young. "Just keep me in the loop."

"I will," said Mann.

He ended the call and picked up the pace, reaching the property gate as the rest of the team started opening SUV doors. Mann hit the auto-start button on the remote he'd pulled from his pocket as he made his way around the front of the Navigator. A few seconds later, their two-vehicle convoy was speeding toward the south gate.

"Who called?" said Serrano, now in the front passenger seat.

"Sheriff Young," said Mann.

"He already heard?"

"No. I'll explain in a few minutes," said Mann. "We need to get clear of this place. And I need to call O'Reilly."

"Good luck with that," said Serrano.

The moment they pulled up to the gate and triggered the automatic sensor that slid the metal barrier to the side, four Ford Interceptors raced up to the entry. Two Minneapolis PD vehicles and two from the Hennepin County Sheriff's Office. The officers inside the vehicles waved frantically at the young woman inside the gatehouse, the inbound gate sliding open a few moments later. As soon as the outbound gate had parted far enough to allow his Navigator through, Mann gunned the engine and sped onto the short access road leading to Cedar Lake Parkway.

He hit speed dial for O'Reilly and waited for her to pick up the call.

"What's up?" said O'Reilly, not one for any kind of formality.

"You want the bad news or bad news first?"

"Did I hear you correctly?" she said.

"You did. I have nothing but bad news to pass along," said Mann, before telling her everything about the Cedar Lake debacle and what he'd just learned about the tragic events in Owatonna.

O'Reilly didn't respond for a few seconds, a sign that she was weighing her options.

"I'll contact Crystal Airport immediately and declare a terrorist emergency. Ground any outbound flights. My guess is they'll transfer to a long-range, private jet," said O'Reilly. "How far are you from that airport?"

"We're too far from the airport to make a difference," said Mann. "And I need to get down to Owatonna. That said, if you somehow manage to keep the plane from taking off, I'll turn around and make my way back up to Minneapolis. There's a good chance our killer will be on board that jet."

"Understood. I'll scramble whatever I can to the airport," said O'Reilly. "Do you need backup down in Owatonna?"

"Do you have people on the books willing to break every rule imaginable?" said Mann. "I don't see this playing out in any kind of career-enhancing way."

"Let me rephrase that," said O'Reilly. "Can you manage this on your own for now?"

"You didn't answer my question."

"And you didn't answer mine," said O'Reilly.

"I asked first."

"I'm your boss," said O'Reilly.

"I think we can handle this for now," said Mann. "I have access to some outside help, if we need it."

"Do I want to know?"

"No," said Mann. "You don't."

The "help" would come from Serrano, who wasn't officially part of their team. O'Reilly knew about Serrano, but more or less pretended that she didn't exist. Which she didn't. Officially.

"Okay. I think I get it," said O'Reilly. "So—just keep what I'm about to say in your back pocket. I have a few levers I can try to pull, if necessary, but I can't guarantee anything. I'm talking about people that have helped me in the past."

"I've heard some stories," said Mann.

"I bet you have," said O'Reilly.

"You're not going to deny them?"

"I'm very sorry to hear about MacLeod and Trejo. Please pass that along to the team," said O'Reilly, not so subtly changing the subject.

Message received.

"I will," said Mann. "And I'll be in touch as soon as I have some news from Owatonna."

"One last question," said O'Reilly.

"Fire away," said Mann.

"If you had to guess—who sent the goons to the lake?"

"I'd say they were either sent by the government or a military contractor with deep pockets," said Mann. "They knew what they were doing. No doubt about that. Even had a backup plan. The seaplane thing couldn't have been easy to arrange."

"All right. I'm going to hang my ass out in the breeze and call in a terrorist threat," said O'Reilly. "Don't screw me over on this, Garrett. Keep me in the loop."

"I will," said Mann. "I mean, I won't—"

"I know what you mean," said O'Reilly. "Just remember. I'll do whatever I can to support you. You have my word on that. And if I can't help you, or if I'm forced to cut you off for whatever reason, I'll tell you straight up, right away. I'll go to my grave before I screw your team over. Copy?"

"Copy," said Mann. "I don't know what else to say."

"You don't have to say anything. Just take care of your people for now. We'll figure out where to go from there," said O'Reilly, ending the call.

"Do you trust her?" said Serrano.

He'd heard stories about O'Reilly. Wild ones. Serious counterintelligence exploits. If any of them were true, they were in good hands. Good enough to know that they wouldn't be backstabbed.

"Yeah. I do," said Mann. "She's a legend at the Bureau—for the right reasons."

"What exactly is going on?" said Mayer. "Why did Sheriff Young call you?"

"Hold on. I'll explain everything I know once we're somewhat clear of the city," said Mann.

A few minutes later, they were headed south on Minnesota State Highway 100, the Navigator's windshield emergency light bar flashing to give them the aura of legitimacy they needed to get as far away from Minneapolis as possible. They'd hit Interstate 494 shortly and turn due east to connect with Interstate 35, which would take them back to Owatonna.

"We're clear now," said Mayer matter-of-factly.

"Yeah. We should be good," said Mann. "I think everyone needs to hear this, so I'm going to pass along what I know over the net. If that's okay."

"No secrets on this team, right?" said Mayer.

"Right," said Mann.

He glanced at Serrano, who had a cigarette in her mouth, a lighter in her hand, and a look on her face that told him he better not leave anything out.

"Roll the window down, Cata. Okay?"

"Only if Jess is okay with it," said Serrano. "We're a team."

"Pass one back, if you don't mind," said Mayer. "I haven't had a cigarette in over a decade, but this feels like the right occasion to break that streak."

Serrano passed one back to Mayer and lit it for her. Mann lowered all the windows. He wasn't about to deny them this simple pleasure. Not after what they'd all just been through—and were about to go through. Mayer coughed a few times before settling in.

"Just like riding a bike," said Mayer. "So. What the hell is going on?"

Mann triggered his radio. "Is everyone up on the net?"

After receiving acknowledgments from everyone in the SUV behind them, in addition to Mills and Jax, he continued.

"I just got a call from Sheriff Young," said Mann. "The SUV recovered at the body dump site has been stolen, and the medical examiner's garage is on fire. A Steele County deputy and an Owatonna police officer were killed in the parking lot at the station, presumably trying to prevent the theft of the SUV. On top of that, Dr. Trejo and Dr. Rostov are missing."

He gave that a moment to sink in. When nobody responded, he finished what he had to say.

"Given the fact that they were working with the bodies inside the garage all day, it's fair to assume that whoever started the fire probably killed them and left their bodies inside the garage. We won't know for sure until the fire is put out and we sift through the mess. We're headed back to Owatonna. Sheriff Young promised us safe haven. I have no idea what that means. We're FBI agents. But a sheriff is an elected position, and they serve as the law in their county. What they say . . . usually holds firm. We're going to set up shop in Owatonna and proceed from there. Questions?"

"MacLeod," said Turner.

It wasn't a question. It wasn't really a statement. It was an acknowledgment.

"Yeah. MacLeod is gone. Trejo, too. Most likely," said Mann.

The net went silent. Not a great sign.

148

"I'm going to make some calls. Figure some shit out," said Mann. "We'll regroup in Owatonna. I'm not going to lie to you—my head is spinning right now. Let's give this some drive-time to sink in. Pass along any and all ideas. Nothing is off-limits."

"This is Baker. What about the plane? Can we ground it?"

"O'Reilly's working on that," said Mann. "She's going to coordinate a local response to deal with the airport."

"They're not going to take this well," said Turner.

"Who?" said Mann. "The FBI?"

"The FBI for one. But I'm thinking about whoever is behind all of this. Whatever *this* is. They may have gotten what they wanted from the lake house—but we cut them deep. Bone deep," said Turner. "They're not going to let this go. Let us go."

"Start looking into motels around Owatonna," said Mann. "We're going to be there for a few days while we sort things out. Defendable motels—in case you're right."

"Oh. I'm right," said Turner. "If I had to guess, I'd say they'll hit us tonight, thinking everyone is exhausted and in complete disarray. Especially the sheriff's department. That's what I would do."

"Then we need to be ready for them," said Mann.

"A trap?" said Serrano.

"Now we're talking," said Turner. "I'll look for a motel that might work for that."

"There's only eight of us," said Mann.

"What about the sheriff's people?" said Turner. "They'll want their pound of flesh. They have a SWAT team."

"Identify a few possible motel options and put together a rough plan. I'll call Sheriff Young before we get back to Owatonna so he can start moving some of his chess pieces around the board—if he agrees to take part," said Mann. "It'll be up to him. He's lost two already, plus their medical examiner. He may not be up for risking any more lives."

"Can't hurt to ask," said Turner.

"No. It can't. And the sooner we start setting this up, the better. The various attacks in Steele County were timed to coincide with the arrival of the team at our target's address," said Mann. "They went for a clean sweep of the evidence—and succeeded. But our showing up at the target house that quickly will change their calculations. They know we're onto them. Know we have the resources and capability to track down the untraceable. We're the last thing standing in their way. Turner is right. They'll come after us sooner than later. If Young will help us, we need to give him time to move his people into place ahead of or shortly after our return to Owatonna. Whoever is behind all of this will be watching us closely. We'll keep their eyes focused firmly on us, while Young does his thing."

"Baker and I will do some Google Maps research and start strategizing," said Turner. "We'll have something for you to pass along to the sheriff in thirty minutes."

"Sounds good," said Mann, ending the conversation.

"I'll start making calls," said Serrano, off the radio net. "But it might take a day or two to get anyone up here."

"You read my mind," said Mann.

"You're an easy read," said Serrano.

"We can fly them in to save time. I have a rainy-day fund," said Mann.

Over the past year, Serrano had recruited a dozen or so disgruntled former Mexican police officers and ex-members of the military that she'd met on the job—and more or less trusted implicitly. *More or less* being the key term. Even she acknowledged that you could never be one hundred percent certain about anyone who worked the job in Mexico.

Realizing her crew's force-multiplier potential north of the border, Mann used ARTEMIS funds to pay for their passports and Border Crossing Cards. He'd even paid for some private tactical training inside the US to boost their general shooting abilities under a variety of conditions, close quarters battle proficiency in tight urban spaces, and emergency first aid skills. Outside of breaking free from their current jobs, which was never guaranteed, nothing stood in the way of their travel to the United States.

"They won't be able to bring any useful gear with them," said Serrano.

"We have a small arsenal of extra weapons, several additional sets of body armor, and some spare night vision goggles. That and a trip to a Cabela's and an Army/Navy surplus store or two should be more than enough to outfit whoever shows up."

"We should have grabbed some of the rifles off the bodies inside the gate," said Mayer. "All our stuff is off-the-shelf, gun store variety."

"We were in a bit of a rush," said Mann. "Jess. Tell me more about the virus transmitter Jax planted in the Suburban. You helped her install it. Did she brief you on its capabilities?"

"She did," said Mayer. "We could have used this kind of tech at SSG, but I think it stayed in the CIA's toolkit until very recently."

"How long until we get a hit?" said Mann.

"It all depends," said Mayer. "My guess is they will assume we've bugged the SUV, so they won't take it anywhere near a location important to their operations. They'll probably drive it into a covered trailer within fifty miles of Owatonna, rendering the conventional GPS cell tower–reliant bugs useless."

"But not the special transmitter," said Mann.

"Yes and no. The virus transmitter won't activate until it loses both GPS and cell tower signals for five minutes," said Mayer. "So if the SUV is in an enclosed trailer, and passes through a cell tower dead zone, it'll go active and try to infect any cellular- or Wi-Fi–enabled device within a certain range."

"What's the range?" said Serrano.

"Depends, according to Jax," said Mayer. "If the SUV is in the back of a semitrailer, I don't think the signal can reach the cab. If it's in something smaller, hitched to an F-350, it's possible. But that's mostly irrelevant. Here's what I think is going to happen. They'll drive the Suburban out to a warehouse in a remote, zero-cell-coverage location, knowing that any of the bugs we may have hidden in the SUV can communicate with GPS satellites and cell towers. They'll probably just leave it out there, never to be found again. Or they might destroy it completely, by burning it with an intense fire that will fry any bugs.

"That's why we set the activation time to five minutes. The bug has about twenty-four hours of battery life, so if it's triggered during transit, it won't be wasted. The daisy-chain effect is its real power. We just need it to infect one device, on one person who's important to their operation—who will hopefully meet with others and propagate the virus. We could potentially map their entire network, if the right person comes in contact with the virus."

"And you can track this with the equipment we have on hand?" said Mann.

"All we need is a cell phone with internet access," said Mayer.

"We'll need to set Jax up in a very secure location, with more than a phone," said Mann. "The bug you planted in that Suburban may be the only shot we have of taking this any further."

"And the plane?" said Mayer.

"I guess we'll know soon enough if that worked," said Mann. "I'm not counting on it."

"I don't understand why they didn't just leave the damn SUV alone," said Serrano. "Why take any risk at all moving it?"

"Because our killer is part of something much bigger. Something *they*, whoever *they* might be, can't afford to lose. Something *they* have invested everything in," said Mann. "That's why *they* are going to so much trouble to cover up his tracks and keep him out of our hands."

"*They,*" said Serrano, "are going to pay."

"You bet your ass they are," said Mann.

CHAPTER 23

Jeremy Powell tried not to run down the hallway to the SCIF. The last thing he wanted to do was look rattled. He swiftly walked past several offices, keeping his eyes focused on the door ahead of him. Once inside, he pulled the lever that sealed the door, rendering it soundproof. The encrypted phone on the desk flashed—his call waiting.

"Hit me with it," said Powell.

"Total disaster," said Litman. "The FBI showed up a few minutes after we pulled onto the property. I have no idea what happened down at the gate to the property, but the FBI wiped out BRAVO team within seconds. They were on our ass less than a minute later."

"Survivors?" said Powell.

"Just me and our VIP," said Litman.

Good. The fewer liabilities the better in this case.

"We're airborne, headed south," said Litman. "Awaiting further orders."

"Okay. I'm going to divert your aircraft to a ghost strip, where another jet will pick you up," said Powell. "That Gulfstream is basically a fifty-million-dollar piece of scrap metal right now. Totally useless to us until we clean it."

"Understood," said Litman.

"Nice job with the backup plan," said Powell. "I told McCall you were the right person for the job. Sounds like this would have been a mission fail if you hadn't been in charge."

"Thank you, sir," said Litman. "The seaplane was a long shot. It almost didn't happen."

"But it did. And it won't be forgotten," said Powell.

"O'Brien—out of the Chicago office—came through at the last minute. He actually flew the plane in and out of the lake," said Litman.

"Well. We'll have to look at him for a promotion," said Powell.

His cell phone rang. *McCall. Great.*

"Gary. I have a call I have to take. Probably the first of many," said Powell. "The flight crew will receive diversion and landing instructions shortly. Make sure they don't flake out. They will not be happy with this. It's a dicey runway in the middle of nowhere—and they'll know it once they do a little research."

"Copy that," said Litman.

Powell replaced the desk phone receiver and answered his cell phone.

"Get to the SCIF," said McCall.

"I'm already in it," said Powell. "Just talked to—"

"Nothing over an unencrypted line," said McCall, before hanging up. The desk phone rang a few seconds later.

"Powell here."

"No shit," said McCall. "Did you hear the news?"

"I just spoke with Litman. Not ideal, but we got Alejandro out," said Powell. "That's all that matters."

"At least we have some good news," said McCall flatly.

"Look. I know the situation in Minneapolis isn't ideal by a long shot, but we kept Alejandro out of FBI hands," said Powell. "Mann's team somehow figured out the license plate. We barely got Alejandro out of there."

"Okay," said McCall.

Okay? That's it? My people pulled off a miracle on that lake, and all McCall can say is okay?

"What's going on?" said Powell.

"Did Zaleski check in with you?"

"She did. The Suburban is in a trailer headed west. Her team is intact. No casualties."

"No casualties?" said McCall. "Is that what she said?"

"That's not what happened?" said Powell.

Part of him hoped that she'd lied, so he could finally put her down like the rabid dog she was. She'd served a purpose in the past, tying up loose ends, but this close to the end game—Zaleski was a liability. Useful to a point, but risky to keep around.

"Well. She didn't exactly lie to you. Her team is completely intact," said McCall. "But she left out the part where she killed two cops in the process of stealing the Suburban, while at the same time setting fire to the medical examiner's office. Presumably to destroy the rest of the evidence collected last night."

"The bodies," said Powell. "Shit. She was just supposed to steal the SUV. I did not authorize the use of lethal force."

"Apparently she missed the memo," said McCall. "And my sources think she may have killed the county coroner and one of Mann's people. Likely the team's medical examiner."

"What do you want to do with her?" said Powell.

"I suppose we put her to work doing what she's good at. Killing people," said McCall.

"Mann's team?" said Powell.

"The sooner the better," said McCall. "Clear the slate. Mann's team has proven to be more resourceful than we anticipated—and now we've pissed them off. Not a good combination. Not with the election only four months away and results to deliver. Throw her at the problem. Augment her team if necessary. I want this ARTEMIS team taken out of the equation immediately."

"Understood."

"And Jeremy?"

"Yes?"

"Under no circumstances is Alejandro's Suburban to get anywhere near LABYRINTH," said McCall. "I guarantee that SUV has more bugs in it than our Moscow embassy."

"It's headed west, away from the site," said Powell. "To be melted down and buried in the middle of nowhere."

"Make sure Zaleski knows she'll be buried in the same hole if she fucks this up," said McCall, ending the call.

Powell took a deep breath and exhaled slowly before dialing Zaleski's encrypted satellite phone. This should be a fun conversation.

PART III

CHAPTER 24

Garrett Mann knocked on the doorframe and peeked inside the conference room.

"Come. Come," said Young, waving him in.

Mann stepped inside, followed by Turner and Baker. The two agents had been in constant touch with the sheriff and members of the county's SWAT team for the past hour and a half, while Mann's entourage drove south from Minneapolis and spent time inside the fire-damaged medical examiner's office. Greg Ulrich, chief of the Owatonna Police Department, and Sam Kilroy from the Waseca County Sheriff's Office stood up to greet them. Kilroy, a senior deputy, ran the regional Tactical Team. Five counties and several towns contributed deputies and officers for the SWAT-style group. Young got up and shut the door behind them while they made their own introductions.

"Sorry about your officer," said Mann, shaking Ulrich's hand. "I blame myself. I suspected that the Suburban might be a target for recovery. I just never in a million years thought they'd kill police officers to get it."

"You didn't kill my officer," said Ulrich. "But thank you."

He shook Kilroy's hand, the two of them simply nodding at each other.

"Agent Mann—" started Young.

"Garrett. Please," said Mann.

"Garrett. I completely share the chief's sentiment," said Young. "None of this was your fault. There's something insanely sinister going on here, particularly given what happened up north. And frankly, if you hadn't taken your team to Minneapolis—I think we'd be looking at a lot more casualties down here. Most of them from your team. Whoever stole the Suburban and burned the bodies in the garage didn't hesitate to lay waste to those two officers, Rostov, or your medical examiner. Imagine if your entire team had been present at the medical examiner's office when they came through."

"I've thought about it a lot. We weren't even remotely prepared for this kind of violent response. Not here or up north," said Mann. "Fortunately, I had these two gentlemen and MacLeod to even things out at the lake."

"We'll take good care of MacLeod's body until it's claimed by her next of kin," said Young. "You have my word on that."

"Thank you. That means more than you imagine," said Mann. "So. I know you all have been talking over the phone pretty extensively, but let me formally introduce you to Special Agents Baker and Turner. Baker spent several years with the FBI's Hostage Rescue Team, and Turner served as a SWAT team leader for several years. They're our team's tactical arm."

"Pleasure to finally meet you outside of a quick roadside chat," said Young, who shook both of their hands.

Ulrich and Kilroy did the same.

"Take a seat," said Young. "Let's go over this in person, so we're all on the same page."

Once everyone settled in, Young turned off the lights and activated the projector on the table, which cast a Google Earth image of a motel and its surrounding area onto the white screen at the front of the room. The Owatonna Roadway Inn sat about a mile north of the Owatonna Degner Regional Airport along Interstate 35.

"It's a solid choice," said Kilroy. "Only two viable vehicle approaches. The overflow parking north of the motel and the main lot around the outdoor pool area. I don't see them using the main lot. It's far too exposed. Then only two ways up to the second level, both in the north-south running breezeway connected to the north parking lot."

"We'll need eyes on the north parking lot," said Mann. "Sounds like that's the most logical approach."

"I think so," said Kilroy. "But I can stage a team in a room facing the main parking lot, just in case. They won't go to waste if the hostiles come in from the north. I'll push them toward the mousetrap once the trap is sprung."

The mousetrap being the two end rooms on the southernmost end of the motel on the second floor. Members of Mann's team would wander in and out of the end rooms, either pretending to talk on the phone or, in Serrano's case, smoke a few cigarettes, to draw the enemy's attention to their location. The rooms were connected by internal doors to the rooms next door, where four FBI agents and four SWAT officers, split between the two adjoining rooms, would wait to ambush anyone who breached the two end rooms.

Twenty-six heavily armed SWAT officers and FBI agents would converge on the scene at that point. Not to mention Baker, who would be in a sniper's nest across from the main lot, targeting any hostiles who managed to slip free and engaging any support vehicles that drove around from the north lot to "come to the rescue."

"Between my police force and Sheriff Young's deputies, we'll have about a dozen additional vehicles on standby a few miles away to rush in and block off all the exits," said Ulrich. "Just need to make sure they're not getting in over their heads when they arrive."

"I'll have a four-person SWAT team in one of the north-facing rooms, covering the north parking lot," said Kilroy. "Your units will be in good hands. Same with the main parking lot approaches."

"And we'll have Baker watching over the main lot, in addition to the ground- and second-floor levels," said Mann.

"My brother-in-law volunteered to provide you with a sniper's nest," said Ulrich. "He's a truck driver—in town for a few days. His truck has a wind deflector mounted on top of the cab. It's hollow, so he can pick you up outside town and park in the semitrailer lot due east of the motel. It's about a six-hundred-foot shot from that parking lot to the target rooms."

"Easy distance," said Baker. "Thank you."

"Don't thank me yet. The weather's supposed to be shit tonight," said Ulrich. "Storm's coming in from the west, so you'll be sheltered from the wind and rain—until your services are required. Then you'll be exposed on top of a rain- and windswept, gigantic metal lightning rod."

"I'm used to it," said Baker.

"Figured you might be," said Ulrich.

"So. We can sneak Baker in no problem," said Mann. "What about the rest of you? Based on the plan passed back and forth, we're looking at a lot of SWAT and police officers occupying rooms at the motel."

Young answered his question. "The assumption is that our adversaries will be focused on your team, so I recommend that you keep everyone here for now. If they're watching your team, which is fair to assume at this point, their attention won't be focused on the motel—until you check in a few hours from now. By that time, we'll have all our units in place."

"I already have rooms reserved and everyone on standby," said Kilroy. "They can start filtering into the motel as soon as you give the order."

"You don't need my order, Sam," said Young.

"Well. This *is* your county," said Kilroy. "So, it's only right to ask."

"Oh brother," said Young. "Sam. Start moving everyone into position. Slowly and discreetly. Greg. Support Sam with whatever and whoever he needs. Garrett. What can you do to make sure we're not nailing our own coffins shut at the motel? I know you come with some organic surveillance and countersurveillance capabilities."

"Yeah. We have drone surveillance capability, which I don't recommend we use. Mostly because our adversaries will be well aware of it. I doubt it escaped their attention up at Cedar Lake. They'll be watching the skies, or at least they should be. Second. Severe weather will render the drone more of a distraction than an asset. What I can provide is a seasoned countersurveillance officer. Jessica Mayer worked with the FBI's Special Surveillance Group. We can sneak her into one of the vehicles you send to the motel. Have her guide them through a short surveillance detection route—what we call an SDR. She'll be able to determine if they pick up a tail."

"Let's go with that," said Kilroy. "I have twenty SWAT officers assembled in the Waseca County station, fifteen miles from here, ready to go. All we have to do is sneak her into my vehicle and I'll drive her out to Waseca. She can head out with the lead team and work her magic."

"That'll work," said Mann. "If she doesn't detect a problem, we should be good to go infiltrating your teams into the motel. Are the rooms taken care of?"

"Yes," said Young, switching the screen to a marked-up version of the same image. "Based on your agents' recommendations, we've secured access to nine rooms. We've already contacted the motel owner and manager. The rooms have been opened. Keys are sitting on the desks inside."

"Easy enough," said Mann.

"I should probably head out with Mayer," said Baker. "I can meet up with Chief Ulrich's brother-in-law outside town."

"That works perfectly," said Ulrich. "He's waiting at a truck stop in Mankato. It's a half-hour drive to Waseca. The ride from Waseca to the motel is fifteen minutes. A long fifteen minutes riding up top inside the wind deflector. But there's no way to get up there from the cab without climbing outside and exposing yourself."

"I'll be fine," said Baker. "I've dealt with worse."

"All righty then. I think this plan is coming together," said Mann. "We get all the SWAT and police units into their rooms at the motel as soon as possible, along with Baker in the parking lot across the street.

An hour or two later, my team will migrate from this station to the motel—hopefully drawing them in."

"They won't know what hit them," said Kilroy.

Mann nodded hesitantly. "Maybe. Hopefully. But don't assume this'll be a cakewalk. We're dealing with highly trained professionals who have already demonstrated that they don't give a shit about killing cops—and for all we know they're better trained than all of us. The element of surprise will be critical. I can't stress that enough. Everything will depend on discipline in those rooms. My team. Your officers. We can't afford a single slipup at the motel prior to the initiation of hostilities."

"I'll drive that point home," said Kilroy. "Hard."

"Same with the backup units. They need to be staged somewhere discreet," said Mann. "No radio chatter at all. Just sitting and waiting."

"I've already worked that out with Sheriff Young," said Ulrich. "Our joint task force will be staged in the county school bus parking lot about three miles north—in Medford. It's an isolated location, and the lot doesn't face any public roads. They can be here in under two minutes."

"Nice. That should work fine," said Mann. "Turner. What are we forgetting?"

"You kind of touched on it already, but we'll need a secure way to communicate," said Turner. "No radios or satellite phones at the motel until go time. If they're scanning the area with a radio frequency detector, like Jax would, they'll quickly identify unusual radio frequency activity. I say we stick with cell phones. Text messages for coordinated action. We'll have to set up a large text group or use an encrypted messaging app like Signal."

"It'll be a clusterfuck to get everyone to download the app and figure out how to work it in a few hours," said Young.

"True," said Mann. "We'll stick with basic text messaging for general coordination. Each user identifying themselves by room before sending."

"Speaking of Jax," said Baker. "Will she be at the motel deploying her usual array of electronic magic? I got the impression you might hold her back."

Mann shook his head. "We can't risk losing her. I'm tempted to send her to the Waseca County Sheriff's Office with Baker and Mayer. Have her set up shop over there for now, where they won't look for her. She's the only one that knows how to track the bugs."

He didn't elaborate any further. The fewer people who knew about the virus transmitters, the better. Turner and Baker got the hint and didn't press the issue. Mercifully, neither did anyone else.

"I can take her back with your other agents," said Kilroy. "Set her up in a secure location inside the station, with a dedicated security detail."

"That would be greatly appreciated," said Mann.

Young checked his watch. "It'll be dark soon. Probably should get this show on the road. A big storm system is supposed to roll through around midnight or so. Be gone by three or four in the morning. Severe thunderstorms and high winds."

"If they hit us, it'll be during the worst of the storm. In the middle of the night," said Mann. "Buy a bunch of instant coffee on the way back to Waseca. They're going to need it to stay alert."

Mann thought about the "go-pills" Dr. Trejo kept locked in the RV's controlled substance locker. Amphetamines reserved for long stakeouts or marathon drives. He didn't think Trejo would have objected to Mann distributing them to the team. Not after what they'd been through this afternoon—and the storm they literally and figuratively faced tonight.

CHAPTER 25

The handrail shook from the last clap of thunder, a massive flash of lightning momentarily illuminating the motel courtyard. Serrano took a long drag on her cigarette and snuffed it out on the railing, before tucking it into the recently emptied Ziploc bag she carried. The boom from the last streak of lightning in the wall of clouds approaching from the southwest was enough to rattle the concrete walkway itself. She probably had time for one more before the rain hit. She was about to light that last cigarette when Mann stepped out of the suite.

"Don't let me stop you," he said. "We might be stuck inside for a while."

She put the pack away, studying the rapidly approaching storm. Mann settled in next to her at the railing, which faced due south.

"I'm good. Maybe I'll trade the nicotine for stims," she said, referencing the "go-pills" Mann had offered earlier.

Several flashes of lightning lit them up like they were being chased by paparazzi. She'd always loved watching storms roll in. Her favorite part was the earliest hints of lightning, too far away for the sound of thunder to reach you. Back and forth across the sky. Above, below, and inside the miles-high clouds. Like a battle raging in the distance. Somewhere else—for now.

"This is going to be one hell of a storm," said Mann.

"I assume you're talking about the weather?"

"That, too."

Serrano laughed louder than she expected. She had to admit. The two of them shared the same sense of humor. Caustic. Sarcastic. Dry. Sparing.

"You think they'll take the bait tonight?" said Serrano. "It's been a long day for everyone. Including them."

"I don't think they have a choice," said Mann. "Not after the smackdown we delivered up north. They may have scored some points down here, tragically, but at the end of the day—they know we can hurt them. Hurt them bad. They'll want to wrap this up as quickly as possible."

"Do you think they're watching us right now?" said Serrano.

"I guarantee it," said Mann.

A raindrop hit Serrano's hand, immediately followed by a few more along her arm. Sizable drops. Dime-size at least. They backed away from the railing and leaned against the wall of the motel, where they were protected by the rooftop overhang.

"I wish we had Jax watching over us," said Serrano. "I feel blind without her."

"Yeah. Me, too," said Mann. "But she can't fly the drone in this weather, and they'd be looking for it, anyway. That, and I don't think their main assault force is anywhere near here right now. Radio frequency analysis might identify some surveillance, but we know they're watching us. When the attack comes, it won't be staged from the IHOP across the interstate. They'll drive in from out of town and hit us hard and fast. The cameras we've set up in all the room windows and wireless motion detectors we've placed on the walkways leading to our rooms should give us all the input we need to react in time."

"I hope you're right," said Serrano. "Not that anyone's going to be sleeping tonight."

"You really gonna take one of the go-pills?" said Mann.

"I don't know. Ask me in an hour," said Serrano. "Caffeine and nicotine have worked for me in the past."

"I took one about twenty minutes ago," said Mann. "And I'm already feeling a bit tweaky."

"Maybe it's better than drinking coffee all night and getting caught in the bathroom when they hit us," said Serrano.

Mann laughed. "I was thinking the same thing."

A dark silhouette turned the southwest corner of the motel walkway, instantly stopping their conversation.

"Turner," she said, recognizing his gait and mannerisms.

"We have this place locked down and I'm still jumpy," said Mann.

"It's going to be a long night," she said.

"No doubt," said Mann.

"You got a cigarette?" said Turner, his face exposed by a flash of lightning.

"Since when do you smoke?" said Mann.

"Since this afternoon," said Turner. "Been that kind of a day."

"Been a cocaine kind of day," said Serrano, getting a laugh from Turner.

"What?" said Mann.

"Just fucking with you," said Serrano, producing her pack. "Cigarettes will do for now. Stims a little later."

"I hate those things, but they work," said Turner.

"Cigarettes or stims?" she said.

"Both," said Turner. "But go-pills are the only thing I know that can keep you alert at four in the morning."

She lit Turner's cigarette, then her own, drawing in what might be her last hit of harsh nicotine-laden tobacco of the night.

Turner had been assigned to lead the SWAT officers hiding in a room on the west-facing side of the motel. His primary job was to mop up any hostiles who escaped the ambush and tried to retreat along the western walkway. His secondary job would be to support the SWAT officers assigned to cover the northern parking lot—the most likely kick-off and subsequent retreat point for an attack on the motel.

To convince any hostile surveillance that the entire team was based in the two suites on the southern tip of the motel's second floor, Turner would have to stick around until about midnight, when he would walk into the western-facing suite, immediately drop to the floor, and crawl outside, slithering along the walkway to the SWAT room. If he hugged the wall and stayed low, he'd remain unseen from any ground-based surveillance teams.

"They're out there watching us," said Mann. "No doubt about that."

"And we're putting on a show for them," said Turner. "Lowering their guard—just enough to draw them in."

"Kilroy's tactical team seems legit," said Mann.

"Not bad at all for a rural SWAT team," said Turner. "Give any big-city team a run for their money."

"Good. Because tonight won't be amateur hour," said Mann.

"Do you think it'll be the same group that hit the station and medical examiner's office?" said Serrano.

"That's my guess, being the closest team. Assuming they didn't fly out already, like the lake house survivors," said Mann.

The rain picked up, a steady downpour that reached halfway toward them along the walkway. Straight down. No real wind yet. Just a few weak gusts from the southwest.

"This is about to go to shit," said Turner. "Time for me to retire for the night."

"What are your SWAT friends up to?" said Serrano.

"Trying to stay awake," said Turner. "That's all any of us will be doing in about an hour."

"Go-pill?" said Mann.

"I haven't taken mine yet," said Turner. "Been waiting."

"No time like the present," said Mann.

"I'll take it after the long crawl back to my room," said Turner.

"Long—low crawl," said Mann. "Knees and elbows scraping the walkway."

Serrano laughed. "What a jerk."

"Normally I'd agree," said Turner, flicking his cigarette over the railing. "But—"

"This is almost exclusively *your* plan?" said Mann. "Including the crawling part?"

Serrano turned around to try to somewhat disguise her laughter. She figured it might not look so good for them from the outside, if they were laughing it up out here right now. Or maybe it didn't matter. Maybe it looked more natural.

"Yeah. Something like that," said Turner.

A long series of lightning flashes lit up the sky in front of them, immediately followed by what sounded like an artillery barrage that vibrated the walkway.

"Time for everyone to turn in," said Mann.

"Yep," said Turner. "Thanks for the smoke."

"Any time," said Serrano, a few moments before the wind kicked up and swept a solid wall of rain across them.

Turner mock saluted them before heading back the way he came. Serrano ducked inside their room, extinguishing her cigarette on the doorframe. Mann followed her in, shutting the door and locking it. Both the doorknob and chain lock. Not that it would make a difference if the breach team used explosives or a shotgun.

"Can't be too careful," said Mann, smiling flatly.

"I think we're well past the point of being careful," said Serrano.

CHAPTER 26

Tara Zaleski wiped her face and flicked the water away. A few seconds later, she refought the same battle, barely able to see through the sideways rain hitting her face. All good. Shitty weather was a battlefield equalizer, reducing visibility and discouraging normal security measures like sentries and lookouts. Significant and understated advantages when attempting to overrun a fixed, defensive position, like the two suites occupied by the FBI at the Owatonna Roadway Inn.

Her surveillance team—parked several hundred yards away in an overflow lot south of the Cabela's sporting goods store—had identified the two southernmost motel rooms as the FBI stronghold. The FBI's RV and SUVs sat in the courtyard parking lot just below one of the rooms. Pizzas delivered an hour or so before the storm hit. Vending machines repeatedly raided for sodas and snacks. Cigarettes smoked on the walkway. All the makings of an FBI task force settling in for the night.

She opened the front passenger-side door of the lead SUV in her three-vehicle convoy and hopped inside, shutting the door as a gust of wind drove a wall of rain inside, soaking the driver and spraying the three operatives in the back seating area.

"Everyone's set. Let's roll," said Zaleski, before removing a satellite phone from her tactical vest and hitting the speed dial button for her surveillance team leader, who answered immediately.

The SUV eased forward, picking up speed as it headed out of the motel parking lot. They'd taken a few rooms at the shittiest possible strip mall–looking place on the western edge of Rochester. Aside from a few hourly paying guests, they were the motel's only customers. Perfect for her team's purposes. It gave them a few hours out of the SUVs and allowed them to switch into the appropriate tactical gear for their impending attack without drawing any attention.

"I still have a light on in the southeast corner room. Maybe an end table lamp?" said Erik Schafer. "The other room has been dark for about an hour. No detectable movement in either room. The motel has been quiet since the storm rolled in. A few vending-machine runs right after the rain hit, but nothing after that."

"Hold your position and continue to observe the motel until we arrive. We're about forty-five minutes from the motel. Maybe a little longer with this weather," said Zaleski. "I'll call you when we're about ten minutes out. You're not going to be happy to hear this, but I want two of you to make your way on foot through the cornfield behind Cabela's and set up on the south side of the road facing the motel courtyard. From what I can tell, you're looking at a four-hundred-yard trip. Bring the heavy-barrel HKs, with as many drums as you can carry. Is that enough time?"

"Give us fifteen minutes. It's shitty out, and we'll need a minute or two to set up," said Schafer.

"Fifteen it is," said Zaleski.

"Do you want us to split up and cover both rooms?" said Schafer.

"Negative. I don't want to stretch you out too thin in this storm. Set up fifteen yards apart facing the main parking lot and cover the two floors facing the courtyard. You're our insurance policy in case there's more to this motel arrangement than appears."

"Copy that," said Schafer.

"We're heading out," said Zaleski. "If anything changes at all at the motel, I need to know immediately. Scan every window of every room you can see from your position. Look for anything out of place. I'd be shocked if they didn't sneak someone into another room."

"We followed them to the motel and watched them check in," said Schafer.

"Yeah. Well, we don't know the FBI team's full roster count in Owatonna," said Zaleski. "What we do know is that at least eight agents hit a target up in Minneapolis earlier today. And they had drone support. That's nine, maybe ten agents total. You've counted six at the motel. That leaves three to four possibly unaccounted for."

"But no drones, thankfully," said Schafer. "We didn't see any airborne prior to the storm hitting."

"We definitely won't have to worry about drones at this point," said Zaleski. "Keep a sharp eye on the motel and courtyard. Watch their vehicles closely. They may have left a few spoilers in the parking lot for us. Or they may have covertly sent a few people ahead of the main group to occupy one of the rooms overlooking the courtyard—long before you arrived. Anything is possible with this group."

"Understood," said Schafer. "We'll all scour the rooms facing the courtyard and parking lot, until it's time to head out. Hopkins will continue to watch the motel while we approach the road."

"No detail is too small to investigate or report," said Zaleski, before ending the call. "All right. Let's get moving."

She didn't have a ton of faith in Schafer's team's ability to identify a problem at this point. Her assessment had nothing to do with Schafer or his team. The weather would hinder or entirely thwart even the most skilled surveillance team's efforts to observe the kinds of details she was interested in.

A curtain out of place, even for a moment. The brief flicker of a flashlight inside a room. A door cracked open. Anything more than her intuition to suggest that something might be off. But not in this weather. And definitely not Schafer's crew. They were longer-range shooters, passing as observers. Snipers and heavy gunners—with the kind of wider situational awareness her door kickers didn't possess, which was why she had chosen them for this job. But not the kind of professional surveillance types she would have chosen, if she'd known ahead of time that her team would be sent back to Owatonna to take out an entire FBI task force.

Hopefully, she wouldn't need them at all. Their drum-fed, heavy-barrel HK416s—similar to the US Marine Corps' IAR (infantry automatic rifle)—would make a mess of the place if unleashed and draw every cop within twenty miles to the motel. Her goal was to avoid attracting that kind of attention, unless absolutely necessary. Blowing doors open with explosives and tossing in flash-bangs would make enough noise, even if she timed the detonations with the thunder. But nobody would mistake the automatic gunfire for thunder. And nothing freaked people out like the sound of a machine gun. Especially these days.

Owatonna's 911 switchboard would light up like a Christmas tree—and then they'd have a real problem on their hands. A few dozen heavily armed cops from the Owatonna Police Department and Steele County Sheriff's Office swarming the motel with a score to settle.

If Schafer's rifles started blazing, they'd have two minutes at most to finish off the FBI team and drive out of here before their cop problem materialized. Maybe less than a minute. If a single police car spotted them departing the motel, an all-points bulletin would go out to every police department within a hundred miles. Escape would be unlikely. That said, she had no intention of letting any hidden FBI agents get the jump on her at the motel.

Her plan was to hit both rooms simultaneously with two teams of four shooters. Doors blasted open with strip charges and flash-bangs tossed through the windows. Easy kill-room drill. Grab all electronics and notebooks. Out of the rooms in a minute. Heading north on Interstate 35 within two minutes. Assuming no hiccups. And there was always a hiccup or two. Hopefully nothing that held them up for too long.

CHAPTER 27

Mann's phone buzzed. An all-unit text coming through.

> This is SWAT north. I have three SUVs entering the north parking lot with their lights out. Drivers are wearing NVGs. I think it's go-time.

Almost two in the morning on the nose. The motel room came to life, the two SWAT officers taking positions at the door connected to the suite next door. Deputy Kilroy, head of the region's multicounty SWAT team, had specifically picked the suites at the southern end of the motel because each suite could be expanded by unlocking doors to the rooms next to them. A cheap but efficient way to add another bedroom and bathroom to the "suite" itself, which was basically a slightly larger motel room with a half wall separating a couch and table from the king-size bed.

Mann settled in behind one of the SWAT officers, quickly typing a response. Suite East is ready.

> Suite West is ready.

Mills, Rocha, and Mayer, plus two SWAT officers, occupied the adjacent room, Suite West. They'd purposefully mixed Kilroy's SWAT officers with the FBI agents, for maximum effect. With Baker hiding in one of the semitrailers across from the parking lot, and Turner in one of the rooms down the western walkway, they didn't have much of a tactical presence.

They'd all extensively cross-trained with Baker and Turner, which meant they could hold their own under the most rudimentary tactical situations—but not something like this. A professional, dynamic assault like the one he anticipated would throw them into a tailspin. Mann and Serrano included. Kilroy's SWAT officers would anchor each room, evening the odds and hopefully tipping them in Mann's direction.

SWAT West is up, answered Turner, who would cover the western walkway once the trap was sprung.

SWAT Courtyard is good, typed the team leader in a room directly above the outdoor pool. Her team of three would cover the courtyard and parking lot.

SWAT Stairwell copies. The four-person team in that room would rush to cover the breezeway stairwells once the trap was sprung, preventing any reinforcements from rushing to help the teams that got caught up in the two suites.

Sheriff Young here. Let's do this. The Steele County sheriff, situated three rooms back from the southern suites with three of his deputies, had just set everything in motion. Mann had made it clear that Young was the senior law enforcement officer in charge of this operation. It was his county. The rest of them were basically guests. Mann removed a round-shaped grenade from the pouch attached to his vest and held it up to the two SWAT officers crowding the doorway.

"They're going to hit the room hard with their own shit," he said. "Breaching charges. Flash-bangs. Maybe real grenades. But none of that matters because we'll be here, safe behind these walls. The moment their shit goes off, I'll toss one of these inside the suite. When mine goes off, we'll hit them with a wall of buckshot."

"That looks like a real grenade," said one of the deputies.

"It's a low-intensity grenade. Specially designed by a retired Marine. A little fragmentation, but mostly blast and flash."

"Does the sheriff know about this?" said one of the SWAT officers.

"Not specifically," said Mann. "But he authorized the use of any unconventional munitions or weapons, as long as my agents employed them—exclusively."

"Okay. Uh . . . ," started one of the officers.

"Hold on," said Mann, before typing a message. Young. This is Mann. Can you restate your unconventional munitions policy?

A few seconds passed before Young responded with a message that would be seen by everyone. FBI is free to use whatever weapons they deem necessary. *Thank you, Sheriff Young.* The SWAT officer gave him a thumbs-up, which Mann returned. They were ready for whatever and whoever was thrown at them. All still unknown. He hadn't bothered to suggest that the units stationed at the motel try to capture any of their assailants. Things would be confusing enough tonight.

Mann typed a quick message. Switch to radios. Things would move too quickly for text messages from this point forward.

CHAPTER 28

Tara Zaleski paused momentarily between the two staircases. This all seemed too easy. A strong gust of wind propelled the rain through the breezeway, blurring her night vision. She wiped the lenses with her sleeve; an acceptable image of the courtyard appeared—until a flash of lightning blinded her momentarily.

"Fuck this," she muttered, flipping the goggles up.

The scene in front of her cleared up immediately. The motel's external lights provided more than enough illumination in the storm to navigate the stairs and walkway.

"All teams. Switch away from night vision," said Zaleski. "There's plenty of light."

She led her team up the southernmost stairway, which deposited them on the walkway leading directly to the eastern suite. The other team would take the northernmost staircase and head left, making their way around the western walkway to the western suite. If all went according to plan, this would be over in less than a minute.

Her team walked swiftly but quietly along the walkway, hugging the wall to stay out of the rain. When they reached the door at the end of the walkway, everyone silently went to work. One of the team members attached a "top to bottom" explosive band along the right side of the door, wrapping the C4 strip around the door handle a few times before finishing the job. Another member of the team crouched next to the window just beyond the door and prepped two flash-bang grenades. When given the signal, he'd toss both grenades in rapid succession through the window. They'd detonate the door explosives when the first grenade exploded in the room, waiting for the second grenade to explode before breaching.

She'd be the first to enter the suite, followed immediately by the rest of the team. The rules of engagement were simple. Kill everyone in the room. No worries about noncombatants. No hesitation. They'd practiced this drill several hundred times, often with multiple complications such as hostages, innocent bystanders, or animals. Tonight would be different. Entirely uncomplicated. Just sight in on anyone in the room and press the trigger until nothing moved or uttered a sound.

The explosives guy gave her a thumbs-up and backed away from the door, crouching next to the operative with the flash-bang grenades.

"East side ready," she said over the radio net.

"West side is almost ready. Ten seconds."

"Copy," said Zaleski.

A flash of lightning illuminated the entire courtyard, followed immediately by a bone-shaking thunderclap that rattled the walkway and windows. She considered delaying the breach, figuring that both rooms' occupants may have been awakened by the thunder, but decided against it. Awake or asleep—it wouldn't matter. Confusion would reign supreme when they set off the explosives. Mann's people might actually hesitate for a moment, wondering if it was another string of thunder.

"West side. What's your status?" said Zaleski.

"West side is ready."

She took a quick look around the courtyard, still a little uneasy about the situation. Nothing. No lights in any of the rooms visible from her position. Exactly what you would expect at a place like this at 2:14 in the morning—in the middle of a severe thunderstorm. Everyone hunkered down, trying to sleep.

"Schafer. Anything?" she transmitted.

"Negative. A light is still on in the eastern suite, but I haven't seen any signs of movement in either room. Same with the rest of the motel."

"Stand by to breach. Grenades in three," said Zaleski. "Two. One. Grenades out."

A loud crack of thunder nearly covered up the sound of the broken glass. She counted to three in her head before giving the order to blow the doors.

"Breach doors in two. One. Go."

The operative directly across the door from her turned away and squeezed the detonator, the door charge exploding at the same time as the first flash-bang grenade. The second grenade detonated a moment before she kicked in the door. Perfect timing.

CHAPTER 29

Mann's radio crackled. "East suite. This is SWAT north. They just pulled the pins on some bangers. Breach imminent."

"Copy that," said Mann. "They'll hit the west suite at the same time. Buckle up, everyone."

Glass shattered a few moments later, a hard object hitting the floor in the adjacent room. Followed immediately by another. *Here it comes.* He closed his eyes to avoid the temporary blindness caused by the eight-million-candela "flash." There wasn't much he could do about the 108-decibel "bang," not that it would matter in a moment. He pulled the pin on the low-intensity grenade and rolled it inside. Timing was everything.

The two flash-bangs detonated a few seconds apart, nearly covering up the sound of the door charge. Flashlights lit the adjacent room, a few suppressed gunshots snapping by the doorway, presumably fired at the fake body created with pillows under the bed's blankets. The "half grenade" exploded a moment later—vibrating the floor under his feet. Mann didn't realize he had been rendered temporarily deaf until he grabbed the semiautomatic shotgun propped against the wall next to him and aimed it at a flashlight in the suite, repeatedly pulling the trigger until the shotgun stopped firing.

Just the muted thump, concussive blast, and hard recoil of seven rapidly fired double-aught buckshot shells. Those—and the fourteen shells fired by the sheriff's deputies a few feet away from him. He'd be lucky to hear again. He tossed the shotgun aside and gripped the compact M4 rifle slung across his chest, then slipped into the suite with the two deputies and Serrano. A quick sweep with his rifle-mounted flashlight identified four badly mangled bodies.

Torsos intact, protected by substantial body armor—not that it did them any good. Their limbs, groins, and faces had been blasted apart by the 189 one-third-inch lead pellets unleashed within the span of a few seconds. The two deputies immediately went to work examining the bodies for signs of life, while Serrano headed to the door, presumably to check for any surprises.

"East suite is a clean sweep. Four hostiles down. Status unknown. Order up some ambulances," said Mann. "Mayer. What are we looking at next door?"

He barely managed to decipher the muffled report that came in through his headset.

"Same. Four hostiles down. Fucked up like nothing I've ever seen before," said Mayer. "That grenade worked like a charm."

From the look of the suite, it may have worked a little too well. O'Reilly wouldn't be happy about the bill for the damage.

"All clear on the walkway," said Serrano, before fully stepping outside.

"Sheriff. I think it's time to release the hounds," said Mann.

Schafer wasn't entirely sure what he'd just witnessed. The only thing he could say for sure was that something had gone terribly wrong. A few seconds after the two teams had breached the doors, flash-bangs lighting up the two suites, a significantly more powerful detonation blew the suite windows into the parking lot. The explosions, which appeared to take place in both suites, were immediately followed by dozens of flashes. Shotguns from the sound of it. Only one member of Zaleski's team carried a shotgun: a compact, pistol-gripped twelve-gauge loaded with breaching slugs in case the team needed to blast open a bathroom door.

From their position at the edge of the cornfield, Schafer and Ramirez couldn't see the entrance to the western suite—only the south-facing windows of each room and the door to the courtyard-facing suite Zaleski had just breached. But based on the flashes he'd witnessed through all the windows, it looked and sounded like the same thing had played out in each of the rooms. And his eyes and ears hadn't played tricks on him. The intense lightning and thunder from the storm overhead were predictable. Flash followed by thunder, even if the thunder came just a few moments later. The chaos inside the rooms had been simultaneous. Zaleski's teams had walked into a trap—and hadn't walked out.

"Z. This is Schafer. What's your status?" he said over the general tactical net.

No reply.

"Z. What the fuck is going on in there?"

Nothing. A steady rain slapped the corn leaves around him.

"We need to get out of here," said Ramirez over the team comms.

Each field team had a secondary channel for close-in coordination. Their headsets piped the different radio nets into separate ears.

"Not until we get some kind of confirmation—from anyone," said Schafer. "They can't all be dead."

He scanned the second-floor walkway, looking for anything out of place. The lights in a few rooms had just been turned on, but that wasn't exactly unusual, given the series of explosions and shotgun blasts that had just rocked the motel.

"Flashlights in both suites," said Ramirez. "Powerful lights."

Rifle- or shotgun-mounted lights.

"Extraction team. You got anything on the north side?"

"Negative. Just people turning on lights in their rooms," said one of the drivers. "About a dozen between the two floors. Are we sticking around? The police are probably already on the way."

"Stand by. I'm trying to make contact with—"

"Is that Zaleski coming out of the suite?" said Ramirez.

Schafer shifted his rifle sight to the walkway next to the suite. A figure stood in the doorway, mostly obscured by the thin cloud of smoke billowing out of the room. Between the rain and the smoke, he honestly couldn't say. A flash of lightning revealed the answer. A muted patch across the figure's tactical vest that read *FBI*.

"Fuck. That's an FBI agent. The breach teams are gone," said Schafer.

"Schafer. This is extraction. Four SWAT-looking officers just emerged from one of the rooms overlooking our parking lot. They know we're here. They just lit us up with their rifle flashlights. What do you want us to do?"

"Get out of there. Now," said Schafer. "The breach teams are out of action."

"Copy. Moving out now."

"We got the same problem," said Ramirez over the team net. "Time to go."

Schafer scanned the walkway again and noted heavily armed SWAT officers pouring out of three rooms overlooking the courtyard. Ramirez was right. There was nothing they could do at this point to try to help Zaleski, except get captured or killed.

"I concur. Let's slowly back out of here," said Schafer, flipping his night vision goggles down over his face.

They'd need the NVGs to find their way back through the cornfield. Anticipating the possibility of needing to make a quick escape, he'd left a trail of infrared ChemLights, invisible to the naked eye, leading to the parking lot. He'd just folded the rifle's bipod when bullets started snapping through the cornstalks.

"I'm pinned down. Taking fire!" said Schafer. "Not sure where it's coming from."

He flattened himself and took a moment to try to determine the direction of the incoming fire. The bullets sounded like they were entering the field from his right. Pretty soon they'd be coming from everywhere.

"Coming from the top of a tractor trailer at our two o'clock," said Ramirez. "I'm taking him out."

So much for slipping out of here quietly.

"Copy. I'll light up the motel," said Schafer, shifting his aim to the eastern suite. "Hit the cops on the walkways after you're done with the shooter on the semi."

CHAPTER 30

Special Agent Baker was done suppressing the target. Time to do some real damage. He'd emerged from the cover of the semitrailer's wind deflector the moment the first flash-bang went off and started scanning the courtyard and surrounding areas. His job had never been to stop the room breach. He watched the hostile team stack up on the door and go to work through his rifle scope, peeking around the corner of the wind deflector. He could have shot and disabled all four of them with his MK17 SCAR LB (long-barrel) in under two seconds, but that wasn't the plan, nor his purpose.

His job was to cover the areas invisible and unreachable by the teams in the motel. Three-hundred-sixty-degree coverage if required, with an initial focus on enemy snipers with a line of fire to the courtyard rooms. He'd almost missed the sniper in the cornfield. The combination of driving rain and frequent lightning made the task nearly impossible, until the shooter made a rookie mistake—and activated their NVGs, the greenish-white light from the device's eyepieces barely appearing in Baker's scope.

The sniper appeared to be preparing to leave, which made sense given the fact that their primary reason for being there had been erased within the span of a few seconds. He sighted in on the barely visible greenish glow at the edge of the cornfield and had started to apply pressure to his rifle's trigger when a dozen or more bullets cracked a few inches overhead, a few rounds shredding the far-right side of the fiberglass wind deflector. Automatic gunfire. He squeezed off two quick, admittedly inaccurate, shots at his target before shifting his aim to the second shooter located about twenty yards west in the cornfield.

In the very brief moment it took him to acquire the second shooter, a long burst of gunfire shredded the top of the tractor trailer—the bullets miraculously missing him. His aim disrupted and his concealment blown, Baker accepted the fact that he had a slim chance of taking out even one of the two shooters before taking a bullet to the face. He grabbed the rope he'd secured to the top of the cab and threw himself over the side as a dozen bullets cracked overhead.

He hit the side of the cab hard but managed to hold on to the rope, then eased himself down to the pavement.

CHAPTER 31

Mann froze. Automatic gunfire erupted somewhere nearby.

"This is Baker. Shooters in the cornfield to the south. Light machine guns. Take cover."

What?

"SWAT North requests permission to engage hostile vehicles. They're making a run for it."

Had SWAT already engaged? Was that what he was hearing?

"This is Sheriff Young. Attempt to disable the vehicles first. If they won't stop or if they fire on you, take them out."

"Copy that," said SWAT North. "Engaging."

Wait. What the—

Dozens of bullets ripped through the south-facing wall of the suite, knocking one of the deputies to the floor—blood spraying from his neck. Mann and the second deputy reacted instantly, dropping down and crawling toward the critically wounded SWAT officer. A second, longer burst of automatic gunfire raked the room just as they reached him. Mann threw himself on top of the injured deputy to protect him from further damage.

When the gunfire shifted away from the room a few moments later, it gave them enough time to drag the deputy into the adjoining room, where the second deputy tore open the compact trauma kit attached to his vest and went to work trying to save his teammate's life.

"I'll get EMTs in here immediately," said Mann, heading back to the suite.

He'd completely lost track of Serrano in all the confusion. A quick peek into the room told him she'd bolted. A torrent of bullets drove him back into the connected room.

"Stay low," he said, before crawling for the door leading to the walkway.

He reached up for the doorknob, a half dozen bullet holes stitching across the middle door before his hand made it halfway. The radio net was complete chaos, every station reporting the same thing. *Heavy machine-gun fire coming from the cornfield to the south.* Then they all started reporting every law enforcement officer's worst nightmare. *Officer down.* Mann had foiled the main attempt to take his task force out, but now everyone was paying the price.

"Baker. What's your status?"

"They had my number up there," said Baker. "Moving to a new position. Reengaging in a few seconds."

"Hurry up," said Mann. "It's a fucking shooting gallery up here."

CHAPTER 32

Sheriff Young low-crawled across the rough concrete walkway, a pair of hands reaching out of the open door in front of him and pulling him inside the room he'd just left. Lying on his back deep inside the room, he stared through the open doorway at a SWAT officer slumped over the walkway railing—bullets slapping into her unresponsive body. Machine guns in the cornfield? That was all he recalled, before a wall of bullets knocked him flat.

He triggered his radio, though he wasn't sure his message would get through given the disordered chatter going back and forth over the net. "SWAT North. Neutralize the getaway drivers immediately."

"Copy. Engaging now," said the team leader. "What's going on over there?"

"Can't talk now," he said, taking his hand off the transmitter.

He glanced around the motel room. Officer Shorey, from the Owatonna Police Department, sat on the floor, his back against the nightstand between the two beds, applying a tourniquet to his left thigh. A thick stream of blood pulsed from a hole just above his knee. Deputy Hamm faced the door, his rifle pointed into the storm.

"Deputy Hamm. Stay back until we can organize a counterattack," said Young. "Help Officer Shorey with his tourniquet."

"I'm good to go over here," said Shorey. "Sheriff Young needs medical attention. Looks like he sprang a half dozen leaks."

"I'm fine," said Young.

Deputy Hamm knelt next to him, giving him a once-over.

"No. You're not, sir," said Hamm, before breaking into his individual trauma kit.

A moment later, someone burst into the room and hip-checked the desk in front of the window, then careened to the floor while yelling, "FBI! FBI! Agent Serrano!"

"Jesus. You almost got yourself killed," said Young, lowering the rifle he'd somehow lifted with his right hand and pointed at her face. "How bad is it out there? I can't make sense of the radio chatter."

"Bad. Two machine gunners in the cornfield south of us," said Serrano. "There's no cover on the walkways, and the bullets are punching right through the walls. Half of your people are down."

"What about your sniper?" said Young.

"One of the gunners got the drop on him," she said. "He's behind the semi right now, talking to Mann. They're trying to figure something out."

A stream of bullets hit the doorframe and shattered the window, spraying glass inside the room. Serrano crawled over to Young and ripped open the trauma kit attached to her vest.

"What's your name?" she said, addressing the deputy.

"Hamm. Doug Hamm."

"Doug. Do you know what you're doing here?" she said, breaking open a combat tourniquet pouch.

"I think so," he said, holding a pouch containing hemostatic, blood-clotting gauze.

"Okay. Listen to me very carefully," she said. "Sheriff Young is bleeding out from a wound just above his left elbow. You need to apply a tourniquet to the middle of his left bicep. The rest of his wounds look non-life-threatening for now. Use the hemostatic gauze on those." She looked at the other wounded man. "What's your name?"

"Shorey. Owatonna PD," said the officer.

"Is that your only wound?" she said.

"Yeah. Unless you see something I can't," he said.

She ripped a flashlight from her vest and gave him a once-over.

"I think that's it," she said. "You kind of look like you know what you're doing, so you're in charge now."

"In charge of what?" he said.

"Keeping yourself alive and making sure Hamm keeps the sheriff alive," she said, before turning back to Young. "You wouldn't happen to have any breaching charges in here, would you?"

"What. Why?"

Another burst of gunfire raked the doorway.

"I need to get out of this room, but I can't go through the front door," she said.

He knew exactly what she had in mind.

"Duffel bag in the closet," said Young. "You'll have to double up the charge to get through the wall. Are you familiar with explosives?"

"Familiar enough," she said.

Young shook his head. "Hamm knows explosives. He's one of our breachers."

"Then I think we should trade jobs for now," said Serrano. "I'd hate to blow us all up."

CHAPTER 33

While Serrano put the finishing touches on Young's tourniquet, Deputy Hamm went to work attaching every ounce of explosives from the duffel bag to the wall in the bathroom that connected to the room directly adjacent to the west. If she could get to the western side of the motel, which hadn't come under fire, she might be able to slip into the cornfields and flank the shooters.

From what she could tell and had heard over the radio, everyone in the suites was pinned down, unable to effectively engage the machine gunners. The SWAT officers who emerged from the three rooms facing the courtyard had been stitched with bullets, the survivors either retreating into rooms or trying to take cover on the breezeway, which was more or less exposed to direct gunfire.

Baker didn't have a direct line of fire to the shooters from the ground, so he was looking at different options. One of them being a climb up the back of an adjacent semitrailer to try to throw off the shooters. Turner and the two SWAT officers in his room remained the wild card. Instead of using her radio, which was filled with panicked reports, she called Turner with her cell phone.

"You're still alive?" said Turner.

"Sorry to disappoint you," said Serrano. "Where the hell are you? What's going on?"

"We're on the walkway next to the west suite. We can't get within five feet of the corner without bullets punching through the wall," said

Turner. "They don't know we're here, but they're doing a damn fine job spreading out the lead."

"Okay," she said. "Here's the deal. I'm stuck on the other side, but I'm busting through with some explosives. Nobody should be in the room next to us. Can you verify this?"

"How many rooms back from the suites?" said Turner.

"Four," she said. "Grab the sheets and blankets off the beds and start tying them to the railing. We're going over the side to take out these machine gunners."

"Sounds like fun," said Turner.

"Where's Mann?" said Serrano. "I hear him over the net, but everyone's talking over each other."

"Stuck in the room connected to the eastern suite," said Turner. "How long until you blow through the wall?"

Young winced and groaned when she pressed the gauze down on his upper shoulder, the sheriff's second most serious wound.

"Hold on," she said. "Hamm! How are we looking in there?"

"Almost done!" said the deputy.

"Thirty seconds," she said into the phone.

"Okay. We're kicking the door in right now," said Turner.

"I'm hearing something on the other side!" said Hamm.

"That's our people," said Serrano. "They're getting ready. Do not detonate those explosives until I tell you. Understood?"

"Understood," yelled Hamm, from the bathroom.

About ten seconds later, Hamm emerged from the bathroom, unspooling wire behind him as he made his way to Shorey—where he started connecting the wire to a detonator.

"Give me a few more seconds. Had to improvise a little," said Hamm. "This is going to be a big one."

Serrano told Turner to clear the room on the other side, before lying across Sheriff Young to protect him from whatever Hamm had concocted in the bathroom.

"I'm ready," said Hamm.

"Turner. You clear?"

"We're clear!"

"Breaching," she said, then nodded at Hamm, who squeezed the detonator.

The explosion blasted part of the bathroom wall into the bedroom, covering them in drywall chunks and splintered pieces of wood. She grabbed Hamm and pulled him toward Sheriff Young.

"Keep patching up the sheriff," said Serrano, before bolting for the bathroom door.

Once inside the smoke- and drywall dust–filled bathroom, she glanced back and gave Hamm a thumbs-up before ducking into the adjacent room. Turner was on the other side with two SWAT officers.

"Welcome to the cool-kid side of the motel," said Turner.

CHAPTER 34

Mann crawled onto the walkway, staying as close to the exterior motel wall as possible, which just barely kept him out of the machine guns' line of fire. Bullets struck the white bricks six inches above him, spraying clay shards all around, and struck the railing, sparking and ricocheting everywhere. The ricochets were his biggest concern. However unlikely, one stray bullet to the face or neck and that was it for him.

He kept going until he reached the southernmost end of the walkway, staying far enough back to remain out of the gunners' direct line of fire. Young transmitted over the radio net.

"All units except for Sheriff Young, Deputy Kilroy, Serrano, and Baker—stay off this channel for now," said Mann. "We're coordinating a counterattack behind the scenes. Switch to the secondary frequency for all other traffic."

"Serrano?" said Mann, over the now quiet net.

"Yeah. You okay?"

"I'm still here," said Mann. "Good to hear your voice. Where are you? What's the plan? I'm pretty much pinned down over here."

"Climbing down to the parking lot from the western walkway," said Serrano. "We're going to move through the cornfield and flank the shooters from the west. Might take a few minutes to get there."

"Who's *we*?" said Mann.

"Turner, me, and two SWAT officers," she said. "We're climbing over the side using sheets and blankets."

"Baker. You still in the game?" said Mann.

"Yep. I'm very carefully climbing on top of another semi," said Baker.

"Coordinate your gunfire with Serrano's approach," said Mann. "Split their attention in two directions."

"Copy. But if I get a shot I can take before Serrano moves into position, I'm taking it."

"Understood," said Mann. "You good with that, Serrano?"

"I don't care how we kill them," said Serrano. "Heading down now. I'll be in touch shortly."

"I'll be here," said Mann.

He inched forward, his rifle canted sideways. Mann kept his head tilted at the same angle as the rifle, maintaining as low a profile as possible. A long series of lightning flashes lit up the courtyard, followed by thunder that shook the walkway—momentarily drowning out the gunfire. He lifted himself about an inch off the concrete, and his targets came into view. Muzzle flashes from the edge of the cornfield. One of them must have spotted him. A maelstrom of bullets hit the railing in front of him. He snapped off a few shots before scooting backward.

While Serrano worked on her plan, Mann decided to take some time to check in with the rest of the motel task force. It felt like the most productive thing he could be doing right now. Taking random, barely aimed shots at the machine guns terrorizing them certainly didn't feel helpful. First things first. He switched over to the secondary net to touch base with the police units.

"SWAT North, this is Mann. What's the status of the getaway vehicles?"

"Drivers are neutralized," said the team leader. "I'm sending two officers down to confirm."

"Copy," said Mann. "Mayer. What's your team's status?"

"Mills took a bullet to his shoulder, but he's fine," said Mayer. "The rest of us are helping to lower Turner, Serrano, and the two SWAT officers to the ground."

"Any survivors among the hostiles that hit your room?" said Mann.

"Unlikely. The shotguns tore them up bad. A few were still making sounds, but they were bleeding out," said Mayer. "We just cuffed them all and got the fuck out of there when the shooting started."

"Same here. No survivors as far as I could tell. We'll sort them out when this is over. Switching back to the primary net," said Mann, before pressing one of the preset frequency buttons on his radio. "Sheriff Young. How are you doing?"

"Back in my room," said Young. "Took a bullet to the upper arm. Severed an artery. Serrano saved me."

"She's resourceful. That's for sure," said Mann. "How far out is our backup and EMT support?"

"Less than a minute," said Young.

"Make sure they stay north of the motel," said Mann. "I know that goes without saying."

"I have some critically wounded officers on the courtyard walkways," said Young. "They don't have much time."

"I understand," said Mann. "But you'll just add EMTs to the casualty list if they try to get to those officers. I have something in the works. This should be over in a few minutes."

"What's the plan?" said Young.

"Flanking maneuver. Serrano and Turner will sweep through the cornfield, toward the shooter from the west. Baker is moving into position to provide sniper cover," said Mann. "I haven't heard anything from Kilroy. Do you know his status?"

"Kilroy was hit coming out of his room," said Young. "He's unconscious but supposedly stable."

"Shit," said Mann. "We need to wrap this up, or we're going to start losing wounded officers. Serrano? Baker?"

"This is Baker. I'm ready."

"Serrano here. We're on the deck and moving toward the western cornfield," she said. "We'll start making our way toward the shooters once we've reached the cornfield."

"Copy that," said Mann. "Sheriff Young. Pass that along to the rest of the officers. Have them sit tight and let this play out. We've lost enough people tonight."

"I'll pass that along," said Young. "But I think we need to keep up some kind of volume of fire, or the shooters might suspect a big move."

"Good point," said Mann. "Just nothing risky. There's no reason to lose any more officers at this point. We'll have this wrapped up shortly."

He hoped. There was no telling what else awaited them out there.

CHAPTER 35

Serrano fought her way through the first few rows of cornstalks. She'd never been in a cornfield before. *Shit. We'll need machetes to pull this off.* And even with machetes, it would take forever. The weather just made it worse.

The lightning and deafening thunder were bad enough. Frightening on a shock-and-awe level for sure, but the heavy rain left her feeling the most uneasy. The constant smacking of the raindrops on the cornstalks made it impossible to listen for movement in the rows ahead of them. The rain had also dropped their visibility to just a few feet. They were looking at a nightmarishly difficult search.

"This isn't going to work. We're moving too slow, and we can't see shit," she said.

"Can I make a recommendation?" said Turner.

"Go for it," said Serrano.

"We can exit the field and make our way along the edge until we get within about fifty yards of them. Then we enter the field again and sweep east in a skirmish line until we make contact. This should save us a ton of time," said Turner.

"Works for me," said Serrano. "Hopefully Baker will have solved our problem by the time we arrive."

"Don't count on it," said Turner. "They're well aware of his general location. He'll be lucky to get a shot or two off before they light him up."

"Maybe that's the key to this," said one of the SWAT officers.

"What do you mean?" said Serrano.

"If we get close enough to put some real heat on the shooters, they'll turn their attention our way—leaving Baker with clear shots."

"That could work," said Turner.

"Yeah. I agree," said Serrano, triggering her radio. "Baker. You there?"

"Yep. I'm on top of a different semitrailer. So far. So good. No incoming gunfire."

"Good. Stay out of sight for now," she said. "Here's the plan. We're on the ground west of the motel. We're going to sneak along the edge of the cornfield until we're within effective shooting range of the machine gunners, then open fire—drawing their attention. Then you take them out."

"That should work," said Baker. "Give me about ten seconds' notice before you open fire, so I can crawl into position."

"Copy that," said Serrano. "We're moving out."

CHAPTER 36

Baker readied himself for what would either be an easy one-two punch or another back-and-forth shoot-out. He hoped for the former. The last shoot-out hadn't worked out so well for him. He inched forward at a rate that would convince a snail that it could compete in the Olympics. With no direct background lighting to silhouette any part of his body, a driving rain that turned the night two shades darker, and constant lightning that played tricks on the eyes, he didn't see how the two gunners could spot him.

When their muzzle flashes came into view, he froze for several seconds, ready to pull back if a hail of bullets snapped overhead and hit the side of the semitrailer. He moved forward a few more inches and stopped, waiting for gunfire to snap past him. Nothing. Baker considered continuing a little farther but decided not to push his luck.

He replaced the SCAR17's twenty-round 7.62mm magazine with a shorter ten-round magazine, so he could keep a low profile on the top of the truck. With the rifle propped up on his left forearm, he sighted in on the closest shooter through the night vision scope. The other gunman was partially visible in the far-right side of the scope's field of view. He'd have no problem immediately acquiring and neutralizing the second shooter.

He triggered his radio. "I have both of them. Easy shots. How far out are you?"

"Still about seventy-five meters away," said Serrano.

"Why don't we do this," said Baker. "On my count, start shooting through the cornfield in their direction. It'll distract them long enough for me to take them out. Then you'll move in and mop up with me covering you."

"We're still too far out," said Serrano.

"I just need you to keep their attention off me, so I can take these shots," said Baker.

"We'll be in position in thirty seconds," said Serrano.

"Some of the officers up here might not have that long," said Mann over the net. "We need to end this now."

"All right. Fuck it. None of us can see shit," said Serrano. "But we're stopped and ready to open fire."

"On my count," said Baker, centering the night vision scope's reticle on the shooter's head. "Three. Two. One. Fire."

He pressed the trigger, the rifle digging into his shoulder as the man's head snapped violently sideways. At the same time, gunfire erupted from the west, slicing through the cornstalks and sealing the second gunman's fate. When the shooter pivoted to unleash a volley of automatic fire at unseen targets on his flank, Baker placed the reticle on the man's upper back and pressed the trigger, knocking him flat.

"This is Baker. Both targets are down. The eastern hostile is down hard. Western took a hit to the back. It's possible that the plate in his vest stopped the bullet. Proceed with caution."

"Serrano. Keep your people back. I can see him crawling," said Mann, gunfire exploding from Mann's prone position on the suite's walkway.

At least a dozen other rifles joined in, the officers and agents shredding the cornfield around the downed target. Baker searched the exploding cornstalks until he finally caught a glimpse of the operator, who continued to slither away. He centered the reticle on what looked to be the hostile's lower back or hindquarters—and fired three times. The figure stopped moving shortly after Baker's third shot.

"Cease fire. Cease fire. I hit him again—and he's not moving," said Baker, switching over to the secondary radio net and repeating what he'd just said.

A few moments later, the guns went silent, leaving them with the night's previous symphony of heavy rain, gusting winds, and booming thunder. And sirens. A lot of sirens.

"Let's start moving the wounded to the parking lot," said Mann. "Ambulances should be here any moment."

CHAPTER 37

Serrano found the westernmost shooter lying on his stomach where Baker had shot him, taking short, seemingly involuntary breaths. More like an abbreviated wheeze. Judging from the amount of blood still glistening on the rain-soaked cornstalks surrounding him—he wasn't long for this world. Still. She wasn't taking any chances. And she sure as hell wasn't wasting ambulance space or EMT time on this guy.

She opened a small nylon pouch attached to her belt and removed a foldable knife. She flicked open the serrated blade and planted her knee in the man's back, ready to plunge the blade through the back of his neck.

"Stop," whispered Turner, suddenly appearing next to her. "How do you think that's going to look on the forensic report?"

"They're not going to spend any time on these *cabrones*," she said.

"No offense, but this isn't Mexico," said Turner. "By dawn, or whenever the storm lets up, this place will be crawling with hundreds of cops and investigators—local, state, and federal."

She put the knife away and stood up, keeping a foot on the man's back. "Then we just let him bleed out?"

"Of course not," said Turner, twisting a sizable suppressor onto the quick-detach muzzle brake of his M4 rifle.

She took her foot off the man and backed up once Turner had finished attaching the suppressor. A flash of lightning lit up the cornstalks, with Turner firing a single shot through the base of the operative's neck when the thunder roared.

"Search him for a phone," said Turner, before triggering his radio. "Mann. This is Turner."

"This is Mann."

"We found the westernmost shooter. Baker did a number on him, and it looks like a few of the bullets fired from the motel found their mark," said Turner.

"Copy," said Mann. "The next one will be easier to find. The body is about five feet into the cornfield."

"Heading over now," said Turner. "Hey. Do you want us to drag the bodies into the grass by the side of the road? Make it easier for the coroner?"

"Negative. We need to leave everything in place for the forensics convention that'll descend on this place after the storm rolls out," said Mann.

"Understood. We're moving on to the next shooter," said Turner, taking his hand off the radio transmitter before turning to Serrano. "See?"

"You were right. Twice," she said, holding up a phone.

"Pocket that," said Turner. "We'll hand it off to Rocha. She might be able to get something useful out of it."

As they started to slowly make their way east, Turner unscrewed the suppressor and tucked it into one of the pouches on his vest.

"It's a different world up here," said Serrano. "These bodies wouldn't get a once-over by detectives or crime scene investigators where I come from. Not even the local cops or National Guard officers. They'd be stripped of their gear, most of it instantly repurposed or stolen by other officers, and the bodies shipped off to the morgue. Even the phone would disappear."

"It's just the opposite here," said Turner. "The bigger the shooting, the bigger the investigation. You're gonna be shocked by how many people show up tomorrow."

"It probably wouldn't be a good idea for me to stick around long enough to see," said Serrano. "Given my situation."

"Shit. I hadn't thought about that," said Turner. "You should check in with Mann the moment we get back. The sooner you're out of sight, the better, especially when they link our team to the Cedar Lake fiasco. We're all going to spend some time in a lone chair behind a table—explaining why we didn't stick around for the aftermath. To be honest, I wouldn't be surprised if they shut us down until they sorted it all out."

"We're too close for that," said Serrano. "We obviously hit a nerve with the Cedar Lake raid. They did not want that man falling into our hands. And they moved fast to retrieve him."

"Maybe none of us should stick around," said Turner. "Who knows how far up this goes, or who's behind it. Could be some of the very people that show up to dig around a little later."

"Now you know how I felt every day as a Mexican cop," said Serrano.

CHAPTER 38

Mann had a half dozen or more wounded officers to evacuate, some critically injured, including the Steele County sheriff and the regional SWAT team leader. Dozens of ambulances and police cars poured into the site—and nobody left standing to coordinate their arrival. The last thing he needed right now was a sidebar with Serrano and Turner. He pulled them into the room where Sheriff Young and Deputy Shorey lay on the floor, barely clinging to life.

"Make this quick," said Mann.

"I can't be here for the inquisition headed our way," said Serrano. "It'll land me in jail or get me deported—and sink ARTEMIS."

"I really don't have time for this," said Mann, heading for the door.

"You need to make time," said Turner, grabbing him by the arm and holding him in place. "ARTEMIS is probably screwed already. The lake—and now this?"

"O'Reilly has our back," said Mann.

"Does she?" said Turner. "Does she know you have a former Mexican police officer posing as an FBI agent on the team? Small detail in the grand scheme of things, but the kind of detail that nails coffins shut. We need to get her out of here immediately."

"She knows," said Mann.

"Damn," said Turner. "Okay."

Young nodded. "I knew she wasn't an FBI agent, but I played along, because you all seemed about as legit as they come—and that's hard to come by these days. I still think you're legit, by the way. Plus, I figured she had some kind of personal connection to these killings."

"My mother was murdered in Ciudad Juárez by the people we're hunting. I tried to track down her killer as a Mexican state cop," said Serrano. "It didn't work out."

"I bet it didn't," said Young. "Shorey. Hamm. Either one of you see a former Mexican police officer here posing as an FBI agent?"

"Nope," said Shorey. "I mean. All these G-folks look the same anyway, right?"

"Right," said Young.

"And I certainly didn't see anyone save your life on the floor here," said Hamm.

"Thank you, by the way," said Young.

"Just doing my job," said Serrano.

"Let me call Sheriff Ulrich, if he isn't here already," said Young. "And have Agent Serrano join Agent Jackson at the Waseca County Sheriff's Office headquarters—though I highly suggest you move both of them to an undisclosed location as soon as possible."

Mann gave the situation some thought, then reached a decision—which would probably come back to bite him in the ass. Then again, this whole day was certain to come back to bite him.

"Have Rocha drive her back to Waseca—and stay with them. She's our computer forensics expert, and we need our tech specialists working the bugs. They might be our last hope of getting to the bottom of this," said Mann.

"All right. I'll grab Rocha and get them on the road," said Turner.

"Before you head out, take a quick look at the shooters in the two suites. Take pictures of their faces. Check for obvious tattoos. Strip their pockets. Grab phones or any other electronic devices. IDs if they're carrying any. And on the way through the parking lot, do the same with the drivers. Also, grab any vehicle paperwork in the glove boxes and snap a shot of the VINs and license plates."

"We took phones off the shooters in the cornfield, but didn't take pictures," said Turner. "I didn't want anyone thinking it was a muzzle flash and lighting us up."

"I don't blame you," said Mann, reconsidering his redeployment of Serrano, Rocha, and Jax. He needed Serrano gone for now.

"Tell Jax and Rocha to relocate with Serrano immediately. Kansas City. They can grab the Expedition stashed in long-term parking at the airport. I strongly suspect we'll be headed in that direction once the circus leaves town. Our killer drove back and forth from Cedar Lake to an unknown location in New Mexico or points south. I guarantee that's where they're taking him. And make sure Rocha and Jax understand that they're not being sidelined in any way."

"They know," said Turner. "But I'll pass it along."

"Same with you, Cata," said Mann. "I mean, technically I'm sidelining you to keep you out of trouble—but I really need you to watch over them. Keep them safe until we get the band back together. Trust your instincts and call me if there's a problem."

"Got it," said Serrano.

"You good?" said Mann.

"It's been a long day," said Serrano.

"Yeah—it has," said Mann.

But not the longest day of his life. Not even close. Yet. Once he finished coordinating the evacuation of the wounded officers—he'd have to wake up O'Reilly with the good news.

PART IV

CHAPTER 39

O'Reilly made her way to the kitchen with Mann on speakerphone. She put her phone down on the counter next to her espresso maker.

"I'm listening, Garrett," she said, hitting the machine's power button. "Just making a double shot of espresso, so pardon the background noise."

"I would kill for an espresso right now," said Mann. "Probably not the best choice of words."

"No. Probably not," she said. "Any chance this was a cartel hit? Possibly related to the Cedar Lake raid or your consultant?"

"No. Unless they're outsourcing their work to former US special operators. We found a few SOCOM-related unit tattoos. Bone frogs, Ranger battalion bravado, Semper Fi—that kind of stuff. No gang-related ink. And only two of the eleven bodies looked Latino. This is something else. Very similar to the crew we took out at the lake."

"Hold on," she said, hitting the double espresso button.

She walked out of the kitchen with the phone while the machine worked its magic.

"Sorry about that," said O'Reilly. "You said eleven bodies. Did any get away?"

"Not as far as we can tell," said Mann. "But the two shooters in the cornfield didn't materialize out of thin air. We plan on reviewing all video from security camera feeds near the motel. There's a Cabela's a few hundred yards from here with enough parking for half of the Midwest."

"Okay. Here's what I'm going to do," said O'Reilly. "I'm going to designate the attack as a domestic terror incident. I'm on shaky ground after the Crystal Airport call, which turned out to be a bust. They took off before my alert reached local authorities and whoever was manning the tower at the airport. But a coordinated, pinpoint attack on an FBI field team falls well within those parameters. This will give me jurisdiction over the scene in Owatonna. For now. I don't know how long that will last, so we'll have to make the best of whatever time we get."

"We took pictures of their faces—those that were still intact—grabbed their phones, emptied their pockets, got their vehicle VINs and license plate numbers. Snapped shots of the unit tattoos. We even broke open a few ink pens to take fingerprints. We'll put this all together and send it back to DC in the morning for CIRG to process," said Mann.

"Nice work," said O'Reilly. "That should give us a solid head start on whatever we're dealing with here. I'll fly out first thing in the morning. Watch your back until I get there. There's definitely more to this than meets the eye."

"Watch my back? What could be worse than a professional hit team sent to kill me in the middle of the night?" said Mann.

"A political hit team sent to kill you in the middle of the day," said O'Reilly. "I'll keep you posted on my ETA. Hang on tight until I get there. You're in charge of that scene. Don't let anyone try to push you out. And certainly don't let anyone try to move you off-site for a debriefing or whatever they claim is necessary."

"Who's this *anyone* you keep referring to?" said Mann.

"I don't know," said O'Reilly. "But I've been around long enough to know that *anyone* can turn out to be your worst enemy."

"That's encouraging," said Mann.

"That's reality," said O'Reilly. "And don't forget it."

CHAPTER 40

"Son of a mother!" muttered Gerald McCall after ending his brief call with Jeremy Powell.

His wife stirred in bed next to him. "What's going on? What's wrong?"

"Oh. Just the usual," said McCall. "Don't worry about it. Always a fire to put out."

More like an entire city burning down.

"Sounds a little more serious than usual," she mumbled, still half-asleep.

"It's all good," said McCall, getting out of bed. "Just need to point a few people in the right direction—at three in the morning."

"Let me know if you need anything," she said, rolling over.

Yeah. I need a tactical nuclear bomb to drop on Owatonna, Minnesota. Got one of those?

"Thank you, honey," said McCall. "Hopefully this won't take long."

"Uh-huh," she said, already on her way back to a deep sleep.

McCall grabbed his robe from the chair next to the bed and slipped it on over his briefs and T-shirt. The phone went into one of the pockets. He considered grabbing a chilled coffee drink from the bedroom mini fridge but decided against it for now. He was wired enough after that call. The caffeine would come later—in copious amounts. Sleep was not in his immediate future. He'd have to pace himself.

After a quick bathroom stop, he made his way to his home office. A cavernous enclave surrounded by floor-to-ceiling cherrywood bookcases. Despite its old-world look and feel, the office was anything but quaint. The windows were laser microphone–proof. The walls were soundproof, incorporating active countersurveillance white noise when occupied. Even the ventilation system, which heated or cooled the office, was attached to a separate system from the rest of the 9,430-square-foot mansion.

McCall shut the french doors and opened a concealed wooden panel to the right of the doors, which revealed a touchpad. After he entered a six-digit code, a low-volume hiss filled the office and the french doors turned opaque—the system shielding his words and expression from any kind of observation, digital or physical. He scrolled through his "most important" contact list and selected a number he'd sincerely hoped he would never have to call. Time to apply some serious leverage. Full leverage to be precise. His call was answered after a few rings.

"Hello?"

Like the man didn't know who was on the other end of the line.

"You have a serious problem on your hands," said McCall.

"At three in the morning?"

"Yes. At three in the morning," said McCall.

A few seconds passed before Daniel Ritter, deputy director of operations for the Central Intelligence Agency, responded.

"Give me a minute to get on a secure line. I'll call you right back," said Ritter, hanging up on him.

McCall clenched his fist as the line went dead. Nobody hung up on him without his acknowledgment. Who the hell did these people think they were? Soon-to-be or already completely irrelevant pencil pushers. That's what they were. His encrypted desk phone rang a moment later. He decided to let the transgression go for now.

"Hello?" said McCall, giving Ritter a taste of his own medicine.

"Funny," said Ritter. "What's going on?"

"What's going on?" said McCall. "I said you have a serious problem on your hands."

"I heard you the first time," said Ritter. "Get to the point."

"The point is that we might have a problem with LABYRINTH, formerly known as SINKHOLE."

"The two are related?" said Ritter.

For a brief moment, McCall gave credence to the question—before the snarky, sarcastic tone hit him.

"Since you sound a little punchy for my taste at three in the morning, I'm going to lay it out straight for you," said McCall.

"Oh. Please do," said Ritter.

"The FBI almost captured one of your former . . . star torturers, slash serial killers, slash sanctioned state murderers yesterday," said McCall. "We managed to intervene and spirit him away at the last second."

"Then it sounds like we're good," said Ritter. "As in—you're good."

"No. We're far from good."

"There's no 'we' anymore, Gerald. We've discussed this exhaustively," said Ritter. "You got what you wanted. Winner. Winner. Chicken dinner. No dessert. No after-dinner drinks. Just the end all, be all—of chicken dinners. So why the fuck am I on the phone with you at three in the morning?"

"ARTEMIS is on the brink of connecting LABYRINTH to SINKHOLE," said McCall.

"A bunch of loser agents corralled into a pointless task force managed to shit on your chicken dinner?" said Ritter. "Is that what you're saying?"

"More or less," said McCall. "Can we cut the bullshit for a minute?"

"Yeah. Shoot."

"Alejandro messed up," said McCall, briefly explaining the situation.

"Jesus. I warned you about him," said Ritter. "This is why we never let him leave the site. He's a fucking degenerate murderer. You seriously set him up in the suburbs of Minneapolis?"

"He demanded it," said McCall. "The power dynamic with these guys shifted after the handover."

"Handover?" said Ritter. "More like a coup!"

"SINKHOLE went to shit under your watch," said McCall. "We filled the gap. Took over."

"Yeah. Things went to shit pretty quickly," said Ritter. "Quickly enough to raise some questions."

"What questions?" said McCall.

"Really?" said Ritter. "Do I need to spell it out for you, or can we just finally acknowledge, at three in the fucking morning on a weekday, what really happened with the SINKHOLE program?"

Maybe it was the lack of caffeine or the fact that he'd been awake for only five minutes—or both—but he found himself at a loss for words. Ritter clearly knew more than he'd ever previously let on. Shit. He felt his negotiating power evaporating by the second.

"Hello?" said Ritter.

Time to go for broke.

"Okay. We undermined your broke-ass program, which wasn't going anywhere," said McCall. "Yeah. A few of SINKHOLE's graduates managed to return and reintegrate into the cartels successfully, but most of them didn't. And they posed a serious risk to the program. That was well before we got involved."

"But you did get involved," said Ritter. "And you fucked us."

"Maybe we saved you from yourself," said McCall.

A few seconds passed before Ritter responded.

"What do you want?"

The sound of victory.

"I need you to shut down ARTEMIS," said McCall. "Not permanently, though that would be preferable, but at a minimum we need them sidelined for a few months while we reassess a few things."

"'A few things' being the psychopaths you've unleashed on America?"

McCall restrained himself. Three in the morning, without caffeine, wasn't the time to parse words—which could ultimately tip his hand. Ritter clearly didn't know LABYRINTH's true purpose. And he had no intention of connecting the dots for him.

"Can you make this happen or not?"

"Shut down or sideline ARTEMIS?" said Ritter.

"Yes. That's all I'm asking for," said McCall.

"And if I say no?" said Ritter.

"We don't need to go there," said McCall.

"Yes. We do," said Ritter. "I need to know exactly where you stand."

"If you say no, then we'll go public with the SINKHOLE information," said McCall.

"Which would sink, pun intended, AXIOM," said Ritter.

"You don't think we have other customers watching our progress here, which has been substantial on levels you can't even comprehend," said McCall. "Do you even know what we're doing?"

"We don't care what you're doing," said Ritter.

"Really? Oh boy. You have no idea. When we're done, you'll be answering to me. Assuming we let you stay in your position," said McCall. "Unless you go public with SINKHOLE and how the CIA sold it to AXIOM. That might complicate things for us. You should be able to watch the hearings, whenever they occur, on the TV in your jail block. Because if you fuck with me on any level moving forward, we will unearth everything."

Ritter responded faster than he expected.

"I'll sideline ARTEMIS," said Ritter. "But I need to make something very clear to you. My next call will be to a very loyal group of special operators—who will kill you and your entire extended family if you ever contact me again. Or, if I fall off a balcony, die in a car bombing, or choke on a . . . chicken wing. Winner. Winner. You're on notice, motherfucker."

The call ended before he could respond, which was probably a good thing. He'd achieved his mission and effectively killed the ARTEMIS inquiry into LABYRINTH. If the conversation had continued, McCall might have either directly counterthreatened Ritter's life or explained exactly why Ritter would go to jail if the details of LABYRINTH came to light. Neither scenario would have been productive for AXIOM, so he let it go and took his finger off the redial button.

CHAPTER 41

O'Reilly had just zipped her suitcase shut when her phone buzzed. She glanced at the screen, which was face up on the bed next to her carry-on-size bag. 4:43 a.m. Camilla James, a.k.a. her boss. Shit. She pressed the green "Accept" button, then switched to speakerphone.

"Director James. How are you?" said O'Reilly, instantly realizing she had just set herself up for a baseball bat to the face.

"Not good, Dana. Not good at all," she said.

"I can't imagine why," said O'Reilly.

"Let your imagination run wild," said James.

"ARTEMIS?" said O'Reilly.

"Can you take me off speakerphone?" said James. "I don't feel like I have your full attention. And I need your full attention."

"Sure. I was just packing," said O'Reilly.

"Packing?"

She swiped the phone off the bed and switched out of speakerphone.

"I'm on the 6:20 flight to Minneapolis," said O'Reilly.

"Not anymore," said James. "ARTEMIS is suspended until further notice."

O'Reilly considered her response. She'd always seen James as an ally. Supportive, yet hands-off. Nonjudgmental about her checkered past at the agency. A close friend of former FBI Director Ryan Sharpe, who lifted O'Reilly up when she was down and shepherded her career. One of the last people on earth she'd want to piss off or disappoint—intentionally.

"Why?" said O'Reilly, keeping her questions simple.

The less she talked, the better.

"Orders from the top," said James.

"How far up?" said O'Reilly.

"Does it matter?" said James. "I'm ordering you to stand down Mann's team. Immediately."

"No, but they've put a lot of blood and sweat into that task force," said O'Reilly. "I owe them something other than *thanks for nothing, time to go home.*"

"Sharpe warned me about you," said James.

Of all the positive things James had ever said about her, she considered her last statement the highest compliment possible.

"He put up with a lot," said O'Reilly, testing the waters.

"Ha! No. He told me you could sound unreasonably reasonable when you had no intention of being reasonable. If that makes sense."

"It does," said O'Reilly.

"You're not going to screw me over on this, are you?" said James. "Like you, I've worked my ass off to get where I am. Mann's task force is doing good work, but they've been involved in two very high-profile, public gunbattles within the span of a day. It's time to hit the pause button on ARTEMIS. Let them cool off. We lost two FBI agents yesterday. Not to mention the police officers and deputies injured or killed."

Cooling them off made some sense. Not that Mann was responsible for any of the deaths. Maybe a short pause would give them time to analyze the evidence and plot a new course of action. One that didn't involve public gunbattles.

"I'll pass along the order and support it from my end."

"Starting with canceling your trip to Minneapolis," said James.

"It might be better if I deliver the news in person," said O'Reilly. "And offer the FBI's more conventional support to the local law enforcement agencies?"

"Sorry. I'm pulling CIRG out of this," said James. "Orders."

"Whose orders?" said O'Reilly.

"The deputy director of the FBI," said James. "Which means the director himself."

"I get that," said O'Reilly. "But who's really behind this? It's too soon for the deputy director or director to be weighing in. Hell. It's too soon for anyone to be weighing in. I haven't reported this yet. We're talking about a rural shoot-out that went down less than two hours ago."

"Oh. We'll get to that," said James. "There's most definitely a little timeline problem here. As in, you not notifying your chain of command in a timely manner. I don't appreciate getting a call from my boss in the middle of the night and not knowing what the hell she's talking about. Puts me in a bad position."

"I'm sorry about that," said O'Reilly. "I was weighing some options."

"Well. The burden is off your shoulders," said James. "Your only option now is to recall ARTEMIS."

"This isn't just about giving ARTEMIS a cooldown period," said O'Reilly. "They're onto something. Something big enough to bring a professional hit team down on their heads."

"Then this is good news for them," said James. "They're off the hit list, because they're suspended until we can sort this out."

Mann wasn't going to take this well. None of them would, especially Serrano. She stifled a laugh. If James knew about her, she'd send an FBI jet to Owatonna to scoop them all up.

"I'll make the call," said O'Reilly. "Get them on the first available flights back to DC."

"No need to make flight arrangements. Send them to the Owatonna airport. A government jet will be there at approximately zero-six-thirty."

Damn. She was scooping them up. "FBI jet?"

"No. ODNI. They'll fly them directly to Andrews Air Force Base for debriefing."

"The Office of the Director of National Intelligence is flying FBI agents around these days?" said O'Reilly. "If I'd known that, I would have requested an ODNI jet to fly to Minnesota. Beats fighting for a seat and overhead space on Southwest Airlines. Send me the flight reservation link when you get a chance."

James laughed. "You didn't hear this from me, but the call to the director of the FBI came from ODNI. Maybe Mann's team stumbled across something of interest to them. For all I know, they'll put ARTEMIS right back in the field after the debrief. Maybe beef up their security. Who knows? All I know is that your division is in the spotlight, which means I'm in the spotlight—which doesn't leave me any wiggle room. I want them at that airport within a half hour. Looks like the motel is a five-minute drive away."

"I'll get them moving," said O'Reilly.

"Call me when they get to the airport," said James. "I've got the deputy director on my ass. I need to report smooth sailing from here on out."

"Understood," said O'Reilly. "I'll call you when they arrive."

"All right. Thank you, Dana," said James, before ending the call.

"Debriefing, my ass," mumbled O'Reilly.

Why the hell would the intelligence community get involved this quickly? It didn't make any sense. She'd been around long enough to know that ODNI's sudden interest in Mann's task force was suspicious. Especially on the heels of yesterday's events.

James wasn't wrong about one thing. ARTEMIS stumbled across something of peak interest to at least one of the US Intelligence Community's agencies. The big question was why that agency cared so much about the fate of a domestic serial killer with former ties to the Juárez Cartel. None of it added up, which was why she had no intention of putting Mann's team on that jet.

CHAPTER 42

Mann ushered the remnants of his team into one of the motel's first-floor rooms. Mayer, Turner, Baker, and Mills—who'd taken a grazing hit to his shoulder. Unpleasant and painful, but not an end-of-mission wound—unless Mills wanted it to be. Mann was well aware that tonight's attack on his task force went beyond the call of duty for all of them.

The past year and a half had been rough on everyone, hopping from one crime scene to the next, with little to show for their exhausting efforts. Frustration above anything else. Not to mention the isolation of being on the road nearly every day. And now this? Finally a lead—and it ended up nearly getting them all killed.

If anyone wanted to walk at this point and return to DC to sit in their empty offices and be absorbed by O'Reilly into another division within CIRG, he wouldn't put up a fight or say a single negative word about their choice. He had nothing but amazing things to say about all of them. They'd be an asset to any team that accepted them. That said, Jax just passed along some encouraging information, and he hoped to keep everyone on board a little longer despite the grave risk this information represented.

"Ray. How are you doing?" said Mann.

"I've been better, but I feel fine. The bullet just grazed my shoulder," said Mills. "I keep thinking about how much I moved around during that initial exchange. Going from window to window firing my rifle.

Constantly checking on everyone. It's pure luck that I didn't take one to the forehead."

"Statistically," said Turner, "you're unlucky to have been shot at all. Most police shoot-outs don't result in gunshot wounds."

"That was hardly a typical police shoot-out," said Baker. "More like a SEAL team raid."

"Exactly," said Mann. "Let's just count our blessings that they weren't as proficient as our SEALs."

"But some of them were ex-SEALs," said Turner. "And ex-Rangers. Marines. Green Berets. People who swore an oath at one point to defend the United States against enemies—foreign and domestic. Now they're the enemy."

The tattoos they'd found on several of the bodies strongly suggested that the assault team had largely comprised highly skilled US military veterans.

"Yeah. That's the problem with all these military contractor groups and companies," said Mann. "They offer our higher-tier operators big money to get out of the military and go to work for them. That money tends to conflict with that oath."

"Scum," said Turner.

"Big business," said Mann. "But yes. In the grand scheme of things. Nothing more than mercenary scum. No better than the Russian Wagner Group."

"So. What's next?" said Turner. "I assume you didn't drag us in here to pat us on the back for a good day's work?"

"What makes you say that?" said Mann.

"Our entire last year and a half working with you," said Mayer.

The room broke out into halfhearted laughter. Everyone was emotionally and physically drained at this point.

His phone buzzed; everyone's attention immediately diverted to the device he'd placed on the nightstand. Jax and company with more information? Maybe a more pinpointed location? He checked the screen. O'Reilly. Could be worse. He accepted the call and put it on speakerphone.

"Dana. You're on speakerphone with agents Turner, Baker, Mayer, and Mills. Is that okay?"

"Yes. I suppose that's fine," said O'Reilly.

She sounded stiff or constrained, like she was about to deliver bad news.

"I was just about to call you," said Mann. "The virus Mayer imported from the Special Surveillance Group—"

"Garrett. Sorry. I don't mean to cut you off, but things are kind of moving fast over here, and I need to get to the point quick," said O'Reilly. "I'm no longer headed out to Owatonna."

Interesting. Something had drastically changed in the last few hours—and not for the better.

"What's up?" said Mann.

"I've been told to pause ARTEMIS," said O'Reilly. "To recall your team from the field. The orders came from the top."

"Dana. We just made a huge—"

Baker shook his head and held up his palm, indicating he should stop immediately. No more information.

He nodded at Baker and continued. "I mean, we have to be on the verge of a big breakthrough here. Someone sent professional killers to take us out. That's not normal. Not even close."

"Garrett. I don't disagree with you, but my orders are specific," said O'Reilly. "And they literally came from the top. The director. With a nudge from the ODNI."

Oh. Now we are getting somewhere.

"ODNI?"

"I guess it was the first available government jet they could scramble. Better than a CIA jet, right?" said O'Reilly.

Baker grabbed the small notepad and pen on the desk and started scribbling. *Another clue?*

"My boss wants you to pack up and report to the Owatonna Degner Regional Airport within thirty minutes. An ODNI jet will pick you up around six thirty and fly you back to Andrews Air Force Base for a debriefing."

Baker raised an eyebrow and shook his head. Turner and Mayer both gave him quick headshakes. They were all in agreement that something was off. ODNI didn't send jets to retrieve FBI agents from the field. As far as he knew, ODNI itself didn't have jets to fly anyone around, except for the director of national intelligence. The CIA, DEA, NSA, DIA, and every other agency that formed the US Intelligence Community had plenty of jets. Nothing about this made sense. O'Reilly must have come to the same conclusion.

"Then it looks like we're headed to the airport. Game over," said Mann.

"Sounds like they just want to hit the pause button for now, Garrett. Two shoot-outs in one day must have been too much," said O'Reilly. "I stressed the point that you'd lose valuable momentum, but they really wanted to render this situation neutral until they talk with you and your team. James seemed to think this would be very temporary. She's a big fan of your team's work."

Render? That was an odd word choice.

"Do you think the new information might change their minds?" said Mann. "We're really close to putting this killer permanently out of business."

"I'll pass it along as soon as we get off the phone," said O'Reilly. "But I doubt they'll render a decision before your flight takes off."

Render again. Rendition. The flight wasn't going to Andrews Air Force Base, or at least O'Reilly didn't believe that would be the destination. Baker held up his notepad and showed everyone in the room.

RENDITION

Mann nodded.

"How long do you think we'll be stuck at Andrews?" said Mann.

"It's hard to say," said O'Reilly. "You know how these things go."

"Yeah. Could be a very long day. Or two. Wish I had a book to read," said Mann. "Speaking of books. Did you ever get around to reading that book I sent you for your birthday?"

"*The Pentagon Papers*?" said O'Reilly. "Every night, right before I go to bed. Funny how I don't have trouble sleeping anymore."

"Hey," said Mann. "You went on and on about getting your hands on that book. Remember?"

"To you?"

"No. I overheard you talking about it with James at some point," said Mann.

"I must have been sucking up to her or something," said O'Reilly. "She's a prolific reader. Me? Not so much."

"I only got 237 pages in before ARTEMIS deployed," said Mann. "There's a copy in my office if you feel like placing it at the edge of your desk to impress James."

"I don't think so. James is like a one-person, walking-talking book club," said O'Reilly. "If she sees that book in my office with a bookmark 237 pages deep, I'm screwed. I don't have time to read 237 pages of anything right now."

She repeated the number. That was a good sign. A few seconds went by before she closed things out.

"Don't miss that flight. Okay?" said O'Reilly.

No mention of the vehicles. The gear. The weapons. O'Reilly was on the same page; she just couldn't say it over an open line. Or she suspected her town house was bugged? Either way, she wasn't taking any chances.

"We'll head over right away," said Mann.

"Call me when you get to the airport," said O'Reilly, ending the call.

"You never gave her *The Pentagon Papers*, did you?" said Mills.

"I actually did, as a joke," said Mann.

"What's on page 237?" said Mayer.

"The number for the burner phone I keep in the Navigator," said Mann. "And a link to an encrypted messaging app."

"We're activating BURN KIT protocols?" said Mayer.

"Jesus," said Turner.

BURN KIT was Mayer's idea, inspired by something she'd seen during her time with the Special Surveillance Group and implemented on the off chance they somehow pissed off a transnational crime organization, like the Russian mafia or a Mexican cartel, with the resources to track them down and no fear of murdering FBI agents. He never imagined they'd be activating BURN KIT to hide from their own government.

They were looking at a complete wipe of any traceable digital activity. Cell phones. Satellite phones. Computers. Tablets. Anything that could be used to track them, including personal credit cards. Everything replaced with devices purchased off-the-books over the past year. Roughly fifteen thousand dollars in prepaid credit cards, and five thousand in cash—to acquire whatever else the team needed. Fake driver's licenses for motel rooms and rental vehicles.

"I don't see any other way. Unless you want to get on that plane," said Mann.

"No thanks," said Turner. "I'd rather not end up in a black site jail cell in Bulgaria."

"Same," said Mayer.

"Baker?" said Mann.

"You had to ask?" said Baker. "We go dark."

"Mills?" said Mann.

"No way I'm getting on that plane," said Mills.

"I'll call Jax and let her know," said Mayer. "They have a partial BURN KIT replacement package in their spare tire compartment. Enough to get them by for now."

"We'll have to figure out a way to link up with the others without using our vehicles," said Mann.

"I've thoroughly inspected and scanned our vehicles," said Mayer. "We're clean. The kit includes several license plates that'll pass muster if they're run through any state systems."

"The bullet holes won't pass muster," said Mann.

"I think they'll get us as far as we need to go for now," said Mayer. "We can switch to rentals in Des Moines."

"We'll have to leave the RV behind. It's too conspicuous. Let's transfer whatever we can to the SUVs, including the assassination team's rifles, magazines, night vision equipment, and helmets. Serrano's people can use the upgrade. We can pick up those automatic rifles from the cornfield on our way out. They might come in handy, given what we're up against," said Mann.

"Remove key evidence in an officer-involved shooting right in front of the locals?" said Mills.

"The story is that we need to hand-deliver the weapons to our forensics people at the Minneapolis field office. Terrorism-related and the clock is ticking," said Mann. "We're in charge here, so I don't expect them to put up much of a fight. And we just need to buy enough time to drive out of town. FBI agents from Minneapolis will be here within the hour. So, let's hustle. And dump all the phones we confiscated from the shooters. Someone will be tracking those shortly. Same with our personal and FBI-issued phones. Sat phones included."

"I recommend that we deep-six all our phones and devices. Toss them over a bridge into a lake or river," said Mayer. "You'd be surprised what the right people can do with a supposedly sanitized phone."

"We'll round up all devices before we head north and toss them in a lake. There seems to be no shortage of lakes in this state. Then we'll turn south," said Mann. "I figure we've got about an hour or so before they start to suspect we've gone dark. O'Reilly can only stall for so long. Her comment about calling when we get to the airport tells me she's been ordered to keep James apprised of our movements. Which means James has no doubt been ordered by someone else to do the same."

"An hour and a half from now, when that plane lands," said Baker, "whoever is behind all of this will scramble every asset at their disposal to find us."

Mann nodded. "And from what we've seen so far, they have some serious assets at their disposal. We may have just seen the tip of the iceberg."

CHAPTER 43

Roughly a half hour later, after slipping away from the motel, they were on Interstate 35, headed north in a two-vehicle convoy. The Navigator and Expedition. The Jeep Wrangler sat in the Waseca County Sheriff's Office parking lot, and the other Expedition was speeding south toward Des Moines with Rocha, Jax, and Serrano.

The prepaid, freshly activated phone in Mann's hand rang, the flip-up screen displaying an unfamiliar number. After this call, he'd have to toss it with the rest of the phones they'd collected. It wouldn't take a digital forensic genius to connect the sudden appearance of a new phone on Owatonna's local cell tower networks to his task force. A burner phone in the true sense of the word. He answered the call.

"Do you really think they had plans to render us?" said Mann.

"Does ODNI offer charter flight service to non-intelligence-related FBI task forces?" said O'Reilly.

"I didn't know ODNI had a fleet of jets," said Mann.

"Exactly," said O'Reilly. "I didn't get too deep into that with James. Mostly because I don't know who to trust right now. There's something seriously fucked up going on."

"We all agree," said Mann. "You should have seen the notes being passed around the room during your call."

"Not to cut you off, but I'm sitting in a bathroom at my usual Starbucks stop," said O'Reilly. "I have no idea if I'm being watched. You know the deal."

He did. Mayer had taught the team the tricks of her very rare trade. If O'Reilly was under surveillance, and they saw her making a call, they'd check the phone records associated with her personal and FBI-issued devices. If the call didn't match up to one of her known devices, they'd know she'd used a burner.

"Yep. I'll make this brief," said Mann. "We got hits from both the jet that flew out of Crystal Airport and the Suburban stolen from the Steele County Sheriff's Office garage. The jet landed in Roswell, New Mexico."

"As in alien abduction, Roswell?" said O'Reilly.

"The same," said Mann. "Several people headed northwest along State Road 246. Their signals went dead about forty miles later, roughly ten miles northeast of the Capitan Mountains."

"El Capitan? Isn't that in Yosemite National Park?"

"Different Capitan," said Mann. "Believe it or not."

"I'll believe just about anything at this point," said O'Reilly.

"The group that drove the Suburban out of the Steele County Sheriff's Office parking lot headed west, deep into Nebraska, where we lost them. My guess is that the Suburban is scrap metal at this point, buried underground."

"Good guess," said O'Reilly.

"Two of the signals associated with the SUV reemerged in northern Colorado several hours ago, and we've been able to follow them off and on ever since. They vanished in New Mexico, about fifteen miles west along State Road 247, which is about twenty-five miles north of where we lost the other group. We've come up with a search area between the two points of disappearance. Based on the cell-tower coverage maps for that area, we're looking at about a four-hundred-square-mile search area."

"Just four hundred square miles?" said O'Reilly.

"We hoped to pull some recent satellite imagery of the area," said Mann. "Or order new imagery?"

"Yeah. I don't think that's going to happen," said O'Reilly. "Not under the current circumstances."

"That's what I figured," said Mann. "Shit. Four hundred square miles in the middle of nowhere. I suppose we can charter a plane or something to try and narrow things down. I have a rainy-day fund."

"I might have a source that can help us out," said O'Reilly. "It's kind of a long shot, but given ODNI's sudden interest in this matter, maybe the government has something going on out there."

"Any help would be appreciated," said Mann. "The plan right now is to head south to Des Moines and link up with the rest of the team. Replace our vehicles. Then drive to New Mexico. We've already gone dark, and I'm going to ditch this phone after we hang up."

"I'll need a way for my source to get in touch with you—if he can help," said O'Reilly. "Not the encrypted app. We need to reserve that for critical communications between you and me."

He turned to Mayer in the back seat. "Can you give me a phone number I can use for a one-time call?"

"Hold on," she said, reading off a number a few seconds later.

"I got it," said O'Reilly, reading it back. "Keep that line open and keep the phone close. I have no idea how long it'll take for him to do some digging, or even if he'll be willing to stick his neck out this far. Hell. I'm not even sure I'll be able to reach him. He's a bit elusive, but I trust him without any hesitation or reservations. He'll help us if he can."

"Beggars can't be choosers, right?" said Mann. "We'll keep our fingers crossed that he turns something up."

"Okay. My time in the bathroom is up," said O'Reilly. "No more calls unless it's a dire emergency. I'll keep this phone with me and check messages every hour or so. I'll also check the encrypted message board hourly."

"Sounds good. I'll let you get to your dry cappuccino," said Mann.

"Sorry about all of this, Garrett," said O'Reilly. "I've seen some shitty things happen to good people in my career. You've probably heard some rumors."

"I have," said Mann.

"This is right up there at the top of that list of shitty things," said O'Reilly. "Just know that I have your back. I'll go to jail before I screw your team over in any way."

"I'll pass that along to the team," said Mann. "It'll mean a lot to them."

"Good luck, Garrett," said O'Reilly. "My source's first name is Karl. He'll reference Ukraine when he calls. If you get a call from anyone using a different name, hang up immediately. If Karl doesn't reference Ukraine in his introduction, it means he can't help you. Politely hang up. Be sure to use my first name in your initial back-and-forth with him. That's his cue that you're not compromised."

"Understood," said Mann. "Watch your back."

"Always," said O'Reilly, ending the call.

Baker commented from the driver's seat. "We're going to need a bigger team."

Mann stifled a laugh. A variation of a classic line from one of his favorite movies.

"Serrano is working on that," said Mann.

"Can we trust Serrano's people?" said Mayer.

"I don't think we have a choice," said Mann.

CHAPTER 44

She'd been summoned. No surprise there. O'Reilly paused on the stairwell landing that led to Executive Assistant Director James's office. James ran the Criminal, Cyber, Response, and Services Branch (CCRSB), easily the FBI's largest and most wide-ranging group. The Criminal Investigative Division alone had nearly six thousand agents, analysts, and staff. Over five hundred of them were assigned to jobs in this building. Considered the backbone of the Bureau, CID was just one of several sprawling and diverse divisions or groups within CCRSB, all of which played critical roles in safeguarding Americans here in the US and abroad.

O'Reilly's Critical Incident Response Group was significantly smaller, but far more diverse. She oversaw everything from the FBI's Surveillance and Aviation Section to the famed Hostage Rescue Team, considered one of the most elite tactical teams in the world. The list was exhaustive, some of the sections so specialized, they weren't found on the rosters of any law enforcement agency—like the Counter-Improvised Explosive Device Section.

But nothing rivaled the uniqueness of ARTEMIS. A team specifically formed to hunt down the nation's most prolific and elusive serial killers along the southern border. The group so unlike anything they'd fielded before, nobody knew where to stick them. CID didn't want them, mostly because Mann had insisted on a level of field autonomy for his team that didn't match that division's bureaucratic and rather by-the-book reputation. The fact that most of the members of the team were castoffs didn't sit well with CID, either. They had a reputation to uphold.

When O'Reilly discovered Mann was looking to find a home for his proposed team of misfit toys, she volunteered to adopt them as a provisional task force. Unfortunately, it looked like ARTEMIS was about to have its provisional status revoked. The task force disbanded. She didn't see any other scenario playing out here. Not with them going rogue. O'Reilly just hoped that they could accomplish their mission before the inevitable dragnet caught them. There was only so much she could do to help them from headquarters.

She was essentially down to three tactics. All of them indirect forms of assistance. Stall for time. Carefully withhold information that could lead to their capture. Gently misdirect efforts to capture the team. And she could only get away with these for so long. James didn't rise through the ranks to lead one of the FBI's most important groups because she was slow on the uptake. O'Reilly had to give the performance of a lifetime in the next few minutes. She swiped her security badge and entered the floor.

The moment she walked into the CCRSB executive suite, one of James's administrative assistants waved her over.

"Director James is ready for you," he said.

No, she isn't. And I'm not ready for her. When the door closed, James shut her laptop and motioned for O'Reilly to take a seat in one of the chairs in front of her desk. No words. Certainly, no morning coffee on the couch in her sitting area.

"I wanted to bring you the news in person," said O'Reilly.

"A few tersely worded emails beat you to the punch," said James. "What the fuck is Mann thinking?"

"He's thinking he can catch this guy," said O'Reilly.

James shook her head. "I hope he's right, because that's the only thing that might, and I do mean might, save his career. Actually. No. His career is over. Catching that serial killer might be the only thing that keeps him out of jail and a full forfeiture of any benefits accrued at the FBI over the years."

"I'm sure he's well aware of that," said O'Reilly.

"What about the rest of his team? They're in the same boat."

"He's not holding them hostage," said O'Reilly. "Hopefully."

"This is a real shit show, Dana," said James. "Did he give you any indication that he would bolt?"

"Other than just being who he is? No," said O'Reilly. "But this doesn't entirely surprise me. I should have stressed that when we spoke. I could have delayed calling him until agents from the Minneapolis field office got there. Had them escort ARTEMIS to the airport."

A little blame absorption went a long way to . . .

"I should have thought of that," said James. "But it was early. And I underestimated his resolve. Now we have a real problem on our hands. I have the deputy director breathing down my neck. Someone bigger than all of us breathing down his."

. . . deflect a lot of blame.

"Do you have any idea what's behind the push to pull him out of the field?" said O'Reilly. "Other than two shoot-outs in twenty-four hours. Is it possible the killer is somehow connected to an investigation or operation sponsored by a member of the US Intelligence Community? Like a confidential informant?"

"I have no idea," said James. "All I know is that someone or some group very high up wants him pulled from the field. And another group wants him dead. Not a good combination for the FBI—or Mann. For his own safety, he needs to surrender himself and his team to the nearest field office. We can protect him. Do you have any way to contact him?"

"No. Every phone or electronic device linked to ARTEMIS went dark several miles north of Owatonna," said O'Reilly. "Did you hear the rest?"

"Just what you told me about an hour ago," said James. "And a growing list of emails confirming that Mann's team did not get on that flight. I was hopeful he might show up at the last minute. Maybe he was just being cautious. I wouldn't have blamed him for that. Not after what they just went through. So. What's the rest?"

O'Reilly figured there was no harm in being the first to tell her news she would soon learn anyway, or revisit information she could access at any time or had already heard in a briefing.

"He took all the assassination team's weapons with him. Same with their night vision gear and helmets," said O'Reilly.

"Helmets?"

O'Reilly shrugged. "I don't know. He told local LEOs something about rushing the weapons up to the Minneapolis field office for immediate forensic examination."

"Wonderful," said James. "Any idea where he's headed? He's clearly not going to the field office."

"No. Heading north has to be a ruse," said O'Reilly. "ARTEMIS had been tracking murders west from Iowa to Colorado and south through Kansas, Oklahoma, Texas, and New Mexico. There's no telling where he's headed. He could backtrack south for all we know."

"Damn it," said James. "Our field offices are already stretched thin. The last thing we need is to divert time and resources to track down Mann. I'm sure he's not a danger, but I've been ordered to stand him down, and I don't appreciate rogue agents. I don't have any choice but to mobilize teams to find him."

O'Reilly nodded. "Do you want me to move some aviation and surveillance assets into the area to assist? Even a Hostage Rescue Team. I could deploy a group to Kansas City or Denver. Just in case. I agree with you that Mann's team doesn't pose a danger to anyone, but their behavior this morning is anything but normal. More like desperate. And desperate people don't always think things through like they should."

Her real intention was to put the group in place to help Mann in case his team ran into trouble they couldn't handle.

"Not yet. Not until we get a better handle on where he might be and what he's up to," said James, glancing at her phone. "Now I get to stand on the carpet and explain this to the deputy director."

"Want me to come with you? Draw some heat," said O'Reilly, really hoping she said no.

"Absolutely not. Your reputation precedes you."

"I didn't realize I had a reputation," said O'Reilly.

"Ha! Why do you think I insisted on keeping you at CIRG after Sharpe left?" said James.

"My charming personality."

"Uh-huh," said James, getting up from her seat and walking around the desk. "Dana. If he reaches out to you, do whatever you can to convince him to come in from the field. I'm not asking you to betray his trust. You could be saving his life—and the lives of everyone on that team."

"I will," said O'Reilly, following her to the door. "And I know."

And she would reach out to Mann to try to talk him out of whatever suicide mission he was planning.

CHAPTER 45

McCall motioned for Powell to take a seat at the small table in the SCIF attached to his office. *Must be nice,* thought Powell. He still had to scurry out of his office to a shared SCIF, like someone with a bout of food poisoning, whenever he needed to conduct highly sensitive business—which happened several times a day. The SCIF scheduled for construction inside his office couldn't come fast enough.

"I have Diego Nataros on the line," said McCall.

Nataros, a former CIA officer directly affiliated with SINKHOLE, now ran the LABYRINTH facility. Nobody—outside of McCall, likely—really knew what role Nataros had when the CIA ran the show. He seemed competent enough and looked the part. Juárez Cartel tattoos, whether fake or real, up and down his neck. A few on his face. His arms totally inked—probably real.

Things seemed to have been under control at LABYRINTH, until a few days ago. They should have seen this coming. He should have seen this coming.

Alejandro had an insatiable appetite for torture and murder. Everyone involved with LABYRINTH understood this. Why the hell had they given him this much room to run? He was nothing more than a celebrity pit bull, kept around to lend credibility to the program and scare new recruits into compliance. Recruits who couldn't be persuaded to join DOMINION became Alejandro's personal property, to be dealt with however he saw fit. Inside LABYRINTH.

That had been their mistake. His mistake, too. Alejandro wasn't a vulture, who ate roadkill or circled around a dying meal until it was time to eat. He was an apex predator, who preferred to hunt live prey on his own terms. A predator who enjoyed the hunt, just as much as he enjoyed the kill. And apparently savored extreme torture.

Feeding him captives was like pushing a dead or injured animal in front of a lion. They'll eat if they're starving, but they vastly prefer to hunt and kill their own prey. Nobody in the program should have been surprised by yesterday's revelations about Alejandro's exploits over the past few years. They let a prolific serial killer drive back and forth from New Mexico to Minnesota, passing through pastures filled with unsuspecting lambs. What the hell did they think would happen?

"Diego. It's Gerald McCall. Are we alone?"

"I have Sergio Alvarez with me," said Nataros.

Sergio Alvarez, LABYRINTH's head of security, looked even scarier than Nataros. Full-face tattoos. Like your worst cartel nightmare. Perfect for the task at hand, but unnerving to be around.

"That's fine," said McCall. "He should be read into this, given the potential threat to the facility."

"What are we looking at?" said Nataros.

"Hopefully nothing. But I'm not one to take chances. Garrett Mann's surprisingly resourceful task force of FBI agents has gone dark. As in not a trace of them anywhere. They drove out of Owatonna a few hours ago and vanished from the grid," said McCall. "After a very spectacular failure to take them out."

"There's no way Mann will find LABYRINTH," said Alvarez.

"For real. This place is virtually invisible. Just rocky desert as far as the eye can see," said Nataros. "No public road for miles. Nothing at all for miles."

"Like twenty miles in any direction," said Alvarez.

"He found Cedar Lake," said Powell.

"Powell is right. His team is resourceful," said McCall. "Does Alejandro understand the predicament he's put us in?"

Predicament? That was an understatement. More like the catastrophic collapse of everything AXIOM had been working toward for the past several years.

"Sergio?" said Nataros.

"I've got that motherfucker locked down hard," said Alvarez. "Full house arrest. And he doesn't like it. But that bitch has to deal with the consequences, yo."

Yo? Sounds like Alvarez might be taking his role a little too seriously. Or he wasn't playing a role. Powell leaned over and whispered, "What do we know about Alvarez?" McCall shrugged. *Seriously? Not good. Jesus.* Who did they have running the show down there?

"Okay. We still need Alejandro's cooperation, so maybe we don't come down on him too hard," said McCall. "We still have about a hundred positions to fill. But we obviously can't have him running amok anymore. His life in Minneapolis is burned, so let's promise him something sweeter. A house in La Jolla overlooking the Pacific perhaps? Provided he stays at LABYRINTH until we're done."

"Can I suggest something?" said Powell.

"Of course," said McCall.

"Alejandro will never stop killing. He might slow down for a while, but he'll never truly stop," said Powell. "He picked Minneapolis for a reason. We didn't force him to live there. He could have picked anywhere in the United States, but he chose Cedar Lake."

"It seemed an odd choice, but nothing too flagrant, so we went along with it," said McCall.

"Exactly—and he chose to drive back and forth to LABYRINTH. Drive. Not fly, like we offered. Why?" said Powell. "So he could kill—again and again. He will never stop killing. If we set him up in a mansion overlooking the Pacific, he'll start killing again soon enough. His methods are unique and unmistakable. Eventually, he'll get caught—and boy will he have a tale to tell. Imagine if Mann had grabbed him at Cedar Lake? Do you really think he'd keep LABYRINTH to himself and spend the rest of his life in a maximum-security prison on our behalf? I'd put a bullet in his head right now and call it good. I'd even consider evacuating and sanitizing the facility before Mann's team shows up and brings hellfire and brimstone down upon us."

"Mann is on the run from his own people from what I understand," said Nataros.

"He is," said McCall. "I've made sure of it."

"And we have a full security team here," said Nataros. "I'm not worried."

"At the very least consider moving the current recruits out of LABYRINTH. Wipe the whiteboard. Remove the computer hardware. Just make the place look a little less like a staging area for an insurgency," said Powell. "At least until we neutralize Mann."

"The current class isn't ready," said Nataros. "They still have at least a month to go before they're ready for deployment. Raul is on his way. He'll seal the deal while they get the last of their training."

"Gerald," said Powell. "We absolutely can't risk having both Raul and Alejandro in the same place at the same time. Ever. If LABYRINTH goes down for whatever reason, we can't resurrect the training program without one of them. And DOMINION isn't ready. We need more operatives."

"We're pretty close to deploying enough operatives to execute our plan," said McCall.

"Pardon the cliché, but *close* only counts in horseshoes and hand grenades," said Powell. "I still have critical positions that need to be filled. We're still three or four classes away from filling them. That's a year. Minimum. We need to do whatever we can to keep the program alive. Get rid of Alejandro."

"Raul isn't exactly a saint," said Nataros.

"None of them are," said Powell. "But he's discreet. And oddly grateful, like any normal person might be under these circumstances. Alejandro chose to live in the middle of the country, so he could trawl the wide expanses of the Great Plains for victims. Get rid of him. He's too much of a liability."

"Mr. Powell has a solid point," said Nataros.

No shit, Sherlock.

"I have an idea," said McCall.

No doubt a bad one.

"Since Alejandro is already on site, let's have him finish the current class's training," said McCall. "Send Raul back to California. Jeremy is right. We can't afford to lose both of them."

"We can't afford to lose the facility," said Powell. "Maybe we kill him and put him in Mann's path. Let Mann emerge as the big hero? Or call our friends at the CIA and hand them the body, so they can concoct a story about how they saved the day somehow. They're good at making shit up."

"It's not a bad idea," said McCall. "Like you said, Alejandro is compromised. He's a serious liability."

"He had a good run," said Powell. "But he got greedy. A cautionary tale for Raul."

"The candidates respond to Alejandro better than Raul," said Nataros. "For what it's worth."

"That's because he's a fucking psychopath," said Powell. "Like—on a different level than Raul or anyone we've come across. He served his purpose. It's time to let him go."

"Diego?" said McCall.

"Yes, sir?"

"We'll keep Alejandro around for now. He'll fill in for Raul until the current class graduates," said McCall. "When the class is deployed, or at the first sign of trouble, put him down. I don't want him falling into the wrong hands. Also, let's start emptying the place out. Jeremy is right. If Mann somehow manages to find LABYRINTH, I don't want him walking away with anything that can shut down DOMINION."

"I'll dilute the operation to the point where we're just finishing the current class's training," said Nataros. "If Mann brings the FBI down on us while training is still in session, we'll terminate the recruits and Alejandro. It'll basically look like an underground university."

"Jeremy?" said McCall.

"Better," said Powell. "But the key here is making sure that a raid on the facility—however unlikely—can't unravel DOMINION. I know I sound like a broken record, but we're too close to the finish line to risk everything on some loser FBI agent who thinks he's just chasing down a serial killer."

"Good. Let's start winding things down at LABYRINTH, until we have a better handle on any inbound threats," said McCall. "Obviously, the situation is fluid. If we eliminate Mann's team or he's pulled out of the field by his own people, we can reevaluate those plans. Likewise, if we detect an imminent threat, we can go scorched earth on the facility. We're close to the finish line, and I'd like to cross it at a full sprint, instead of limping along."

McCall gave Powell a thumbs-up, which he dutifully returned. Hopefully his face reflected the same level of faux enthusiasm.

"Do you want me to beef up security?" said Nataros. "Or would that not be in line with reducing our footprint?"

Powell shook his head. If anything, he'd recommend reducing LABYRINTH's security footprint to the minimum level required to exterminate the guests if the government raided the facility. That's all that mattered. That and removing any sensitive information sooner than later.

"Let's keep the current security posture," said McCall, giving him another thumbs-up. "We can always adjust it up or down as the situation dictates."

Powell feigned a smile and nodded.

"Sounds good, sir," said Nataros. "LABYRINTH is in good hands. You can count on us."

"Thank you, gentlemen," said McCall, ending the call.

McCall turned to Powell and sighed. "You want to firebomb the place, don't you?"

"Nuke it from orbit. It's the only way to be sure," said Powell.

"Okay, Hicks," said McCall, surprisingly catching the reference from the movie *Aliens*. "We'll keep that option on the table as a last resort."

"Maybe I should head down there," said Powell. "Nataros knows what he's doing. He was part of the original SINKHOLE program. But I don't know about Alvarez. He strikes me as more of a prison guard than a paramilitary professional."

"Isn't that essentially a big part of his job?" said McCall.

"I suppose," said Powell. "But we can't afford a major fuckup down there. I can better prioritize the evacuation of DOMINION materials if I'm down there. That's my biggest concern. That and making sure nobody with knowledge of the program is taken alive."

"Including yourself?" said McCall.

"If the place is raided while I'm down there, and I can't escape," said Powell, "I'll gladly suck in several lungfuls of hydrogen cyanide. It's the price of doing business. I'm just not convinced that Nataros and Alvarez will see it the same way."

"It's up to you," said McCall. "I don't think we're going to have a problem at LABYRINTH, but your presence would undoubtedly make a difference if Mann pulled off the impossible."

"Then I'll get down there right away," said Powell.

CHAPTER 46

Serrano nudged Mann from the driver's seat, waking him out of a shallow sleep. Something buzzed nearby.

"Your phone," she said.

He'd passed out somewhere west of Kansas City. After meeting up with the rest of the team on the outskirts of the city and replacing their bullet-riddled, very FBI-looking convoy for two slightly less conspicuous full-size SUVs and the spare Expedition, they headed toward Colorado. A straight shot south by southwest to New Mexico would be too obvious. They'd take a more circuitous route and stick to side roads, before turning south toward New Mexico.

"Thank you," he said, rubbing his face vigorously to shake off the sleep.

He grabbed the phone from the center console cup holder, not bothering to check the caller ID.

"This is Special Agent Mann."

"Like an updated version of the Johnny Rivers song," said a dry voice.

Mann shrugged. He had no idea what that meant. "Sorry. The reference is lost on me."

"Before your time, I guess," said the caller. "My name is Karl, and I heard you were interested in travel recommendations to Europe."

"Yes. Our mutual friend Dana highly recommended you," said Mann.

"Dana's kind of partial to Ukraine, but with the ongoing conflict, I'd look more into Central Europe right now. Poland, the Czech Republic, and Austria are wonderful this time of year."

"I was thinking of something in the desert," said Mann.

"Okay. We can cut the bullshit now," said Karl. "Based on the search area Dana gave me, I asked a source to see if we ever had anything going out there. I figured it wouldn't be hard to find on the books if anything ever existed. Central New Mexico is outside our normal purview. To my surprise and the source's, we did have something there at one point. Rather recently in fact. I have some coordinates for you."

"Give me a few seconds to grab a pen and something to write on," said Mann, glancing back at Mayer, who handed him a notepad and pen. "Okay. Ready."

Karl relayed a ten-digit GPS coordinate, which Mann repeated back.

"So. Here's the deal," said Karl. "I just gave you the coordinates to what we called a service entrance back in my day. A kind of back door for a cleaning crew. But not the kind of crew that vacuums floors and dusts shelves. The kind that comes in to perform a deep clean—if you catch my drift."

"I do," said Mann.

"Because of the very nature of their purpose, the locations of these service entrances are never known to the occupants. In this case, the service entrance is a half-mile-long tunnel. It won't be illuminated. It may not be ventilated. It may be blocked at some point by a natural or intentional cave-in. As you can imagine, these service entrances weren't very popular with site occupants."

"I can imagine," said Mann, frantically scribbling a note for Mayer, which he handed back to her.

Research and order emergency escape breathing devices— EEBDs—15 minute capacity. Need ASAP. Access to facility may be unventilated. ½ mile tunnel.

She nodded and started typing away.

"My source didn't have any details on where it would put you in the facility, but typically it'll dump you somewhere out of the way. Bring explosives, crowbars, blowtorches, thermite. The works. Typically, the breach points are designed to provide quick and easy access to the facility, but there's no telling what you'll find at the end of that half-mile tunnel. Someone may have unknowingly placed a wall of lockers against the breach point."

"Got it. Thank you," said Mann. "Do you have any information on the facility itself?"

"All my source told me was that the site is listed as deactivated," said Karl. "And that it's underground. Well, I assumed that based on the tunnel description. But I think it's a fair assumption."

"Is there any way it's listed as deactivated but is still active?" said Mann.

"I asked the same question, and the answer is—you won't know until you breach the facility. Sorry. Bad joke," said Karl. "I think it's fair to say, based on my source's reputation for accuracy, that the original owners have moved out. If the site is currently occupied, it's under new management. May I offer you a word of caution?"

"Of course," said Mann.

"If the site is operational—it wasn't taken over by the local school district," said Karl. "We custom build sites like these to serve very specific purposes. The new owners probably haven't strayed too far from the original purpose of this location. Expect it to be well guarded."

"Good advice," said Mann. "Can you say which agency originally occupied the site?"

"You just answered your own question," said Karl.

"I can think of more than one agency," said Mann.

"But which one did you think of first?" said Karl, ending the call.

The Central Intelligence Agency. Made sense given what he'd said earlier about central New Mexico being outside their normal purview. But why would the CIA have a covert, underground site in the middle of New Mexico? The answer? Back to what Karl said. *They wouldn't know until they breached the facility.*

"Mayer. What's the price tag on the breathing devices?" said Mann.

"Six hundred a pop."

"Cata. How many of your associates are headed north?" said Mann.

"Eleven. And it's a solid crew," said Serrano.

Eleven plus eight. Nineteen. Times six hundred.

"Thirteen thousand dollars, with tax," said Mayer, reading his mind.

"That's a big hit to our budget," said Mann. "But I don't see any other option. Unless we open the door, or whatever we find at the coordinates, and blow air into the tunnel? We can rig up some fans to a battery, right?"

"No," said Serrano and Mayer at the same time. Mayer continued, "If the tunnel is devoid of oxygen, and sealed off at one end, we'd need the kind of fan you find attached to the back of one of those swamp boats. Even that might not be enough. We're talking about a half mile. Twenty-six-hundred feet."

"Then we have to order the breathing devices," said Mann. "If we show up at these coordinates, and we can't breathe in the tunnel, we've hit an impasse."

"For two days," said Serrano. "We could open the tunnel and test the air. If the air is shit, we order the breathers. If the air is good, we proceed."

"It's not a bad idea," said Mann. "I just don't know how much time we have until *they* find us."

"*They,*" said Serrano. "Who exactly are *they?*"

"That's the big question," said Mann. "What exactly did we stumble on? And how deep and far does it go?"

"And how much time do we have? Realistically," said Mayer. "Before *they* catch up with us."

"Order the breathers," said Serrano. "We can always resell or return them. The sooner we get this done, the better."

"Okay. Order the EEBDs," said Mann. "And order two gas detectors that can measure oxygen levels."

"I need somewhere to send them," said Mayer. "Should I look for an Airbnb in Albuquerque? That would give us a mailing address."

"Yes. Shit. I didn't even think of that," said Mann, before turning to Serrano. "Can your associates meet us in Albuquerque?"

"That's fine," said Serrano. "It's less than a half-day drive from Ciudad Juárez."

"Then that's that," said Mann. "We'll plan the op and drive south when we're ready. It's a three-hour drive from Albuquerque to the coordinates Karl gave me."

"Do you think he's CIA?" said Serrano.

"Sounds like it," said Mann.

"Dios ayudanos," said Serrano.

"Sí," said Mann. "We're going to need all the help we can get."

CHAPTER 47

Three well-worn, classic American SUVs idled outside the team's sprawling eastern hills rental estate, waiting for Serrano to let them in. She pressed the remote control that opened the property's streetside sliding gate and guided the drivers into a small parking area under a canopy of ash trees. When the collection of classic American four-wheel-drive vehicles—two rust-spotted Broncos and a boxy Jeep Cherokee—had pulled into the shade, Serrano's associates emerged.

They formed a loose gaggle behind the vehicles. Eleven in total. Nine of them women. Serrano gave them a once-over, recognizing everyone immediately. Sofia, a former Mexican Army officer and the de facto leader of the group, nodded and gave her a thumbs-up. She triggered her radio transmitter.

"We're good," said Serrano.

If Sofia or anyone on the team assembled behind the vehicles had given off bad vibes or even the slightest hint that something was off, she would have calmly walked back into the house—and Mann would have taken them into custody. Within moments of Serrano's transmission, the entire ARTEMIS team emerged from various concealed locations surrounding the property's parking area and assembled around Serrano.

"This is a serious-looking crew," said Mann. "Welcome? I'm not sure what to say. Thank you is probably a better starting point. *Muchas gracias. Estamos en dueda contigo.*" We are in your debt.

"*Habla español?*" said Sofia, her question aimed at Serrano.

"Pasable pero limitado," said Serrano. *"Mismo con el resto."*

Passable but limited. The same with the rest.

"Bien," said Sofia. "The same for most of us with *inglés*. A few members of the team speak very little English. Just what they've seen on TV. Cata. *Tu inglés es impresionante."*

"Cuando en Roma," said Serrano, before turning to Mann. "Are you following most of this?"

"Más o menos," said Mann. *"En serio, Sofia. No puedo agradecerte lo suficiente. Todos ustedes. Bienvenido."* Seriously. I can't thank you enough. All of you. Welcome.

"I like this guy. His Spanish is textbook, but he's clearly made an effort," said Sofia, stepping forward. "Good to see you."

Serrano embraced her, and the two held each other for several seconds. Sofia's mother had gone missing a few months after Serrano's mother. The two of them had gone through the Chihuahua State Police Academy program together, Sofia graduating first in the class and earning a transfer immediately upon graduation to Heroico Colegio Militar—Mexico's military academy. Four years later, she was back in Ciudad Juárez. Assigned to a long-standing, corrupt counternarcotics military task force. Like Serrano, her days in government service had been numbered from the start.

"He can be trusted to do the right thing, and that's all that counts in this business," said Serrano, before turning to Mann. "Don't let that go to your head."

"Believe me. It didn't," said Mann, holding up his hands. "So, the sooner we get through the introductions, the quicker we can feed everyone. I imagine it's been a long day for your team, Sofia."

"It's not my team in the . . . uh . . . *cómo se dice 'en el sentido tradicional'?"* said Sofia.

"In the traditional sense. I get it," said Mann. "I'd like to think I'm in charge of my team, but I'm not entirely sure that's true, either."

Pretty much everyone laughed, understanding his joke. A few of Sofia's people chuckled politely, clearly not getting what he said.

Nothing against them—but he took note. A language barrier in a fire-fight spelled doom.

"Que bueno," said Sofia. Excellent.

"Three teams?" said Mann.

"Sí. Navaja is my team," said Sofia, two of the Mexicans gathering around her. A male and a female. "Mateo is a former Guardia Nacional. Machine gun operator. And Malena is a former Chihuahua state police officer."

"Navaja?" said Mann.

"Named after the traditional Spanish fighting blade," said Sofia.

Serrano produced her *navaja,* flicking it into the open position, provoking smiles and nods from the Mexicans. Mann examined the blade in her hand, somehow having the sense not to ask her to hand it to him. You never relinquished your *navaja.* It was considered an extension of your essence as a fighter.

"That's one hell of a knife," said Mann. "Is it a family heirloom?"

"No," said Serrano, noticing that Sofia and most of the Mexican team didn't understand the term. *"Reliquia de familia."*

"Ah. I see," said Sofia, producing her own. "No. Not typically. Unless one of your parents was a thief or a murderer with roots back to nineteenth-century Spain."

"Never know, right?" said Serrano, closing her knife and putting it back in her pocket.

"Hacha. Or axe," Sofia said, pointing to three members of the team who had clustered together to her left. "They're our—*cómo se dice*—heavy hitters? Is that right?"

"Sí," said Mann.

"Bueno. Javier is former National Guard SWAT. Amelia and Daniela are former, seasoned Chihuahua state police officers with serious counternarcotics experience," said Sofia. "Last but not least, is *Lanza."*

"Spear," said Mann.

"Muy bien," said Sofia, turning to Serrano. "He's not bad."

"Don't let him fool you," said Serrano, getting a laugh out of pretty much everyone.

"*Claro que sí,*" said Sofia. "*Lanza* is more of a stealth, precision team. Zita is former Naval Infantry. A Marine?"

"*Sí,*" said Mann.

"Tianna and Bianca are former Chihuahua state police officers," said Sofia. "They specialized in surveillance. Stakeouts. But on the street. Not sitting in a van. And then we have Neva and Gloria, who were state police academy candidates, but dropped out to take care of their families after their mothers disappeared."

Mann turned to Serrano. "Can you translate for me? I don't want any of this to get lost—in translation."

"Of course," she said, kind of worried about what he planned to say.

"I'll keep this short and simple," said Mann. "For my own benefit—but especially yours."

When Serrano translated his words into Spanish, the entire Mexican contingent briefly laughed—and seemed to relax just a little. Their deeply lined faces softened. Shoulders relaxed.

"Everyone here has lost someone, somehow to the inexplicable darkness out there—with no real closure. Some of the victims have been found. Most haven't. Justice certainly isn't something any of us have experienced," said Mann, pausing so Serrano could translate.

The buy-in was immediate. She could see it on their faces.

"That's why we're all here, on some level," said Mann. "From what Cata has told me over the past year, the Mexican system either forced all of you out or you quit—because you couldn't accept their *official* narrative about why your family members, spouses, friends, and neighbors disappeared or were murdered. You originally joined the military or the police to make a difference, but found out that the powers that be either didn't care or were powerless to help. Unfortunately, it's not that different up here."

Serrano struggled to keep her emotions in check. She knew Mann's story. And Mann knew hers. She knew all the ARTEMIS stories. She used to think that some of the agents, like Turner, had less of a stake in the task force, but listening to Mann right now, Serrano understood that everyone was here for the same reason.

"Justice," said Serrano. *"Justicia."*

Mann looked at her and nodded. "Exactly. I don't know how that works given what we're up against, but what I do know is that the serial killer we've been tracking in the United States for the past year and a half uses the same methods that were used for close to a decade in Ciudad Juárez. The team's medical examiner strongly felt that this was not a coincidence. He was burned alive, by a US-based team somehow affiliated with this serial killer."

"How are they affiliated?" said Sofia.

"We don't know," said Serrano.

"But we think we've tracked this killer to a specific location about three hours south of here," said Mann.

"Think?" said Zita, SPEAR team leader.

"I'll explain in detail later," said Mann. "But for now, we've received intelligence about a former CIA facility in central New Mexico. We're fairly certain this is where they took our killer."

"What kind of intelligence?" said Sofia. "And who are *they*?"

"*They* are still a mystery," said Mann.

"But the intelligence is solid," said Serrano. "Even if it's a bit sparse."

"How sparse?" said Sofia.

"We have the coordinates for a back door to a facility that the CIA claims is inactive," said Serrano. "And it's underground."

"That's it?" said Zita.

"That's it," said Mann. "What we know is that our killer disappeared in the general vicinity of a former CIA bunker of some kind. We just don't know a damn thing about the facility. That's the whole point of this party. To figure out exactly why the occupants of that site are protecting a prolific serial killer. He's killed dozens north of the border over the past few years."

Javier, AXE team leader, raised his hand. Serrano nodded at him.

"Do we have any idea what we're up against?"

"No," said Serrano. "All we know is that we'll be taking a half-mile-long, supposedly secret tunnel into the facility."

"Supposedly?" said someone.

"It's a back door, built specifically for covert entry into the facility if the occupants went rogue," said Mann, Serrano quickly translating. "No light. Maybe no air. Everyone will have their own oxygen source. A personal breathing device."

"And weapons?" said Javier.

"Plenty of weapons and ammunition. Some night vision. Some body armor and helmets," said Mann. "Not the over-the-counter stuff we'd originally stockpiled for you. Serious shit. Suppressed rifles. Drum-fed automatic rifles similar to the M27. Grenades. Flash-bangs. The works. We're going in heavy. Hopefully we won't need to."

Mann gave Serrano a look and nodded. They'd discussed this part in advance of her associates' arrival.

"If you want to head back home," said Serrano. "That's perfectly fine. *En serio. Está bien.* We have no idea what we're walking into, but we'll be heavily armed and well equipped. If it turns out to be too much for us to handle, we'll turn back. That's a promise."

"Prometo," said Mann. *"Esta no es una misión suicida."*

"His Spanish isn't bad," said Sofia. "Is he married?"

Everyone laughed for a few moments, before Sofia turned to her team.

"Qué dicen todos?" What do you say?

Everyone voiced their approval. They were here to stay.

"Thank god," muttered Mann.

"Did you think some of them would go home?" said Serrano, under her breath.

"I expected *all* of them to go home," said Mann. "It's the smart thing to do."

"I never said they were smart," said Serrano, loud enough for Sofia to hear.

Sofia laughed. "I scored higher than her on my academy entrance exam, just in case you're curious."

"Oh. I'm very curious," said Mann. "Tell me more. Cata's like a closed book. That smokes a lot of cigarettes."

"Not a word," Serrano told her.

"Okay. Okay," said Sofia. "So. Are you going to introduce us to your new friends? Or is this going to be like one of those awkward *quinceañera* dances, where the girls and boys avoid each other for five hours?"

"Yes. Sorry," said Serrano. "Garrett? Introductions?"

"Me?"

"Sí," said Serrano. "Turner won't like what I have to say about him, and he's a little sensitive."

"Seriously?" said Turner. "Oh. She's definitely doing the introductions. This should be fun. Game on."

"Then let the games begin," said Serrano.

CHAPTER 48

They'd been at it for a few hours now, everyone up around dawn shaking off the cobwebs from the previous night's tequila shots and beer. That hadn't been Mann's idea. Certainly not ahead of tonight's mission. But Serrano's associates had brought the party favors, and who was he to deny them a proper reunion? And they needed an icebreaker, if the two groups were going to work together. A few hours of drinks and stories, over grilled meats, grocery store–prepared sides, and junk food, wasn't unreasonable.

His only firm ask was that the alcohol stopped flowing by 9:00 p.m., a request strictly honored by everyone. They understood what was at stake tomorrow. The house went close to silent around 10:00 p.m., only Serrano, Sofia, and a few others remaining around the firepit for another hour or so. A disciplined crew. Before turning in last night, Mann felt as good as possible about whatever lay ahead of them.

"I think we've balanced the teams nicely," said Mann. "Serrano and I will accompany KNIFE as the command-and-control team. In addition to sweeping and clearing assigned areas, we'll do our best to maintain overall situation awareness and direct efforts."

"Situation awareness *es muy importante* underground. It's not easy," said Javier, the former Mexican SWAT officer. "I've lost a lot of officers because nobody could talk to anybody."

Mann nodded. "When we get inside the complex, Agent Mayer will try to analyze their underground communications system. From the little I understand, they run cables through the tunnels, and the cables are designed to pick up radio transmissions and send them through the complex. It's called a leaker feeder system?"

Mayer nodded.

"If we can't piggyback onto their underground system, we think we have a workaround. Our handhelds can be turned into basic repeaters. They won't increase signal strength, but if we place them strategically, within rough line-of-sight of each other, we should be able to maintain some semblance of communications. Assuming this isn't a massive complex. We have a limited number of spare radios. If that doesn't work, we'll have to scavenge radios from whoever we find down there and switch frequencies."

"Whoever we kill," said Serrano.

"More or less," said Mann. "AXE will be our heavy-hitting sweep team. They'll clear and cover the most ground. Turner will carry one of the automatic rifles we took from the team in the cornfield back in Minnesota, in addition to his regular load out, just in case we run into unexpected resistance and need to either break through a tough spot or hold our ground. You'll be issued most of the grenades and explosives."

Turner high-fived Javier, Amelia, and Daniela—Mayer politely turning him down.

"We're ready to rock and roll," said Turner.

"SPEAR, led by Baker, will serve as our primary digital evidence collection team, after they've executed their sweep-and-clear duties. Rocha, my team's digital forensics expert, will work with Bianca, who was sent to the US by the Chihuahua State Police to learn digital forensics a few years ago," said Mann. "The two of you take whatever you can with you. We can analyze it later. Anything that can't be carried out and looks important will also be your responsibility. Rocha has a number of tools at her disposal to drain those machines of their data. Make sure to spend time today with Bianca so she can work on her own. I don't know how much time we'll have at the site."

"We'll make sure she has all the time she needs," said Baker.

"She has a computer science degree," said Rocha. "She knows what she's doing."

"Excellent. That leaves the EYES team. Jax will fly the Albatross overhead, with Mills watching the feeds. Neva and Gloria will provide security. The other automatic rifle will go to them," said Mann. "EYES will range ahead of us, stopping about five miles out to scan the ground and sky in the direction of the coordinates for drones or security. They'll stay there for the duration of the op. What else?"

"There's no information on the bunker?" said Sofia.

"No. We don't even know if it's actually underground," said Mann. "Google Maps doesn't show anything, other than an old ranch and a few outbuildings within a mile of the coordinates. We know the secret entrance is a half-mile tunnel. That's pretty much it. Which is why we're bringing so much shit with us. Night vision. Breaching charges. Shaped charges. Emergency oxygen tanks, which should be delivered this afternoon. We will be improvising from the moment we enter that tunnel."

"Have any of your agents been inside a cartel bunker or tunnel system?" said Javier.

A quick visual survey of their faces confirmed what he already knew.

"A few of us have been on tours of bunker systems on the border," said Mann. "Compliments of your government."

"Yeah. Well. This is going to be a steep learning curve for your people," said Javier. "Pretty much everyone here has taken part in raids on tunnels and bunkers. It's a shit experience. They turn out the lights, and it gets bad real fast. Your enemy knows the tunnels. You don't. They set traps everywhere. Cameras watching. It's like your worst nightmare."

"I don't doubt it," said Mann. "Which is why we're grateful you're all here. We're going to be relying on you. All of you. And you have my word that if things get out of hand down there, or it becomes clear that we're just not a big enough force to take down the facility, we'll retreat the way we came. The breathing devices are good for a two-way trip. This is not a suicide mission. I want this just as badly as the rest of you.

Trust me on that. I've been working up to this moment my entire career. But I won't sacrifice you to get what I want. *Prometo.*"

"Rules of engagement?" said Serrano. "We should clarify those."

"*Sí,*" said Mann. "Very simple. Take down anyone carrying a weapon or attempting to raise the alarm. We'll all have suppressed weapons and knives. Hog-tie the unarmed. Hands-to-feet so they can't get up and sound the alarm. Assume everyone is hostile. Take no chances."

"Vehicles?" said Zita, the Mexican Marine. "Are we bringing all of them?"

"Only what we need to keep our travel profile somewhat smaller," said Mann. "We need to transport nineteen. That's four vehicles. Five per vehicle."

Zita shook her head. "No. I think we need to bring all of them. Look, I trust you as far as Serrano trusts you, which is far. But my compadres and I will need to head south immediately when this is done. Your government will not give us medals and treat us to a fancy steak dinner. They'll throw us in jail, or worse—turn us over to La Guardia Nacional."

"She's right," said Serrano.

"Then we bring your three SUVs and one of ours," said Mann. "If we walk out of there alive, I'll make sure you get back home safely."

Baker checked his watch. "Cabela's opens at nine. Same with Surplus City. How about we nail some breakfast and do some shopping."

"Sounds good to me," said Mann. "Cata? Any last questions for now? Anything we didn't discuss that we need?"

"Thermal blankets," she said. "Basic Mylar foil blankets. Migrants use them at night to hide from thermal imaging. They're not perfect, but they'll reduce our infrared signature significantly during the hike from the vehicles to the back door. They're cheap and effective. We can cut holes to see and breathe through."

"Add Mylar blankets to the shopping list," said Mann. "What else?"

He hoped that was it. The current list was pretty extensive—and expensive. The entire Mexican contingent needed new hiking boots, military-style backpacks, CamelBak hydration systems, tactical vests with ammunition pouches, balaclavas, gloves, knee pads, goggles—pretty much everything. They couldn't risk bringing anything like that over the border with them. Despite their completely legitimate travel documents, US Border Patrol might have flagged or detained them if they tried to cross with paramilitary-looking gear. Mann wasn't sure how far their remaining credit cards and cash would stretch. They were about to find out. Serrano took a close look at the list.

"GoPro cameras would come in handy," said Mayer. "No need to stop and remove a digital camera while on the move. Just turn and point your body at whatever you want to document. The video is high-res. We can sift through the footage and create images later. I recommend that we equip two members of each team with a GoPro."

"How much?" said Mann.

"Four hundred a pop," said Mayer. "Another fifty or so for a viable vest mount."

They were getting close to squeezing their budget dry.

"We'll need documentation of what we've found," said Mann. "O'Reilly will stick her neck out for us, but she'll need something she can bring to her boss. I think we need the cameras."

"Beats taping a cell phone to your rifle or helmet," said Turner, getting some laughs.

"All right. Add six GoPros to the list," said Mann. "What else?"

"A thermal imaging scope might come in handy to spot sentries on the approach to the back door," said Serrano. "Do they even sell those in stores?"

"They probably do, but I don't think that's in the budget," said Mann. "Not with all the ammunition we still need to buy."

"We brought some *dinero* with us," said Sofia.

"You've given up enough to be here. Risked enough," said Mann. "I don't want you spending your own money."

"How much are we talking?" said Sofia.

"Seven hundred dollars for a basic handheld scope that should do the job," said Baker.

"That's steep. Like a month's pay," she said. "But we have the money—if you think it'll make a difference."

"It might," said Baker. "But the back door should be shielded from observation. Wouldn't be much of a secret entrance if it wasn't."

"And the drone is equipped with a thermal camera," said Jax. "It'll detect sentries in the open. I can steer you around them."

"But what if they're not fully in the open?" said Sofia. "What if they're under a tarp?"

"Then we could be looking at an ambush before we reach the door," said Baker. "At the very least some sniper activity. Most definitely a serious security response inside the facility."

"If you run out of money to buy the scope," said Sofia, "we'll buy it."

"I'll wire the money back to you if we end up needing it," said Mann.

"Deal," said Sofia.

"Then let's fire up some breakfast and go on a shopping spree," said Mann.

While the two groups teamed up to cook breakfast for nineteen, the Mexican team leaders, Serrano, Turner, and Mann gathered for a moment in front of the map displayed on the great room's massive, wall-mounted flat-screen TV.

"We really have no idea what we're up against?" said Javier.

"None. All we know is that the virus pinged two groups, who approached this general area, before their signals went dead. No cell or Wi-Fi coverage, no more pinging," said Mann. "A source in our government confirmed that there's an inactive CIA site within the search area. They gave us the coordinates to the back door. That's pretty much it."

"And the two teams we tangled with in Minnesota—"

"Tangled?" said Zita.

Serrano translated the meaning of *tangled*.

"The two teams were professional, well trained, and well equipped," said Turner. "We can expect the same inside this site."

"But you smoked them," said Javier. "Both times."

"More or less, we got the jump on them—both times," said Mann. "We can't count on that here, and we'll be fighting on their turf."

"*Sí.* That's bad news for us," said Javier. "Every doorway. Every hallway corner. Every stack of crates. Every dark room. Every single one of those represents a threat."

"Maybe we can smoke them out," said Zita. "I've seen that work."

"And I've seen it not work," said Javier. "Way more than it worked. They'll have masks. Powerful ventilation blowers. That trick only worked for so long before they adapted—and turned it against us. They masked up and used thermal scopes to pick us off in the tunnels."

"We're gonna have to do this the hard way," said Mann. "Room by room, until we find our killer. That's our primary mission. Whatever else is going on down there is secondary. Someone else can clean up that mess."

PART V

CHAPTER 49

Garrett Mann sat cross-legged with Jax and Mills, huddled around the laptop displaying the Albatross's drone control screen. The rest of the teams stood in a semicircle behind them, the entire group dimly illuminated by the screen. They'd picked this location as a drone control point and line of departure for the team because it was naturally screened from the provided coordinates, and presumably the target site, by a sizable rise in the desert landscape identified on a topographic map they'd downloaded online.

Not that it would matter for now. They sat well out of traditional thermal detection range, and Jax hadn't identified any aerial surveillance. The ultrahigh (UHF) or superhigh (SHF) line-of-sight frequencies used by commercial and military drones would have pinged the radio frequency (RF) detection antennae shooting thirty feet into the night sky behind them. In fact, they'd picked up no RF activity at all in the area.

"I think you're clear to move out," said Jax. "When do you want us to launch the drone?"

"Assuming the site hasn't mounted the kind of IR sensor you'd find on an Apache helicopter to a tower above them, we're most likely dealing with military grade or high-end, off-the-shelf thermal scopes. Best in market can detect a human at four thousand yards. Two point three miles," said Mann. "We'll be wearing the Mylar blankets, which should cut that down considerably. To be safe, I think you should launch when we're two miles out. You'll be able to steer us around any problems inside of that detection range."

"Sounds good. We'll have the drone ready to launch," said Jax. "Mills will place it on the county road when you give us the signal, assuming there's no traffic coming from either direction. Not that we've seen a single vehicle on this road since we turned south off State Road 246, twenty miles from here. It's about a quarter-mile hike back to the road, so Neva will accompany him for security."

"And sanity," said Mills. "It's so quiet and dark out here, you could lose your mind—and not in a bad way."

"Yeah. It's pretty amazing," said Sofia. "You don't see stars like this back in the city."

"The Milky Way galaxy is visible to the southeast," said Rocha. "Or something cool."

They all turned to take in the clearly visible, densely packed band of distant stars and faint gases that reached from high above and terminated on the horizon. They'd been out here for close to an hour, and he hadn't noticed it until now. Mann let them enjoy a few more moments of awe before moving things along.

"If you need a smoke, do it now," he said.

Half of the Mexican team chain-smoked like Serrano, but nobody took him up on the offer.

"I'm good," said Serrano. "Too nervous to smoke."

"That sounds a lot like an oxymoron," said Mann.

"I'm going to pretend you didn't just call me a name," she said.

"I didn't. It means—"

"I know what it means. Just fucking with you," she said. "You need to lighten up a little."

He paused, cocking his head.

"Close to an oxymoron?" said Serrano.

"You're getting the hang of it," said Mann, before turning to the others. "All right. Let's do this. Switch to night vision."

The group formed up in as straight a line as one could expect in the near pitch darkness of a moonless night in the middle of the desert—even with night vision goggles. The teams staggered their departures by roughly twenty yards, SPEAR setting off first with Zita walking point. She had extensive experience patrolling in the desert with Mexico's Marines. All the Mexicans had spent considerable time on counternarcotics patrols outside Ciudad Juárez or deep in Chihuahua—far more than anyone on ARTEMIS.

AXE followed the lead element, their harder-hitting capability just a radio call or whistle away if SPEAR detected or ran directly into trouble. KNIFE brought up the rear. Mann didn't like walking in the back, but from a command-and-control perspective, it made sense to keep both him and Sofia, the Mexicans' de facto leader, together where they could coordinate a response to any threats encountered on the way to the service entrance. Mann checked the muted screen on his GPS receiver. Five point two miles to the coordinates provided by mystery man Karl and his mystery source, who Mann suspected were one and the same.

CHAPTER 50

The hike took just under two hours, the mid-fifty-degree temperature and steady breeze keeping them comfortable the entire way. They took a short break around the one-hour mark to let Jax scan the area ahead of them with the Albatross drone's IR camera. Their path to the back-door coordinates was clear, but she identified eight human heat signatures roughly a half mile southwest of their destination—forming what looked to be an expansive 360-degree ring.

The presence of sentries a half mile away eased the fear that Serrano had dragged her compadres away from their lives for nothing. At the same time, she felt a little nauseous. They were about to descend into the unknown, and given the number of guards spotted on the surface, they could expect significant resistance down below. Some of them wouldn't walk away from this. It was a shitty burden to carry.

The service entrance Karl referenced had been easy enough to find. A weather-beaten, substantial-looking metal door set into the steep, rocky slope of the rise that kept them out of the sentries' line of sight for the duration of the hike. Easy to locate. Not so easy to open—quietly. The door had been secured to its steel frame with three heavy-duty, shrouded Master Locks. They couldn't use bolt cutters on these, and thermite cutting charges would light up half the desert. She knew the answer to their dilemma the moment she saw the padlocks.

"Anyone have the combinations?" said Turner.

Nobody laughed.

"I'll rig the C4 charges to detonate simultaneously," said Baker. "If we're gonna make noise, there's no point in making it easier for them to find us."

The sentries were unlikely to venture a half mile away from their posts unless they felt confident about the direction of the sound. A single detonation would give them a general idea of the direction. Multiple detonations, even tightly spaced, might allow them to better pinpoint the source. The security teams underground would likely be placed on a high-alert status due to the explosion, but if the topside sentries managed to find the door, security inside could be focused in the direction of the team's approach through the tunnel.

"I'll let Jax know," said Mann, "so she can watch for a reaction. You sure they won't see the explosion?"

"Not with this hunk of earth in the way," said Baker. "And not in the quantities I'll need to pop the locks. If we had a tree canopy above us, they might see a quick flash reflected off the leaves and branches."

"All right. I'll let you get to work," said Mann, before triggering his radio. "We're going to blow the locks open, which is going to make noise. We'll need to move fast to get out of sight in case they send people over or launch a drone to investigate. Prepare your emergency breathing devices."

Serrano quickly translated, so everybody was on the same page. A few minutes later, everybody was ready. Fortunately, it was pitch dark out because they would have looked utterly ridiculous. The emergency breathing devices were basically orange plastic hoods that sealed to the neck, connected by a hose to a cylinder tank you slung over your shoulder in what resembled a small nylon duffel bag. One minute they looked like a special operations team, the next—aliens from a low-budget science fiction movie.

Mann and team leaders walked up and down the line formed to the left of the door, checking everyone's gear with red-lensed flashlights. Each member of the team carried a flashlight with a red lens, for use under limited outdoor circumstances. They'd use the high-lumen tactical lights attached to their rifles and pistols for illumination in the bunker.

Mann checked in with Mayer, who stood nearby. "What do you think about leaving one of the repeater radios at the entrance? If the tunnel is a straight line, would the signal travel a half mile underground?"

"I don't see why it wouldn't," said Mayer. "It won't be the clearest connection, but as long as the tunnel is straight, it should work to some degree."

"Okay. After Baker blows the door, place one of the makeshift repeaters in the entrance," said Mann. "Contact Jax on the secondary frequency with any instructions she might need to access the signal."

"Got it," said Mayer.

Mann turned to Serrano and gave her rig a once-over, then patted her on the shoulder.

"All good. FYI. I'm going in right behind AXE," he said. "In case it gets too tight for us to squeeze by each other. I need to be able to assess and react as quickly as possible to whatever we run into. I hope you don't mind bringing up the rear."

"Why would I mind?" she said, hoping she didn't sound pissed off.

Because she was. Serrano had seen herself as one of the first inside the bunker, ready to drill holes in whoever had harbored the serial killer who butchered her mother.

"Because I know you," said Mann. "Once we're inside, it's payback time for all of us. I won't let you miss a moment of it."

"You better get moving," she said. "Or they'll die of old age before we get to them."

"Funny," said Mann, before moving back down the line.

His voice returned in her earpiece a few moments later. "Baker. Everyone is set."

"Copy that," said Baker. "Three. Two. One. Fire in the hole."

The Mexicans pressed their hands against the sides of their hoods to preserve their hearing. Serrano and the FBI agents remained still, the noise-canceling capabilities of their earpieces reducing the detonation to a safe, one-time level.

Several members of the team rushed the door after the blast, applying a combination of brute strength and a few crowbars to pry it open. It didn't look hopeful at first. The door didn't budge. Mann had been worried about that from the beginning. A door left exposed to the elements, and presumably unused for several years, felt like a big risk to take. A possible showstopper.

Which was why he'd brought enough explosives to blast through whatever they encountered, but only as a last resort. Not only would an explosion that big draw the sentries right to the door, but they ran the risk of collapsing the tunnel. Serrano started to walk over to the gaggle working on the door when a creaking sound cut through the night as the door swung open.

"We're in. Turn your oxygen on. *Activa tu oxigeno*," said Mann over the radio. "Cata. Don't bother trying to shut it behind you. It's heavy and the hinges are rusted. We barely got it open."

"Want me to rig a surprise inside?" said Serrano. "In case one of the sentries finds it and gets curious?"

"We don't have the time. The tanks are only good for fifteen minutes," said Mann. "And we may need to return the same way. In a hurry."

"Got it," said Serrano, motioning for Mateo to enter the tunnel.

Mateo pulled the lanyard protruding from the bag slung across his chest, which triggered the oxygen bottle's actuator and started the flow of oxygen. They'd all practiced this dozens of times throughout the afternoon. To stop the flow, they'd have to dig around a little inside and replace the cotter pin attached to the lanyard. He stuffed the lanyard into one of his trouser pockets and stepped into the tunnel.

"This is Turner. Oxygen levels are very low."

Damn. She'd really been hoping that the shaft was ventilated. The tunnel promised to be claustrophobic enough. The hood would take it to the next level. She pulled her lanyard and jammed it in one of her pockets, before trudging forward into what promised to be the longest half-mile walk of her life.

CHAPTER 51

Jeremy Powell woke to a knock at his door. It took him a moment to remember where he was. Fifty-something feet below ground, sleeping roughly the same distance away from a serial killer. Why had he insisted on coming here? He checked his watch. It was 2:10 in the morning. No way he was opening that door. A more insistent knock came a few seconds later.

"Mr. Powell. This is Sergio Alvarez. We might have a situation."

Might? What the hell did that mean?

"Hold on!" he said, before turning on the lamp on the nightstand and getting out of bed.

He slipped on a pair of pants and sandals, before making his way to the door. A quick look through the peephole confirmed it was Alvarez, and not Alejandro looking for a new plaything. He opened the door a crack to confirm that Alvarez was alone. This place had a way of getting under your skin. Powell had no idea how any of these people could stand working here for very long. He'd been here just over twelve hours and couldn't wait to get out.

"What's going on?" said Powell.

"The topside sentries heard what they described as an explosion. The ground didn't shake or anything like that. No flash. Just a single high-explosive detonation," said Alvarez. "I don't know. Could have been a sonic boom. We get those from time to time."

"Have the sentries heard sonic booms before?" said Powell.

"Yes," said Alvarez.

"Did they describe this as a sonic boom?"

"No. But White Sands Missile Range isn't that far from here," said Alvarez. "There's always something new going on outside."

"Is Mr. Nataros up?"

"Yes. I just woke him up, and he sent me here to let you know."

Powell feigned a smile. "Well. If you felt it was important enough to wake up Mr. Nataros, and Mr. Nataros felt it was important enough to wake me up at two in the morning, then I think it's time for a trip to the control room. Do you mind waiting a minute while I get dressed?"

"There's no rush," said Alvarez. "We'll be in the control room."

"I'd actually prefer if you stayed here," said Powell. "I haven't gotten used to having a serial killer around."

"Alejandro has never caused any trouble here. Not for the staff," said Alvarez. "The recruits? That's a different story. We have to keep a close eye on him around the women. He's ruined a few very good candidates."

"Stick around, please," said Powell, shutting the door.

Ruined? That was one way to put it. The sooner they filled the DOMINION roster, the better. Just a few more classes. Not that anyone here had any idea how close they might be to finishing the recruitment and training phase. Nor would they ever. When the time came to shut this place down, they'd ship in a new batch of recruits like usual and pull the plug a few days into their training. Every recruit would go to sleep one night—and never wake up. Except for the night duty staff. Their bodies would simply cease functioning, and they'd drop dead within minutes. Or if they happened to be in the wrong place at the wrong time, they'd die from a suppressed gunshot to the head.

He finished dressing and followed Alvarez to the control room, where Nataros stood in front of a bank of screens displaying the compound's dozens of surveillance camera feeds. He apparently hadn't considered the situation at hand to be too concerning. He was dressed in gray sweatpants, a dark-blue T-shirt, and flip-flops.

"Sorry about this, Mr. Powell," said Nataros. "It's probably nothing, but—"

"Better safe than sorry," said Powell, "when your boss is in town."

"There's some truth to that," said Nataros. "But we typically assume an enhanced security posture when something we can't readily explain occurs. This falls in that bucket."

"Don't let me stand in your way," said Powell, before heading over to the wall of video feeds.

"The first thing we do is check the perimeter motion sensors. They start a quarter mile out from the center of the sentry circle, with a quarter-mile bump out to the west to cover the vehicle tunnel exit. Multiple layers. Obviously, you'd be hearing an alarm right now if one had been triggered, so we'll run diagnostics to make sure all of them are working. If we find one down, we'll send a team to investigate," said Nataros.

"How many do you send?"

"The four-person rapid response team on duty at the time," said Nataros. "Equipped with thermal scopes. I've already mobilized a backup team to take their place if we need to send them out."

"And the topside sentries have thermal scopes?" said Powell.

"Correct," said Nataros, pointing at a section of the screens. "And we have a camera system up there with three-hundred-and-sixty-degree night vision and thermal coverage. If a team were to parachute into their perimeter and try to take out the sentries, we'd see it happen from here and send reinforcements. As you can see right now, everything looks normal."

The control room duty officer swiveled his chair toward them. "Diagnostics show no issues with any of the sensors."

"Thank you," said Nataros.

"And then what?" said Powell.

"What do you mean?"

"What comes next?" said Powell.

"That's it," said Nataros.

"That's the enhanced security posture?"

"We'd lock down the recruits and send nonduty staff to their rooms, but it's two in the morning. Recruits are locked down at ten, and any of the staff you see out and about are on duty," said Nataros.

"What about the rest of the security team?" said Powell. "Shouldn't you at least wake them up to ask if they've ever heard a noise like that before?"

"None of the shifts have ever logged a noise like that before, so it's safe to assume it's a novel sound," said Nataros.

Powell shook his head, wanting to say something snide, but let it go. Instead, he nodded.

"Given the circumstances surrounding ARTEMIS," said Powell, purposefully using a word that should mean nothing to the duty team in the control room, "why don't we take opportunities like these to test the security posture and procedures of the site—just until ARTEMIS is resolved. No need to sound any annoying alarms or flashing lights. How about a soft security drill, if that makes sense."

"It makes perfect sense, Mr. Powell," said Nataros, before nodding at Alvarez. "Soft wake-up for the entire security detachment. Send the rapid response team topside. Muster everyone else in the armory."

"Got it," said Alvarez, without a hint of disapproval. "The backup rapid response team is already in the armory, gearing up. We'll buzz them into the control room through the door that connects to the armory when they're ready."

Powell could see that on one of the screens. Four security officers donning body armor and readying weapons. While Alvarez sent a code to the security detachment quarters, rousing the rest of the garrison, Powell studied the screens more closely, picking up on something he hadn't noticed before.

"I don't see any coverage of the VIP area," said Powell.

"Cameras aren't permitted in the VIP area," said Nataros.

"Why?"

He glanced at Alvarez, who shrugged and shook his head.

"Honestly. I don't know," said Nataros. "I just assumed the facility was designed that way for privacy reasons back in the day. I don't think it ever had cameras."

"It didn't," said Alvarez, who had been stationed here by the CIA *back in the day*.

Powell subtly shook his head, eyes darting to the duty officer. Nobody currently employed at the facility, except for Nataros and Alvarez, knew how long this place had actually existed and who previously owned it. For a good reason.

"Speaking of VIPs," said Powell. "How do you keep esteemed guests from wandering around during a security drill, or heaven forbid, a real problem?"

"We can't," said Alvarez. "The VIP quarters' locking system can always be opened from the inside. We can lock people out of the VIP area. Same with the staff quarters and other sensitive parts of the facility, like the armory and control room."

"Too bad," said Powell. "I'd sleep in one of the staff rooms if you could lock it down."

"He doesn't like to be constrained or restrained in any way," said Alvarez.

"That's an understatement," said Powell. "If Alejandro understood the concept of restraint, I wouldn't be in your hair right now—and we wouldn't be running a security drill at two in the morning."

CHAPTER 52

Javier held up a fist, which halted the team in place; the same signal was sent back through the column by everyone else until the entire group had stopped. He hadn't turned off his rifle light, which told Mann that they weren't in danger. If Javier had detected movement ahead, he would have killed his light.

"I think we have a problem," said Javier, over the radio.

Mann squeezed past Mayer and the two former Mexican police officers to join Javier and Turner, who stood at a fork in the tunnel, each of them pointing their rifle lights in a different direction. Turner straight ahead, and Javier to the right down a similarly constructed, wood beam–reinforced shaft that broke off from the original passageway. Neither light revealed an end point.

"Karl didn't mention a split?" said Turner.

"Yeah. Did I forget to mention it?" said Mann.

"Which way, boss?" said Javier.

"Boss?" said Mann.

"It's a term of endearment," said Turner.

One of the women behind them snickered.

"I'm sure it is," said Mann. "Why don't we take the road less traveled."

"Doesn't look like anyone has traveled either way," said Javier.

"It's a poem," said Mann.

"I know," said Javier. "Robert Frost."

"They made you study Robert Frost in Mexico?" said Turner.

"You learned about Pancho Villa, right?"

"I really can't tell if he's fucking with us," said Mann.

"Siempre jodiendo contigo," said Javier.

"Always fucking with you," said one of the ex-cops behind them.

"That's what I thought," said Mann.

He checked his air cylinder gauge. Eight minutes left. He didn't have time to give this too much thought. Not if they had to take the same route out of here. Certainly not if they had much farther to go, though he strongly suspected they didn't. They'd maintained a good pace on the way in, the tunnel completely intact and passable so far.

"What's going on up there?" said Serrano over the radio.

"The tunnel branches off to the right," said Mann. "Go ahead and drop your picks and shovels. I don't think we'll be needing them anymore."

While the tools clinked to the rock floor, Mann patted Turner on the shoulder.

"I think this is where we part ways. AXE and SPEAR will keep going straight. KNIFE will take the side tunnel," said Mann. "We can't break people off into different teams, so I'm going to gamble a little. Put two teams down the tunnel I think was designed to be the primary breach point."

"Sounds reasonable to me," said Turner. "Javi. WWJD?"

"Qué?"

"What would Javi do?" said Turner.

Mann stifled a laugh.

"Both tunnels look the same in terms of construction," said Javier. "If we had more time, I'd split the group up evenly. And just so you know—I'm telling Jesus on you."

They all laughed briefly.

"Maybe they built these with an inside source in mind," said Mayer. "Someone who could send them a signal somehow and let them know which entrance to use based on interior patrols or other factors. And that's why they look identical."

"I guess we'll find out soon enough," said Mann. "Jessie. Set up one of the repeaters at the fork, so we can tell each other what we've found."

"Will do," said Mayer.

"Activate the GoPros when you reach the end of your tunnel," said Mann. "I want everything documented."

While Mayer tied one of the repurposed handhelds to a wall beam facing the fork, Mann quickly passed the plan to the rest of the team. Sofia arrived with the rest of KNIFE several seconds later, turning into the tunnel that branched right. Serrano brought up the rear of the column.

"You again?" said Serrano as she walked by him.

"Still here," said Mann, wondering how many of them wouldn't be here when their business had concluded.

CHAPTER 53

Sofia crouched and turned off her rifle light. The rest of KNIFE did the same. Like the other team leaders, she walked about twenty feet in front of the rest of her team, scanning ahead and keeping a sharp eye out for trip wires or other hazards. Mann slowly counted to ten in his head before contacting her, hoping to give her enough quiet time to better assess whatever had caused her to go dark. The fact that she hadn't issued a warning over the radio indicated she didn't detect an immediate threat.

"What do you see?" said Mann, remaining still.

"I think it's the end of the tunnel," said Sofia, reactivating her light. "Just being cautious. I didn't see any light peeking through or hear anything. Not that I can hear much with this hood on. Activating my GoPro."

"Same," said Mann.

He pressed the shutter button on the top of the camera, activating the QuickCapture feature they'd enabled back in Albuquerque. The camera would continue to record video until he pressed the button again. Mann moved forward, motioning for the rest of the team to follow. He knelt next to Sofia and activated his light. The tunnel ended at the far reaches of their combined light beam.

"Let's move up," said Mann.

The team approached the end of the tunnel together, finding a hinged metal door fitted with a substantial pull handle and a surprisingly simple dead bolt lock. He swept the doorframe and the walls around the frame for a switch or lever. Mann found it hard to believe that they were looking at something as simple as a door with a dead bolt. But why not?

"That's it?" said Serrano.

"Looks like it. I guess they figured if you had the combinations to the padlocks outside—you belonged in the tunnel," said Mann, grabbing the dead bolt and the door handle at the same time. "Lights out."

When the tunnel went pitch dark, he slowly turned the dead bolt counterclockwise, surprised at how easily it moved. A reasonable tug on the handle swung the door on its hinges, revealing the back of a steel shelving unit stacked with clear plastic bins containing PVC plumbing parts. A strong draft rushed through the team; the air headed in the direction of the tunnel entrance a half mile behind them.

Beyond the shelving unit, which had been placed directly against the section of wall he'd just opened, lay a well-lit, expansive room packed with humming and whirring machinery. Pipes, vents, and cables connected to the industrial-size equipment covered the high ceiling, heading in every direction. He didn't detect any human activity in the room.

"What the hell is this?" said Serrano.

"Looks like the facility's mechanical room," said Mann, producing his red-lensed flashlight from a pouch on his vest.

"Do we just push the bins out of the way and climb through?" said Serrano.

"I don't think so," said Mann, searching the back of the shelves with the red light.

He found a variation of what he expected. A series of three vertically spaced pull-action latches, where the shelving unit in front of them connected to the unit next to it. He opened the latches and pushed the metal shelf frame, which effortlessly swung the entire unit inward and out of the way.

"Clever," said Sofia.

"Yep. It's gone undetected all these years," said Mann.

"Hopefully," said Mayer. "Or we just triggered an alarm."

"Check the air," said Serrano.

Sofia pulled the gas monitor out of one of her cargo pockets and checked the screen. A few seconds later she gave them a thumbs-up.

"We're good," she said, before yanking off her hood.

He triggered his radio. "AXE. SPEAR. This is KNIFE. Do you copy?"

Both teams responded, the makeshift repeater still able to transmit between teams.

"We reached the end of the tunnel and found a door with a dead bolt. Nothing more complicated than that," said Mann. "We opened it and found ourselves behind an industrial shelving unit, which easily swung out of the way after opening a few latches. Looks like it was built that way. Easy access. The door opened into what looks like the facility's mechanical room. The air inside is good. My guess is you'll find yourselves in a similar easy-entry situation. We'll enter at the same time once you've figured out your end."

"Copy. We can see the door now," said Turner. "Looks the same. I'll let you know when we're ready. Out."

Mann removed his hood and stuffed it in the cylinder bag, then stopped the airflow from the cylinder. He locked the actuator in the closed position with the cotter pin attached to the lanyard he had stuffed in one of his pockets and checked the gauge. Five minutes of air remaining. Enough to jog out of here, if necessary, though he suspected that the entire tunnel shaft was filled with breathable air by now—which may have just created a problem he hadn't thought of.

Did they just disrupt the entire site's air handling system by venting it to the outside? Would that raise alarms somewhere? If the answer was yes, they'd send people here first to check on the air handlers.

"Shut the door and swing the shelving unit back in place," said Mann, before triggering his radio. "AXE. SPEAR. We need to breach immediately. I didn't take the site's air system into consideration. We probably just set off a bunch of air pressure alarms somewhere by opening this door."

CHAPTER 54

Nothing like rushing into the unknown. Mann's last transmission bumped up their timeline. Urgency was paramount. No time to pause and listen. They needed to breach the facility immediately.

"Here we go," said Turner, yanking the door open to reveal—another wall.

Shit. Thankfully, it wasn't constructed of hard-packed dirt and wood beams like the rest of the tunnel, or they'd be headed back for the tools they dropped at the split. It looked like some kind of dull metallic material. Maybe a panel? Mann said the other door opened behind a shelving unit, which swung open like it had been purposefully designed that way. Maybe this would be a similar situation.

He searched the edges of the panel, finding several bolt latches, which he slid open before lightly pushing on the metal. The panel swung inward to reveal a softly lit hallway with polished concrete floors and metal wall panels directly in front of them. He scanned the ceilings for cameras, finding nothing obvious, before yanking off his hood and stuffing it in his bag. Turner pushed the panel open a little farther to reveal another hallway to the left. This one with three doors on the right side. No cameras as far as he could tell.

Turner stepped into the hallway and crouched, replacing the cotter pin on his air cylinder. He zipped the bag shut and motioned for the two teams to enter.

"KNIFE. This is AXE. We're in," said Turner.

The reply came back garbled, but he got the gist of it. Mann was aware that they had breached the facility. Now for the fun part.

"Gear up, everyone," he said, swinging his backpack in front of him and unclipping his NVG- equipped helmet.

When everyone had stowed their hoods, turned off their air, and prepped their gear, he passed along instructions.

"SPEAR will provide security while AXE clears these rooms. I see two more hallways ahead. Probably more doors. Watch those hallways," said Turner over the radio, before turning to Javier. "Ready to bust some doors down?"

"Fuck yeah, man," said Javier.

"Let's see what we're dealing with here," said Turner, approaching the closest door while SPEAR moved down the main hallway into covering positions.

He stared at the keyless, electronic door handle for a moment, hoping they didn't have to break all these doors down. They'd be here forever, making a ton of noise. Especially if the other two hallways had three doors each. He drew his suppressed pistol and pulled the handle downward, relieved that it opened. Turner pushed the door open an inch, seeing nothing but darkness inside. A few more inches and a soft light activated somewhere inside the room. He burst inside, expecting to find someone getting out of bed.

"Automatic light. Nobody's home," said Turner, scanning the room over his pistol sights. "Check the next door."

He looked around, bewildered. The place looked like a hotel room. Nightstand and a lamp. Full-size bed with tightly pulled linens and cozy-looking comforter. Desk with a lamp and ergonomic office chair. Flat-screen TV mounted to the wall opposite the desk. A dresser. Hangers, a shoe rack, and a luggage stand in the closet. *What the hell?*

An open door to his left led to a tight but well-appointed bathroom. White marble floors. Black granite counter and undermounted sink. Glass-enclosed tile shower. A toilet with buttons and an LED display. *Buttons on a toilet?*

"The second room is unoccupied," said Javier. "Looks like a hotel room."

"That's what I was thinking," said Turner, exiting the room and heading to the last room, at the end of the hallway.

He pushed the handle down and swung the door open. The moment the lights activated inside, he quickly backed up and crouched. The bed linens had been stripped, leaving a bare mattress. A glass tumbler and an empty bottle of something fancy-looking sat on the desk. Tissues littered the nightstand. He didn't get the sense anyone was inside the room, but he wasn't taking any chances. The rest of the team had already gathered along the wall on the opposite side of the door.

Mayer stood in the doorway of the second room, slowly shaking her head. A look of concern clouded her face. She was thinking the same thing. Something was really off here. With the team in position, ready to pounce, Turner entered the room, followed by Javier, who split off and checked the bathroom.

"Bathroom is clear," said Javier. "Looks like whoever stayed here just checked out. Housekeeping hasn't been around yet."

"You keep reading my mind," said Turner, searching for personal items and coming up empty.

All he knew for sure about the recent occupant was that they had expensive taste in tequila. The empty bottle turned out to be Gran Patrón upon closer inspection. Javier exited the bathroom and eyed the bottle.

"Damn," he said.

"Two hundred dollars a bottle," said Turner. "Let's take pictures of each room and move on to the next hallway."

The first two rooms were identical. Tidy and unoccupied. He noticed a thin layer of dust this time, something he'd missed in the other rooms. Nobody had used these rooms in a long time. He pushed downward on the last door's handle, and it didn't budge. Somebody might be home. Daniela reached over her shoulder and slid a compact crowbar out of her backpack and offered it to Javier, who shook his head and pointed at her—then the door. She nodded and gently wedged the straight end of the crowbar as far as she could between the frame and the door, immediately adjacent to the handle.

"I kick first. You shoot," said Javier. "If the door snags on an interior lock, you kick it again and I shoot."

Turner was familiar with the drill. "Do it."

Daniela hit the round heel of the crowbar with her left palm, jamming the chisel end deeper, before grabbing the shaft with both hands and yanking it toward her. The lock mechanism immediately gave in to the levered pressure, Javier's front kick opening the door wide. The automatic light activated as Turner rushed in; a man who could pass for a ragged-looking Antonio Banderas quickly slipped out of the bed and opened the top nightstand drawer. Turner applied pressure to his pistol's trigger.

"*Alto!*" yelled Javier and Daniela, which stopped the man in his tracks.

"*Quién eres?*" said Javier.

"*Nadie. Nadie,*" said the man, his eyes darting back and forth from the doorway to the nightstand. "*Un prisionero.* Get me out of here."

"*Asesino en serie?*" said Javier, Turner getting the gist of the question. Assassin. Series. Serial killer.

"What are you talking about?" said the man, his body ever so slightly edging toward the nightstand.

Turner applied a little more pressure to his trigger. If this was their killer, they couldn't afford to give him an inch. The guy hadn't survived for this long because he was slow or sloppy.

"Serial killer," said Turner. "We almost got you at Cedar Lake."

The man's eyes betrayed him, their snakelike neutrality expressing surprise. Not a wide-eyed, holy-shit look, but just enough to tell Turner that his words had struck an odd chord. He'd seen it before serving high-risk warrants. The smallest tells predicted bad outcomes. Turner applied the last few ounces of pressure to the trigger, just as the man thrust his hand into the nightstand. The bright-red mess on the lampshade and the wall next to the bed told him that he didn't need to press the trigger again.

"Was that him?" said Daniela.

"I think so. But I don't know," said Turner, suddenly feeling weighed down by the gravity of the situation. "Maybe Serrano will know."

Had he just shot the serial killer they'd been hunting for a year and a half? They had no photographs to reference. No DNA. No way to know. No real closure. Turner opened the top nightstand drawer, finding a compact Glock pistol. Whoever he had been, he certainly wasn't one of the good guys.

"What about fingerprints?" said Javier. "They must have pulled some prints from the SUV."

"They did. But they didn't match anything in our system or yours. But now we have a reference. You nailed it," said Turner, triggering his radio. "Kim. We need you here right away with the forensics kit. We need to take some fingerprints."

"On my way," said Rocha.

"When she's done with the prints, I'm taking his hands," said Javier, unsheathing the kukri knife attached to his belt. "We need to be sure. Actual fingers are about as sure as it gets."

Turner put his hands up. "Take whatever you want. After Rocha takes his fingerprints. I can't throw a pair of hands on our boss's desk and call it good. His face is still intact, so we need to take pictures. Someone in your government or ours has a file on our killer. If he's our man, we'll figure it out later with the prints and pictures. *Ándale. Ándale.* We have another hallway to clear."

"Technically, it's *apurarse*," said Javier. "*Ándale* means come along. Not very urgent."

"Okay. I'll file a complaint with Duolingo later," said Turner. "Right now, we need to clear this area and move on. Link up with KNIFE and figure out what exactly the fuck is going on here."

Speaking of KNIFE.

"Mann. This is Turner," he said over the radio. "Do you copy."

The transmission was beyond distorted this time, but he passed along the information they'd gathered anyway.

CHAPTER 55

Mann paused, straining to hear what one of the other teams was trying to pass across the radio net. He still had a relatively straight line of sight to the repeater, which indicated that AXE and SPEAR had taken some turns along the way, weakening the signal strength to the point that Mann could no longer understand what they were saying. All he knew was that they had successfully entered the facility undetected and had found some doors. The rest was a staticky mess.

"What's up?" said Serrano.

"I don't know. A lot of radio traffic from the other teams," said Mann.

"We can all hear it," she said. "It doesn't sound frantic."

"I guess," said Mann, not believing his own words—or hers.

"Whatever they're dealing with, they have it under control. Or they don't. There's absolutely nothing you can do about that right now. Right?"

He nodded. She was right. They needed to press on without hesitation. Their presence in the facility wouldn't go unnoticed for long.

"Any luck with the door?" said Mann, referring to the electronically locked, windowless hatch they found to the left of the secret entrance.

"Negative," said Malena, putting away her makeshift electronics kit. "The lock is either too complex or too simple."

Malena was a former Mexican police officer who specialized in wired and electronic surveillance. She'd brought what she called a "brute force" electronic entry kit with her, which she'd previously used to break into hotel rooms to plant listening devices and concealed cameras as a police officer.

"It was worth a try," said Mann.

"We still have another door," said Serrano. "Which doesn't appear to be locked from this side."

"Yeah," he said, grimacing.

"What?"

"We didn't find any cameras in here, but I can't shake the feeling that we set off a bunch of alarms," said Mann. "And they're just waiting for us on the other side of that door."

"There's only one way to find out," she said. "We don't have any choice but to move forward. The other teams are relying on us. And this is the only way we get to the bottom of whatever was going on between our killer and this facility."

He looked over the rest of the team, seeing no hesitation on their faces. Sofia cocked her head.

"Are you actually worried about us?" she said.

"Yes," said Mann, surprised that he so easily admitted his only real fear right now—getting all of them killed for nothing.

Sofia shook her head. "Hey. Drop that shit right now. We're here for us. Not you. This is our choice. Every single one of us came here prepared to die. Nobody expects to walk out of here alive. But we need to make whatever we do here count. And we can't do that if you're . . . ah—*cómo se dice*—wishy-washy?"

"*Wishy-washy* sounds about right," said Mann.

"We need you in charge or out of the way," said Sofia. "Because we're going through that door right now, with you leading the way or bringing up the rear."

Mann glanced at Serrano, who offered him nothing but a shrug. He looked them over, sensing no harsh judgment—but certainly no shoulder to cry on. They wanted exactly what he wanted. Some form of closure, whether that meant getting to the bottom of this facility's link to the killer or dying.

"Stack up on the door," said Mann.

When everyone was in position, he pulled the handle down and yanked the door inward. The team spilled inside, following standard room-clearing protocol. Mann peeled off to the right. Sofia went left. The rest of the team formed a tight wedge a few feet in front of the door, scanning for targets.

"Clear," said Sofia.

"Clear," said Mann.

"What the hell is this place?" said Serrano.

"Looks like a border tunnel access hub," said Mateo. "But we're like a hundred and fifty miles from the border."

Mann scanned the room, which had to be fifty feet long and half as wide. Maybe fifteen-foot-high ceilings? Same as the mechanical room. A dozen or so wood picnic tables sat in the middle of the room. Six narrow tunnel openings ringed three sides of the room. Two on each of the sides. Plus, three windowless doors. Two on the tunnel-less wall to their left. One on the opposite side of the room. None featuring the same electronic lock they had found on the door in the mechanical room. A quick look at the ceiling told Mann that their presence in the facility was no longer a secret. He raised his rifle and fired a single shot, shattering a dome camera—its pieces falling to the floor.

"Cover the entrances. I expect company soon," said Mann.

Sofia positioned Mateo and Malena facing the right side of the room, covering two of the doors, before ranging forward with her rifle pointed at the third.

"Six tunnels," said Serrano. "Six sentries topside. I bet these tunnels lead up to the surface. Things could get really busy down here—really fast."

He jogged over to the closest tunnel and looked inside.

"I think you're right," said Mann. "The shaft goes about thirty feet straight out, before dead-ending at a ladder."

They couldn't possibly cover ten points of entry, without splitting up and assigning specific breach points for each group to cover. He glanced around the space, coming to the only conclusion possible to cover all entrances without killing each other in a cross fire.

"Sofia. Take Mateo and Malena to that corner of the room," he said, pointing to their immediate right. "Serrano and I will take the corner diagonally opposite on the other side of the room. Shoot anyone that emerges from the tunnels or doors, except for the door directly adjacent to our position. It's too close. We'll take care of anyone that comes through it. Malena. Rig our last repeater radio to the door leading back into the mechanical room. If we can reach Jax, we can get a heads-up if the topside sentries head down the ladders. Cata, please translate that."

Serrano fired off a rapid string of Spanish, which spurred Sofia and the others into action. A few seconds later, the two groups crouched in their assigned corners, waiting for the inevitable.

CHAPTER 56

Powell wasn't exactly impressed with the level of urgency in the control room. The duty officer, a drone of a man dressed in khaki pants and a dark-blue polo shirt, swiveled left and right in his chair like a confused idiot. His assistant, dressed in the same ridiculous outfit, appeared to make herself look busy, examining a bank of digital control screens related to the equipment in the mechanical room—where the alarm originated.

While she pressed the touch screens, silencing the alarms, Powell witnessed a group of five heavily armed, body armor–clad operators appear at a door on one of the screens labeled "topside tunnel access point." He pointed at the screen, which went blank the moment he lifted his hand.

"There! Damn it. Armed intruders!" he said. "How many alarms have to go off before you mobilize the proper response?"

"It was an airflow alarm. Happens every time we open or close one of the exterior access points, like the topside sentry hatches or vehicle tunnel door," said Nataros. "How the hell are we supposed to—never mind. The rapid response team is en route to the mechanical room. They should arrive any second."

"Well. It's too late now," said Powell. "They're inside the facility."

"Where?" said Nataros.

Alvarez pointed at one of the "dead" screens. "Tunnel room."

"Lock it down," said Nataros. "Restrict it to entry only."

"Done," said the duty officer, scanning the screens on the wall. "I don't see them on any feeds coming from the adjacent spaces. Their only way out is to go back the way they came, through mechanical."

"The rapid response team just accessed mechanical," said Alvarez.

"Then that's it," said Nataros. "They're trapped."

"Trapped?" said Powell. "How the hell can you trap a team that materialized out of thin air!"

"It doesn't matter right now," said Nataros. "They're isolated from the rest of the facility."

"That's actually the worst possible room to get stuck in," said Alvarez.

"Really? Why is that?" said Powell.

"The room has ten access points. We can simultaneously breach the room from every point and end this in a matter of seconds," said Alvarez. "They can't possibly repel that kind of attack. How many did you see enter the space?"

"Five. I think," said Powell. "And they didn't look like they were messing around."

"Well. Neither are we," said Nataros, turning to Alvarez. "Swarm the room and end this now. We need to figure out how they got inside before anyone else pops in unexpectedly."

Powell wondered if they used the escape tunnel connected to the VIP lounge. He had no idea how they would have known about the tunnel, since it was installed immediately after the CIA turned over the facility and before AXIOM staffed the site. Obviously, it wasn't in his best interest to bring up the tunnel with Nataros or Alvarez, because he had no intention of bringing them along if he had to pull the plug on LABYRINTH.

"Mr. Nataros?" said the duty officer.

"Yes?"

"We have a second intrusion," he said. "Ten heavily armed hostiles just exited the VIP door."

"What the—" started Nataros.

"And—they just shot out the camera," said the duty officer, pointing at a blank screen. "We're blind."

"Did you see anyone else with them?" said Powell.

"Everyone I saw was armed with a rifle and wearing tactical gear. Serious-looking vests and night vision–equipped helmets."

"Are the topside sentries still alive?" said Powell. "Are we looking at a large-scale government raid?"

"The sentries are still in position," said the duty officer. "Our topside camera feed confirms this."

"Send teams from the armory to intercept. A pincer move if possible. One through the staff quarters. The other through the staff recreation area," said Powell.

Alvarez dashed to the door connecting the control room to the armory and punched in a code that opened the door. He barked a few orders, before shutting the door and returning to their huddle in front of the screens.

Powell turned to Nataros. "I need them out of here."

"The duty staff?"

"Yes," said Powell.

Nataros nodded at the duty staff, who quickly exited the control room through the door leading to the staff quarters.

"Is that door locked from the outside?" said Powell.

"Yes. What's going on?" said Nataros.

"Can you lock it so it can't be accessed from the outside?"

Nataros glanced at Alvarez, looking for an answer. *How does this guy not know every single detail about a facility he's run for close to two years!*

"Yes," said Alvarez.

"Then lock it down," said Powell. "We don't want any of our uninvited guests swiping themselves in."

"The duty team won't be able to get back in," said Alvarez.

"We don't need them right now," said Powell.

Alvarez made his way over to the duty officer station and pushed a few buttons on the three-foot-wide touch screen in front of the empty chair.

"We're locked down," said Alvarez.

"Okay. Here's the deal," said Powell. "We need to sanitize LABYRINTH immediately. Two hostile teams managed to covertly enter the facility."

"Sanitize? As in kill the recruits?"

"As in kill everybody," said Powell. "The physical evidence left behind will be bad enough, but there's nothing we can do about that. But we can't have the recruits or staff talking about the program."

"What about the security detachment?" said Alavarez.

"Well. If you've been following the strict protocols established for all interaction between security and DOMINION zone staff, I don't see any reason why they should be included in the sanitization procedure."

"We have. I know what's at stake," said Nataros.

"Do you want me to redirect security to the recruit quarters?" said Alvarez. "To take care of them?"

"I appreciate the initiative, but that won't be necessary," said Powell.

"So. How do we sanitize the facility?" said Alvarez.

"I can't disclose that right now," said Powell. "But what I can say is that we'll need to equip security and ourselves with the masks stored in the armory. The ones with the canisters. Sooner than later."

"Jesus. Poison gas? How?" said Nataros. "We don't carry anything like that here. We can shut down the air handlers and seal the exits. Eventually the oxygen levels will drop, suffocating everyone."

"Two teams just breached the facility through secret entrances, which vent directly to the surface," said Powell. "Correct me if I'm wrong, but if you shut down the air system, won't that create negative pressure and potentially draw air into the facility?"

"If we shut down the air systems, the air exchange should be neutral," said Nataros. "Nothing in. Nothing out. Everyone will suffocate. We can station security at every known exit to—"

"That's too much to ask of your security team. Trust me. It won't work," said Powell. "I have a built-in plan to get the job done. We just need to clear a path to make it happen."

"Should I cancel the order to bring the topside sentries down and have them seal the surface hatches?" said Alvarez. "Recall the teams ready to storm the tunnel room?"

"No. We need them to wipe out the hostile force in the tunnel room," said Powell. "They're in the way, unless we want to take our chances heading straight through the staff quarters area."

"The ten hostiles that emerged from the VIP section were headed straight for the staff quarters," said Alvarez.

"Which is why I strongly suggest we take a slightly longer, alternate route," said Powell.

CHAPTER 57

Baker shot the two dome cameras attached to the ceiling, before giving Zita the green light to start clearing rooms along the long hallway. They'd emerged from the luxury quarters section of the facility to an area that looked more like an underground lair. The polished concrete floors had given way to dull, scratchy concrete. The walls transitioning from boutique-looking metal panels to modular, office space construction. And no more soft up lights. Harsh fluorescent tubes hidden behind translucent plastic ceiling panels cast a sickly greenish-white glow.

He stationed Bianca, a former Mexican cop, facing the long axis of the hallway to protect them while they worked in groups of two to breach the rooms. They used the crowbar-and-kick method demonstrated by AXE in the VIP area but moved things along faster. From what he could tell, they had ten rooms to clear in this hallway alone, which he guessed represented only a fraction of the rooms required to staff a facility this massive.

The first room, which resembled a basic military barracks room, contained a middle-aged woman who put up no resistance. They ordered her to lie face down on her twin-size bed and hog-tied her with plastic flex-cuffs. The second room's occupant, a fit Caucasian male in his late twenties or early thirties, lashed out at the breach team—taking a bullet to the forehead before his right hook completed its arc. SPEAR wasn't fucking around.

Bianca moved forward as they made progress, keeping her rifle pointed down the hallway. The next two room breaches ended peacefully, if you consider being shoved face down onto a concrete floor or mattress and abruptly hog-tied to be a nonviolent encounter. Suppressed gunfire erupted in the hallway, drawing everyone out. Bianca sat against the left side of the wall a few rooms down, firing repeated, single shots down a side hallway that opened to the right. A bright-red, basketball-size blood splotch stained the wall a few feet above her.

"Four of them. Two down," she said over the radio—her voice sounding weak.

Baker reached her first, taking a quick peek around the corner with his rifle. A figure at the end of the short hallway leaned out to take a shot at Bianca, his head snapping back from Baker's double tap. Two bodies lay in the hallway, halfway between Baker and the man he'd just killed. Zita pulled Bianca out of the line of fire and summoned Tianna, who broke open the team's trauma kit and went to work on their wounded comrade.

Judging by the stain on the wall above Bianca and the rapidly expanding pool of blood on the floor beneath her, Baker wasn't optimistic about her chances of survival. And even if Tianna could stabilize her, they couldn't stop clearing rooms. Every one of these doors represented a potential threat. Not to mention the fact that their serial killer could be in one of these rooms.

As much as he'd like to believe that Turner put a bullet through their killer's head, they had a duty to clear every space and room in the facility searching for potential matches—and taking more fingerprints. It was the only way to be sure.

"How is she—"

Bianca's head tilted sideways, her eyes wide open but lifeless.

"Fuck. I'm so sorry," said Baker.

"We need to keep moving," said Zita.

Gunfire erupted from the end of the short hallway, several bullets striking the corner next to Baker and the wall where Bianca had been fatally injured. Baker removed a flash-bang grenade from a pouch on his vest and pulled the pin, then tossed it in the direction of the shooter. The grenade detonated, a flash momentarily lighting up the hallway. The "bang" muted by his noise-canceling earpieces. He leaned to the left, watching the end of the hallway over the barrel of his rifle. Several seconds later, a head emerged—its owner probably wondering why his position hadn't been rushed after the grenade detonated. Baker pressed the trigger once, spraying the security officer's brains against the wall behind him.

"Zita. I'll cover this hallway," said Baker. "You clear the rest of the rooms."

Rocha settled in next to him, breathing shallowly. "I think I'm having a panic attack. I'm shaking."

"Welcome to the club," said Baker, before taking a deep breath and exhaling.

Rocha followed his lead, repeating the same breathing cycle a few times.

"Feel better?" said Baker.

"Not really."

"Good. If a few deep breaths can calm you down in a situation like this, I must be doing something wrong," said Baker, his own hands trembling from the adrenaline.

CHAPTER 58

Turner took a moment to take it all in. They'd just entered an unlocked space that looked like an expansive chain hotel lobby combined with a shopping mall food court. Half of the room contained furniture clusters, simple but comfortable-looking couches and lounge chairs arranged around coffee tables. A few of them oriented toward the flat-screen TVs on the far wall.

The other half featured a few dozen square cafeteria-style tables, surrounded on each side by stackable metal chairs. A long, stainless steel buffet table, with space for several trays, stood in the middle of the dining area. A drink station featuring a soda dispenser with several choices and the kind of industrial coffee maker you'd expect to find behind the counter at a Waffle House sat against the wall just beyond the tables.

He hustled to catch up with the rest of AXE, which had already split up between the two doors on the far side of the facility's recreation-dining area. He settled into place next to Amelia and Mayer, who had crouched next to the leftmost door.

"What is this place?" said Turner.

"Who the hell knows," said Mayer. "I've never seen anything like it."

"You ready?" said Amelia.

Both Turner and Mayer nodded.

"We're ready," said Amelia, over the radio net.

"Copy," said Javier. "Opening the doors in three, two—"

"Hold on," said Turner. "What if we find a hostile in the hallway between your door and ours?"

"You back up immediately," said Javier. "We'll take them out."

"Copy," said Turner.

Close Quarters Battle (CQB) situations required constant thinking and planning. Every movement had to be choreographed. Lines of fire had to be studied and deconflicted. Every angle considered. Fortunately, they were dealing with only one level here. He'd taken part in multilevel operations where they had to consider ceiling and subfloor shooters. You never knew where the next bullet might come from.

"Starting the count over," said Javier. "Breach in three, two, one. Go!"

Mayer yanked the door inward, making room for Amelia and Turner to rush the hallway. Amelia rushed out first, instantly going limp in an explosion of gunfire. Turner reached out and grabbed the drag handle on the back of Amelia's vest as she fell and pulled her out of the line of fire, where Mayer took over and dragged her farther inside while he covered the door. A fury of suppressed gunfire, presumably from Javier and Daniela, immediately followed—quieting the hallway.

"I think they're all down," said Javier. "You want to make sure?"

"Yeah," said Turner, returning to the doorway.

A quick peek into the hallway revealed a heavily armed, four-person team flattened to the concrete floor, a few of them still moving. Turner poked the automatic rifle he'd taken from the motel shooters through the doorway and fired a short burst into each of the downed hostiles, his noise-canceling radio earpieces turning the unsuppressed gunshots into Bubble Wrap pops.

"Hallway is clear," said Turner, over the radio.

"Copy," said Javier. "We're on the move."

"Amelia is gone," said Mayer.

Turner glanced over his shoulder as Mayer lowered Amelia's head to the floor. She had taken two bullets to the face, the entry holes so small they looked like deep-red blemishes on her cheek. The dark-red goop spilling out of her helmet told the full story. Amelia never knew what hit her. She'd died instantly. This shit could be so random.

"Amelia is KIA," said Turner, over the radio.

"Ah . . . fuck," said Javier. "Okay. Uh . . . there's a substantial-looking door to your left. We'll cover you while you investigate."

"Moving out," said Turner, taking his finger off the transmit button. "Jessie?"

"Yeah?"

"Watch the door we used to access this room," said Turner. "We can't afford any more surprises."

"Yep," she said, shifting her attention and rifle to the door at the far end of the room.

"Be right back," said Turner, stepping into the hallway.

Describing the door as substantial turned out to be an understatement. He hit the brushed metal hatch with his fist, feeling nothing but unmovable steel. No signs indicating what they might find on the other side. Just a thick slab of steel with a biometric fingerprint scanner to the right of the doorframe. And a camera mounted in the left corner of the ceiling next to the door. He drew his suppressed pistol and shot the camera.

"I don't think we brought enough explosives to get through this door," said Turner.

"Is it key card activated?" said Javier. "Maybe one of those guards has the right key card."

"Fingerprint," said Turner. "It's a biometric scanner."

"Okay. Or the right finger," said Javier.

"Let's keep moving," said Turner. "There's a door next to the team you cut down. Key card activated. And I see some key cards on the bodies."

They stacked up on the door and used one of the guards' key cards to open it. Turner went first, finding himself in what looked like a locker room. The walls to the left and right, which extended at least fifty feet, were lined with two-foot-wide, six-foot-tall steel lockers. Two rows of benches lined the room from front to back.

The disturbing thing was that all the lockers were open—and mostly empty. The only items left behind in the few lockers he examined near the door were tactical gloves, rigid plastic knee protectors, and a few pairs of shooting goggles. Useless shit in this kind of a situation. Turner counted the lockers on one side. Twenty. Times two. Forty security officers. Six topside. Four dead. Leaving thirty on the loose inside the facility? He scanned the ceiling for cameras, finding none, before returning to the door.

"This looks like the security team's staging area. Possibly their living quarters. About forty in total," said Turner. "The team we hit must have just geared up and exited. Shitty luck for them."

A quick sweep of the sprawling space confirmed Turner's theories. The locker room connected to an expansive bunk bed–style barracks area with forty empty beds. They also found another very unbreachable-looking door at the far end of the barracks. This one without any kind of obvious access mechanism. Turner assumed the door led to the armory, and entry could only be granted from some kind of central control room. It made sense to connect the armory to the security detachment's living quarters, but not grant them unlimited access to weapons.

He hadn't seen an obvious camera, but there had to be some way for the control room to verify identities before buzzing them in. Not that it mattered since nobody in their right mind would ever open the door for them. Unless SPEAR or KNIFE took over the control room.

"SPEAR. KNIFE. This is AXE. Do you copy?" said Turner, wanting to relay the information they'd gathered.

Nothing. UHF radio signals should be able to penetrate a few walls. SPEAR couldn't be that far away. They just split up a few minutes ago. He repeated the call with the same negative result.

"I think some of the interior walls are stone," said Javier. "The radios won't penetrate. We had this problem all the time clearing cartel bunkers. Perfect comms one minute. Garbled the next. Gone after that."

"All right. Let's keep moving," said Turner. "We have another door at the end of the locker room."

They followed the same procedure, Turner opening the door and slipping inside to scan for threats. What he found defied explanation.

"Holy shit," said Turner, over the radio.

"What is it?" said Mayer.

"You have to see it to believe it," said Turner. "The room is clear."

The rest of the team entered the space, muttering to themselves when they took in the room.

"Looks like a real drug lab," said Tianna.

"Just like the labs we found in the cartel bunkers, but bigger. I see meth cooking stations. Other shit I don't recognize. Maybe some kind of new drug?" said Javier. "What are we looking at?"

"I don't know," said Turner. "But we definitely stumbled into something far bigger than a serial killer's hideout."

"You sure this isn't government sponsored?" said Javier. "The dudes we iced in the hallway were not cartel. Latino. But not cartel muscle."

"Pretty sure. Though I'm starting to reconsider that assessment," said Turner.

Tianna examined the closest meth cooking stations, shaking her head. "I don't think this is real. It looked real from a distance, but up close—it's all wrong. And they wouldn't just leave it out like this. Unguarded."

"She's right," said Javier. "None of this makes sense."

"Nothing we've seen makes sense," said Turner, before triggering his radio. "SPEAR. KNIFE. This is AXE. Urgent traffic to pass."

Very urgent. As in "we need to get out of here right now" urgent. Nothing was what it seemed down here.

CHAPTER 59

"KNIFE . . . copy?"

Serrano put a hand to one of her ears, thinking she could push the earpiece in a little farther to better hear the staticky transmission. Mann responded before anyone else.

"This is KNIFE. Send your traffic."

"Topside . . . vanished. I think . . . recalled . . . site."

"Jax. Is that you?" said Mann. "I don't understand your transmission. Send again."

Instead of trying to communicate normally over a radio net that was spotty at best, Jax simply repeated the same message over and over again, presumably figuring that all the words would get through eventually—and make sense. Which they did.

"Topside . . . Topside . . . your way . . . heading," she said. "Way . . . topside . . . way . . . your. Topside . . . heading."

"Copy. Topside sentries headed our way," Mann said a few times over the radio, before turning his attention to KNIFE. "This is it. They're going to try and smoke us out. Watch your cross fire."

Serrano aimed her rifle between the two tunnel entrances she'd been assigned to cover. At the first sign of movement in either tunnel, she'd shift her aim and open fire—back and forth between the two.

"Yes . . . Yes . . ."

A new transmission hit the radio net, overriding Jax's acknowledgment.

"SPEAR. KNIFE. This is AXE. Urgent traffic to pass."

"Turner. This is Mann. Solid copy. Where are you?"

"We're in a fake drug lab. Looks real enough on the surface, but our Mexican friends have confirmed that it's just a prop," said Turner. "We have one KIA. Amelia. What's your status?"

"We found something similar. Sofia and Mateo described it as a border tunnel hub," said Mann. "Where the cartels stage drug shipments to be transported by mules through the tunnels. But the tunnels lead to the topside sentry posts. Jax just reported that they're heading down. I have to cut you off. We're about to have company."

"Understood," said Turner. "We must be close to you if we can talk. We'll keep moving. Have you heard from SPEAR?"

"Negative," said Mann. "I need to go."

Serrano detected movement and shifted her rifle to the leftmost tunnel opening.

"Hold on," said Mann, pulling the pin on a flash-bang grenade and hurling it into the same tunnel after a long pause.

The grenade detonated several feet inside, their eyes shielded from the flash and their earpieces reducing the "bang" to an easily tolerable crunch. A man rushed out, firing wildly. Serrano pressed her trigger three times in rapid succession, dropping him to the floor behind the picnic tables. She sent two more bullets into him to be sure. Mann's rifle snapped twice, spinning the figure that emerged from the adjacent tunnel in place—180 degrees. Both Serrano and Mann fired twice, propelling him back into the tunnel.

"Cover the mechanical room," said Mann.

His warning came just in time. Two figures appeared in the doorway, firing blindly into the room. Serrano's first shot caught one of them in the face, the shooter stumbling forward and staggering into the tunnel room. Bullets from multiple directions knocked him to the ground, his body motionless the moment it hit the concrete floor. The second shooter fired a long burst of automatic fire into the room, forcing Serrano and Mann to lie flat as bullets chipped the stone-and-dirt wall above them.

The door several feet to their left burst inward, four body armor–clad, heavily armed security officers spilling into the room. Serrano instinctively flipped her rifle's selector switch, firing several long bursts into the group and sending them to the floor. While she reloaded, Mann finished the group with single shots placed through their faces or necks.

"We can't keep doing this," said Mann, swapping rifle magazines. "Eventually, they'll swamp us."

A vicious firefight erupted just beyond the door to their left, the shooters in the two tunnel entrances facing Sofia's team unleashing a coordinated hail of gunfire. The firefight went back and forth for several seconds, until it died out.

"Sofia. What's your status?" said Mann.

"Not good. Mateo is gone. Malena is hit," said Sofia.

"How bad is she?" said Mann.

"Not bad," said Sofia. "Took a bullet to her right hip. She's still mission capable."

"Copy. Did you hit any of them?" said Mann.

"We took out the shooter in the leftmost tunnel. The one closest to you. I can see him. He isn't moving," said Sofia.

"Okay. Keep an eye on the rightmost tunnel," said Mann.

Serrano was done with this. "How many of those half grenades do you have left?"

"Three," said Mann.

"Give them to me," said Serrano.

"I don't think—"

"I don't care what you think," she said. "We need to end this now."

To emphasize her point, gunfire erupted from the door leading to the mechanical room, forcing the two of them to the floor.

"What are you thinking?" said Mann.

"You'll see," said Serrano. "Just cover me. Hit the mechanical room door hard when I make my move."

He transferred the three lower-intensity grenades to Serrano. She stuffed two of them in one of her cargo pockets and pulled the pin on the third. While Mann methodically unloaded a fresh magazine on the mechanical room door, she released the grenade's safety lever and sprinted past the first tunnel entrance to the right, pausing momentarily before tossing the grenade into the rightmost of the two tunnels.

The grenade exploded a second later, ejecting the guard that had been hiding inside the shaft into the tunnel room. Two bullets struck his face the moment he looked up.

"Keep going," said Mann. "I got you."

She removed another grenade and pulled the pin before dashing past the smoking hole she'd just created. Sliding along the room's outer wall, while Mann alternated his fire between the two tunnels ahead of her and the mechanical room entrance, she pulled the pin on the grenade in her hand and underhanded it into the next opening. The security guard inside let out a quick string of obscenities before bursting out of the tunnel, gun blazing. Mann's bullets instantly tossed him aside before Serrano could raise her rifle. The grenade detonated, throwing dirt and rock into the room, completely obscuring her view.

Serrano dashed through the cloud of dust and put her back against the wall between the previously blasted tunnel and the next, retrieving the last grenade from her pocket.

"Cata. I can't see the tunnel entrance. Too much dust from the grenade," said Mann.

"*Mismo,*" said Sofia.

She was on her own for now. No problem. Serrano drew her pistol and shifted it to her off hand. Risky, since she couldn't hit the broad side of a barn with her left hand. A helmet-encased head peeked out of the tunnel next to her, Serrano snapping off a few quick shots that couldn't possibly have hit the mark. She pulled the pin on her last grenade and considered her options. If she somehow banked it into the tunnel, the shooter would rush out, firing in her direction.

Serrano decided on a different approach. She released the safety lever, starting the grenade's four-to-five-second countdown. Two seconds later, she rolled it directly in front of the next tunnel entrance, immediately backing up and taking cover in the tunnel she'd just cleared. The muffled blast was joined by an agonizing scream.

They needed to get out of there immediately. This room would chew them to pieces eventually.

"Garrett. I'm going to link up with Sofia," she said. "We'll bring Malena to your position. Cover us."

"Yep," said Mann. "Be careful. We still haven't heard from the two sentries in the tunnels next to Sofia. I'm watching the two openings, but this room is filling up with dust and smoke."

"We'll return the way I came," said Serrano. "Keeping to the outside of the room. I might send Malena topside through one of the tunnels I cleared. Get her out of the way."

"I'm fine," said Malena, over the radio.

"We should send her up immediately," said Sofia. "Jax can watch over her. They'll be able to talk to each other. She can guide Malena around any remaining topside security."

She'd forgotten about Jax.

"Garrett?" said Serrano.

"I agree. Send her up," said Mann. "Have her report what we've encountered so far. A fake cartel bunker and a lot of security. Still no sign of our killer."

Mann's last statement nearly stopped Serrano in her tracks. In all the chaos, she'd forgotten about their entire reason for coming down here. To find their killer. Serrano broke through the dust to find Sofia crouched next to Malena, who looked worse than she had sounded on the radio. Her hip bled profusely. No spurting or pumping, but the blood flowed freely, despite the hemostatic gauze Sofia pressed into the wound. Serrano slid into place next to Malena and covered the two tunnels to their left. Mateo lay a few feet away, his body curled up in a fetal position. A pool of blood spreading underneath his head.

"Malena. Are you sure you can climb out? It could be fifty feet up. Maybe more," said Serrano.

"I can do it. Just get me to one of the tunnels. Now," said Malena. "I don't want to slow everyone down."

"We can stick together," said Serrano.

"No. I'll be fine," she said.

"Okay," said Serrano, triggering her radio. "Garrett. We're moving. Cover us."

"Give me a few seconds to reload," said Mann. "In three. Two. One. Go."

Mann's rifle barked steadily as they carried Malena to the second tunnel on the outer wall. The dust cloud kicked up by the grenades was thicker here, providing them with some concealment. Serrano waited at the tunnel opening while Sofia helped Malena to the ladder deeper inside the tunnel. Sofia emerged from the darkness alone several seconds later, joining her at the edge of the tunnel.

"Is she gonna make it up the ladder?" said Serrano.

"I think so," said Sofia.

"Her wound looked serious," said Serrano.

"Yeah. The bullet dug deep into her hip. I couldn't stop the bleeding," said Sofia.

Serrano activated her radio. "Malena. How are you doing?"

"Almost out," she said.

Another transmission broke through. "Go . . . down. Danger. Back down. You're . . . danger."

"Shit. Jax just told me to head back—"

A muted burst of gunfire echoed through the tunnel, followed by several clangs and a heavy thud. Serrano aimed her rifle into the shaft and triggered her rifle light. Malena lay in a bloody heap at the bottom of the ladder. She deactivated the light and turned to Sofia.

"We need to make our time down here count," said Serrano. "Which means we're going to kill every one of these fuckers."

CHAPTER 60

Powell turned away from the screens. Whoever breached the facility had become quite adept at finding and neutralizing the cameras. About the only thing the video feeds were good for at this point was roughly tracking the hostile force's progress. Another dead camera feed meant more ground gained by ARTEMIS—if this was in fact Mann's crew. He still didn't know for sure. The numbers suggested it might be something else. Fifteen heavily armed intruders had entered the facility through different access points. Seven more than Mann had at his disposal based on the latest reports from Minnesota.

He glanced at the site map on the wall across from the screens. From what he could tell, the ten-person team first appeared in the VIP quarters. Reports from various teams, combined with the camera outages, suggested that this group had split up and moved through the staff and security living areas. One of the groups appeared in the drug lab, having emerged from the security detachment's quarters. He counted four before they shot out the cameras.

The other group must have cleared the staff quarters. Alvarez received an abrupt radio transmission from the team that had been assigned to that area. A quick enemy contact report, then nothing. He couldn't risk taking that route to reach the mechanical room or the escape tunnel. These people were making short work of Alvarez's security team.

Powell briefly considered heading through the armory into the security detachment's quarters, assuming that the area might be safe since it had already been cleared by the hostile force—but just as quickly dismissed the idea. With the cameras out, they could walk straight into a second force that they hadn't seen yet. His only viable option with the cameras out was to use a route that Alvarez's security officers controlled.

Unfortunately, reports from the tunnel room didn't sound encouraging. His people controlled the mechanical room, but Powell couldn't access that room without going through the staff quarters, which felt like a bigger gamble than throwing everything at the tunnel room. All he needed to do was get into the mechanical area alive, with enough security officers to repel any counterattack from the tunnel room. At that point, he was home free.

"Alvarez," said Powell. "How many security guards do you have left?"

"Twenty-two," said Alvarez.

That was quick. He'd expected Alvarez to spend some time counting. Maybe he wasn't entirely useless after all.

"I just heard from the last two topside sentries," said Alvarez. "They popped someone trying to climb up one of the ladders."

"Where are all of your officers right now?" said Powell.

"Two up top. Four with us. Twelve in the armory," said Alvarez. "And four in the DOMINION zone."

"Do you need the officers in the DOMINION zone?" said Powell.

"It's standard protocol to have four guards in there at all times," said Alvarez. "But given the circumstances—"

"If they have a team waiting by that door, we run the risk of a critical breach if we bring them back in," said Nataros.

"He's right," said Alvarez.

"Then I guess we'll have to do without them," said Powell. "Eighteen should be more than enough to get us into mechanical, then out of here."

"Why mechanical?" said Nataros.

"We built a fail-safe into the system, in the event that the facility faced imminent capture," said Powell. "We're going to gas the facility with hydrogen cyanide. That's the sanitization procedure."

"Are you serious?" said Nataros.

"Very," said Powell.

"How?" said Alvarez.

"The red key card in that safe," said Powell, pointing at a small gray electronic safe on the floor under the duty officer's desk, "opens a hidden panel in the mechanical room containing a propane tank–size canister of hydrogen cyanide. A few twists of a few valves, and the gas is released into the air handlers in vapor form. Everyone should be dead within ten minutes. Incapacitated in under two."

"I always wondered what was in that safe," said Nataros.

"There's a reason we didn't tell you. If word got out—you'd have a mutiny on your hands," said Powell. "If you reported an attack likely to overrun the facility to the AXIOM emergency response center, they would have given you the combination to the safe, which contains the key and instructions on how to sanitize the site."

"I'm surprised you can't do this remotely," said Alvarez.

"Too risky," said Powell. "One computer glitch and *adios* to the entire facility."

"Fuck. This is grim," said Nataros.

"It's a grim business," said Powell, heading toward the safe. "Shall we?"

"And these masks will keep us safe?" said Alvarez.

"Yes. We chose this type of mask specifically with this in mind," said Powell, picking up a full-face gas mask with an attached filter canister. "Just make sure you have a snug fit."

"That's not funny," said Nataros.

"It wasn't meant to be," said Powell. "Bring the rest of the security team into the control room for a quick mission briefing. The vehicle bay cameras are still intact, so we'll start there and work our way through the tunnel room to the mechanical room. Have the two topside sentries make their way down one of the ladders and wait for us to approach the tunnel room door. They'll be our distraction."

"On it," said Alvarez, heading to the armory door.

"And have them bring me a semiautomatic shotgun with a pouch full of shells," said Powell.

"We have Saiga-12s with ten-shell magazines or Benelli M4s," said Alvarez.

The Benelli was more reliable, but only held seven shells, plus one in the tube. And he'd have to manually reload it one shell at a time.

"I'll go with the Saiga," said Powell. "Four mags should be enough."

"You got it," said Alvarez.

"Hold on," said Nataros.

Nataros was starting to annoy him. "Yes?"

"How do we get out after activating the gas?"

Powell entered the safe combination and removed two key cards. One red. One green.

"You follow me. The green key card gets us out of here."

CHAPTER 61

Turner moved toward the open bay door on the far side of the "drug lab." Whoever was running this place didn't know a damn thing about security. His team shouldn't have been able to infiltrate this far into the facility. Doors should have been locked. Security teams should have been tactically deployed to deny them access to certain areas of the site. It wouldn't have taken an overly serious effort to thwart them. It's not like his team was a Delta Force detachment. A bare minimum of competence could have trapped them somewhere along the way.

As he got closer to the opening, a dozen or so vehicles came into view. All 4x4s, ranging from armed dune buggy–looking contraptions to sleek black Range Rovers with tinted windows. Turner reached the right side of the bay door, motioning for everyone else to stack up behind him. He peeked around the corner, noticing an open door at the far end of the vehicle bay and one of those very solid-looking doors halfway between his position and the far door.

"KNIFE. This is AXE. Do you copy?"

"Copy," said Mann. "You have to be close if we can talk."

"I agree," said Turner. "We're about to leave the fake drug lab and enter what looks to be the site's parking garage. Lots of 4x4s in here. I see an open door at the far end. I'm thinking you're not far from that door, or we would have a hard time talking. We've heard gunfire, which must have come from somewhere beyond that door. Everything's quiet right now."

"I wish I had a better sense of where we are right now, but I don't," said Mann. "We've been fighting for our lives here. I have two KIA. Mateo and Malena."

"No. No," muttered Javier, crouched next to Turner.

"Do you have any unsuppressed weapons?" said Turner.

"Our pistols," said Mann.

"Fire three shots. If I can hear it clearly, we'll head for that door and link up," said Turner.

"Copy that," said Mann. "Have you heard anything from SPEAR?"

"Negative," said Turner. "Silence on the line."

"Same here," said Mann. "They can't be that far away."

"Maybe they got wiped out," said Turner.

"I doubt it," said Mann. "Baker is crafty."

"Yeah. He is," said Turner. "And his team is solid."

"Ready for that shot?" said Mann.

"Do it."

Three small-caliber gunshots echoed through the space.

"You have to be just inside that door," said Turner. "Can you throw something through?"

"No. We're pinned down," said Mann. "My only way out of here is heading up one of the ladders."

"Ladders?"

"The six tunnels in here lead topside to the sentry posts Jax identified," said Mann. "Our Mexican friends say it resembles a tunnel hub at the border. They stage drug shipments and carry them through the tunnels to various businesses or apartment complexes immediately adjacent to the border wall."

"This whole place is fucked up," said Turner. "Hey. In case my team doesn't make it out, I think we took out our serial killer. We entered the facility in what looked like a luxury hotel floor. Only one of the rooms was occupied—by a guy that didn't respond well when I mentioned Cedar Lake. He went for a gun, and I shot him."

"Did you take fingerprints?" said Mann.

"And both of his hands," said Turner. "Javier's idea."

"You're welcome, boss," said Javier.

"Thank you, Javier," said Mann. "Hey. I just tossed an empty rifle magazine at the door. I think it ricocheted inside."

"I saw it bounce in and hit the ground," said Javier.

"I'm right inside that door," said Mann. "To the left."

"We're heading in your direction," said Turner, stepping into the open.

Before he got more than a few feet, the reinforced steel door between the drug lab and the tunnel room burst open, a hail of automatic gunfire forcing Turner and his team back. Turner flipped the selector switch on his heavy-barrel rifle to automatic and poked it around the corner, unleashing the entire seventy-five round drum at the figures that filled the vehicle bay. Turner's salvo lasted several seconds, flattening a third of the group that had burst through the door. He backed up and detached the drum, immediately retrieving another from a pouch attached to his vest, while the rest of the team pounded the room with gunfire.

"What's going on out there?" said Mann.

Turner peeked around the edge, while inserting the fresh ammunition drum.

"You have about a dozen hostiles headed in your direction," he said.

"Copy. We're headed topside," said Mann. "That's too many for us to deal with."

Turner flipped the rifle's bipod open and dropped to the floor before thumbing the button that released the bolt and chambered a fresh round from the drum. Turner's automatic rifle blasted away at the gaggle of security officers headed for the tunnel room door, dropping a few more before the security team finally organized their return fire and drove him back.

A frenzy of gunfire snapped through the garage door–size opening, ripping into the drug lab behind them. Mayer stumbled backward, falling to the ground. Javier immediately grabbed her and dragged her out of the line of fire.

"What's Mayer's status?" said Turner, keeping an eye on the vehicle bay.

"I'm fine," she said, the words barely coming out. "Took a few to the vest. Knocked the wind out of me."

Turner reloaded the rifle with his last ammunition drum, before cautiously scanning the vehicle bay. No more obvious threats. Just a few creepers. He sighted in on a security guard toward the far end of the garage, who crawled slowly toward one of the SUVs. A quick burst from Turner's rifle cut his journey short. Turner examined the rest of the downed guards for any signs of life that might pose a threat to his team. A few guards twitched and coughed, but that was about it. Anyone who had evaded AXE's torrent of gunfire had already made it into the tunnel room.

As he swept the rifle's magnified sight over the bodies, he noticed something that he'd missed during the gunbattle. The masks. They all carried full-face gas masks with side-mounted canisters. The kind issued to soldiers and Marines to wear with full NBC suits (nuclear, biological, chemical). Out of place in the overall context of this raid, unless the guards planned on using tear gas grenades. Nothing was out of the question at this point.

"Garrett. You still there?" said Turner.

"Yes."

"Do you see the masks?"

A few seconds passed before Mann responded. "Yes. That's odd. They're gas masks in the truest sense of the word, with no self-contained oxygen supply like our hoods. They're solely designed to clear contaminants from the air."

"They're up to something."

"I agree," said Mann. "We all need to get topside immediately. They might try to release some kind of gas to flush us out of the site. Tear gas or something a lot stronger."

"That's what I was thinking," said Turner. "I might try to drive a few of the vehicles out of here."

"Don't bother. They would have taken the vehicles if that was an option. Probably locked down the vehicle exit and didn't want to leave it open for us. Did they try to go for the vehicles?" said Mann.

"Negative. They went straight for the door that leads to the tunnel room."

"They're moving fast. A few of them are already in the mechanical room. I think they plan on bypassing this room entirely," said Mann. "You might be able to slip in here right behind them without anyone noticing. It's a one-second dash to the closest tunnel."

"It's not a bad idea," said Turner.

"Take an immediate left when you enter the door. You'll see the tunnels right away. Duck into the first tunnel. There's a ladder at the end, about thirty feet or so inside. Maybe a fifty-foot climb."

"Got it," said Turner. "I'm sending Mayer, Javier, and Daniela your way."

"Where are you headed?" said Mann.

"To find SPEAR," said Turner. "A lot of these walls are solid rock. They're probably hunkered down somewhere, waiting for orders."

Gunfire erupted ahead.

"Shit. They spotted me," said Mann. "I'm headed topside. You should head back the way you came, through the service entrance tunnel. They've formed a defensive position on the mechanical room door. They'll cut at least one of you down if you try to enter."

"I'll send them back through the hotel-looking area," said Turner.

"Move fast and wear your breathing devices on the way out. If they . . . gas. Vent . . . tunnels."

"You're breaking up," said Turner.

The gunfire stopped.

"KNIFE. This is AXE," said Turner.

Nothing. He repeated the call one more time. Same result. Mann was either dead or headed to the surface.

"Jessie. Can you walk?" said Turner.

"I'm good," she said. "Just got my bell rung pretty hard."

"Okay. Follow me. We need to upgrade some of our gear," said Turner, leading them into the vehicle bay.

CHAPTER 62

Mann struggled with the climb up the metal rung ladder. Hauling himself fifty feet vertically, carrying close to fifty pounds of gear, turned out to be far harder than he imagined—and he considered himself to be reasonably fit. He focused on the starlit sky above him as he pushed off each rung and grabbed the next. When he reached the surface, two pairs of hands grabbed him by the shoulders of his vest and yanked him over the edge.

"The old man made it," Serrano said to Sofia, not a hint of exhaustion in her voice.

She easily smoked two packs of cigarettes a day, and the climb hadn't bothered her in the least. Maybe it was time to start smoking.

"Anyone else up top?" said Mann.

"Not that we can tell," said Serrano, her night vision goggles in place.

Mann flipped his down, automatically activating them. A quick scan confirmed her assessment. The two topside sentries must have stayed with the main group of guards moving into the mechanical room.

"Jax. You there?" said Mann, over the radio.

"I'm a few thousand feet above you to the southwest," said Jax.

"You can fly now?" said Mann.

"Pixie dust," said Jax. "I didn't want to share any."

"Understandable," said Mann. "Do you see any heat signatures up here other than the three of us?"

"Negative. You're the only show in town right now," said Jax.

Mann glanced at the sandbag-lined sentry posts, coming up with a quick solution to seal the hatches for now.

He turned to Serrano and Sofia. "Shut all the topside hatches and stack several sandbags on each of them. I don't think we can lock them from up here, but the sandbags will make them very difficult to open. Three or four sandbags per hatch should work. Each bag weighs around thirty pounds. I got this one."

"Got it," said Serrano, the two of them taking off.

Mann swung the wood hatch next to him shut and started to pull one of the sandbags off the three-sandbag-high sentry post.

"Jax. Here's what you missed while flying around like Peter Pan," said Mann.

"Funny," said Jax.

"The site appears to resemble a Mexican cartel border bunker, except it's obviously nowhere near the border and fake as shit on close inspection. Turner thinks they may have popped our serial killer, but we won't know until we compare fingerprints to what we took from the SUV in Minnesota," said Mann.

"That's good news, right?" said Jax.

"Yes. But we've paid a heavy price to get those prints," said Mann, heaving the sandbag onto the hatch. "At least three KIA, and we can't raise Baker on the net. SPEAR is MIA right now. Turner is looking for them. The rest of his team is headed out the way we came."

"Copy. I'll keep an eye out for them," said Jax.

"I think the facility security team is about to release some kind of gas. A poison or some kind of irritant to clear the site. It's important that you contact our people immediately when they exit, and make sure they don't take off their masks until they're at least fifty feet from the hatch," said Mann, barely freeing a second sandbag. "Even the smallest traces of something like hydrogen cyanide can mess you up pretty badly. We're shutting the six hatches topside to prevent any immediate leakage in our area."

"Between Mills and me, we can keep a close eye on the topside area and the service entrance," said Jax.

"Sounds good. From what I could tell, the security team consisted of about ten to twelve guards," said Mann. "We're putting sandbags on top of each sentry tunnel to make it as difficult as possible for them to open them, but I have this gut feeling that they'll use a different exit. Something we haven't seen yet."

"We have you covered."

"Fingers crossed that they make it out in time," said Mann.

"They'll make it out," said Jax.

"I sure as hell hope so," said Mann.

CHAPTER 63

Powell turned left upon entering the mechanical room and headed straight for the hidden panel that contained the poison gas. How he had survived those several seconds in machine-gun alley would remain one of life's great mysteries. Guards had dropped all around him during that fifteen-yard dash, half of the security detachment going down in a hail of gunfire. How Nataros and Alvarez had also survived would go down as one of life's great disappointments.

He could have used a little help with them. Especially with Alvarez, who seemed a lot quicker on the uptake than Nataros. He'd have to be extremely careful with how and when he chose to take them out. Alvarez was a survivor. He'd been around since the original SINKHOLE days. The only former CIA employee brought back for the facility's revival. A testament to skills Powell had no intention of underestimating.

"Set up a blocking team at the door. Nothing gets through," said Powell. "Is there any other way to access mechanical?"

"There's another door on the other side of the room," said Nataros. "It leads directly to the staff quarters."

That was the door he planned on taking out of here. It emptied into a short passageway that ran between the staff quarters and VIP area, where they would take a hidden ladder in the VIP lounge to the surface, after he disposed of Alejandro—if the hostile force hadn't done so already.

"Who can access that door from outside this room?" said Powell.

"Just the engineers," said Nataros.

Who had either been shot dead or tied up in their rooms right outside the door.

"Put a few guards on that door," said Powell. "We don't need any surprises right now."

Alvarez barked a few orders, which moved two of the remaining guards to the other side of the room.

"How many security officers are left?" said Powell.

"About nine," said Alvarez.

"Tell them to hold the line," said Powell.

He placed the key card against a slightly discolored, playing card–size rectangular spot on the outer wall. A few muted clicks later, a panel disguised as rock popped open next to the hidden key card reader. A black cylinder the size of a five-pound propane tank with no markings sat inside. He glanced at the instructions card, though the procedure for releasing the gas looked simple enough. Open the valve attached to the top of the cylinder, followed by the two marked Do Not Open!

"Masks on!" said Powell, the order passed along almost instantly.

Powell pushed the facepiece firmly in place against his face, making sure his nose aligned with the nose cup, and pulled the rubber straps over his head. He tightened the straps until the mask felt slightly uncomfortable against his face, taking several breaths to verify that the filter wasn't obstructed. Now for the moment of truth. He pressed his hand against the filter and took a breath, the mask adhering to his face. A successful seal test.

"Is the team ready?" said Powell.

"Just a few more seconds," said Nataros. "The guards are taking turns donning their masks, so they can keep the mechanical room secure."

"Ten seconds—and I'm releasing the gas," said Powell. "I need the door to the staff quarters opened. We'll head straight through and to the VIP area. We're headed to the VIP lounge."

"We'll clear the way," said Alvarez, his voice muted by the mask.

Powell silently counted to ten, his hand on the valve. He hoped they didn't run into any delays on the way out. The concentrations of hydrogen cyanide inside the facility would likely exceed what the masks could handle within five minutes of release. Under "normal" concentrations of hydrogen cyanide, the masks provided around thirty minutes of protection. The fail-safe system had been designed with overkill in mind, to prevent its intended victims from stumbling upon a mask and somehow escaping.

"Last call!" said Powell, having reached ten.

"Everyone's good!" said Alvarez.

He twisted the main valve counterclockwise, before turning the other two in the same direction.

"Let's go. Move!" said Powell, taking off for the door leading to the escape hatch.

They reached the VIP lounge without incident, a blessing and a curse. He'd hoped to lose a few more security officers along the way—to make his job a little easier in the end. Then again, with the entire remaining security force thinking he'd led them to safety, they wouldn't expect a betrayal.

"Stay here and make sure nobody gets through the VIP access door," said Powell.

"Where are you going?" said Nataros.

"To make sure our guest can't talk to the feds," said Powell, breaking off from the group with Alvarez.

They sprinted to the end of the main VIP quarters hallway and veered to the right, where they found that the three rooms in the farthest hallway had been crowbarred open. A quick look inside Alejandro's suite erased any doubt about the serial killer's fate while raising an interesting concern. Both of Alejandro's hands had been chopped off at the wrists. Most likely for fingerprinting, which would match the prints taken from Alejandro's Suburban. Or possibly because the team thought his hand might grant them access to restricted areas of the facility. Not the case with Alejandro, though it could pose a problem if they found the biometrically secured door to the DOMINION zone.

He led them back to the VIP lounge, where he placed the green key card against a blank electrical wall plate behind the espresso bar. A three-foot-wide, six-foot-high panel next to the espresso bar shifted slightly a few moments later. A gentle shove swung the portion of wall inward to reveal a pitch-black passageway.

"There's a ladder about a hundred feet down this tunnel," said Powell. "It'll put us well outside the sentry circle."

"Should we send security first?" said Nataros.

"No. I'll go first," said Powell, activating a handheld flashlight. "The two of you follow closely behind. We need the security team to make sure nobody finds this and follows us up."

"I'll have half the team stay here," said Alvarez. "The other half will follow close behind."

"Sounds good," said Powell, not wanting to raise any more suspicion with Alvarez than he may already have.

When he reached the metal rung ladder leading up, he turned and considered doing the deed—his thumb on the shotgun's safety lever. Alvarez appeared unexpectedly, his rifle in the ready position. Trying to take them out now was mutually assured destruction.

"Where's Nataros?" said Powell, feigning concern for the site's administrator.

"Here! I'm here!" said Nataros, appearing over Alvarez's shoulder. "Are we headed up?"

"Yes," said Powell. "Ready?"

"God yeah. I can barely breathe in this thing," said Nataros.

Powell climbed the ladder until he reached the top, a hatch marked by muted strips of tritium, a relatively harmless radioactive isotope that glowed in the dark. Tritium itself didn't emit a color, but in this case, it was enclosed in a green radio-luminescent paint. If they'd been wearing night vision goggles, they would have seen the hatch from the bottom of the ladder. He placed the green key card against the hatch. A few clicks and clacks later, he climbed out of the LABYRINTH.

"You didn't say anything about using the key card at the hatch," said Nataros, stumbling out of the hole.

"It was on the instruction card," said Powell, handing it to Alvarez.

The moment Alvarez took the card, letting his rifle hang limp by its sling, Powell raised his semiautomatic shotgun and placed it against the man's face—thumbing the safety lever into the fire position. The twelve-gauge, double-aught blast removed most of Alvarez's head. He then turned the shotgun on Nataros, who stood a few feet away, and pressed the trigger.

Nataros remained upright after the blast to his face, a dark figure frozen in place for a few moments, before collapsing to the desert floor. Powell turned and fired twice at the shadow emerging from the hatch, knocking the security guard back down the hole. A flurry of confused screams erupted from the tunnel, as the body collided with whoever followed closely behind.

Powell knelt next to the opening and poked the shotgun into the darkness, pressing the trigger repeatedly until the magazine ran out of shells. He reloaded the shotgun, still hearing voices below, and emptied all ten shells from the fresh magazine into the darkness. Screams and cries of agony echoed upward, quickly dying out to moans and croaks. He slammed the hatch shut and pressed the key card against it, a few clicks telling him that it had sealed the rest of the site's security team underground. In a few minutes, they'd all be dead—and he'd be driving out of here.

CHAPTER 64

The first shotgun blast got Mann's attention. The second, a moment later, made him take a knee. He scanned the horizon to the south, his ears pointing him in that direction. These blasts were far enough away that he wasn't immediately worried. A series of repeated blasts and distant flashes made him reconsider that assessment. Better safe than sorry. He dropped to the ground, aiming his rifle in the direction of the flashes.

"Serrano. Sofia," said Mann. "What are you seeing?"

"Nothing," said Serrano. "I'm hugging the dirt."

"Same," said Sofia. "It came from the south. I saw some muzzle flashes."

"Jax?" said Mann.

"Three heat signatures popped out of the ground about two hundred yards south of you. Maybe a fourth," said Jax. "I think one of them just shot the others. I have a lone figure heading toward the cluster of run-down structures to the southwest."

"Could they be friendly?" said Mann.

"AXE. SPEAR. This is Jax. Report any topside positions. I repeat. If you're topside, report immediately. We're about to engage a runner headed southwest."

No response.

"KNIFE. You're clear to engage the fleeing target," said Jax. "That can't possibly be one of ours."

Must be someone important to the organization operating this facility. The kind of person who would shotgun people who trusted them. Without a doubt someone who would gas an entire facility. Mann scrambled to his feet and started running in what he hoped was a southwesterly direction. Two hundred yards was well out of shotgun range.

"Am I headed in the right direction?" said Mann.

"Affirmative," said Jax. "Do you want me to lasso your target?"

"Please," said Mann.

Lassoing meant identifying a target with an infrared laser visible only to night vision. The laser operator would typically circle the target repeatedly with the laser, clearly identifying it for attack or pursuit.

"Serrano. Sofia. What's your status?" said Mann.

"Up and moving," said Serrano.

He saw them ahead, dashing from the westernmost sandbag position toward the one closest to the fleeing target.

"Start shooting as soon as you're in position," said Mann. "I'll be there in a few seconds."

The sharp crack of a dozen or more 5.56mm rounds hit his ears, Serrano and Sofia already firing.

"Target is still on the move," said Jax, politely letting them know that they'd missed.

Mann picked up the pace, reaching them while they reloaded. He hit the sandbag wall hard and saw the laser, which poked downward from an invisible point in the sky like a green tattletale. He lined up his rifle with the target, a figure sprinting toward a one-story, flat building at least three hundred yards away, and triggered the IR laser affixed to his rifle's handguard. His holographic rifle sight was essentially useless in the dark and completely useless at this range.

"Jax. Hold the laser on the target," said Mann.

"Copy," said Jax, the green sky beam steadying on a single point.

"And please keep an eye on the nearby sentry hatches," said Mann. "We didn't sandbag all of them yet."

"I'm on it," said Mills.

"Good to hear your voice, Ray."

"Good to hear yours," said Mills.

Mann aligned his rifle's laser with the terminal end of the drone's beam and pressed the trigger three times, then readjusted his laser and repeated the process. Serrano and Sofia rejoined the fray with fresh magazines and their IR lasers activated; four green lasers chased a lone figure across the desert. When Mann had expended his thirty-round magazine, he deactivated his laser.

"Jax. Is our target still up?" said Mann. Serrano and Sofia still fired short rifle bursts.

"Affirmative," said Jax. "Shit. I lost the heat signature. Looks like they just reached the building."

"Cease fire!" said Mann, the rifles going silent.

He moved closer to Serrano. "Reload. This might not be over."

While they inserted fresh rifle magazines, a bright light illuminated the desert floor to the west of the building.

"Jax. You seeing this?"

"Yeah. But the drone is east of the building. I can't see what's going on inside."

"Headlights?" said Mann.

"I really can't tell from this angle," said Jax. "But that's a lot of light."

The light started to shift across the rocky landscape, a vehicle emerging a few seconds later. It looked like some kind of boxy SUV. Probably a Range Rover or Mercedes G-Class. Something that could travel over boulders if necessary.

"Hold your fire," said Mann.

"Why?" said Serrano, taking a few shots.

"You're taking PFM shots," said Mann.

"PFM?"

"Pure fucking magic," said Mann. "They're out of range. And the vehicle is most likely armored."

"We can at least try," said Serrano.

"Don't waste your ammo."

"What else do we have to shoot at?" said Serrano.

"Nothing for now," said Mann.

"So that's it?" said Serrano. "Jax. Can you fly that drone through that vehicle's windshield?"

"Affirmative."

"Even if it's bullet-resistant glass?" said Serrano.

"A ten-pound drone striking at a relative speed of about a hundred miles per hour should still do the trick," said Jax.

"We're not pulling a kamikaze trick with the drone," said Mann.

Serrano grabbed him by the vest and spun him around. "What the hell is wrong with you? We need whoever took off in that SUV. Dead or alive."

Mann knocked her hand loose. "Alive would be better."

"And how are we supposed to pull that off now that he's a half mile away?" said Serrano. "Your stupid PFM?"

"Kind of," said Mann. "Jax. I need you to follow that SUV with the drone. Whoever's driving it will undoubtedly make an urgent phone call to report their escape. I want Jax's virus infecting every piece of communications gear in that vehicle."

"Copy that," said Jax. "Bringing the drone around. Intercept in two minutes."

"Stay with the vehicle as long as possible," said Mann. "We can pick up the drone wherever it runs out of battery charge. I want to make sure the virus does its job."

"The drone can fly for another two hours at this speed," said Jax. "I can lock it on to the vehicle and let it fly autonomously about twenty feet above the SUV until the battery runs dry."

"Whatever it takes," said Mann. "Any sign of the others?"

"Not yet," said Jax. "And our eye in the sky is already west of the site. You'll have to warn AXE and SPEAR not to take off their masks until they're clear of the door."

"Understood," said Mann. "I'll let you focus on the drone. Good work, Jax."

"Easy peasy. Out," said Jax.

"Shouldn't they have made it out by now?" said Sofia.

"Soon," said Mann, not wanting to openly admit she may be right.

At least ten minutes had elapsed since Turner had sent his team back to the service entrance tunnel. Someone should have surfaced by now if the gas hadn't gotten to them first. He wasn't hopeful about their chances. The last time he checked his emergency breathing device's gauge, the cylinder held five minutes of air. The other teams had been in the tunnel longer before reaching their breach point. Not enough to get them out. They'd run out of air before reaching the exit, forced to breathe the air flowing out of the site through the tunnel, and with it . . . whatever had been released into the air system.

"Let's sandbag the rest of these hatches and head toward the service entrance. They'll be exhausted," said Mann. "We can debrief there and decide what to do next."

His earpiece crackled.

"Jax. This is Mayer. Do you copy?"

"Jessie. Where are you?" said Jax. "My drone is off-site. I can't see you."

"We're at the service entrance," said Mayer. "Turner and the rest are a few minutes behind us."

"Don't take your masks off until you're at least fifty feet away from the door," said Jax.

"Make it a hundred feet," said Mann. "How are you feeling?"

"What do you mean?" said Mayer.

"Just clear the door and stay put," said Mann. "We'll be right over. Jax. Can you send one of the vehicles to them? We may need to drive to Roswell if they start to show signs of neurological damage."

"Garrett. We're fine," said Mayer. "We swapped the orange hoods for the masks we found in the armory. Brought a few more with us in case we want to head back down."

"I'd love to head back down and make sure we put an end to this," said Serrano.

"An end to what?" said Mann, off-radio. "The site below us is part of something way bigger than a serial killer. This is just the beginning."

"I'm still going down there," said Serrano.

"So am I," said Mann. "Just not right now. We need to let the gas vent for a few hours. Then we'll take a look. Deal?"

"Deal," said Serrano, producing a pack of cigarettes from a pouch on her vest. "Can I smoke now?"

"We just escaped poison gas," said Mann. "Why not?"

PART VI

CHAPTER 65

Powell waited until he turned south onto County Road B7 before trying to reach out to McCall. The hard-packed dirt road leading away from LABYRINTH wasn't well maintained, and the last thing he needed was to blow a tire with a team of commandos chasing him.

He checked his cell phone first, not surprised to see No Service on the screen. He dug through his tactical vest pouches until he found his sat phone, which he powered up. Several seconds later, his phone was tracking at least three satellites. He pressed one of the preset buttons and prepared himself for one of the least pleasant phone conversations of his career.

"Confirmation code," answered McCall.

Not this shit.

"The Cubs suck," said Powell.

"That wasn't very nice," said McCall.

"I'm not in the mood," said Powell.

A long pause ensued. "Do you want to know who else isn't in the mood?"

"Sorry. It's been a night."

"What happened?"

"LABYRINTH was covertly breached by two teams, using two separate entry points. I still don't know how—"

"I got all of that from your urgent sitrep," said McCall. "The site. The personnel. The hostile force. What's the current status? I assume you didn't call to say hello."

Powell took a moment to compose himself. He wasn't in the mood to take shit right now, but he didn't appear to have a choice.

"I'm the only one that made it out—as far as I know," said Powell. "I gassed the site. Took out Nataros, Alvarez, and the few security guards who tried to escape with us. The rest are locked inside. I made Alvarez lock the vehicle bay doors with his personal override code, which vaporized along with his head. A few members of the hostile force made it topside by climbing up the sentry post ladders. If any of our people try to exit using one of those six ladders, the hostile force will probably eliminate them—and very likely inhale a lethal dose of poison in the process. Nobody with any real knowledge of what's going on down there is getting out."

"Well. I guess you're not fired," said McCall.

"Oh. Okay," said Powell.

"That's a joke. None of this is your fault," said McCall. "Are you certain that the gas released?"

"I followed the instruction card," said Powell. "Nobody was keen on testing the air."

"I guess we'll have to trust the system and hope for the best."

"Nataros, Alvarez, the staff involved in the DOMINION training, and the recruits themselves were the only direct liabilities at the site," said Powell. "Nataros and Alvarez are dead. The staff were instructed to lock themselves in their rooms until the security alert ended. With the amount of gunfire in the facility, I can only assume they stayed in place and are now dead. The recruits were locked down in their bunk rooms. Should be the same result."

"Alejandro?"

"Dead from a single headshot," said Powell, leaving the part about the severed hands out of the discussion for now.

"Good. And the training center itself was empty when the gas was released?" said McCall. "It's a new addition—running on a separate air system."

"The recruits are locked in their rooms by ten," said Powell. "My guess is they were all asleep when the gas was released. The door to the training facility is heavy duty enough to dampen the sound of gunfire. They keep four security officers in the recruit living area at all times, but they can neither access the school nor open the door leading back into the rest of the facility without authorization from the control room— which we did not grant."

"Then that's it," said McCall. "I guess we hold our collective breaths and hope Mann doesn't piece enough together to see the bigger picture until we can properly muddy the waters."

"I can't say for certain that Mann hit the facility," said Powell. "We had a minimum of fifteen intruders breach the site. ARTEMIS was down to eight by my count, and I can't imagine him wrangling another seven FBI agents to come along. He was radioactive enough before all this went down. After Cedar Lake and the motel, joining up with him would be career suicide."

"We've already examined the security feed footage you managed to upload before leaving the control room," said McCall. "They made short work of the cameras, but we managed to isolate some high-enough-resolution frames to positively identify Mann and most of his team."

"Then who the hell did he recruit to help him?" said Powell. "Mercenaries?"

"We're still working on that. From what we can tell, the others are all Latino," said McCall. "And the only Latinos originally on the team were Dr. Trejo, who Zaleski torched at the Owatonna medical examiner's office, and a still-unidentified female FBI agent. I'm starting to wonder whether she's actually an FBI agent."

"She's been with the group for a while," said Powell. "Past surveillance has shown her wearing FBI-labeled equipment and flashing an FBI badge."

"But we can't identify her," said McCall. "All we know about her is the name Serrano, and the two Serranos in the FBI database are not her."

"Maybe she's part of an exchange program?" said Powell. "A Mexican federal agent of some kind?"

"Flashing an FBI badge?"

"That would be odd," said Powell. "Could she be a former cartel *sicario* that Mann somehow turned? That could explain the additional personnel they brought into the facility. Former cartel heavies. They tore our security apart."

"We're about to do a deep dive into her identity," said McCall. "The bigger problem right now is figuring out how Mann found LABYRINTH and Alejandro's house at Cedar Lake."

"Has to be a well-placed insider. A present or past CIA employee," said Powell.

"I agree, but Mann doesn't have any connections to the CIA, unless we've missed something in his profile," said McCall.

"What about Assistant Director O'Reilly?" said Powell. "I've heard stories about her."

"We all have," said McCall. "But that door is shut hard for now. I don't know how she pulled it off, but as far as the FBI and the federal government are concerned, her career only goes back to the point where she was promoted to head the Critical Incident Response Group."

"That's impossible," said Powell.

"We ran a full background profile on her a year ago, after ARTEMIS started tracking Alejandro," said McCall. "She's a ghost prior to her current job."

"Interesting," said Powell. "I heard she played a key role in taking down True America. Maybe she negotiated a clean sweep of her service record to avoid scrutiny after Ryan Sharpe retired."

"It's entirely possible," said McCall. "Rumors are rumors. Paperwork is the truth."

"She's not the kind of senior FBI director we want digging into our business," said Powell. "Especially if she has past connections to the CIA and other groups that I've heard rumors about."

"I agree," said McCall. "Maybe it's time to preemptively remove Mann's nexus to these groups and the kind of sensitive information that can tank a multimillion-dollar investment in AXIOM's future. I don't take LABYRINTH's loss lightly. I just pray it's not a showstopper."

"Mann has proven resourceful, but only with some very targeted help," said Powell. "I'll reach out to our other friend. O'Reilly has a bad habit of tearing things down, and old habits die hard. I think it's time they crossed paths."

"Not a bad idea. It's not like he's busy now that LABYRINTH is gone," said McCall. "Where are you now?"

"Heading south on a dirt road," said Powell. "I should hit a paved state road in about ten minutes. My plan is to turn east and head to Roswell."

"I'll send a plane to pick you up," said McCall. "You'll have an encrypted communications suite on board. Contact our friend and get that ball rolling. We'll wait and see where the rest of the pieces fall before making any drastic moves beyond that."

"I'll reach out to him when I'm airborne," said Powell.

"All right. I'll be in touch," said McCall, ending the call.

Powell lowered the windows, letting in the cool night air. What a disaster. On one hand, he wished he'd never volunteered to babysit LABYRINTH. On the other, he acknowledged the likelihood that the entire facility would have fallen into Mann's hands if he hadn't been there. Nataros was borderline useless. Alvarez was good, but not committed enough to pull off the gas trick.

In the end, Mann would have retreated to the surface and called in reinforcements. Within hours, LABYRINTH's staff and recruits would have been in federal custody, singing songs about DOMINION. He just hoped that McCall understood that Powell had fundamentally saved the program, or at the very least—extended its life span long enough to fulfill AXIOM's multibillion-dollar contract. And seal their positions as kingmakers.

CHAPTER 66

The eastern horizon glowed deep orange. Serrano took a deep breath and exhaled, a technique Mann had tried to teach her—and that she'd entirely ignored until right now. She was desperate for some kind of calm, but too nervous to smoke. Tonight was the first time that had happened. She'd taken the pack in her vest out at least a half dozen times over the past twenty minutes, shoving it back into its pouch before repeating the process. Now she was doing Mann's Buddhist crap. End-times for sure. No exaggeration.

She was about to climb down into the facility, with no idea if the mask and filter, taken from the site's armory, could handle the level of gas, or whatever may have been released into the air system. Maybe they hadn't released anything at all, and the security guards carried the masks as standard procedure in the event of an attack on the facility. Lots of unknowns, which they'd pondered for the past four hours while giving the atmosphere below time to clear.

They'd opened the topside hatches and left the service entrance open. Unfortunately, only one of the breach points remained open at the terminal end of the service entrance tunnel. They had closed the door in the mechanical room, worried that the entry might be discovered by a team responding to an air system alarm. She remembered the strong draft that had washed over them the moment they opened that door, the site's air vacating at an alarming rate. Closing the door had been the right call at the time.

Turner had left the other door open, giving her hope that she wouldn't immediately die after climbing down one of the topside sentry ladders. They'd attached a climbing rope to her vest's drag handle, a reinforced, one-hand nylon grip located at the top of her vest, just below the nape of her neck. She'd climb down and proceed into the tunnel room, where she'd wait for fifteen minutes. If she felt fine at that point, Serrano would climb back up. If she experienced any symptoms of nausea, dizziness, shortness of breath, euphoria—the list went on— she'd return to the ladder and climb back up.

If she couldn't climb, the team would pull her back to the surface. Mann had assured her that the mask would keep her safe, but everything had its limits. She'd essentially volunteered to be the team's "canary in the coal mine." A risk she was willing to take to verify the death of her mother's murderer for herself, and to help forward whatever efforts ARTEMIS would take to track down the killer's apparent benefactors. Turner's description of the luxury accommodations beneath them had turned her stomach. These people, whoever they were, had harnessed that sick killer for their own purposes. She wouldn't stop until they were all dead or in jail.

"Ready?" said Mann.

"Not really," she said. "But yeah—let's get it over with."

Mann placed the mask against her face and pulled the straps over her head.

"You'll be fine. I promise," said Mann, tightening the straps. "Take a deep breath."

She inhaled, no air entering her lungs—the mask hugging her face.

"I can't breathe!" she said.

He raised his hands. "Try now."

She took a deep breath, drawing air into her lungs while realizing he had been testing the mask's seal.

"I'm good," she said.

"Then off you go," said Mann, grabbing her wrist.

"Yes," she said, before laughing.

"Yes?" said Mann.

"I accept your proposal," said Serrano, lifting the hand in his grip.

"Nice try. But I forgot the ring," said Mann. "You'll have to settle for me setting your wristwatch alarm for fifteen minutes."

"Lucky me," said Serrano, holding her arm out while he set the alarm.

"Any signs of trouble, you tug on the line and head back to the ladder," said Mann. "Use your radio. If this place is toxic, we'll have to call it in and let O'Reilly deal with it. Don't be stubborn about this. You can't be a part of the solution if you're dead. Copy?"

"Copy," said Serrano, turning toward the open hatch behind her.

Fifteen minutes later, she'd reemerged without any signs of poisoning. Mann ushered her away from the opening, before removing her mask.

"Anything?" he said.

"Not a sound. The place is a tomb," she said.

"No. Not that," said Mann. "What about you? Are you feeling okay?"

"I guess—uh, I'm fine?" she said, surprised by his concern.

Mann could be shockingly aloof most of the time. Almost pathologically practical. She didn't really know how to respond. He smiled for the first time in what seemed like a month.

"Good," he said, nodding slightly. "Are you okay to go back down?"

"The moment you change this canister, I'm climbing back down that ladder," said Serrano, holding up her mask. "There's no telling how much time we have left before the people operating this place send a recovery team."

They'd spent the past four hours exploring the surrounding area in groups of two, the rest of the team stationed topside with the automatic rifles, waiting for a retaliatory response that still hadn't arrived—and at this point probably wouldn't. Not that they planned on letting their guard down anytime soon.

Their patrols had found several motion sensors outside the topside sentry perimeter, about a quarter mile out. The service entrance had clearly been placed outside the sensor zone. They also located the vehicle entrance to the west, a well-worn dirt road steeply dropping underneath a wide desert-camouflage net and ending at a rolling, retractable steel garage door.

"Let's do it," said Mann, turning to the team that would descend first.

Turner and Baker would join Mann and Serrano for the team's initial postattack reconnaissance of the site. They'd spend no more than twenty minutes below, moving quickly through the areas already explored to assess the situation and verify that the facility was clear of any potential threats. They'd stop along the way to collect more masks and canisters.

The goal of the second trip, conducted by the same team, would be to explore areas they hadn't accessed or traveled through during the initial breach. Specifically, the door secured by the biometric scanner. They'd carry a sack given to them by Javier, which now included the hands of the two headless men found a few hundred yards south, next to a sealed hatch used by the site's single escapee. It was only a theory, but the two looked like they might be important, which meant that their hands might open the door Turner's team found on their way through the southern part of the site.

Turner led them on a quick tour of the previously explored parts of the site, having seen most of them during his travels with AXE and his search for Baker's group. Serrano counted nine bodies in the vehicle bay, all with gunshot wounds. A few injuries less severe than the rest. They probably died when their gas mask canisters finally failed.

The drug lab turned out to be just as fake as previously reported. All the lab gear, raw cooking materials, and refined products looked real enough, but when you got up close—you could tell something was off. Why would they go through the trouble of creating a fake drug lab? The same question could be asked about the tunnel room. Why simulate a border tunnel transport hub? Maybe for training? Were they creating an undercover team to infiltrate the cartels? Why would a decades-past Ciudad Juárez serial killer be part of the operation? Hopefully they'd get some answers.

But the first order of business as far as Serrano was concerned was to confirm that they'd killed the man responsible for hundreds of gruesome murders just south of the Texas-Mexico border. The man who had robbed Cata of her *madre* when she was seventeen—on the cusp of heading out into the world to make the one person who had sacrificed everything for her proud. She feigned as much interest as she could muster while exploring the facility, itching to get to the room that contained his body.

Serrano had to see it for herself. Then she needed to verify that the fingerprints from the body matched the Suburban used to dump the bodies in Minnesota. Only then would she truly feel that her mother's murderer had been brought to justice. She'd deal with the implications of the rest of this place later.

They took a quick detour into the armory to load up on more gas masks and canisters, which they tossed in their backpacks. Mann suggested that they confiscate all the ammunition and select pieces of gear, like night vision goggles and thermal scopes, on another trip down. Their status with the FBI was still in question. They would likely remain fugitives, even after calling this place in—and their money was running low.

Turner brought them to the very solid-looking, reinforced steel door that featured a biometric scanner. They'd tackle this obstacle during the next trip down, armed with a bag full of hands. After moving through the staff's recreational area and quarters, which contained a few dozen hog-tied corpses and a bullet-riddled security team, they finally reached the hotel-like accommodations Turner had described.

The first room they encountered was a swank lounge complete with a fully stocked bar, an espresso station—and several dead bodies. A few of them had no apparent bullet wounds, victims of whatever gas had been released hours ago. A compact doorway next to the coffee station stood open, three bodies piled up at the bottom of a metal rung ladder leading upward. Their heads and shoulders riddled with jagged holes suggesting that they'd been shotgunned from above. A detail that matched what she and Mann had heard while topside. A dozen or more shotgun blasts in the distance. Someone cleaning house.

The moment of truth was near. Turner stopped them for a moment outside the lounge. She glanced past him at the hallway, which branched off into two separate passageways.

"The room at the end of the first hallway is what you're looking for. The other rooms are empty," he said, nodding at her. "The second hallway is interesting. Two empty rooms, then the room we found recently vacated. We're coming up on twenty minutes, so don't linger."

Serrano blew past him the moment he stopped talking, turning right into the first hallway. She was inside the killer's room a few seconds later. Brains on the wall. Hands missing. He looked old, his black hair a mess. A quick look around the room revealed nothing. No luggage. No personal items. The bathroom told a similar story. A small toiletry pack sat on the counter. The kind of convenience pack hotels provide when your luggage is lost while traveling.

"How are you doing?" said Mann, startling her.

"It's a bit surreal to think that this might be him," said Serrano.

"We won't know for sure until we match the prints," said Mann. "But all the signs point in that direction."

"We'll see," said Serrano. "Turner said he found a bottle of Gran Patrón in the recently vacated room. I don't see a bottle here, but he just arrived."

"I don't understand," said Mann.

"The guy I tracked down and killed in Ciudad Juárez had a La Línea tattoo—"

"You told me that already," said Mann. "That's the Juárez Cartel faction that carries out all the executions and runs their intimidation operations."

"There's something I never told you," said Serrano.

"Okay," said Mann.

"I always knew there was no way that guy worked alone," said Serrano.

"Right. It's logistically impossible," said Mann. "There were two of them."

"Actually. Three of them," said Serrano.

"Three? You said two," said Mann.

"Anyway," she said, ignoring his accusation. "After torturing him for hours and getting nowhere, I killed him."

"Cata. I already know all of this," said Mann, checking his watch. "But now there are three of them?"

"I never told you the real story about the tattoo," said Serrano, flicking open a serrated knife. "I need to examine his La Línea ink."

"Jesus," said Mann, before triggering his radio. "Turner. We're going to need another minute or two."

"That's cutting it close. Everything okay back there?" said Turner.

"Nothing to worry about," said Mann. "Are we ready to head back up?"

"Yeah. But I think we should send Mayer and Rocha back down to scour the room at the end of the last hallway for fingerprints and other forensic evidence," said Turner. "Whoever stayed in this room left very recently."

"Sounds good. Let's start moving everyone out of here," said Mann. "We'll be right behind you."

Serrano started in the most obvious place. Right shoulder. She cut at the shoulder and yanked the long sleeve down his arm. Nothing. The left arm yielded the same result.

"No tattoo," said Mann.

She shook her head, before tearing open his loosely fitting button-down shirt with her bare hands to expose the La Línea tattoo on his upper left chest. Two flaming skulls flanking a third skull adorned with a WWII Nazi helmet, which sat under the letters "n.c.d.j" and above a wavy banner declaring "La Linea 727."

"That's a pretty messed-up tattoo," said Mann. "Has to be your guy, right?"

"Yes," she said. "And no."

"And no?" said Mann.

"He's part of the triad," said Serrano.

"Damn it, Cata," said Mann. "Triad? What are you talking about?"

"The guy I killed in Ciudad Juárez had the same tattoo. The Gran Patrón symbol added to the very bottom of the La Linea 727 banner. I stripped that guy down and examined every inch of his body, looking for anything that might set him apart. I took hundreds of photographs before I burned his body to a crisp. It took me a while, but I finally saw it. That was their sign. The bee—Gran Patrón's logo. Bees swarm the blue agave plant."

"I see the bee," said Mann. "And something else."

"Exactly," said Serrano. "The bee is ringed with the word *tríada*. Triad. And a Roman numerical stamp. II/III. Second out of three. The guy I killed had III/III on his tattoo. Third out of three."

"So we're still missing the first of the three," said Mann.

"Yes. And whoever was staying in the other room. The room with the bottle of Gran Patrón. That's the last killer in the triad. Until he's dead, I won't rest."

Mann nodded. "Understood. We'll take prints from the other room and see where those lead us. My hunch is that the final killer in the triad is living the good life. This guy owned a multimillion-dollar property. Whoever runs this place treats their more esteemed guests very well. We'll get to the bottom of that soon enough. But we can't ignore the bigger implications of this facility. We need to process this scene methodically and unemotionally."

"As long as I have your word that you won't screw me over on this," said Serrano. "I will find the killer, no matter what this place turns out to be."

"You have my word," said Mann.

"And the bodies?" said Serrano.

"Bodies?"

"Mateo. Malena. Amelia and Bianca."

"Right," said Mann. "We'll bring them to the surface and figure out a way to get them back to their families. I don't know how, but I'll make it happen. I promise."

"Thank you," said Serrano.

CHAPTER 67

Mann stood in front of the brushed metal door, contemplating the fingerprint scanner. The drop pouch attached to the right side of his vest contained three pairs of severed hands, each pair placed into a separate, gallon-size Ziploc bag. Two of the bags contained a key card, each taken from the headless bodies found at the escape hatch. The bag without identification belonged to the man they strongly suspected to be their serial killer. The hope was that at least one of these hands would open the door.

"So. I just start pressing fingers against the biometric scanner?" said Mann.

"Your guess is as good as mine," said Baker.

"Control room. Are you ready?" said Mann.

They'd left Rocha and Mayer in what they'd identified as the control room in case the biometric scanner triggered a remote verification method, like a camera feed accessible to the duty team. Mayer had rigged a series of radio repeaters along the hallways so they could talk to each other. Given the limited amount of time they planned on spending down here on each trip, they didn't want to waste any time trying to decipher the site's radio communications network.

"We're standing by," said Mayer.

Mann lifted one of the bags out of the oversize pouch and checked the key card through the plastic. Diego Nataros. The other set of hands belonged to Sergio Alvarez. Neither key card indicated their rank in the facility. He opened the bag and removed a hand without looking, placing the index finger against the scanner. Nothing.

"Garrett," said Mayer. "One of the workstation screens just activated. It's asking for key card verification to permit access to DOMINION."

"DOMINION?" said Mann.

"There's a small key card–size scanner next to the keyboard," said Mayer. "I think you need to run one of the cards back to us. But not the one linked to the hand you just used."

"That makes sense," he said, pulling the other two bags out and handing the one with a key card to Baker. "Run that back to Mayer and Rocha."

"Got it," said Baker, taking off with the bag.

About a half minute later, the outline of the biometric scanner turned bright green—a series of four heavy thumps inside the door immediately following.

"Turn your GoPros on," said Mann. "We have to document everything."

"Including the bag of hands?" said Turner.

"Good point. Let's hold off on the GoPros until the hands are out of sight," said Mann. "Unless you want to go to jail."

"I think we're already going to jail," said Turner.

"Probably," said Mann.

"That's not funny."

"It wasn't meant to be," said Mann.

Mann grabbed the thick metal handle and pulled, the door opening without any detectable resistance. Four security guards lay on the gray tile floor just beyond the hatch, their unmasked faces twisted in agony. He imagined them frantically pounding on the door at the first sign of respiratory trouble. A futile effort, considering they had been left to die here by Nataros and Alvarez, who he presumed were the two top dogs at the site.

"It worked," said Mann. "The door is open. We found four dead security guards inside."

"Excellent," said Mayer. "We'll stick around in case there are any more double verification processes. Baker is on his way back. We're holding on to the other bag of hands for now."

"Lucky you," said Mann.

"Yeah. It's a dream come true," said Mayer. "When I joined the FBI, I told myself—whatever you do, make sure you find yourself holding a Ziploc bag containing two severed hands before you retire."

"Damn. Talk about achieving your career goals," said Turner. "Time to retire."

"That's what I was thinking," said Mayer. "But I still have eleven years to go before I'm eligible."

"Retirement?" said Baker. "Shit. We'll be lucky if we don't end up in prison after this."

"Good point," said Mann. "But Mayer?"

"Yes?"

"At least you'll go to prison knowing you achieved everything you set out to achieve in the FBI," said Mann.

"Since when did you acquire a sense of humor?" said Mayer.

"I don't know. Maybe after my third near-death experience today?" said Mann, getting a laugh out of Serrano and Turner.

Baker appeared at the end of the hallway, reaching them a few moments later. "Wait. You're funny now?"

"Apparently," said Mann, nodding at the open door. "I don't think we're going to find anyone alive inside, but you never know. Watch your corners. Check every single body you come across. Make no assumptions."

Mann stepped inside, feeling like he'd just crossed the threshold of something inherently evil. Something that wouldn't let them go back the way they came.

"Grab their ID cards," said Mann, stepping through the small gaggle of dead guards. "They double as key cards."

They faced their first decision about twenty feet down the utilitarian, industrial-looking hallway. A tight, dimly lit passage broke off to their right. The left side of the corridor featured six similar openings. They needed to work methodically.

"Baker. Stay here while we sweep this passage," said Mann.

"Got it," said Baker, taking a knee in the middle of the main hallway, his rifle pointed toward the other openings.

"Turner," said Mann. "Lead the way."

Mann and Serrano fell in behind Turner as they navigated the single passage that appeared to extend as far as the main hallway. They found the half dozen doors on each side of the corridor to be unlocked, each revealing a basic interrogation room. Rectangular metal tables bolted to the floor, with iron-shackle loops welded to the center of each table. A single chair on each side. Dome camera in the corner of every room.

All the rooms looked well worn. The tables dented. Chairs crooked. Walls scarred—presumably by the feet of the chairs. A few dried bloodstains. This area had seen some serious business. Twelve rooms in total? A sizable operation. But what kind of operation? Time to find out. Mann led them down the first hallway to the left, which featured a dozen reinforced metal doors. They tried all the door handles, finding them locked.

"Let's crack these open," said Mann.

Turner and Serrano pulled crowbars from their backpacks and wedged them between the doorframe and the door handle.

"Try the key card things we took from the guards first," said Baker.

"Someone's thinking," said Mann.

The first two yielded nothing. The third card opened the door. Its owner must have been the four-person team's section leader.

"Fucking genius," said Turner.

Mann pocketed the two that didn't work, plus the one they didn't use, before pulling the door open. A twenty-something Latino male, with tattoos up and down his arms, lay face up on a narrow bed. Eyes closed. Arms hanging over the sides. He'd died in his sleep. They opened a few more doors a little farther down the hallway, finding a mix of men and women—all in their twenties or thirties, most with similar cartel tattoos. He handed the key card to Turner and asked him to check a few rooms in the next hallway.

Serrano knelt next to the woman in the last room they opened, taking a closer look. She leaned in, examining the woman's neck—turning her head left and right a few times.

"What's up?"

"Her neck tattoos have been removed," said Serrano. "You can still see some vague outlines, but with a few more laser treatments and a little more time, they'd be gone."

"Can you tell if the treatments are recent?"

"Uh—recent enough," said Serrano.

"What about the arms?" said Mann.

She lifted the woman's T-shirt sleeve to the top of her shoulder, exposing a fully inked arm.

"No signs of any attempt to remove these," said Serrano.

"Interesting," said Mann.

"You can hide arm tattoos, but you can't wear a turtleneck in Phoenix—or anywhere else for that matter during the middle of the summer—without drawing attention," said Serrano.

"Mann. I opened two doors and found the same shit," said Turner over the radio.

"Copy," said Mann. "No need to check any other rooms right now."

Everyone was dead. Mann ushered them to the windowless door at the end of the hallway, where he pressed one of the security officers' key cards against a card reader under the door handle. The door buzzed and clicked, Turner opening it to reveal a cavernous, two-story space—twice the size of the area they'd just explored. The football field–size space looked like a Hollywood movie set.

To their left, two full-size two-story houses, with real grass lawns, flanked the start of "Main Street," as the sign ahead of them declared. They walked along the concrete sidewalk until Main Street came into full view. Beyond the houses, several structures lined the street, looking like a cross-section of various types of housing found in the United States.

A standalone town house. Half of a duplex, with its side completely exposed like it had been cut in half by a laser. A one-story ranch house. A two-story apartment building that took up half of one side of the street. Toward the far end of the street, Mann saw what looked like frontage for a movie theater, grocery store, small city bodega, coffee shop, and tattoo parlor, which he guessed was where they got their tattoos removed.

"What the hell is this?" said Baker.

"Ever read *The Charm School*?" said Turner.

"Yeah. I'm getting those vibes," said Mann.

"Big-time," said Mann.

"I don't get it," said Serrano.

"It's an old spy novel," said Mann. "The Soviets took American pilots captured in Vietnam and forced them to train spies that would operate in America as sleeper agents. They created an American town to make the training as realistic as possible."

"Dios mío," said Serrano. "Why would they do that with cartel thugs?"

"That's exactly my question," said Mann, his voice trailing off.

A single metal door on the wall to their right competed for his attention. Serrano followed his stare.

"Another biometric scanner," said Serrano. "I wonder which hand will open it."

"Shit. I left Alvarez's hands back in the control room," said Baker. "Sorry about that."

"Mayer. How much time do we have left on the canisters?" said Mann.

"Three minutes until you hit twenty," she replied.

Out of an abundance of caution, they'd agreed not to exceed twenty minutes.

"Let's open the door, take a quick look inside, and get out of here. GoPros off, please," said Mann, pulling one of the bags out of his pouch.

He'd grabbed the unmarked bag; the hands inside belonged to their suspected serial killer. Why not give it a try? If the killer's hands opened the door, they were looking at a level of cooperation between the people who ran this site and the killer that they hadn't yet considered. He removed one of the hands and pressed its index finger against the scanner; the console instantly turned green, followed by a few muted clicks inside the door. No double verification required for this door. Very interesting.

Mann opened the door, then closed it, the console going red for a moment before it returned to its original state.

"Why did you do that?" said Serrano.

"I'm curious about something," he said, offering the hand to Serrano. "Hold on to this for a second?"

Turner laughed. "He is getting funnier by the minute."

Mann retrieved the hand he'd used to open the first door and pressed the index finger against the scanner. Nothing. He tried a few more fingers with the same result. Something told Mann he did not want to see what was on the other side of this door.

"Cata?" said Mann, putting the hand back in the bag.

She held the killer's finger against the scanner, opening the door.

"This can't be good," she said, crossing herself.

"None of this is good," said Mann, pulling the door open.

Mann stepped into a dark antechamber, a second door visible a few feet in front of him. He searched the walls next to the door, finding a light switch, which triggered an overhead fluorescent tube. The light flickered for a few moments, before bathing the room in a sickly greenish-white pallor.

The next door was constructed of the same steel, also windowless—but didn't appear to have any locking mechanism. He opened the door to a pitch-dark space; the slightest hint of chlorine bleach hit his nose. Nothing but the strongest odors should be able to penetrate his mask's filter. He wasn't sure he wanted to see what waited for them in the darkness.

"Do you smell that?" said Serrano.

"Yeah. This is going to be really bad," said Mann. "Baker. Wait outside and cover us."

"I think I'll wait outside, too," said Turner.

"Cameras on," said Mann, activating his GoPro.

"I found the light switch," said Serrano.

"Do it," said Mann, instantly regretting his words.

The off-white light cast by several exposed fluorescent tubes revealed a scene that would likely haunt Mann for the rest of his life. Glistening white tile covered the walls and floor of the roughly twenty-by-twenty-foot room. An oversize circular drain sat in the middle of the floor, a stainless-steel ventilation hood directly above it.

A sizable steel barrel, mounted to a raised, wheeled metal frame, sat in one of the corners, next to a plastic shelving unit. The bottom two shelves held several five-gallon plastic gasoline cans, each labeled SODIUM HYDROXIDE. Lye. The third contained an industrial-size propane heater. Three twenty-pound propane tanks sat on the other side of the shelving unit. One-gallon bottles of bleach sat on the top shelf.

A thick, pinkish rivulet led from the drain to an ancient-looking wooden workbench set against the far wall. A wall-mounted, industrial-grade tool rack ran the length of the wall behind the table, featuring a chain saw, a small circular saw, two reciprocating saws, and a variety of machetes, hatchets, handsaws, tin snips, and scissors. A dull wire garrote with wooden handles hung from a hook, next to a tight spool of wire. The Piano Man's trademark tool.

He'd heard about places like this but had never seen one. They went by several nicknames. Bathhouses. Roach motels. The Bermuda Triangle. Chop shop. The names got worse toward the end of the list. The process was simple: If the cartels wanted to make a body disappear, they'd bring the corpse to a place like this for disposal. The body would be cut into pieces that could be stuffed into the stainless-steel drum, which would then be filled with the sodium hydroxide.

The propane burner would be placed under the drum to bring the lye to a slow boil, dissolving the flesh, innards, and all but the most stubborn bone pieces, within twelve hours. The resulting "soup" would be left alone to cool, before it was poured down the drain, essentially erasing any traces of the victim.

"Garrett?" said Serrano.

He didn't like the sound of her voice.

"Yes?"

"Over there," she said.

He'd been so focused on the ghastly workshop that he'd missed the worst part. A woman sat against the wall directly across from the workbench, her hands shackled to one of three metal rings attached to the wall. She had been stripped down to her underwear, exposing a body full of tattoos. Judging from the lack of bruising and abrasions beneath the cuffs on her wrists, she hadn't been here long. At least she hadn't suffered. Only the serial killer's fingerprint opened the door to this room—a twisted and evil "perk" of working for whatever organization ran this place. She must have been brought in within the past twenty-four hours, as an offering to the psycho.

"We need to go," said Mann, tapping his canister. "We'll start here when we return."

As they started to leave, the woman cried out. *"Por favor!* Take me with you. Don't leave me here!"

How is she still alive?

"Turner. Bring me one of the extra masks," said Mann.

"It's not a good idea to change masks," said Turner. "One whiff of whatever they pumped into this place could be lethal."

"We found a survivor," said Mann.

"What?" said Turner.

"Just bring me the mask and your bolt cutters," said Mann.

"We need to be careful with her," said Serrano. "She has some serious Juárez ink."

"I have a feeling she's not going to give us much trouble," said Mann, removing a pair of flex-cuffs from his vest. "But better safe than sorry."

Ten minutes later, pushing the boundaries of their gas mask canisters uncomfortably close to the half-hour mark, they were topside with one of the facility's only two survivors, a Juárez Cartel *sicario* named Elena. And she had one hell of a story to tell.

CHAPTER 68

Dana O'Reilly finished watching the forty-three-minute video for the second time—her hands trembling.

"I'm getting too old for this shit," she mumbled.

She called Mann, who picked up immediately.

"Pretty bad, huh?" said Mann.

"Is this for real?" said O'Reilly.

"What do you mean?"

"You haven't gone off the deep end, right? Hired a Hollywood production company to create this video?" said O'Reilly.

"You got me, Dana," said Mann. "We all drew from our 401(k)s to create a video in a desperate attempt to salvage our careers."

"I'm not joking, Garrett," said O'Reilly. "Because what you sent me represents a clear and present danger to the United States. I don't know how, exactly, but I do know that nothing good can come of whatever was going on in that facility."

"Dana. This is all very real," said Mann. "We spliced it together using footage taken with GoPro cameras. Elena is real. The Starbucks-branded coffee shop, fifty feet underground, is real. The fifty-four cartel members that we found gassed in their cells are real. All of it. The first set of coordinates in the video correspond to the tunnel entrance we used to access the site. The second set is for the topside hatches. The third is the vehicle bay entrance."

"I know," said O'Reilly. "I believe you. I just had to ask—so I can say I did with a straight face when everyone asks me the same question."

"I understand. It's all very overwhelming. I'm still trying to process what we found. The first part of the facility barely made sense. Fake drug lab. Simulated border tunnel hub. It all seemed totally random, until we broke into the second part of the site. There's nothing random about it."

"What do you mean?" said O'Reilly, thinking she knew where he might be going with this.

"Based on what Elena told us, which you witnessed," said Mann, "whoever is behind that facility wanted their *recruits*—Elena's word—to think they were in a bunker on the Texas-Mexico border. When they were brought to the site, she caught glimpses of the tunnel room and drug lab while they escorted her to the training area. She became convinced that she'd been hand-picked for some kind of special training."

"And you're sure this isn't some kind of Juárez Cartel operation?" said O'Reilly.

"It's entirely possible that I might be wrong about that," said Mann. "We found no corporate logos or paperwork suggesting any specific company was behind this, but your contact stressed that this was no longer an agency-run site."

"CIA?"

"Yes," said Mann.

"He told you that specifically?"

"No. But he gave me enough verbal cues to make the connection," said Mann. "He sounds like an interesting guy."

"That's Karl in a nutshell," said O'Reilly. "If his past exploits weren't so highly classified, you'd find his bio listed first under the Google search—*been there, done that.*"

"Another thing," said Mann. "The fingerprints we took from the guy we found in the luxury-suite part of the facility match the prints taken from the Suburban spotted at the scene of the body dump in

Minnesota. We're confident he's the serial killer we've been tracking. That's the good news."

"Okay," said O'Reilly. "So. What's the bad news?"

"Serrano is convinced there's another killer loose in the US, sponsored by whoever ran that site. The evidence we collected supports her theory, and this killer is part of whatever the hell was going on underground at the site. A triad of serial killers. Two dead. One still out there."

"Three killers?" said O'Reilly. "What happened to the first killer?"

"Long story—for another time," said Mann. "Just trust me on this."

"Don't you mean . . . trust her?"

"Yes. Her information checks out," said Mann. "Two down. One to go. But that's the least of our problems."

"Agreed," said O'Reilly. "I'm far more concerned about that aspect of your discovery."

"Yes," said Mann. "But the two are directly connected. If we find the last killer, we shed more light on the insanity we discovered down there."

"I don't disagree," said O'Reilly.

"So. Where do we go from here?" said Mann. "We have no intention of surfacing without assurances."

"What kind of assurances?" said O'Reilly.

"Do I really have to recite a list?" said Mann.

O'Reilly had a tough call to make. If she brought this to her boss, one of two things would happen, with little middle ground. Either James would embrace it all, wipe ARTEMIS's slate clean, and dedicate significant resources to investigating and shutting down a possible Juárez Cartel sleeper network in the United States—along with the network's benefactor. Or. She would muster every resource available to her to bring Mann's team in, thinking he'd gone off the deep end.

"What do you want me to do?" said O'Reilly, testing the waters.

"Bring this to James," said Mann. "Without institutional buy-in, I'm not sure what we can accomplish on our own. The site contained no paperwork connecting the dots beyond the desert, and none of the staff survived. We have one current or former Juárez Cartel *sicario* spinning stories. Based on what we saw down there, I believe her, but will anyone else?"

"I believe it," said O'Reilly.

"Then we need you to sell it," said Mann. "Without getting yourself fired."

"I don't care if I'm fired," said O'Reilly. "This isn't my first career-jeopardizing rodeo."

"That's why I approached you with the ARTEMIS concept," said Mann. "Your reputation preceded you."

"Good to know, for better or worse," said O'Reilly. "I'll bring this to James as soon as we hang up. We should probably switch to a new encrypted chat room on a different app. I'll have to access the video in front of James from the current site. If anyone is watching either of us, which I suspect they are at this point—they'll be all over our current chat room soon enough."

"Okay. Call me at the following number from a burner phone in a secure location," said Mann, passing along a new number, which she quickly scribbled down on a notepad that she intended to burn the moment she left the office.

"Got it," she said.

"We'll set up something entirely new," said Mann. "And Dana?"

"Yeah?"

"Thank you," said Mann. "That comes from all of us."

"Don't thank me yet," said O'Reilly. "Bringing this to James might not go well."

"Trust me on this. James is well aware of whatever history you bring to the job," said Mann. "She wouldn't have kept you around if she didn't believe you were a salty-as-fuck asset to her branch and the FBI. Sell this as a chance for her to join whatever secret club you belonged to."

"Who said I wasn't still a member of that club?" said O'Reilly.

"Now you're talking," said Mann. "Let's touch base tonight."

"Sounds like a plan," said O'Reilly. "If you don't hear from me by tomorrow morning, I'll either be in an interrogation cell at headquarters or relaxing in a hammock on a beach in Nicaragua."

"Nicaragua sounds nice," said Mann. "But I don't think it'll come to that."

"We'll see," said O'Reilly. "Good luck. Stay off the radar for now. How are you doing for funds?"

"We were down to a few hundred dollars yesterday, but we may have stumbled across several hundred thousand dollars while exploring the facility."

"I didn't hear that," said O'Reilly.

"Hear what?"

"Exactly," said O'Reilly.

"Watch your back," said Mann. "I have a bad feeling about this."

"Been there, done that," said O'Reilly, ending the call.

Instead of wasting any time second-guessing herself, she dialed Director James's direct line. Better to rip the Band-Aid off than to peel it away slowly.

CHAPTER 69

Mann removed the SIM card and battery from his burner phone and tossed everything into the pool. Serrano must have been watching him, because she opened the patio slider the moment his phone hit the water. She made her way over and sat down on the patio chair next to him.

"How did it go?" she said.

"O'Reilly believes us," said Mann. "She's going to show the video to her boss."

"That's good, right?" said Serrano.

"Maybe. Maybe not," said Mann. "I know we can trust O'Reilly. I just don't know if we can trust her boss, or whoever *she* takes this to."

"Have you thought about contacting any of the nearby field offices?" said Serrano. "Even if they've been warned to watch out for you, they'd have to be curious. Right?"

"You'd think they would be," said Mann. "But there's no telling how they'd react."

"They'll send a team out, and when they see this place, it'll raise questions. Hard questions," said Serrano. "How couldn't it?"

"It depends on who's behind the site," said Mann. "We still can't rule out government involvement, despite what O'Reilly's contact told us."

"True. But not the FBI," said Serrano. "The CIA wouldn't have handed over a place like that to the most straitlaced law enforcement organization in your country. That's a recipe for disaster. They most likely turned it over to a private entity—possibly retaining some kind of authority?"

He'd been thinking the same thing. Nothing inside the facility screamed government. It was the small stuff that he noticed first. The pens, notepads, and other office supplies hadn't been sourced through "the system." Then weapons and gear in the armory. High-end stuff by government or FBI standards. Finally, the two-hundred-thousand-dollar-a-pop armored Mercedes G-Wagons and Range Rovers in the vehicle bay. If the crown prince of Saudi Arabia owned the site, the vehicles might make sense. But not the US government. They were looking at a privately owned facility. An individual or corporation with very deep pockets.

"If I don't hear from O'Reilly by tomorrow, I'll send the video and coordinates to major field offices in California, Arizona, New Mexico, Texas, and Colorado. Let them sort it out," said Mann. "We nailed our killer. It came at a steep price, but we did it. We should be celebrating."

"But we're not," said Serrano.

"Yeah," said Mann. "Because there's still another killer out there—and what we found at the facility far overshadowed what ARTEMIS had originally set out to accomplish. This isn't the kind of group that just walks away from a Vegas blackjack table after winning a few hands. This is a go-for-broke kind of team."

"Which is why I hounded you to be a part of it," said Serrano. "I could tell you were serious. Willing to bend the rules if necessary. We did good today. But we're not done. My vengeance isn't complete."

"I know. We're nowhere close to done on that front or the rest of it," said Mann, before getting up and jumping into the pool.

He let himself sink to the bottom, next to his burner phone. Something about sitting underwater calmed him like nothing else. After several seconds, Mann pushed off the bottom, breaking the surface to find Serrano standing at the edge—contemplating the water.

"Hop in," said Mann. "It feels amazing."

"I can't swim," she said, shaking her head.

"Then use the stairs in the shallow end," said Mann.

"I've never been in a pool or any kind of water before," she said.

"How tall are you?" said Mann. "In feet. I don't feel like doing math."

"Five feet, six inches."

Mann swam to the shallow end and stood up, the water coming to his sternum.

"I'm five feet, ten inches," said Mann. "That's a four-inch difference, and the water is at least a foot and a half from my mouth. It's even shallower by the stairs."

Serrano made her way to the shallow end and took off her shoes and socks, before dipping one of her feet in the water.

"I don't have a bathing suit," she said.

"Did you see me wearing a bathing suit?"

"I don't know," she said.

"Trust me," said Mann, extending a hand. "You'll be fine. I'm here. I'm a qualified lifeguard."

"No, you're not."

"No, I'm not. But you can't drown if you can stand up in the water," said Mann. "I know that much."

She took his hand and walked down the stairs, until her feet touched the bottom. The water came up to her midabdomen.

"This is nice," she said.

"You've really never been in a pool before?"

"No. I never saw a pool until I joined the police," said Serrano. "And I waived the pool test, which limited my career opportunities."

He pulled her a little farther into the pool, until the surface of the water reached the bottom of her shoulders.

"Incredible," she said. "I feel like I'm floating!"

"What a difference one day makes," said Mann, still holding her hand—even though he no longer had to.

CHAPTER 70

Raul took the call poolside, slightly annoyed to be disturbed on a near-perfect summer day on the outskirts of Sacramento. Days like these had become rare over the past decade. In a few weeks, the temperatures would reach borderline intolerable levels, the air barely breathable from the wildfires that would inevitably break out in the drought-stricken Bay Area. They were in the third year of one of the longest and severest El Niño stretches in history. A recipe for wildfires. Maybe it was time to head north. He could always fly down to New Mexico when summoned.

"Hello?" he said, acting like he didn't recognize the number.

"Raul. How are things?"

"I'm guessing they're about to get worse," he said, assuming this wasn't a social call. "What do you want?"

"You're lucky you got out of New Mexico when you did," said the voice he knew only as Mr. Clean, because the man's head was shaved bald. "The facility was hit last night. The program is no longer operational."

"When will it be back up and running?" said Raul, admittedly relieved by the thought of an extended furlough from his duties.

"The program is finished. The facility was completely wiped out," said Mr. Clean. "We're doing what we can to cover our tracks. I don't see any exposure that would jeopardize your safety."

"That's good to know," said Raul, deciding to test the waters. "So. Is it fair to say that my obligation to you is satisfied, given the unfortunate circumstances?"

"Not yet," said Mr. Clean. "Alejandro was killed in the raid."

"I'm sorry to hear that," said Raul, not sorry at all.

"We're fairly certain that his escalating lack of discretion brought about the end of the program," said Mr. Clean. "We're not sure how they tracked him to New Mexico, but within a few days of his making a serious mistake on the way back to Minneapolis, we lost the facility."

"Once again, I'm very sorry to hear this," said Raul, once again not sorry at all. "I did warn you about him. He is—was—a very different breed. You have nothing to worry about from me."

"We've always appreciated your discretion, and your service," said Mr. Clean. "I wish we had heeded your warning."

"So. What are we looking at here?" said Raul.

"One more job," said Mr. Clean. "I need you to copy down an address."

"Can you text it to me?"

"You're kidding, right?"

"Hold on." Raul got up and made his way into his expansive River Park home, where he grabbed a pen and notepad from one of the kitchen counters. "Ready," he said.

Mr. Clean passed along the address, and Raul had him repeat it for good measure.

"I assume this won't be an easy job," said Raul.

"All I can tell you is that the address belongs to a senior-level FBI director," said Mr. Clean. "She's single and lives alone."

"Doesn't sound very difficult," said Raul. "We're talking termination?"

"Correct," said Mr. Clean. "But do not underestimate her. She's not your typical FBI bureaucrat. She's hands-on. Been around the block a few times."

"I'll be careful," said Raul. "Timeline?"

"The sooner the better."

"Sounds good to me," said Raul. "The sooner I get this done, the sooner my obligation to you expires. Correct?"

"In a sense," said Mr. Clean. "It'll get you very close to the finish line. We're going to do some deep digging into the team we suspect is responsible for the raid on the facility. I intend to use your unique skill set to take them down. You pull that off, and your obligation to us is over."

"Can I get that in writing?"

"Funny," said Mr. Clean. "You'll have to take my word for it, and the promise of a three-million-dollar kicker. One million for the assistant FBI director. Two for the others."

"Very generous," said Raul. "I'll keep you updated through our usual back channel."

"We're counting on you," said Mr. Clean.

"I always come through," said Raul.

"Yes. You do," said Mr. Clean, ending the call.

Raul stared at the address and shook his head. He'd do the job and take the money if the offer was real. But he'd stay off the grid the entire time and disappear when it was done. If what his handler said was true about the facility in New Mexico and Alejandro, these people would clean house soon—sweeping him away with the rest of the operation's key liabilities.

He glanced at the modified La Línea tattoo on his deeply tanned left shoulder—the Gran Patrón bee instantly grabbing his attention—along with the roman numerals I/III. He was the first and now last of the *tres amigos*. The sole survivor. A title he intended on maintaining until old age claimed his damned soul.

ABOUT THE AUTHOR

Photo © 2022 Bellomo Studios

Steven Konkoly is the *Wall Street Journal* and *USA Today* bestselling author of *Wide Awake, Coming Dawn,* and *Deep Sleep* in the Devin Gray series; *The Rescue, The Raid, The Mountain,* and *Skystorm* in the Ryan Decker series; the speculative postapocalyptic thrillers *The Jakarta Pandemic, The Perseid Collapse, Event Horizon, Point of Crisis,* and *Dispatches* in the Alex Fletcher series; the Fractured State series; the Black Flagged series; and the Zulu Virus Chronicles. A graduate of the US Naval Academy and a veteran of several regular and elite US Navy and Marine Corps units, he has brought his in-depth military experience to bear in his fiction. Konkoly lives in central Indiana with his family. For more information, visit www.stevenkonkoly.com.